— PRAISE FOR *DANCING ON THE SPIDER'S WEB* —

"In *Dancing on the Spider's Web*, Sasha Paulsen weaves her own irresistible web. Her characters are so alive in their complexity and her prose is so vivid that I began to believe Sarah, Gabriel and Rory must be living just down the street. All I wanted was to find out what they would do next. A sparkling and utterly engrossing debut."

— MARGOT LIVESEY

The New York Times bestselling author of *The Flight of Gemma Hardy*

"A funny, joyful story of young love lost and found again in the tumultuous time of Haight-Ashbury. You'll adore Sasha Paulsen's quirky band of misfits, especially Sarah, who fears love even as she chases it. A touching debut novel that takes you back to a bygone era when seeking mattered more than finding."

— SANDRA DALLAS

The New York Times bestselling author of *The Last Midwife*

"Sasha Paulsen has set her debut novel in San Francisco, Napa and Berkeley in the pivotal '70s. She manages to deftly capture both the spirit of those times and the essence of a cast of zany, appealing characters. Highly recommended."

— JAMES CONAWAY

author of *Napa*

DANCING ON THE SPIDER'S WEB

a novel by

SASHA PAULSEN

DANCING ON THE SPIDER'S WEB

a novel by

SASHA PAULSEN

TEMPEST

ISBN 978-1-7327768-0-7 (ebook edition)

ISBN 978-1-7327768-1-4 (paperback edition)

ISBN 978-1-7327768-2-1 (paper on board edition)

ISBN 978-1-7327768-3-8 (hardcover edition)

Library of Congress Control Number: paw18753

Printed and bound in the United States of America

First Printing April 2019

Design by Dorothy Carico Smith

Published by Tempest Books, Ltd.

tempestbooksltd.com

For Ariel, Sam, and Pip

"They danced down the streets like dingledodies, and I shambled after as I've been doing all my life after people who interest me, because the only people for me are the mad ones, the ones who are mad to live, mad to talk, mad to be saved, desirous of everything at the same time, the ones who never yawn or say a commonplace thing, but burn, burn, burn like fabulous yellow roman candles exploding like spiders across the stars…"

— Jack Kerouac, *On the Road*

PROLOGUE

JUNE, 1977

THE LOVE LIFE of the male tarantula is so dismal it could make the average human feel he is an honored guest at a lavish, perpetual banquet of satisfaction. The huge, hairy spider spends his first years alone in an underground hole, reaching up into the light only to snare his meals. When he finally emerges at puberty, his sole purpose is to mate and create more tarantulas. Driven by nature, he searches for a female who may kill and eat him, whether she accepts him or not. If he survives, he limps on, with whatever legs he has retained until he finds another mate. He doesn't eat; he wastes away, and after one summer of love, he dies.

Of all this natural tragedy, Rory McIntyre was unaware. He had studied literature and history at Harvard, and physics and astrophysics at MIT, but he had not taken a biology class since tenth grade at Napa High School. He had, therefore, no compassion and certainly no empathy for the weary tarantula lumbering across the lonely desert road at sunset. He had stopped only because he didn't want squashed spider parts on his wheels.

"God, you are ugly," he said. The spider stopped; it was looking at him. How many eyes did it have? He could see its fangs. "I didn't run over you," Rory pointed out. Another tarantula appeared and another and another. Did they roam in packs? He didn't know. He watched the procession with a horrified fascination and thought of Napoleon's army in retreat from Russia, bloodied, limping, missing limbs.

He closed his eyes and when he opened them, the spiders were gone and the sunset's brief flames were subsiding into twilight. He glanced at his watch. He had no wish to linger in this place, dwarfed by an immeasurable sky and surrounded, he now knew, by spiders.

He sped on, finding some comfort in the thought that maybe, maddened by the sun, he had been hallucinating, but then, against all reason, he began to imagine that one spider had climbed up onto his tire and was riding along with him, munching its way through the floorboard. Unaware that a sex-seeking tarantula would have traveled over him as indifferently as it would have crossed a rock, Rory decided that the creature was waiting only for darkness, when it would crawl up his leg and cause him to drive off the road into a canyon, where he would be found years later, a bleached skeleton sitting in a heap of rust inhabited by hundreds of its spider descendants.

He had other things to think about such as: he might be on the wrong road, it might not be a road at all, and he had not done such a crazy thing ever, at least not of his own free will. Nonetheless, his thoughts, bobbing through his head like tumbleweeds, kept returning to this idea of the hitchhiking spider. He had thought he was alone. He had not seen another sign of life except cactus and sagebrush, which looked dead even if they were not.

Before the last of the light vanished, he stopped and knelt on the dusty road to inspect the underside of his car. There was no tarantula. What he would have done had he found one did not, like most of his thoughts, bear close inspection. As he stood back up, the impulse to hurry on faded for a moment and he studied the fading landscape.

Mexico. In first grade he had made a clay map of it, a lumpy green and orange arrangement on a piece of cardboard he had painted bright blue to represent the sea. He had not understood that it was a real country made of earth and filled with people until the day he and his father met the girl in the vineyard.

In the fog of a late-summer dawn, they discovered her perched on the fence, feeding grapes to a waiting deer and sampling some herself. When Joe McIntyre harrumphed, the deer bounded away but the girl stayed, motionless, clutching a mangled cluster of grapes and regarding him with dark, enormous eyes. She was barefoot, slight, and delicate, and her veil of black hair spilled over a white dress splotched with mud and grape juice. Joe later said he thought he might have come upon a species of vineyard fairy. "Are they any good?" he asked.

She nodded.

It was only a small vineyard. Joe had left his family farm in Nebraska determined to be anything but a farmer, and he had never tasted wine in his life until World War II landed him in Italy. It was only chance and the injuries he suffered at Salerno that sent him to recuperate in a little valley north of San Francisco called Napa. Walk, his doctors told him; you are lucky to still have both your legs.

This was how he had discovered, at the end of a country lane, a farm stand tended by a dark-haired girl named Jean. This was how Joe came to eat so many tomatoes and zucchinis, he miraculously regained his health. This was the story Joe told to Rory and his five siblings, offspring of the marriage of Joe and Jean, any time they recoiled from eating vegetables.

Jean was the last of a family of pioneering immigrants who had come to Napa Valley, planted grapes, and built a winery from native stone. They had survived earthquakes, fires, and infestations, but the government had provided an insurmountable, unnatural disaster with its plan to create a nation of teetotalers, Prohibition. Their winery closed, but the family held onto their land as long as they could, replanting vineyards with walnut trees and vegetable gardens. By the time Prohibition was repealed in 1933, Jean's father was dead and her mother failing. When Joe arrived in 1945, the Arenti land had been sold, and the winery was one of many old stone ghosts scattered throughout the valley.

Like Joe, Jean had no interest in farming. When they married, they moved to the southern town of Napa, and the only thing from the Arenti winery they kept was a splintered, old, wooden wine press, because Joe had taken a romantic fancy to it.

Joe went to work as a mechanic, and, chance again, he was sent out to the country to repair a truck belonging to a farmer named Rudy Avila. Rudy was seventy-nine years old and he had eleven acres, all that was left of a large land grant that had been given to his grandfather a century earlier. His family had been cattle ranchers, but as their land holdings diminished, his father planted grapes, and these hardy vines had survived both phylloxera and Prohibition. Now, the only farming Rudy did was to tend his old vines, and every year he made a barrel of wine. He poured Joe a glass and they sat in the sun and talked about Italy. Before Joe left, Rudy had agreed to sell one of his acres. Joe built Jean a modern house there. She planted flowers in the wine press, but Joe planted a few grapevines and he started making wine with Rudy. The past, Rudy said, had a way of slipping into the future.

The McIntyre children thought the wine Joe made was disgusting stuff, and the day they found the girl on the fence, Rory had only gone into vineyards with his dad to escape the relatives visiting from Nebraska. He was expounding his theory that Aunt Margaret and Grandma McIntyre traveled by broomsticks not airplanes when they came upon her.

Joe invited her to come back to the house for breakfast. She went with them only as far as the backyard where she sat down on the tire swing slung from an oak tree. The hospitable McIntyres brought breakfast outside to the picnic table. "If she was eating Joe's grapes, she must be hungry," Jean murmured, but the girl only surveyed the pancakes, eggs, and bacon warily.

"Would you like a snail?" Joe asked, offering her a plate of pastries. "Or how about a bear claw?" Her eyes widened and she shook her head worriedly.

"Mexican," Aunt Margaret declared. "I think she's a Mexican."

"*Sí!*" The girl's voice was soft but clearly astonished. "*Soy de Mexico y —*"

"You must speak English," Margaret interrupted, "or people will think you are very stupid."

"I know what she said," Rory muttered. "She came here on a tornado. She's looking for the broomstick of the Wicked Witch of the West." The girl smiled at him. "I guess we can keep her."

"You most certainly cannot," Margaret said. "She must belong to someone. She must be able to say something."

"Would you like to swing?" asked John, the eldest McIntyre child. He pushed her gently, but Rory, of the opinion that a girl who traveled by tornado might prefer a better ride, shoved the tire soaring into the air. When it slowed, the girl looked dizzy but her eyes were sparkling.

"*Yo lo vei,*" she said to Rory. "I saw it. Mexico." She turned to Margaret. "Yes, we came from Mexico. My father is Dr. Glass, and he bought the white house at the end of this road, but I am going back to Mexico because there the sky is blue, not white, and the people are happy. My name," she added, "is Sarah Glass."

It was some time before the McIntyres learned that she had just chosen the name Sarah from several she had been considering as she sat on the fence eating Joe's grapes.

Rory McIntyre, two decades later, was not much given to looking back; nor did he care to dwell on the future, being none too certain he had one, or much of one, at any rate. In the dusky light, the Mexican desert was taking on a ghostly, chiaroscuro aspect. A breeze rustled the dry bushes and prickled his neck.

"No, no more ghosts," he said aloud, but as darkness flung a cloak over the sky and the silence magnified his involuntary solitude, he remembered the grapes, the swing, and the girl. He got back in his car and drove on, watching for a light.

PART ONE

AUGUST, 1976

CHAPTER 1

THE DEPOSIT CHECK hadn't bounced. The keys opened the door. The electricity had been turned on without complications and all four burners on the gas stove worked. Sarah Glass, setting down the last of her three boxes of possessions, was overtaken by an unfamiliar, irrepressible fit of optimism. She felt it distinctly if warily: an inexplicable notion that an invisible hand was arranging these things, a gift for following the bizarre impulse that had brought her here.

She did not believe in unseen things, she reminded herself, but neither could she insist the sensation was only the biochemical result of living for three days on peanut butter. She, who had never done a wild thing, had done this. She flicked the light switch on and off. Light bulbs, too.

With a fluting call, a scrawny black cat came in through the window and rubbed against her ankle. His ear was torn, his tail bent. He had been left, along with the light bulbs, by the previous tenant.

"Are you still here?" Sarah asked. "I still don't have any food. I won't until my check arrives. You might want to go somewhere else."

The cat, unconcerned, began to groom his paws. This was his realm, a flat no larger than the pocket on a mouse's apron: a tower with a minuscule kitchen and bathroom patched on in the corners. It also had a fireplace, an empty window box, and a balcony framed by climbing roses. Sarah had paid all but three dollars of her available funds to move in.

She unrolled her sleeping bag on the floor. The cat tested his claws on it and settled down to scratch fleas and watch her unpack one box: a battered pan, a coffee pot, two chipped coffee mugs, two blue Chinese bowls.

The last item, wrapped carefully inside a frayed, gray flannel bathrobe, was a pottery statue of a woman with an enormous belly and eight arms, two of which grew from her back, wing-like. Two arms held out an empty plate, two were raised above her head, and the last two served as legs. Sarah set it on the fireplace mantel. The cat leapt up to inspect it. He sniffed the empty plate and looked at Sarah.

"I know," she said. "It's ugly. She might have elephantiasis, and maybe jaundice. Also, a genetic weirdness. It was a gift." The cat stared at her unblinking. "I suppose it is rude to leave her plate empty," she admitted. "I'll see what I can find."

She went down the stairs. Close the front door at all times, the landlord had warned her, and soon he would repair the lock. Although this elegant Victorian sat on a San Francisco hill with others of her class, below it lay the exotic, unpredictable Haight Street where people slept in the Paradise Laundromat and Madame Sophie's purple fluorescent sign for psychic readings blinked off and on all night. Her street sloped steeply down to Haight like a giant's asphalt sliding board. Sarah ventured onto it.

She walked swiftly, as was her habit, but gradually she slowed to study her surroundings, still scarred with the detritus of an era of peace, love, and tie-dye: The Ho Chi Minh Inn; Used Rubber; Metal-Xtasy; Bella Moonflower, Witch: Enchantments and Consulting. She read the menu of the Psychotic Ostrich's Vegetarian Delights and, snared by the scent of wild strawberries, she went into Mother Earth's Organic Produce. She examined the mounds of apricots and eggplants and calculated that she could afford to buy half a peach.

"Can you feel it?"

The speaker, the only other person in the shop, was a hefty woman whose cloud of raspberry-colored hair complemented her rainbow-striped caftan: Mother Earth herself.

"It?"

"It has been hot and sunny for three days in a row. Do you know why?"

Sarah shook her head no, although she had heard that such odd summer weather in San Francisco had people speculating the great earthquake was imminent. Mother Earth spread her arms and her gown billowed like a hot air balloon rising. "It is the end. The planets are aligning in a straight line. Do you know what that means?"

"No, not really."

"Something heavy is going to happen. California will finally fall into the ocean, and we will return to where we belong."

As goes California, Sarah recalled, so goes the rest of the nation. In this case, she was not sure it would be an honor. It is possible to live nearly all of one's life in California and still feel inept in these conversations. "That would be heavy," she agreed. "Volume times density — "

"You are missing the big picture."

Sarah nodded. This was often her shortcoming. "I've been away."

"You are a native?" Mother Earth raised an eyebrow.

"Yes. Well, no. Not of San Francisco. I grew up in the country. Nowhere, really."

"Yes. I see."

Sarah departed. Her legs were glad to be moving. She had been driving for three days, for two thousand, nine hundred and eight miles, until she had run out of land in San Francisco. Why she had done it, she could not explain, even to herself, except she retained a memory of being lost in this city, of wandering through it, thinking that some kind of magic was afoot in its noise and motion, its lights and gaudy, clashing colors. Whether she was seeking a new adventure or an old memory made up of lost and broken pieces, she did not really know. Her life since then had contained little that could be called magical, although several times she had found parking places in Los Angeles and New York.

At least, she mused, unlike many who had given way to such a vagary and bolted from their life, she had a clear passage back. In one month she would repack her car and return. She had opened a door to another world, but she would not lose sight of it. She could retrace her flight. This adventure was reversible in time.

She came into a new neighborhood where the shop signs were in Spanish. She entered a market, making her way past bins of chilies, dried beans, and bundles of herbs to a stack of tinned cat food. They had no price, so she held out one can and a dollar bill to the woman at the cash register, who returned most of the money, murmuring, "*Gracias.*"

"*Soy un gato,*" Sarah ventured. "No, no, not *soy* — "

"*Tengo?*"

"*Oui.* No — yes. Sí. That is, I don't really have a cat but — yes, thank you."

"I TOLD HER I was a cat," Sarah said to her new roommate as she emptied the cat food into a blue Chinese bowl. "She must have felt sorry for me. She gave me a bag of day-old cookies."

The cookies were pink and green, rock hard. Sarah tasted one and put the rest of it on the winged statue's plate. A stale cookie was, no doubt, inadequate, but she didn't really believe in anything, least of all that an offering to a lump of clay could change her life.

Beyond her window, fog was moving in from the sea, weaving

ghostlike through a grove of eucalyptus trees. "I should have asked Mother Earth how soon we are going to fall into the sea," Sarah said to the cat. "I wonder if we fall all at once or crumble slowly in pieces."

She went back outside; this time she hiked up the street. Where it ended, she could see the towers of the Golden Gate Bridge disappearing in clouds and mist. She wandered on, eastward into a trendy neighborhood where shop windows were filled with bright and lovely useless things. She read restaurant menus and inhaled the aromas that wafted out as people glided in: women with men, women with women, men with men. She was extremely hungry.

She read the flyers tacked to walls. *Having a Transit? What To Do When Neptune Conjuncts Pluto. Metaphysical Jogging: Running for Light. Let the Universe Find You Love. How to Grow Asparagus. The Art of Death and Dying.* Of these, she estimated that her best bet was growing asparagus. As for love, hadn't the universe just provided her with a cat?

The street ended at a pawnshop where a fantastic jumble of jewels, furs, feathers, and watches was locked behind a metal grill. A necklace suspended in the air was fashioned from two gold acrobats wearing enameled tiger skins. They dangled by their knees from the chain, each holding the edge of a gold star and presiding over the finery, which had served its purpose, cast the necessary illusion, and been abandoned.

"Excuse me."

The low voice behind her made Sarah jump. She turned and looked into the face of a slight, fair, agitated man.

"Damn," he said. "Sorry. I didn't mean to scare you but I was just wondering" — he glanced around, anxious and bird-like — "would you have dinner with me? Jesus, this sounds awful, but my sister and her husband are here, and you don't know them — well, of course you don't — but I just saw them, and look, I'll pay for it."

"Gabriel!" a voice trumpeted. "My God, Gabriel! I thought we'd never get here. These mountains! Why did they put a city here? And the way they drive! Don't they know there are rules? Pete wanted to go fishing, but I said no, we had to see how Gabriel is doing in San Francisco. But my God, Gabriel, this place! And the people! I can't even say what I've seen."

The owner of this voice was a handsome, strapping blonde whose features were so ample they could hardly fit comfortably on one face: a wide mouth and many teeth, a prominent nose and bulbous eyes. It was a passionate, extravagant face; its owner could have dressed in silk robes and raked in coins for her prophecies, but instead she was wearing a tight, lime-green, polyester pantsuit. Her lipstick, cotton candy pink, matched the two spots painted on her cheeks like symmetrical insect bites. One hand clutched a scarf, printed with cable cars, covering a frizz of curls, and the other held the arm of a colorless man who stood, jaw tight, hands clenched, waiting, it seemed, for a car to spring onto the sidewalk and mow them down.

"Hullo, Lydia," Gabriel said.

"You didn't tell me you were bringing a girl," Lydia replied. "So there, Pete, he does know people. Mother will be glad." The woman's eyes appraised Sarah's dusty blue sweatpants, gray sweatshirt, aged running shoes, and hair tied into a long black ponytail with a packing string. "Maybe."

"She's a good friend," Gabriel said. "A really good friend. We both feel the same way about the city, that it's really exciting and full of things happening."

"How nice," Lydia said. "Does she have a name?"

"Rebecca."

Lydia showed them her day's worth of shopping: Malaysian bells for her sister who collected bells, an English teacup for her mother who collected everything, and for herself the cutest sculpture of the Golden Gate Bridge made of seashells with little clam people walking on it. "And guess where it's from, Gabriel? China! I didn't see the tag until I'd paid for it. Pete said, 'I won't have a Red thing in my house.' 'But Pete,' I said, 'it's not red; it's all different colors.' Well, dinner — " Having bought San Francisco, she now wished to eat it.

Her own vote was for Ye Olde Haufbrauhaus, San Francisco's Favorite Since 1937, but she agreed to Gabriel's choice, a restaurant in vogue that month not only for its inventive cuisine but its ambiance. The chef specialized in rare, weird ingredients; one might find truffles, cow eyeballs, and nasturtiums all on one plate. The interior was entirely black and lit by the flames from open grills. The waiters wore chains, rags, and safety pins.

Sarah, borne along with them, entered the establishment cautiously. She had read the menu earlier, and she could have eaten there instead of renting an apartment. The dark obscured her clothes but made it difficult to find her way. Still, she fared better than Pete, who upended a table and demanded to know why the place had not paid its electrical bill.

They were seated. While she could not see, she was content to breathe the air, redolent of wine, thyme, and garlic. The waiter brought a candle with the menus and by its light, Sarah studied this person, Gabriel.

He was beautiful. In him, his sister's too-large features had been brought under control and proportioned so the result was a harmonious, epicene, mathematical perfection. He might have been dipped in glowing moonlight: his hair was pale, his skin fair, and his eyes stone gray. His fit of nerves evaporated, he exuded charm as effortlessly as a flower gives off scent.

"An aperitif, Rebecca?" he asked. "The usual?"

"What? Oh. Yes."

"We'll have two French Kisses," Gabriel told the waiter.

"There he goes again," Pete said. "Why can't he be normal?"

"Because," Gabriel replied. "What will you have, Pete?"

"Beer. Not a foreign one."

"And Champagne," Lydia added. "We must have Champagne."

Pete opened his menu. "*Porc farci*. Sounds indecent."

"It might be good," Lydia said. "What do you think, Rebecca?"

"Yes," Sarah said, "if you like pork."

"Don't you? Are you Jewish? You must be! Who else doesn't like pork?"

"Hindus," Gabriel said. "Muslims."

Lydia looked again at Sarah. Dinner, Sarah told herself, it's dinner. A weightless feeling was overtaking her, and although she knew it was the effect of vermouth falling on an empty stomach, she was not sure science alone could explain it. She was not Sarah; she was Rebecca, dining in fashion with a handsome stranger. Besides, soon they might all fall into the ocean.

"Yes," she said to Lydia. "I am a Muslim." No, she added to Gabriel, she would not object to the *fruit de mer* appetizer.

"I thought you must be foreign," Lydia said. "You have the longest eyelashes I've ever seen. Are they real?"

Gabriel winced. Sarah asked, "Shall we try *agneau à deux*? We wanted it last time we were here, but they had run out. Gabriel was so disappointed."

He recovered, crowed with laughter, and ordered the lamb. Lydia chose lobster, and Pete, chicken. "Dammit, though," he said, "they should have steak. Why don't they have steak?"

"What have you been doing, Gabriel?" Lydia asked.

"Having a transit. Neptune conjunct Pluto."

Pete groaned. Lydia took a check from her purse. "Daddy sent you this, and he wants to know when you are going to get a job. Rebecca, why don't you tell him he should get a job?"

Sarah demurred. "See?" Lydia asked. "She thinks you could make better use of your time. Don't you, Rebecca?"

"Well, yes and no," Sarah replied, draining her drink.

"What are you, a politician?" Pete asked.

"We don't really know anything about you," Lydia added. "Gabriel never calls home. What are you?"

As the vermouth collided with her empty stomach, Sarah felt the pleasant fog it was dispersing through her nervous system, and she pulled an answer from the ether. "I am a physicist," she said speculatively, just as Gabriel said, "She's a dancer."

"A what?"

"A physical dancer," Gabriel explained.

"That must be different," Lydia said, and Pete's expression indicated that it fell in a class with *porc farci.*

"Yes," Sarah agreed. "It is."

"I keep asking her why she doesn't get a real job." Gabriel sighed, and the Champagne arrived. Under the cover of the uncorking, Sarah slipped a prawn into her pocket.

"I'm sure your family is happy to help you out," Lydia said.

"Actually, I'm an orphan."

"Oh, I'm sorry."

"I'm not." Sarah added a crab's leg to her pocket.

Gabriel's fingers brushed hers beneath the table. "I love this city," he said. "It's so wicked and wild and golden."

"It is pretty." Lydia drained her glass and held it up for more. "Do you know what I'd like to do? Go to a fortune-teller. Wouldn't that be too fun?"

"No," Pete said. "It would be too expensive."

"I went to a fortune-teller," Sarah recalled. "She said, 'You should have been a dancer.'"

"I was the fortune-teller," Gabriel said. "It's how we met."

Servers brought the food. Lydia's enormous lobster sprawled over a

plate draped with seaweed, and the waiter required a kind of axe to reduce Sarah and Gabriel's lamb to manageable portions, but Pete's plate
was by far the loveliest, with slivers of chicken and elegantly crossed
green beans sitting on a bed of greens, purple pansies, and an orchid.

"Damned fairy meal," he muttered. "Should send it back." He
moved the flower garden to his bread plate and munched the chicken
in gloomy silence.

Sarah tasted the lamb; it had been raised on honey and nectar. She
slipped pieces into her growing stash. Gabriel, watching her, added a
chunk of Lydia's lobster, along with a handful of Pete's flowers. Presently, Lydia groaned. "I couldn't eat another thing."

I could, Sarah thought. I could.

Gabriel requested the dessert cart and took the mango mousse,
Lydia, the peanut butter cheesecake. Sarah, with delight, chose the wild
strawberry tart, and Pete, the chocolate cake.

"The Decadence. A fine choice," the waiter said to Pete, who slumped
down and declined to taste his cake. Lydia ate it.

"You'll come home for Christmas, won't you, Gabriel?" Lydia's
words rolled together. "It's the reunion. Bring Rebecca. She's an orphan. She can come. And I'll tell everyone that everything's all right."

"We have to go." Gabriel tossed a handful of money onto the table.
Sarah felt his hand grasp her elbow. As swiftly as she had been transported into the restaurant, she was whisked out.

Having no experience of being picked up in the street, she was not
sure where she should be set back down, so she kept pace with Gabriel as he flew through the fog, around corners, up a hill and down
another. He stopped, at last, in front of a dilapidated house hidden by
untrimmed bushes. Its windows were smashed, its doors boarded, its
gingerbread trim splintered.

"Want to go in?" Gabriel shoved open a rusty gate.

"The sign says no trespassing."

"I come here all the time." He led the way through weeds to the back of the house. There, in a tangle of wild roses, an old wooden caravan rested on one remaining wheel.

"It looks like an old Gypsy thing," Sarah said, examining its faded, painted designs. "How do you suppose it got here?"

"They sold it to a Victorian who led a secret life. Victorians were good at that." Gabriel sat down on a broken step. Sarah sat down too. "I'd like to steal it," he said. "I wonder where we could find a horse."

The wind rustled the roses. Sarah shivered. The fog was wrapping around them. The heat spell was over. "So," he said, "tell me about virtual particles."

"I believe they are particles that have such a short life span they die before they are detected."

"Now there's a useful thing to look for. Sounds like love. I'd rather look for the Grail."

"The what?"

"The Holy Grail."

"Oh."

"What's wrong with that?"

"Nothing. Except it's a myth." He looked affronted; she faltered. "Maybe it exists. Or it did in another time."

"What about quarks?"

"Quarks? I — I don't know. I really only like physics theoretically. That is, I wonder if there really is system of order in the universe that anyone can discover."

To her surprise, this made him laugh. He pulled a handful of white roses off a bush and began to weave them into a circle. "Thanks for eating with me. You know how families are — or maybe you don't." He tilted his head to study her. "I had a dog. I left him with my parents while I moved here, and when I went back to get him, my mother had had him killed because he shed. She said you should never love anything so much you can't lose it."

"That's awful."

"Why? Do you believe in love?"

"Well, I don't know — "

"Do you have a dog?"

"No, but a cat seems to think he lives with me."

"Is that who you were bagging food for? Did you get enough to eat?" Sarah nodded wistfully. "Well, then — " He handed her the unfinished wreath of roses. "Goodbye."

She trailed him back to the sidewalk but he was gone in the fog. Sarah had no idea where she was. She wandered through the mist, searching for a familiar sign. When the shape of a man emerged, she breathed easier until he turned toward her. He was gaunt and bearded, wearing a ragged black robe and a necklace made of bones. He held a wooden staff. He grinned; he had no teeth.

She ran. How she found her flat, she never knew. She collapsed onto her sleeping bag. The cat sniffed her pocket. He purred as he ate the lamb and the lobster.

"Don't get used to this," Sarah said. "It won't happen again."

CHAPTER 2

S HE HAD LEFT the tower window open and in her absence a spider
had begun to spin a web in the frame. If she closed the window
now, she would ruin its work. Instead, she watched it.

"A curious evening," she said to the spider and the cat. "The sort
that fades away in the morning and has no connection with reality."

She was interrupted by the telephone's harsh ring. This was odd.
She had given the number to only one person, and her roommate in
New York had already called to say the check was in the mail.

"Well," a voice said, "Isn't this something? That strange woman in
New York said you'd gone to San Francisco. Not, of course, that I expect anyone to think of telling me because, like we said at my group, if
you don't expect anything, you won't be disappointed. But you might
like to know what happened at my group last night. We had a revolu-
tion. We kicked the men out. We decided that as long as there are men
in the group, we'll never get anywhere. They always stick together. So
what is the point of having a group to discuss what went wrong in a
relationship if all the men do is agree they never did anything wrong?
That's what your father did. When we went to a marriage counselor,
what did he say? 'Everything is fine.' So the counselor told me it was
all in my head. Well, where else could it be? The men said women
never agree on anything, but last night we agreed that the men had

done some things wrong. If only I had realized this, I could have broken away from your father's domination years ago."

"He left years ago," Sarah said.

"You don't remember. Aaron does. So does Cecily. The worst thing a woman can do is get married and have children and then have to explain what she did."

"You don't have to."

"My group says I should. They say I need an outlet for my anger. They say I should write a book. Well. San Francisco. You certainly get all the chances."

A scattering of pebbles hit her window, and from the sidewalk, came a hooting call. "I have to go," Sarah said. She hung up, and leaning out over the balcony, she asked Gabriel Dinesen what he wanted.

"Rebecca at last! I followed you home. I didn't realize I'd have to run. I'm hungry again. Would you like to go to Hamburger Mary's?"

He led the way to his car, a new, silver BMW. It was a gift from his father by way of apology for the dog, he explained. A useful thing, guilt.

Hamburger Mary's was well lit with chandeliers, although most of the bulbs were blue and orange. They sat near a statue of the Virgin who stood between two furry pink flamingos. Their sandwiches arrived speared through the center with steak knives. As Sarah began to feel full, she wondered if Gabriel would ever ask her name, but she didn't offer it. Whoever Rebecca was, she certainly had more fun on dates — if this was a date — than Sarah ever had.

"Where next?" Gabriel asked. "Have you been to the biker bar that serves sake? No, wait, I've got it: let's dance."

At a club called Niners, he vaulted out onto the dance floor. Sarah trailed behind him, dazzled by the giant murals of miners, madams, football players, and robber barons. The real people were dull in comparison, except for Gabriel. He was a dancer, moving like quicksilver in the flash of a strobe light. He caught her hands. She tripped, but he turned her stumble into a twirl. He spun her in loops. Her feet slid toward the door; they were leaving and she knew she should follow them.

"I can't do this," she whispered. "I hate it."

"What?"

"I only have a month — "

"Really? Then we'd better keep dancing."

Just as he could dance with no help from her, so was he able to carry on a solo conversation as they returned to her flat. He told her where he had been born: Chicago; where he had been raised: all over; what he did all day: messed about; and what his ambition was: to make a better kite than he had last year.

She stopped at the front door, but he took her arm and climbed the stairs. "Do you think I'm a serial murderer?" he asked.

"I hadn't thought of that."

"Then we're off to a good start. Where are you from?"

"Nowhere."

"I knew it! All my life I've wanted to meet the Princess from Nowhere. I read the story when I was a kid, except I thought it was nowhere. I called her the Princess from Now-here."

He strolled about the room, flipped open the two unpacked boxes, saw that they were filled with books, feigned terror, and sat down on the sleeping bag. He looked up at her thoughtfully. Oh, Sarah thought, here we are. Gabriel was struck too, not so much by the expression on her face as by the claws that pierced his thigh.

"I'm so sorry." She gathered up the cat, who was preparing to launch a second attack. "Be nice," she admonished, even as she wondered why a cat must be nice to a stranger who had sat down, uninvited, on his bed. "I've given up sex." She blurted this out; she'd had no idea she was going to say it. Alarmed, she squeezed the cat and he jumped out the window.

"Oh no," she exclaimed. "He might run into traffic. I have to go get him." She ran back down the stairs.

The cat had vanished. Sarah was relieved. What would she do with a cat? She lingered on the sidewalk watching the door. Why didn't Gabriel leave? A distant siren broke the silence of the night, and then the shrill ring of a telephone. Sarah bolted up the stairs, but before she reached her landing, Gabriel's voice brought her to a halt.

"Who? Sorry, you must have the wrong number. There's no Priscilla here." Through the open door she could see him. He had got himself a cup of water and he was sitting on a box grimacing as he turned the pages of one of her books.

"The woman who lives here is named" — he squinted at the inside cover — "Sarah Glass. What? Oh, I see. She changed it? Really? Actually, I prefer Sarah too, although I think she is a Rebecca. And you are? Ah, her mother."

Sarah slunk back down the stairs but Gabriel's cheerful chirping followed her. "I wouldn't take it personally, although I do agree — based on extensive experience of myself —that all men are crazy. No, I wouldn't say you were a fool because you thought you were happy. Maybe you were. Yes, that is a good point. Yes, I'll tell her. Who is Cecily? Ah, her sister. Yes, I have it: Cecily will be in San Francisco to buy her wedding dress, and Sarah should see her but not make fun of her. Why would she do that? Oh, her fourth? Well, practice makes perfect. Who wrote a short story about that? Her brother? No kidding? But even if it wasn't a nice story — no, no, I've never read it, but I'm fundamentally illiterate. It was nice to meet you. No, I do mean it. Yes, I really do."

Outside, Sarah leaned against a tree growing up through a crack in the sidewalk. Its branches rustled in the wind; a few leaves broke loose and flew away. Finally, Gabriel came out, glancing around as he walked to his car. When the taillights of the BMW disappeared, she went inside.

On the mantel lay his wreath of roses, imperfect flowers, white, and scentless. She hung it around the neck of the homely statue, and there she left it, long after the roses had faded and dried and crumbled at a touch, long after she had untangled Gabriel Dinesen from the trappings of their meeting, the candlelight, the wine, the food, and the fog.

She felt something brush against her leg. It was the cat.

CHAPTER 3

THE NEXT DAY, Sarah received her check. It was not a huge amount, as the world goes, but it was more than she had ever possessed. The Miriam T. Hawkley Prize had purchased this adventure, this stolen month. It had let her run away.

She took it to a bank and when she had produced enough identification to persuade them to accept it, she left with the magnificent advance of twenty dollars and went to the nearest grocery store. There, she was confounded by choices. Which honey? Which tea? She could even afford the organic carrots. As she considered the possibilities, a shopping cart collided with hers.

"Isn't this a coincidence!" a man exclaimed. "Running into each other in the frozen food!"

Sarah blinked. She had heard that all the men in San Francisco were gay, but this did not seem to be the case. She didn't know this short, plump, balding person, and yet he said, "So, beautiful, what are you doing here?"

"Having a transit. Neptune conjunct Pluto."

"So you're into astrology." He turned his cart to accompany her as she moved away. "That can be heavy. Ah, I see you're buying coffee. I guess you're not into health food. Do you know what coffee does to your vitamin B? I used to drink coffee, but now I have a great coffee substitute and what a difference! Changed your mind, did I?" he added as Sarah pushed on past the coffee. "So, what's your name?"

"Jemima."

"Just like the pancake mix! Another coincidence! My name is Earl. So, Jemima, would you like to get together to try my coffee substitute?"

"No, thank you."

"Do you have other plans today?"

"I'm going to a lecture on death and dying."

"Wow. So, you're into death. I'm into personal relationships myself. Hey! I have an idea: we can go to this lecture and then try my coffee substitute. Don't be shy. I can tell you are. I used to be shy too. I had real problems relating to people, I mean, women. But then I figured out there are other ways to meet women than picking them up in bars. Like this: crash, here we are. I use ideas like this in my shyness seminar. You'd get a lot out of it. It costs ten dollars, but everyone says it's worth it."

She darted away into the pet food aisle. "Why me?" she mumbled, tossing cans of Kitty Stew and Chicken Divine into her cart. "I'm not nice. I'm not pretty. And I'm not — "

"I think you are pretty."

Sarah looked down to a pair of brown eyes nearly hidden by a mop of copper-colored hair that topped a small girl wearing purple shorts, a red T-shirt printed with a moose, one orange sock, one blue sock, and yellow sneakers on the wrong feet.

"Are you going to eat all that food?" she asked.

"It's for a cat."

"What's its name?"

"I don't know. He's not my cat."

"Whose cat is he?"

"He doesn't seem to be anyone's."

"Then you should give him a name."

Sarah considered this. "Maybe — Widdershins."

"That's silly."

"No, it's a good word. If you say it while you run backwards, you might fall into another world."

"Why?"

"Because you want to, I guess."

"Do you?"

"Sometimes."

"My name is Lucy. I'm almost five. And this is Avery," she added, as a red-haired boy crawled out from under a cereal display. "He's my brother. He's only three. He's bad." Avery grinned at Sarah, and she did not doubt it.

"We're getting food for Widdershins," Lucy informed Avery. The pair were adding cans to Sarah's basket when Earl reappeared. "Ah, here you — "

"This is our mother," Lucy said. "And we have a cat."

Earl pushed on without a word.

"Thanks," Sarah said. "I really mean it. Thanks."

They hooted and leapt onto Sarah's cart. They pumped it around a corner and out of sight.

"No, not another cart!" a woman shrieked. "You must not steal other people's carts!"

The cart returned with Lucy and Avery riding on the prow. The woman pushing it stopped short. "Good God," she exclaimed. "Sarah."

CHAPTER 4

"KATE?" IT WAS the best Sarah could manage, but when you have run off to be invisible in a far-away city, you do not expect to find your long-lost best friend in the corner grocery store.

Was it Kate? She had not seen Kate since the year after they graduated from Napa High School. Sarah had never intended to return to Napa, but she had to be maid of honor as Kate, the devotee of *Seventeen* magazine, morphed into *Modern Bride* and disappeared into a cloud of lace and color-coordinated flowers.

Kate? This hefty woman looked like she had slept in her baggy T-shirt and frayed blue jeans and cut her own hair, maybe with a butcher's knife; but Kate's mother had always called her daughter a walking newspaper and this woman was talking, even as she returned six boxes of corn flakes to a shelf: "I didn't know you were in the city, Sarah! Where are you living? Why are you here? Isn't this wonderful?"

It was Kate.

Limply, Sarah followed her through the checkout stand. Outside, Kate loaded potatoes and oranges into the backpacks Lucy and Avery wore. "It slows them down," she said. "We're walking. Are you?"

"What? Oh, yes, yes, I am."

"Which way?"

"Stanyan? Yes. Stanyan."

"But we're on Stanyan, too! Oh, this is amazing! Which house?"

"It's pink, shades of — pink."

"Not the Rose House? I love that house! We're further down the hill in that square modern building. It's ugly, but it was cheap."

They set off. Kate's conversation continued even as she darted to retrieve children from bushes, trees, or under cars. Sarah trailed along, communing with the unseen powers in which she did not believe. She would make an effort, if only they would stop showing off. She had never possessed Kate's boundless enthusiasm for life.

"Didn't Mom tell you we'd moved to San Francisco?"

"Maybe." Kate's mother always sent Sarah a Christmas card, and Sarah always intended to send one back.

"You look so shocked."

Sarah nodded. She knew the symptoms of shock. She had correctly diagnosed them in a man who had been hit on the head by a frozen turkey thrown from a frat house window, but she had never had to identify them in herself. "I just never expected to see someone from my past."

"You say that like you've escaped from a loony bin."

"I've been living in New York."

"I know," Kate said. "Med school. Mom and Dad are so proud of you. And Dad's glad your biology has improved. He still remembers the time you told Rory the facts of life."

Sarah felt the sun, hot on the back of her neck, and was relieved that they had reached her house. She stopped; so did Kate.

"This is the perfect house for you, Sarah. It's so romantic."

"I rented it over the phone. I didn't know it was pink."

"It reminds me of Cecily's pink and white wedding. Although I liked the lemon and lime one the best. Remember how beautiful she was?"

"I remember how hysterical she was when the lime sherbet dresses turned out to be washing machine avocado. Have you seen the black house with eleven colors of trim? Maybe she can use that scheme for her next wedding."

"Is she getting married again?"

"Number four."

"Is that why you're here?"

"No, no. I'm only here — I've only got a month."

"You say that like you've only got a month to live."

Sarah tried to laugh, but it came out in a nervous spasm that turned into a fit of coughing. She opened the front door; still, Kate lingered.

"Is that Widdershins?" The black cat had come out onto the stoop, and Lucy and Avery chased him up the stairs. "Why did he run away?" Lucy called.

"Would you like to come in?" Sarah asked Kate.

"I'd love to!" Kate followed Sarah up the stairs. "It's my day off. I wanted to do something special but I never thought — oh! what a great place! It's like Sleeping Beauty's tower! Do you remember, Sarah, when we were weird? The stories we made up? All those handsome men dashing into our lives, sweeping us off our feet. Where did we get our ideas?"

"*Sleeping Beauty. Snow White. Gone with the Wind.*"

"Not from real life at any rate."

"No," Sarah said. "Would you like coffee — oh, damn, I forgot to buy it. I'll just run — "

"And we'll go with you!" Lucy, abandoning the search for the black cat, startled Sarah by taking hold of her hand. Avery took her other one.

Sarah expected Kate to object, but she only said, "Have fun!" Sarah departed with her two appendages. She could not remember if she had ever held the hand of one person, let alone two, and both inclined to hop rather than walk.

※

LEFT ALONE, KATE stood perfectly still for several seconds. Then she threw up her arms and stretched with delighted abandon. She did ten knee bends. She spun in a circle that turned into a waltz. She danced around the room and sank into a deep curtsey.

"Thank you, your highness," she murmured.

"Enchanted, of course."

Kate looked up and fell over onto the floor. Standing in the doorway was a prince holding a bottle of wine and what looked like a garden of white roses.

"So it is true that all California girls are beautiful," Gabriel Dinesen remarked as he opened the wine. He had also brought glasses and a corkscrew. He should have brought chairs, too, he observed, but he joined Kate on the floor and clinked his glass against hers.

Laughing, Kate explained that no one before had ever mistaken her or Sarah for a true California girl, that fabled compound of teeth, legs, and hair. Kate was tall but round and rosy. Her eyes were hazel, her hair chestnut brown, and the time she dyed it blonde was one of her more painful adolescent memories. Sarah, short and skinny, with soot-dark hair and eyes, missed the mark entirely.

"Where is the lady of the house, by the way?" Gabriel asked.

"She just ran out the door."

"Ah. Is this a habit of hers?"

"Oh yes."

"I see. And you are her best friend?"

"Did she tell you this?"

"No. So you know her?"

"Only since kindergarten."

"Sometimes I amaze myself," he mused, "and this is a feat, considering the wonders I've seen." He poured more wine. "Can I ask you something?"

"If I drink enough of this wine, you can probably ask me anything."

"Excellent! What's her name?"

"Sarah."

"Who is Priscilla?"

"Oh, it was Priscilla, but she changed it in kindergarten. She found out that her dad had changed his name from Guevara to Glass and so she thought she'd choose a new first name too. She found it in a library book. Sarah could read anything, even before she ever went to school. She found a book called *Sarah, Plain and Tall*."

"But she's hardly plain or tall."

"Oh, but she thinks she is," Kate said. "It's because her mother and sister are beautiful, tiny, pink and gold. Her mother was Miss Long Beach."

"No."

"Yes. They used to make fun of Sarah because she was so different, well, dark, and when she grew to five-three, they always said she was like someone's Aunt Josephine the Giraffe who was six feet tall and died from hitting her head on the ceiling or something. That's when Sarah and I started drinking coffee to stunt our growth. It might have worked for her, but I still grew."

"I love evil stepmothers and wicked stepsisters."

"Oh, but, Isabelle isn't Sarah's stepmother. And they weren't that bad. Well, maybe they were. One time, Cecily gave Sarah a present, a pottery vase, a reject, all squashed and misshapen. She said she knew Sarah would like it because she'd found it in a box marked 'unloved things.'"

"But Sarah was just the fairest in the land."

"No," Kate said, "but she was really, really smart, and everyone said she got it from her father, which offended her mother. I don't suppose Sarah has told you any of this."

"Not a word. More wine?"

"Oh, thank you."

"So her father was smart?" Gabriel prompted.

"Brilliant. My mom went to high school with him. She said no one expected him to be smart, because his parents were farmworkers from Mexico and they could hardly read or speak English. But they stayed in St. Helena so he could go to school, and he won scholarships to Berkeley. Then he went to med school and came back to Napa as Dr. Glass, married to Miss Long Beach."

"Napa?" Gabriel exclaimed. "You grew up in paradise?"

"No, silly, Paradise is a town further north."

"But you have all that wine."

Kate shrugged. "When we were kids, the valley was mostly prunes and nut trees. And most people just knew about Napa's mental hospital. It was called the Napa Asylum for the Insane but then they had to change it. Still, at football games, the other side always called us the Napa Nuts. We all left as soon as we could."

"Where's Dr. Glass now?"

"Well, at first it seemed like he'd run away, but it turned out he was dead," Kate said. "And he'd bought such a great house, down the lane from our house. It was the original Victorian from an old farm, although most of the land had been sold. Still, it was great. Sarah and I used to play games there, like we were arriving at a hotel and which room did we want? And we used to spy on Cecily from the balcony to see what happened when she came home from dates. I was sorry when Sarah's mom sold it. I think Sarah was too, but she never said so."

Gabriel refilled her glass. Kate went on. "Sarah liked our house. I never knew why. It was such a madhouse: six kids, never a place to be alone. Even in the bathroom, someone always wanted you out. Well, she liked us, after she got used to us. She did run away the first time my dad did his gorilla act, but my brother Rory got her to come back.

She was like one of the family after that. She went on trips with us. One time we lost her in San Francisco, but Rory found her. Sarah was only surprised that anyone had missed her.

"She was always different. At my house, everything was laid out: This is what you do, this is what you believe, from the time you got up in the morning. But no one at her house bothered with Sarah, so she just figured things out for herself. Like the name changing. I'd never have thought of doing it, but because she did, I changed mine too, at least a dozen times, except I always chose names like Aurora and Cleopatra.

"And God: Sarah didn't have to believe in Him. She didn't even know about Him. One time when my terrible Aunt Margaret was visiting, she told Sarah to say grace at dinner, and Sarah didn't know what grace was. We didn't always say it; Mom was usually too busy to pray. But Aunt Margaret kept insisting Sarah had to know, and Sarah was almost in tears until Rory said he would say it. But Rory was a failure at religion. He only was an altar boy once, because he took the candle snuffer apart during Mass and so many people were distracted watching him that Father Anselm didn't want him back. The only prayer he knew was *mea culpa, mea culpa, mea maxima culpa*. It shocked Aunt Margaret so much she forgot about Sarah; it was almost like he did it on purpose."

Gabriel looked unimpressed with this tender recollection; Kate explained: "Rory always liked Sarah, even when he hated girls, because no one could holler at him when she was around. If Dad even raised his voice, her eyes would get so big, he'd give up. Sarah was Dad's favorite; we didn't mind, and it came in handy for Rory, especially the time he blew up the kitchen with a rocket. I think Sarah liked him too. She believed anything he told her. She probably still thinks *mea culpa* is grace. If it weren't for Rory, she might still believe she's a boy."

"Oh, really?"

"Yes, you see, we went on a field trip to see the Sea Scouts, and we decided to join, but the leader said it was only for boys. So Sarah said we would just have to be boys. She said if we kept junk in our pockets like Rory and walked like Rory, then we were boys. We thought we were boys until Sarah told Rory. He laughed like anything when she explained why. But then we fell in love with Paul McCartney and we knew we couldn't be in love with him if we were boys. So we knew we had to choose."

"And you chose love."

"In its best form," Kate agreed. "Unconnected to reality. We'd make up stories and pretend we'd dreamt them. Like, there I was in Paris — for Sarah, it was always Paris — and a man on a runaway horse trampled me and it turned out to be Paul and he came to the hospital — "

"Oh God, I love this."

"Oh! Sarah! Hi!"

Two children, dusted with cookie crumbs and drizzled with melted ice cream, danced into the room. Sarah followed, carrying a bag containing two half-eaten jelly donuts, cat treats, four unpeeled bananas, two exploded cartons of chocolate milk, a ripped bag of potato chips, a box of Cheerios, and coffee. She had not had to buy the disassembled salad spinner, although she had offered.

She had been thinking, with more compassion than she had formerly felt, of the dazed faces she had observed on parents in pediatric wards. If she had found Kate sitting in the empty room babbling to herself, she would have understood, but the sight of Kate, sprawled on the floor against a backdrop of white roses, emptied Sarah's head of all thoughts. Lounging next to her was Gabriel Dinesen. Between them was an empty wine bottle.

"Hullo there," Gabriel said.

"Sarah!" Kate called. "I met Gabriel! I think there's some wine left. But maybe not."

"I'll make coffee."

Sarah escaped into the kitchen and set a pan of water on the stove to boil. Rebecca, mysterious and wild, or at least interesting, was evaporating. What her mother had not decimated, Kate would have finished. Kate's mother had always warned her family to never say anything in her presence that could not be safely repeated during Sharing. This was Walking Newspaper Tipsy on Wine.

"D'you know, Gabriel," Kate reflected, "I've often wondered if we weren't a little crazy."

"Nonsense," Gabriel replied. "You were just good Californians. If you don't like reality, you find another one."

Sarah drowned out Kate's voice with the coffee grinder. When the beans were pulverized, Kate was still talking.

"For a long time, it was satisfying to be in love with Paul McCartney. Then I fell in love with James Bond, and Sarah had a thing for Einstein, although he was dead by then. But all of a sudden, we were sixteen, and we'd never been out on a date. You know how high school is, once your reputation is set. We were smart and so we were hopeless social failures.

"Then one weekend a teacher took a group of us to visit UC Santa Cruz. And we went to a dance at a place called the Wild Gold Shore. Boys asked us to dance because they didn't know us. The next Saturday night we took Sarah's mother's car and went back. We paid a dollar and we danced again. We got hooked. We went every Saturday night that we could. We never saw the same people twice. We made up names and tried out different personalities. We even tried being dumb, just to see what it was like. And we danced."

"Your secret life: the dancing princesses!"

"Until Sarah found the real thing."

"No," Gabriel protested. "She didn't. She couldn't."

It was now or never. Sarah would have preferred to go out the kitchen window and sit in a eucalyptus tree with the birds, but she carried in the coffee and an exploded milk carton. She only had chocolate milk.

"Sarah! I was just about to tell Gabriel about the time you found the real thing," Kate said. "Of course, I won't if you don't want me to."

"No coffee for me, thanks," Gabriel said. "I only stopped by to see if you will come tonight. Unless you'd rather go dancing." His silver eyes twinkled at Sarah. He tucked an envelope in the roses and departed.

"Wow," Kate sighed. "Who is he?"

"I don't know."

"It really happens."

"What does?"

"Flowers and dancing, and he looks like Prince Charming. What else do you want?"

"I don't know."

Kate, who once would have leapt to a vigorous defense of love, was strangely silent, and her enthusiasm dimmed further as she described her life. She was working at a bank and going to night school. She didn't have a major, but since she only took one class at a time, there was no pressure to decide. Her husband, Sterling, was out of work just now. They had moved to the city for his job, but three months later he was laid off. Did Sarah remember Sterling?

"But you're doing things, Sarah," she said, "just like we planned."

"You have your children." They were cute, now that they were sound asleep on her sleeping bag. The cat was curled up with them

"Lucy and Avery?" Kate asked. "Oh, they're not mine. They're Rory's. He's divorced now and he ended up with the kids. They've just moved back to California. He had to get permission to leave Massachusetts. They're staying with us while he looks for a place to live. He hasn't said what he's going to do. Well, he has to work. He had thousands of dollars in legal fees. I think he's sorry he didn't go to law school after all."

"He didn't? I thought he was going to go into politics and save the world."

"That was a long time ago, Sarah. I'll bet he couldn't even tell you who the president is now. He still drags his books everywhere. All he brought from Boston, besides the kids, are books, but most of them are about physics, of all things."

"Physics?"

"Weird, isn't it?"

"Yes," Sarah said. "Well, maybe not."

"He had to go back to Boston for one more court thing, so I said I'd keep the kids for him. He also wanted to hear a talk at MIT about whether someone might have made a mistake, which would mean the universe is only nine billion years old instead of eighteen billion, or something like that. You might like talking to him," she added.

CHAPTER 5

WHEN SHE WAS alone again, Sarah opened Gabriel's note: "The Scoundrels of Leisure," it read. "At home today. Follow the map." The hand-drawn web of roads was highlighted in yellow. "I suppose," she said to the cat, "I could just drop by."

She followed the map out of the city over the Bay Bridge and into the crowded flatlands of East Bay. The route twisted up into the Berkeley hills until, near the summit, it came to a road lined with a hodgepodge of houses in Spanish, Tudor, and Colonial styles. The "x" on the map marked a modern house, made of glass and metal and perched half on land, half in the air, like an airplane, hovering but never able to land.

Sarah parked her car. She always had enough courage to go so far but then no further; in this case, it was the driveway. Before she backed up, she lingered to admire the view, the cities below, the bay, and San Francisco, sparkling in the afternoon sun. Beyond the Golden Gate, dark clouds were gathering at sea.

A storm? It never rained in the summer. In Napa, summers were day after day of sun, varied only by the amount of fog that made its way inland from the ocean. Rain wasn't supposed to fall until after harvest. Crops needed rain, but only at the right times, not too soon or too late, and not too much, because then the Napa River flooded.

Sarah had grown up thinking that rain was something like love: unpredictable and rare, yet everything depended on it.

Unexpectedly, her little car trembled. Gabriel was bouncing on the fender. "Hullo!" he called. "It's about time."

SARAH WAS NOT entirely sure how she had landed in a leather chair by a glass wall that commanded a view of much of the Pacific Ocean. The chair was revolving and she could not figure out how to turn it off. She accepted a glass of red wine but declined marijuana and cocaine. The spinning chair was enough of a challenge for her senses, compounded by pounding music and smoke. Already she had lost sight of the door.

The room resembled a dusty museum filled with spears, masks, statues, jugs, jars, and books, but, by far, the most intriguing collection was its inhabitants. The Scoundrels of Leisure were Gabriel's best friends, ever since his arrival in the Bay Area a month earlier. They shared the house, which belonged to Gabriel's uncle, an anthropologist on sabbatical; the professor had bought the house with his inheritance, not with his salary, Gabriel explained. He was in the South Pacific, but Sarah decided he was missing an opportunity to observe a group as unique as any newly discovered tribe on an overlooked island. The Scoundrels of Leisure had their own vocabulary, rituals, and mythology. They also had, collectively, more names than she and Kate had ever adopted.

James, "The Roach," had been working for several years on a thesis on rats' ears. Mark, also called Flake, was in his fifth year of law school. This day was his turn to swallow a fish from the aquarium, but he had not done it. Philip, aka Crotch, had been rejected by thirty-seven medical schools; still, his only ambition for as long as he could remember — this time might not exceed two weeks — had been to be a gynecologist. Harry, also known as Harry the Swinger or the Human Chimney, was an unemployed teacher with enough muscles for four men. Led by Gabriel, who was only called Gabriel, they were an affable band of lost souls: irrelevant, irreverent, uncommitted, unsuccessful, unstressed, and happy. It is easy to feel that way, Sarah mused, when you do not have to pay rent.

The tribe did have its taboos, the chief of which involved answering the telephone. The professor had let Gabriel use the vacant house with only one stipulation, that he live there alone. Gabriel's mother, who mistrusted everyone in California, called often. She could ruin everything, Gabriel warned. A respectful silence prevailed when the phone rang. There are rituals of survival as well as celebration, Sarah decided, and she named her study: "The Magical Rites of the Scoundrels of Leisure: Creating a World within a World and Keeping the Other One Out."

Gabriel perched on the arm of Sarah's chair to rotate with her. It reminded him of Berkeley's cyclotron, he said. "I don't know why anyone wants to accelerate particles, but here I can identify with them. What do you think?"

"I think there are reasons for accelerating them."

"I mean about all this."

"It doesn't seem quite real."

"Neither are you."

"But I want to explain everything."

"Good. Start with gravity."

"He's not really going to eat that fish, is he?"

"He has to," Gabriel said. "It's the rule."

More people arrived. "Ah, business," Gabriel murmured. He bounded up to meet a cherubic young man, whose companion, an ethereal, possibly anemic woman, drifted towards Sarah. The weight of her turquoise jewelry might have been all that kept her from floating out the window. Sarah offered her the chair. The woman rotated with an untroubled air.

"Who are you?" she asked when Sarah was in view.

"Sarah."

"What does that mean?"

"It means — it's what people call me."

The woman's name was Sunset. She loved the chair. "It's so nice," she said. "I was so tired. It takes so long to get here. It's because our car is Italian, or is it Swedish?"

"Where do you live?"

"Nowhere. Our house isn't finished. Grover keeps changing the windows so he can see the sunset."

"But the sun's position in the sky changes."

"I know," Sunset agreed. "It moves all over."

"Actually, it's the earth — "

"The earth goes around the sun," Sunset recited uncertainly. "And the sun moves too. No wonder it's so mixed up."

Abandoning this subject, Sarah asked where their house was. Much effort on her part established the site somewhere in California, in the mountains, but not the real ones.

"Do you mean the foothills? Gold country?"

"Oh no. That's Colombia. Or maybe Mexico."

"It must be nice to live in the mountains."

"It isn't," Sunset said, her expression mournful. "The helicopters make me so nervous. I can't sleep when they buzz. It's worse than the mosquitoes."

"Whose helicopters?"

"The sheriff's, or maybe it's the army's."

"What's Grover's business?" Sarah asked.

"Real estate. And Gabriel is one of his best customers. He is so cute. I thought Mildred was his girlfriend, but maybe she's Harry's. She's real heavy, too, like you. We have to go now." Sunset wafted up out of the chair. "It's been real."

Sarah watched Gabriel hand Grover enough money to buy the city of Oakland. "Let the wild rumpus begin," he announced. "Ah, and here's Mildred!"

Mildred had just come from her class, part three of five sessions on discovering her body. As she shared this, she threw off most of her clothes, revealing a form so abundantly in evidence that Sarah wondered, with only the slightest trace of envy, how Mildred could ever have lost it. Mildred was, indeed, heavy.

"I have to leave," Sarah said to Gabriel. "It's been real."

"But you can't go now. I'm going to cook dinner."

Mildred looked Sarah over. "Gabriel does only bring home women who can cook."

"Wrong." Gabriel steered Sarah into the kitchen and around several overflowing bags of trash. "I bring home women who will admire me as I cook. Have you noticed that I've introduced you without telling anyone your name? Can I say it's Rebecca?"

"But it isn't, really."

"I supposed you've never read *Ivanhoe.*"

"Gabriel, I have to tell you about my class." Mildred came into the kitchen. "It is the first time I have ever really felt integrated. Can you imagine," she asked Sarah, "walking into a room and taking off all of your clothes?"

"No," said Sarah, conjuring up a wicked image of Mildred carrying her unintegrated body parts about in a shopping bag.

"It's so healing."

"Healing of what?"

"Energy."

"How do you heal energy?"

"Do you know anything about the human body?"

"Not very much, no."

Far away, a shimmer of lightning flashed through the clouds as

Mildred discussed the effect of healing energy on passion. Becoming integrated had changed her life; more importantly, it had changed her relationships.

"How?" Sarah asked wonderingly.

"Love."

"I've never figured out what love has to do with relationships."

Mildred explained. Fundamentally, she had always believed she should love all men, but she had gotten herpes in the process. Men had only loved her for her body, which she now knew was not an integrated thing to do. By the time she had described, in lachrymose detail, all the men who had loved her only for her body, Gabriel had sautéed several chickens. Mildred's experiences had been so disillusioning she had done the unthinkable: she had given up sex.

"This is a discouraging trend," Gabriel said.

It was true, Mildred declared, she had been celibate for nearly two weeks before she met Harry. As she neared the gripping climax of her tale, in which she had made love with her entire body, so overcome with passion she had not noticed that Flake and Roach were in the room — she was drowned out by a roar of thunder.

"Earthquake!" shouted Flake. The Scoundrels of Leisure all tumbled into the kitchen. They stared in astonishment at the window.

"It's raining," Harry said. "Now this is weird."

He was answered by more thunder. The lights blinked and went out. Without lights, music, or the prospect of dinner, a chill descended over the gathering. Mildred put her clothes back on. Gabriel proposed a solution: "We'll leave."

The group followed him, without question, through the rain, thunder, and lightning to his car. Sarah branched off toward her own.

"Sarah!" Gabriel sprang after her. "Where are you going?"

"Home."

"Your wish is my command!"

"You had better go or you'll be hit by lightning."

"I'd love it."

"No, you wouldn't."

"Then you had better save me from my worst impulses and come too. Otherwise, I will stand here until I melt into a mere stump of my former self."

CHAPTER 6

SARAH SAT IN the front seat with Gabriel, and just how Mildred, Harry, Flake, Roach, and Crotch fit into the back, she did not wish to know. She rode warily, like a tourist who suspected she had got on the wrong bus but could only understand a few words in the banter of the natives. They were singing, "We all live in a yellow submarine."

She was curious as Gabriel skidded over the wet streets and onto the highway. Did no one else wonder where they were going? Her unease grew as they headed north, past the fairyland of lights disguising the oil refineries on the Carquinez Strait and glittering C&H Sugar plant sign. They crossed the bridge into Vallejo, just south of Napa. Through the blur of rain, she saw the exit to Napa.

"You said you wanted to go home." Gabriel chuckled as he swerved onto it. "That fortune-teller you went to, was it the one on Highway 29? When she looked at my palm, she ran screaming from the room. Isn't that the old Victorian where murder was done? Haunted, of course. But nothing beats the Napa Asylum for the Insane. Once a Napa Nut, always a Napa Nut, eh? Don't look now," he murmured, "but Mildred is sucking Harry's thumb. I am so inhibited."

Only when they had swept through the town of Napa did Sarah begin to breathe more easily. She did not care where Gabriel's magical mystery tour was going, as long as it was not to meet her mother. They sped onto the Silverado Trail, which ran north from Napa along the eastern hills of the valley. Abruptly, Gabriel swung his car off the Trail and onto an unmarked gravel road. Narrow and unlit, it zigzagged up a hillside. He stopped in a grove of oak trees.

"End of part one," he announced. "Everyone out." He vanished into the dark.

Why did they all do everything Gabriel commanded, Sarah wondered as she joined the witless band huddled beneath the dripping trees? The rain had ended, and the moon, still shrouded in clouds, gave only a faint clue that they were on a narrow ridge above a wrinkle in the hills. A light wobbled into view: Gabriel was driving a Jeep that lurched and sputtered and had only one working headlight.

"Part two," he announced. "The wild ride."

They all got in and the Jeep shot off, heading for a tree. Gabriel veered around it, cackling. They bounced down a steep dirt road pitted with holes. Bushes scratched the Jeep. "Lean left! Lean right!" Gabriel shouted as they careened around boulders. "No brakes!" The others echoed his manic laughter. Mildred cried, "How wild!"

Sarah clung to the roll bar, recalling the time when she was thirteen and discovered a lump beneath her chin. She diagnosed cancer and earnestly mourned her impending, premature death. Now she promised to resurrect a reverence for life if only she would not be smashed into a tree.

They screeched to a halt. They were in the dark, but as the moon drifted into view, it illuminated a huge, dark ruin of a building: It was a castle, hidden in the forest and overgrown with brambles. Gargoyles leered down from a tattered balustrade. One tower still stood; the other was shattered. Black holes, like blind eyes, peered through the tangle of thorns.

Gabriel led the way down a ragged path to an enormous wooden door that creaked and groaned when he pushed it open. They crept into a room permeated with the musty smell of locked-away things.

"Welcome to the Castle Paradise," Gabriel said, lighting a candle that sent shadows gamboling over wraith-like shapes of furniture covered with dusty white sheets. "At least that's what the man who built it named it. Have a seat. Make yourself at home. Just look out for spiders. It's their home now."

When each had sat down carefully, Gabriel continued: "It was built by a banished European count, or so he said he was. He came to California during the Gold Rush and made a fortune selling shovels to miners. He found this little valley inside a valley, and he wanted it, despite warnings that the native people who had been driven from it still haunted and protected it. An earlier settler had built an adobe house and a chapel here but he put his house on the ancient burial site; it collapsed on him in an earthquake.

"This count, who had a dozen different names, wanted a winery; it was all the thing in 1865. He built this place to remind him of his lost home, possibly the Castle Bran. He planted vineyards, but he never made a bottle of wine. He vanished one night and was never seen again. The story was, he was burying treasure in a lost cave in these hills. His nephew inherited the castle, but sold it when phylloxera wiped out the vineyards. The new owner replanted and was wiped out by Prohibition. It was abandoned when my father found it.

"My father is a shrink, so he knows the reasons for all the bizarre things he does, why he bought this place and why he leaves it empty now but won't sell it.

"We came here after my parents had split up, after my mother burned down our house; she was never much of a cook. My father's plan was to create the ideal commune here. He was in his liberal phase then; he and his colleagues were almost admitting they were not much of an alternative to insanity. They decided they'd lost touch with the right side of their brains, the intuitive, creative, and spiritual side, as compared to the rational, mathematical left side. In order to find it, they needed to free themselves from an urban setting. The idea was they would make wine to support the commune. They probably would have been better off looking for the buried treasure.

"It was a great life for us kids here, though. The grown-ups had more trouble adjusting. Once my father and the co-leader, Abe Barkham, a Jungian, came to blows over how much white flour they could put in whole wheat bread. And then there was the fireplace. The chimney had collapsed. They spent six months rebuilding it and planned a celebration around lighting the first fire. When the room filled with smoke, no one would admit anything was wrong. Every night we had to light a fire, even though it was July, until Jed Barkham and I dismantled the chimney. This caused another fight about whose kid was more maladjusted.

"We lived here until my mother showed up and everything ended. The commune split up and we went to live in Texas, like none of this had ever happened. Except my father has never sold the place. He's writing a book about it. It's called *In Search of the Lost Mind*."

Gabriel proposed a tour. He blew out the candle but produced a flashlight. "Sometimes the ghosts blow up flashlights," he warned. "Let there be dark."

They went out into a courtyard, past a broken fountain to a path that led to the adobe chapel, which the commune had used as a store-room and workshop. A loom, a spinning wheel, and bags of mildewed yarn shared the space with statues of Jesus and Mary; sacks of seeds sat with candlesticks on an altar. The tour went on, but Sarah lingered at the foot of a set of stairs.

"Touch the spindle," a voice behind her warbled. "Touch it, I say." Gabriel sprang out of the dark. "And so," he hummed, "Rebecca wondered, why were their fates entwined? Why had he brought her to Pemberley?"

"Manderley."

"So you do read romances."

"Not anymore."

"So what was this real thing you didn't want Kate to tell me about?"

"Nothing."

He picked up a candlestick and tried to stab himself in the heart.

"It wasn't real. He was a football star. Rob Hamilton. Kate always wanted to drive by his house to see what it was like to be groupies."

"There's his car, Sarah! He's in the garage! Drive past again!"

"No! He might notice."

"He won't know who we are. God, he's cute. Sarah, slow down."

"I can't. I know him, sort of."

To Sarah's relief, Gabriel put down the candlestick. She said, "He was in my government class."

"I can't drive past his house again, Kate. He's moved to the desk behind me."

"Oh, god, have you talked to him?"

"No. Mostly he just puts his feet on my desk."

"Doesn't the teacher say anything?"

"Are you kidding? Mr. Garzoli?" The government teacher was also the football coach.

"Sarah, maybe he likes you!"

"Don't be crazy, Kate. I'm not a cheerleader. And I don't think he has a brain at all. He just sits and sniffs Magic Markers."

"He started standing by my locker."

The first bell rang; lunch was over.

"Sarah! He's there again, standing in front of your locker!"

"Can you loan me your book, Kate?"

"You have to go to your locker sometime."

"Just loan me your book."

"And then he talked to me. At least, I guess it was a football player's way of talking."

Enormous feet landed on her desk, one on either side of her. A paw tugged on her hair.

"Hey, where's your book?"

"I forgot it."

"Here, take mine. I never use it. Hey, are you going to the game on Friday night?"

"I don't know."

"You should. It'll be great. We're going to kill them."

"Oh. That's great."

"Yeah. You'll see them in the film Garzoli shows today. It's the game from last year. A couple of good plays, and the rest is pitiful. No defense. No offense. After the game, I'll look for you at Round Table."

"Kate and I went to a football game. Afterwards, everyone went to Round Table."

They sat in a corner. Sarah tried to be invisible.

"Kate, stop looking around."

"I can't help it. This is so exciting. Do you like him?"

"I don't know. I've tried a few dreams on him."

"Like where you're walking on the beach and a wave knocks you down and — "

"No, just the simple ones like, you know, we're in Paris and we're talking —"

"Oh God, there he is!"

"Don't stare, Kate. What's he doing?"

"He's getting a drink. Root beer. His hair is wet. He must have taken a shower. He's wearing a Pendleton. Red. Oh. He's talking to Sherry Duvall."

"He probably forgot."

"Now he's looking around. Oh God, he's coming this way."

"And he talked to us."

A hand rocked her shoulder. Rob Hamilton, who had scored the winning touchdown, sat down at their table. They were conspicuous. Kate was dying.

"Hey, what did I tell you? We killed them."

Sarah's brain shut down. Kate valiantly carried on the conversation while Sarah tried to think of something to say to this bruised and freckled object of admiration. She gave up and wished she were far away, dancing with strangers. Maybe he wished he were back on the football field, killing people. He drank his root beer, stood up, and rattled her bones once more.

"See you in class," he said.

"What happened?" Kate asked.

"Nothing," Sarah said.

Not long after this, Kate had her own fling with reality, in which she told one of her dancing partners her name and went as far as the parking lot with him.

"What happened?" Sarah asked.

"Not too much," Kate said.

"And that was that," Sarah said to Gabriel.

"That's it?" Gabriel asked. "You are my kind of woman, Rebecca." He smiled at her, and briefly Sarah considered changing her name one more time.

The last stop on the tour was a pond. "Here is where we look for ghosts," Gabriel said. "The count dug it where the first adobe house had stood on the burial grounds. One story says that ghostly hands reached up and pulled him under when he was swimming. It might be why my father built a swimming pool, but maybe it was because no one liked to swim in mud."

"Oh hell," Harry the Swinger mumbled. "I believe in ghosts."

"Don't think of them as ghosts," Sarah said. "Think of them as advanced technology."

"No," Gabriel said. "You have to think of them as ghosts."

"I see one!" Harry shrieked and fell down as the others scattered and ran for the Jeep.

An hour later they were back in Berkeley. The electricity was on, and everyone returned to their previous places as if they had only left for a fire drill, except for Sarah, who slipped away, back to the city. She took Flake's goldfish with her.

CHAPTER 7

THE CAT'S COLD feet on Sarah's neck woke her up. Her doorbell was buzzing. A dense fog covered the world outside, and standing in it, at the front door, were Lucy and Avery McIntyre. Lucy was wearing a sleeveless cotton dress. Avery was barefoot.

"Hello," Lucy said. "Kate went to work, so we came to see you."

"Are you all alone?"

"Yes, only Sterling is there. Rory got tied up at the airport, but we don't know who did it. He said he would ask you, is it all right?"

"Of course it is."

While she called Kate's number, they fixed themselves Cheerios with chocolate milk. When she hung up, Avery was investigating the cupboards, and Lucy inspecting the purloined fish, floating listlessly in a bowl.

"I think it's dead," Sarah said.

"Why?"

"I don't know. We could dissect it — cut it up. It's how you find out what things look like on the inside."

It did not occur to Sarah that dissecting cadavers was probably not on any list of activities for preschoolers. She said they first should be sure it was dead and found her stethoscope. They listened to heartbeats: their own, the cat's, and the fish's. It was dead; they cut it up.

When the carcass was mangled, the children looked about for another subject. The cat had fled.

Unsure how to reclaim the knives, Sarah suggested they draw the dead fish in her lab book. Lucy traded in her knife for a pencil and Sarah's lab book. Avery took a pencil, but preferred to work on the wall. This was not so bad a thing, Sarah decided, hiding the knives.

"What does this say?" Lucy asked, studying the words on the title page of the lab book.

"Things I Might Not See Again."

Sarah had only begun making drawings in this book. The first ones were awkward and unfinished: a man's face, obscure but handsome; a Gypsy cart; a torn-eared cat; a spider in its web. "Yuck," Lucy commented.

"Is it that bad?" Sarah asked.

"I don't like spiders."

"Don't you? I've always thought they're interesting. They are so little, yet they know just what to do to take care of themselves."

Lucy looked doubtful. "Do you see this web?" Sarah asked. "It's the one I was trying to draw. The spider spun it while the window was open and now I can't close it or I'd destroy her web. Widdershins loves it, because he can come and go whenever he wishes. I've noticed he is careful not to hurt the web. I think they might be in cahoots."

They drew the fish and named its parts; they named their parts, too. Lucy's nose was Rose; Avery's feet were Macaroni and Cheese. "I have a tail," he told Sarah. "So does Rory. Lucy doesn't."

Here, the doorbell buzzed wildly, and Kate burst into the room, followed by a plump, panting man whom Sarah instantly recalled as a man whose best opinion of himself was his own: Kate's husband, Sterling.

"Lucy, that was very bad," he began.

Kate cut him off. "I called home, and they were gone."

"I told him, Kate," Lucy said. "He said tell me at the commercial."

Kate sighed. Sterling said, "I only watched television while I was working on my résumé."

"I thought you were going to do the laundry."

"You know I hate laundry. Anyway, you're lucky I remembered Sarah had called."

"Never mind," Kate said. "Let's go, shall we, kids?"

"No," Avery said.

"Rory will be home soon."

Lucy wavered. Avery said, "No, thanks."

"You can't stay here all day."

"Sarah doesn't mind," Lucy said.

"I don't." Sarah was oddly surprised. "Don't you have to go back to work?"

Kate relented. Sterling frowned. "This is wrong, Kate. As I have said, although Rory doesn't seem to hear me, raising children is very difficult if you change your mind." He followed Kate out the door to finish making his point.

Lucy shut the door. "Now, what shall we do?"

They walked to the store to buy lunch. Sarah fared better than she had the day before. They left the store with alphabet soup, Oreo cookies, peaches, crayons, two plastic bowls shaped like monkeys, and a package of sunflower seeds. Their progress home was slow because they had to explore the wonders to be found on a sidewalk.

"Dog poop," Avery said reverently. "Shall we put it in our bag?"

"Well, no," Sarah said.

"One time Avery ate dog poop," Lucy told her.

"Oh no. Really?"

"Yes. But only Rory threw up."

They ate lunch and planted all the seeds that Avery didn't eat in the window box. Avery ate the pink cookie from the statue's plate.

Lucy replaced it with an Oreo. They wanted Sarah to sit with them on her sleeping bag. Avery snuggled up against her and fell asleep.

"Now we can read the book about spiders." Lucy said, opening the lab book. "Once upon a time, the spider said, 'We're in cahoots,' to the unicorn."

She leaned against Sarah, too. This coziness was an unknown sensation for Sarah, who observed people but touched them only when she had to. She said, "What unicorn?"

"There." Lucy pointed to Sarah's first drawing of the cat. "Did you see one, Sarah?"

"No, not really."

"They have to hide or they will end up in a zoo. That's what Rory said."

"Did he? He sounds rather smart."

"He is. Well, you know him. He said so." Lucy whispered, "There's one outside, Sarah."

"Where?"

"It wants you to draw a picture."

"It does?"

"Yes. Of a world. For a unicorn and fairies."

"What fairies?"

"The fairies that ride on the unicorn. Can you see them?"

Sarah squinted at the window. "Maybe you should draw their world."

"No, they want you to do it."

Sarah drew a web on the grid of the lab book. She added a creature at the edge, but it looked like a cat, not a unicorn. She drew flowers winding through the web.

"The unicorn and the fairies are on the other side of the flowers," Sarah explained. She looked up from her work. Lucy had gone to open the door.

"Here's Rory," she said.

When Sarah had last seen Rory McIntyre, he was eighteen and shining in the glory of an American high school Renaissance man: the handsome, popular scholar and athlete, the student body president, the star of *Guys and Dolls*, and the National Merit Scholar whose experiment with bean plants had been launched on a NASA satellite.

In the intervening years, he had clearly suffered some sort of blight. He was still tall, but thinner, pale, and bearded. He had exchanged the fastidious khakis and button-down shirts of the high school elite for faded jeans, battered running shoes, and a moth-eaten sweater unraveling at the cuffs. His copper-colored hair was long and shaggy. His green-gold eyes had shadows beneath them, and in them a guarded look, which, Sarah allowed, could have been the result of living any amount of time with Sterling.

"Hello." With a nervous spasm, he picked up Lucy and glanced at the door.

"Avery ate the seeds," Lucy told him. "And we cut Sarah's fish up, all to pieces."

"The seeds shouldn't hurt him," Sarah said swiftly, for Rory's unease had turned to alarm. "They were sunflowers."

"Oh no — believe me, it's not the worst thing he's eaten, but your fish — "

"It was dead."

"We were dissecting it," Lucy said. "And we listened to hearts. The fish's heart was dead. We can listen to your heart too."

"We have to be going," Rory said. "Thank you, Sarah."

"You said we could go see her," Lucy pointed out.

"But I didn't mean immediately, did I?"

"You might have." Lucy patted his cheek. Rory put her down and came to collect Avery, who woke up and, in a burst of affection, threw his arms around Rory's neck and crashed his head into his father's nose. Sarah heard a dreadful crunch and saw the blood drain from Rory's face until he was as white as the wall. He sank down onto the floor. She hurried into the kitchen to concoct an ice pack.

"Thank you," Rory said, when he could speak again.

"It's quite painful."

"I saw stars. That hasn't happened since I got hit by a baseball bat."

"Is your nose dead?" Lucy asked.

"Just unconscious," Rory said. "No, you cannot dissect it."

"Do you mind — " Sarah knelt beside him but was too shy to touch his nose. "It might be broken. I've only seen a broken nose once, but when the doctor touched the man's nose, he fainted. I'd hate to make you faint."

"So would I."

"It's probably all right."

"Yes. Well, we should be going."

"But I'm hungry," Avery protested.

"Me too," Lucy said.

"We have trespassed enough."

"No, we haven't," Avery said. "Sarah has Cheerios."

"And coffee," Lucy said. "You could have some."

Sarah was effectively prompted. "Would you like — "

"He would," Lucy said. "He always would like coffee."

While Sarah made coffee, she listened to the conflict of wills transpiring in the other room, wherein Lucy and Avery were insisting on pouring the milk. Rory came into the kitchen once to find something he could use to mop the floor. When Sarah brought in the coffee, the floor was clean and the two children were eating. Rory was staring at the cereal floating in Lucy's bowl.

"Capillarity," he said to Lucy, who continued eating, unimpressed.

"Do you take milk?" Sarah asked. "Do you mind if it's chocolate? What about capillarity?"

"It's the force that causes — the attraction — it's what makes the Os float together. But, you probably already know that. Black coffee is fine. Thanks."

He tilted the mug and studied it, as if he were wary of its contents. Finally, he took a sip, just as Lucy jumped up to hug him. The cup flew out of his hand. Sarah dropped her own cup to try to catch his, and so both smashed. Rory collected the pieces while Sarah wiped up the coffee. Avery filled in the silence: "Damn, oh damn. Jesus Christ. Goddammit, not again."

"I'll get more," Sarah said.

"Only if you have a plastic cup with a lid."

"Actually, I only have bowls."

"That's fine." Rory reached out to catch Avery, who was edging towards the kitchen. "Don't touch anything."

"There's really nothing he can break — " Sarah was cut short by a crash as her vase of flowers went over.

"Damn," Rory said. "Goddammit."

"It's only water."

"We'll leave now."

"But I have to go to the bathroom," Lucy said. "Alone." She went into the bathroom. Sarah poured more coffee into her two Chinese bowls. Rory held a bowl with one hand and the back of Avery's shirt with the other. They drank their coffee, bereft of conversation.

"We can name your parts," Avery suggested. "I named my tail George."

Rory thought of something to say: "Kate said you're going to med school."

"Oh. Well. Yes."

"Here?"

"No. New York."

"Then why are you here?"

Before Sarah could think of a reply, Lucy waltzed out of the bath-room wearing Sarah's nightgown. Her face was painted with tooth-paste. "Now I can go to the ball," she announced.

When Rory and his children were gone, Sarah sat still for a mo-ment, contemplating her scattered roses. Then she pressed her fingers onto her wrist to count her pulse. "Nothing," she said to the cat. "Not a flicker. But why didn't I ask him how old the universe is?"

CHAPTER 8

JUST HOW SARAH Glass had fallen in love with Rory McIntyre was as odd as it was unexpected, for it was devoid of romance as either Kate or Sarah imagined it. Their theories did differ, but if Kate ever noticed, as the heroes of their lunchtime dreams began to deviate in form from Paul McCartney, that Sarah's had taken on a striking resemblance to her older brother, she never remarked on this.

Kate's heroes were all black-haired, blue-eyed, mysterious, and brooding, tormented by secrets that had to be revealed and put right by the end of one lunch period. Sarah's stories were sadly lacking in passion. As much as she admired Kate's high dramas, she could not fashion one for herself; her heroine was more like a villain, and the crime not believing in love. She could not imagine a thrilling rescue such as Kate routinely constructed, although she agreed it was probably easiest to fall into someone's arms if you were leaping from a burning building. Kate's stories also had fiery kissing scenes, although neither really believed that a man would really do so odd a thing as put his tongue in someone else's mouth. Sarah's characters rarely got beyond giving each other meaningful looks. Kate had to step in to spice things up: "And then he swept you into his arms and kissed you until you couldn't breathe."

"Maybe you can't breathe if someone's tongue blocks your windpipe."

"Sarah, he has to kiss you sometime. Everybody kisses everybody, all the time. Don't you like kissing?"

Sarah knew that Kate came from a family where everyone kissed everybody else all the time, but if anyone had ever kissed her, she didn't remember what it was like.

That Rory could be the hero of a romance did not occur to Kate, who did not understand how he managed to be so popular. When they arrived at Napa High School, Rory was a big man on campus, even though he didn't play football because he didn't want to be hit on the head and he only played baseball because he liked it. He played piano in the Jazz Band, and his best friend Matt Biagi, who had been a running back of great promise until he wrecked his knees, played trumpet; and they made band acceptably cool. Even what might have been the greatest strike against Rory — he was an outstanding student — didn't cast him into social oblivion. He was so personable, so handsome and good-humored, he was deemed to be smart only by accident.

His brains were further excused by his car, an antique roadster he had restored in his father's auto shop. He drove Kate and Sarah to school and, although unpopular themselves, they garnered a gratifying degree of prestige when they were seen in his shining burgundy MG.

They could fit into the passenger seat if Sarah sat in the middle, an unnerving arrangement that rendered her unfit to make conversation, intelligent or otherwise. The other blight on these rides was Kate's tendency to begin recounting her newest story. Sarah was never sure how far Rory was taken in by her efforts to imply she only listened to Kate as an exercise in friendship, but sometimes he winked at her. When he did such an astonishing thing, she felt an interior upheaval, like an earthquake, and this was even before she fell in love with him.

Sarah was living with her sister and mother in the house that her father had bought; although he had been gone for nearly a decade, he had left her this elegant, white Victorian with its Juliet balcony, its gardens and creek and trees. She loved the house. Everyone admired it, although no one knew what it was like to live inside it. Sarah didn't try to explain what she herself could not understand.

Isabelle had kept the house, although it was a constant reminder of the perfidy of her husband, a man who had not only left her but died too, but she had gotten rid of most of his things, including his books, paintings, and furniture he had bought. What to do with the three children she'd been stuck with was another matter. Aaron, the eldest, bolted early. Cecily, so perfect a replica of her mother, was sometimes excused for existing, but Sarah, the youngest, the dark, bright, awkward changeling, was doomed.

She had learned early to stay out of her mother's way, but as she grew, it did not take much more than a passing encounter to provoke a flood of ugly words more painful than blows. Many nights, Sarah would take her books and study in her mother's car; if Isabelle locked the house, she slept there. In the morning, when the door was unlocked, she slipped inside to change before Kate and Rory arrived to pick her up, and she could escape to school.

She fell in love with Rory the same month she turned fourteen, when a sweltering summer lingered into October. One night, it only took the sight of Sarah reading as she ate a solitary dinner to provoke Isabelle. Sarah fled to the car, and as she read by flashlight, clouds moved in. The first rain since May thrummed on the roof throughout the night, and she didn't wake up until a car pulled into the driveway. She sat up, and, in alarm, saw Rory's bewildered face looking at her through the window.

"I'm not ready," she gasped as he opened the door. "You don't have to wait for me."

"I don't mind," he said. "I'm early. Kate's sick."

Her panic increased as he walked to the house with her. He had never been inside it. She ran up the stairs, but no matter how fast she changed, she knew he would still have time to see the bleak and dusty emptiness.

"Ready." She ran back down to where he stood waiting in the entry.

"Don't you want to eat breakfast?"

At his house, she knew, everyone ate breakfast. His mother cooked it, just as she did dinner. Sarah didn't know which would be worse, to tell him she never ate breakfast or to have him follow her into the kitchen and see where her mother had flung a coffee pot against the wall. It would still be lying on the floor in a puddle of coffee grounds.

"I'm not hungry," she said, but her voice was drowned out by a louder one. Cecily.

"It sounds like the idiot has come in."

"Really, Cecily," came the reply. "How can you say 'idiot,' when she is so brilliant? If only we knew everything! Imagine to be so smart, you go around telling the world you are Mexican!"

When Sarah was in second grade, she had told her teacher about her grandparents, who lived in Mexico, and Isabelle had never forgotten this because the principal had called the former Miss Long Beach to ask if she needed help translating school documents.

"Mexican!" Isabelle said. "I would send her to live in Mexico, if only anyone wanted her. Then she'd find out that her father the saint didn't care about her or anyone else. But who am I to try to tell anything to someone who knows everything? And I will sell this house. I hate every stick in this white elephant. I will sell it and she can just find somewhere to live. Mexico."

Through a haze of pain, Sarah felt Rory touch her arm. "We better go," he said. "We'll be late."

He drove in silence, and the road to school stretched like a rubber band until it was twice as long as usual. Sarah was mortified; she was sure it was fatal. She had spent many cold nights in the car wondering how long a night could be, but always in the morning, the world resumed its order under the healing balm of a day like all the rest: classes in, classes out, and for tomorrow, read the following pages. Now she was unmasked, and there could not be a worse witness than Rory McIntyre, the paragon of normal. She only didn't understand why he stayed in the car when he finally reached the school parking lot. He rubbed his steering wheel and diffidently he said, "You know you can always come to our house, don't you?"

"It doesn't matter. It's better to be locked out than locked in." Her voice broke; tears spilled down her cheeks. Her humiliation was complete. She found the door and ran.

She did the unthinkable that day: she didn't go to school. She walked until she was numb and hollow from her head to her feet. She returned to her house only because she had nowhere else to go. She had no plan except to avoid Rory McIntyre for the rest of her life.

As soon as she opened the door, the telephone rang. Kate needed to borrow her geometry book. "Rory was supposed to ask you," she said, "but he couldn't find you after school. He said he'll come and get it, but first he has a million things to do. He's so important, he might die of a fat head any day."

"I'll bring it over." Sarah was sure she could be gone before Rory finished a million things, but once inside the McIntyres' house, amid all the wonderful uproar — the twins had put suntan oil in the aquarium and killed all the fish — she was caught, as always; she didn't want to leave.

Kate was resting on the sofa. "Cramps," she sighed. "I suffered, but I thought up a great dream. Do you want to hear it?"

"No."

Undeterred, Kate began to recite her newest creation, in which she was locked in an attic of a desolate mansion until she was rescued by a black-haired, blue-eyed man who had been roaming the bleak countryside pondering his problems.

"Why were you locked in the attic this time?" Sarah asked.

"I haven't worked that out yet, but this time I had cramps. I thought I might die. I was in anguish. He took me in his arms, and I wept on his shoulder. But how could I explain to him why I was suffering?"

This was a dilemma that had puzzled Kate and Sarah ever since fifth grade, when all the girls had been told to line up to leave the class with no explanation. One boy said they were going to get shots, which caused three girls to go into hysterics. It turned out that they were only going to watch a film about the menstrual cycle, but they concluded they were being told a secret of life guarded from men. Only Sarah spotted a paradox, in that the film had been made by Walt Disney. How did he know?

"I wonder," Kate continued, "how do you cry on someone's shoulder? Sitting or standing, it seems like it would be awkward."

"I think it sounds stupid."

"Why?" Kate was dumbfounded; Sarah might not like passion as much as Kate did, but she was always as concerned about technical details.

Just then Rory walked into the room. Sarah felt her face turn hot, then cold, then hot again. Kate stared at her with undisguised interest. Rory said, "Sal, I was looking for you."

Joe McIntyre always called her Sally, which made her feel like the name she had given herself was really her own, but this was the first time Rory had made his own version of it.

He picked up a ball of yarn from his mother's knitting basket, unwound it and wrapped it around his wrist, and when he was in danger of cutting off his circulation, he tried to untangle it. "We need some monsters for a Halloween party, and since you can draw, I was wondering if you would draw them. I'll paint them, and Kate, if she lives, can wash the brushes." He dropped the yarn ball and chased it as it rolled across the floor.

Later, Sarah realized that this might have been when she fell in love, but she had never been in love with anyone she had seen in person, so she didn't recognize it at first. She only knew that, after this, everything he said or did was suddenly magnified as if she were seeing it under a microscope. She drew a gallery of creatures for his party and did not know why he insisted they were great when they were so glaringly inadequate. Once, while she was working on the floor, he stepped on her hand, and when he rubbed her fingers to see if they were broken, Sarah did not feel pain as much as confusing bliss, but she would not have guessed this had anything to do with love.

Halloween arrived. Kate and Sarah spent the day at Queen of the Valley hospital making masks for sick children. They returned to Kate's thoroughly depressed by their good works. Rory was going to his party. John, Kate's oldest brother, was going to a party. The younger children were going trick-or-treating, although they had also been invited to parties.

Rory, dressed as Merlin, left last. When his father said, "Be home by midnight," a cool, arrogant look flashed across Rory's face. Sarah, too, was astounded that anyone would tell the magnificent Rory what to do.

She and Kate answered the door for trick-or-treaters. Kate spun a limp story about a stranger at a masked ball. By eleven o'clock, the night was much too long. They went to bed.

Long past midnight, they were awakened by a banging on Kate's window. "Would you let me in?" Rory called. "Door's locked."

Kate and Sarah went to the door. Rory's friends propped him against the porch and left. Rory tried to stand up, sagged, and collapsed, vomiting into the grass.

Lights went on in the house. Footsteps pounded down the hall. Joe and Jean McIntyre rushed outside to where Rory lay sprawled on the lawn. Jean shooed everyone back inside, but still they could hear the ruckus of Joe's shouting, Jean's weeping, and the retching sounds of Rory being sick again.

"I think he's drunk," Kate whispered, and the thought that Rory might die in agony kept Sarah awake the rest of the night.

On Sunday morning, Joe decreed that Rory would attend the first Mass; when Rory refused, another storm of shouting ensued. Sarah's shock as much as her courtesy told her to leave. She was fleeing down the lane to her house when a car pulled up beside her. It was Rory. "Do you want a ride?" he asked.

He looked gruesome, like a trampled Halloween mask, greenish-white with bloodshot eyes. He said nothing until they reached her driveway. "Could I come in?" he asked.

The house was cold and silent. Cecily was gone for the weekend, and Isabelle was never an early riser. "God, it's quiet here," he said. He slumped down onto the black and white tile floor. "I think I'm going to die."

Isabelle appeared at the top of the stairs. "It's Rory McIntyre," Sarah stammered. "He thinks he is going to die."

She held her breath while her unpredictable mother approached the inert boy. "Maybe you would prefer to sleep in a bed," Isabelle said. She told Sarah to get him coffee and aspirin and show him to Aaron's room. To Rory, she said that although he might wish to die, he probably would not. Then she left to play golf. It was the first time in many months that Sarah thought she might like her mother.

Rory flopped into Aaron's bed, and Sarah told him the only comforting thing she could think of: Thomas Jefferson had died of diarrhea, and Charlotte Brontë of morning sickness, but she didn't know of anyone who had died of a hangover. He almost smiled and closed his eyes. He slept most of the day. It was dusk when he came to Sarah's bedroom door. He did not look so bad, but still he flinched when he saw her peanut butter sandwich. She put her book on it.

"I just wanted to say thanks," he said. "And if you will thank your mother for me, too, well, I guess it's off to the guillotine."

Of the following Monday, Sarah remembered every detail. She wore a purple heather skirt and sweater; Rory wore khakis and a yellow shirt. He was quiet on the drive to school, but Kate was talking enough for all three. Rory was in huge trouble, she reported. He was grounded forever, and his parents were going to make him go to Catholic school and become a priest.

"Kate," Rory interrupted, "it's raining. Do you want to walk?"

Sarah asked Kate if she had understood the math. Kate, deeply disappointed, discussed geometry. It wasn't until lunch that Sarah had a chance to ask Kate if her parents could really make Rory be a priest. "Probably not," Kate said. "He'd be pretty bad at it, but he has to go to Mass, because he was rude to my mother and said she believed in myths for idiots."

"He has to, even if he doesn't believe in it?"

"That doesn't matter. Sarah, he was gone all day yesterday, and Mom was so upset, partly because he'd been rude about God, but mostly because they didn't know where he was. When he came home, he didn't look so bad until Mom started crying and Dad was hollering, and Rory cried too, and he never cries, at least not so people can hear.

"I made him a Bloody Mary, like in F. Scott Fitzgerald, except we only had tomato juice and celery. But Rory drank it. Then he told me that at the party, a girl he'd gone out with once, just once, told him she was pregnant, and he got so nervous he drank eight Jack Daniels, three beers, and two piña coladas. Then she said she hadn't meant it was him, and he was so relieved he drank more of everything. He said he made a mistake trying to explain this, and that's why Mom flipped out, and they made him feel like he was the worst person in the universe." Kate paused to let the profound implications of these revelations sink in. "I guess he's not so bad, in spite of his fat head."

No, Sarah agreed, he wasn't. The first bell rang; lunch was over. As she headed to class, the object of her thoughts materialized in front of her. She had never seen Rory alone at school. He was moving so slowly, she would have passed him, except when he saw her he said, "Hey, Sal," and he began walking with her, causing her such mental disorder, she didn't know if she was on her head or feet. He talked quite normally. He told her about the Winter Show and asked if she could paint a giant Santa Claus for it. He wondered if changing the name from Christmas Show made any difference. He agreed when she said no, not when it was filled with the same things. He paused in front of his classroom and said, "See you later."

The second bell rang. Sarah looked around in a daze. She was supposed to be in biology, but instead she had walked with Rory McIntyre to the wrong side of the campus. Where was she? Nothing looked the same. The world had spun out of its orbit, and she was floating in a bright, soft, glittering place where gravity didn't work. She would be late, but she didn't care. Finally, she understood: she was in love.

IT WAS A hopeless love, and because if Kate knew, she would tell Rory, it was also a secret one. Rory, Sarah discovered, bore an amazing resemblance to James Bond, Mr. Darcy, Mr. Rochester, and the Scarlet Pimpernel. How had she missed this before? Where he deviated from these heroes (his passions were for *Star Trek*, baseball, and a pompom girl name Diane Crupack, called Cupcake) and where he was not quite heroic (he had aversions to spiders, lima beans, and a purple acrylic sweater his mother had bought him), his glow remained untarnished.

Nor did seeing him daily diminish his magic. Each morning when he arrived at her house, the lights of the world turned on. When he talked to her, she missed most of what he was saying due to the pounding of her heart. Once he bumped her knee as he shifted gears and she very nearly fainted.

As she grew more used to being in love, her heart did not thunder so tumultuously in his presence and she was able to hear better. She memorized everything he said and replayed these tapes in her head at night. She agreed that Mark Twain wrote better than Jane Austen, that history was more important than chemistry, and that the Giants should win the pennant this year.

At school, he belonged to another world. She could recognize him from across the campus and each sighting struck her with fresh awe. She knew him. She knew he had a rash caused by the purple sweater. She planned her route so their paths would cross, but whenever he saw her and said hello, her brain shriveled into a useless lump. When he smiled at her, it dissolved entirely. She could only think: it really happens.

Other than stalking him, drawing for him, and memorizing his conversations, she had few outlets for so great a love, and this was why she went to Mass with the McIntyres on the first Sunday of Rory's penance. Sarah had never been inside a church, and the rich mystery of the rituals was almost as fascinating as watching Rory squirm, slouch, sigh, and look for things to read. At Sunday dinner after Mass, Rory asked, "So what did you think, Sarah? Was it weird, silly, or just plain dumb?"

"I don't know anything about God," Sarah admitted. "I suppose a person has to begin much younger than I am to believe in things, so a service at a synagogue or Buddhist temple might seem just as strange."

She had not meant to please Rory with her answer, and yet he beamed at her. "There's an idea," he said. No one had specified which church he had to attend. Even if he was limited to Christians, there were still Baptists, Methodists, and Jehovah's Witnesses. Diane Crupack was a Mormon; maybe she would go out with him if he converted. On Monday, Kate reported that Rory did not have to go to Mass anymore, and Rory murmured to Sarah that he owed her one.

That winter on a school skiing trip, Martha Harris broke her ankle and got to drive home with Rory, who had taken his own car to the mountains instead of riding on the bus. Sarah suffered more than Martha; why had she not thought of breaking her leg? She did, however, create a fine variation of the story for Kate, who said that Sarah was getting better at dreaming.

Spring came gloriously and painfully. Rory played baseball, and Diane Crupack noticed him. Sarah had been reading the Greeks, so she understood that heroes must have their flaws. Rory's surely was that he didn't notice that Diane, although pretty, bouncy, and blonde, was dumb past all hope and probably couldn't read; she had trouble distinguishing Rory at games, even though his name was written on his back. "Where is he?" she would squeal. "What did he do? A home run? Really?"

Sarah hated her heartily and created a story for Kate in which a baseball star was smitten by a vapid, selfish, shallow dimwit who was not that pretty and who abandoned him heartlessly when he suffered a crippling injury rescuing her poodle. He found true love, however, with the doctor who treated his elbow. Kate loved this story, and perhaps this was the first time Sarah considered going to medical school.

That spring, Rory ran for Napa High student body president and recruited Sarah to paint his signs. She and Kate, prodded by Sarah, campaigned for him so relentlessly that Rory's opponent tried to win them to his side. Rory won and, rightly, invited Sarah and Kate to his victory party.

They went like awestruck shepherds invited to Mt. Olympus. They huddled in a corner. The loser, a good sport, asked Kate to dance, but she mutely declined. Sarah left their spot once to get root beers, and as she paused in a doorway to marvel that they were there, a hand touched her waist. She looked around. Rory was standing behind her. Her knees turned into Jell-O; then she understood that she was blocking the door. She wobbled out of his way, and Rory, with the Cupcake, went on through. Sarah sat back down by Kate and swung her feet vigorously until Kate asked what was the matter. "Sex," Sarah said.

IN THE SUMMER, Rory worked in his father's shop and so did Sarah and Kate, answering phones and ordering parts. Sarah concluded that her heart must be a small, weak thing to fill with joy when Rory asked her to help him install a distributor, and to break just as easily when Diane Crupack strolled into the shop wearing short shorts and a skimpy halter top and sucking on the straw of a Pepsi. Rory's brain would turn into pink, bubblegum-flavored slush, and Diane's giggles echoed as they sauntered out of sight: "Rory, don't! You'll get grease on my clothes!"

Kate, rolling her eyes, asked, "What clothes?"

Each summer, the McIntyres went camping in Yosemite. Sarah had always gone with them, and now she wondered how she could have been so oblivious to Rory. She and Kate had spent the previous holiday tracking a ranger named O'Toole, who resembled Sean Connery. This year, Sarah let herself dream of what might happen, only to come up against a nightmare: Diane Crupack was invited too. She would share a tent with Sarah and Kate.

Heart-stricken, Sarah decided not to go. Instead, she languished at home. She read *Anna Karenina*, *Tess of the d'Ubervilles*, and *Romeo and Juliet*, but no tragedy compared with hers. In the mountains, her dreams were coming true, for Diane Crupack.

"You should have gone," Kate told her when the McIntyres

returned. With only mild prompting, Kate described how Diane had been bitten by mosquitoes, terrified by bears, and dive-bombed by blue jays. She had spent most of each day in the bathroom, combing her hair and putting on makeup. She got a blister and couldn't walk. She wouldn't eat anything and only drank Pepsi. By mid-week, Rory was hiking off without her, and Kate had to suffer her company. Rory and Diane were a thing of the past.

That summer, too, Cecily, newly graduated, got married, and Isabelle, as she had been threatening to do for years, sold the white house. She announced she was moving away, maybe to Australia. Sarah made plans to live with the McIntyres as a servant, but then Isabelle only moved into an apartment in town.

Sarah's sorrow was mitigated by one thing: Rory continued to drive her to school. He said it was on his way. She dared not hope, and yet it came to this: nothing else mattered, not her mother's cruel words, not even the heartbreaking glimpses of others happily living in her house, if she could be near Rory McIntyre, hear his voice, and sometimes see him smile at her.

THAT YEAR WAS 1968, a year like a winter after a summer of love, a year of violence, assassinations, riots, and protests. There was a war, faraway in Vietnam, and the country was so divided over it, no one knew what would bring it together again; but little Napa, sheltered by its green mountains, had other concerns. Newcomers were arriving. Some, intent on reviving its once-thriving wine industry, were removing prune trees to plant grapes. Others eyed the open fields and orchards, not as new vineyards, but as prime real estate that could feed the growing appetite for shopping centers, housing tracts, highways, and parking lots. Ironically, it was some of the newcomers who were most adamant about saving the little valley — look what had happened to other farmlands in places like San Jose and Los Angeles.

Joe McIntyre became part of a movement, which, that year, successfully passed an Agricultural Preserve to declare agriculture the highest, best use of land in the county and drastically limit development. If no longer hidden, the valley would be protected.

Rory rolled his eyes at his father, a mechanic who had never gone near a college, spouting facts and figures in a debate over something as inconsequential as how many parcels a pasture could be divided into; yet the Ag Preserve was what brought David Ilillouette into his life.

Ilillouette, an aide to the local congressman, came to Napa High for a debate on the state of the world: was there a future or not? Young, idealistic, and handsome as a Greek god (better-looking even than Robert Redford, Kate decided), he was more dazzling that the average political aide. Everyone knew he had been the lover of a famously raunchy rock star, and he had gone to Vietnam on a fact-finding trip and ended up saving a platoon of soldiers. He had marched with Martin Luther King for civil rights and with Cesar Chavez for farmworkers. He had been with Bobby Kennedy on the night he was murdered. He was biding his time until he was old enough to run for his boss's job and save the world. And this magnificent fellow, shaking hands with the ASB president who would introduce him, said to Rory: "McIntyre? Are you Joe McIntyre's son? I've been wanting to meet him."

Thunderstruck, Rory asked, "Why?"

"This Ag Preserve — you guys are the first in the country to do something like this. It's one good thing that happened in this nightmare year. It gives you hope when it's almost run out."

"It's just a small thing, not that important."

"Small things add up," Ilillouette said. "Don't you think saving the place where we live" — with a gesture, he encompassed the entire world — "will be the most important work we do?"

Rory took Ilillouette to McIntyre's Repair and listened to him talk to Joe about war and peace and life and death as if the older man had something worthwhile to say. If Rory remained unimpressed with his father, David Ilillouette changed everything else for him. He lectured Sarah and Kate on their drives to school. Did they know there was a world beyond the bubble where they lived? Did they realize that when he turned eighteen, Rory would have to register for the draft? He, of course, would go to college and escape, but others — friends —could be sent to fight and die in a war that no one understood, that Ilillouette said could never be won. What did people in Napa care about? Saving pastures, pancake breakfasts, Fourth of July parades, and who was Harvest Queen.

"I've got to get out of here," he said.

This new perspective did not, however, interfere with his reign as a hometown all-star. He escorted the homecoming queen, hit home runs, and played Skye Masterson in *Guys and Dolls* (Sarah went to every performance to watch him sing to a character named Sarah.) For the Spring Show, he and his best friend Matt Biagi wrote a parody of *The Music Man*. Years later, Sarah was a terrified pre-med student observing in a hospital emergency room when "Till There Was You" played over a loudspeaker. Instantly, she was transported from the blood and fear around her back to the Napa High Auditorium on a rainy spring night, watching Rory and Matt warble their way through the song. She nearly believed in love again, although she had long since fallen out of love with Rory McIntyre.

Rory had applied to Harvard because David Ilillouette encouraged him to try, and when he was accepted with scholarships, it was such a notable achievement *The Napa Register* interviewed his parents to ask what they had done to raise such a prize son. The McIntyres said they really didn't know.

That summer in the auto shop, Rory asked Sarah to help him so often that Joe paid her as a mechanic. Kate, who didn't like grease, still answered phones, but Sarah learned to adjust carburetors and replace brakes. It became the happiest summer she had ever known.

In the afternoons, she and Kate swam in the pool at Sarah's apartment, and sometimes Rory and his friends joined them. Matt had appraising looks for Kate, who had become as round and luscious as an ice cream cone. He threw her into the pool so many times Sarah wondered if this might be the preliminary mating ritual of a football player. She could not imagine anyone, least of all Rory, picking her up to toss her squealing into the water. Perhaps it was just as satisfying to talk to him, she thought wistfully. She could finally finish a sentence in his presence without thinking it was the stupidest thing anyone had ever said. She had grown so comfortable around Rory she worried that she might be falling out of love with him, until, with a twist of pain, she would think: this will all end; this summer will end, and he will leave.

WHEN THE McINTYRES made their annual trek to Yosemite, Sarah went with them and she stored away treasures, like how Rory's hair looked all tousled in the morning and how grouchy he got when he was hungry. Of her own presence, she was sure he was unaware, until the night he said to her and Kate, "D'you two want to hike up the Mist Trail tomorrow?"

Kate said no, it was a stupid hike, overrun with people, and there was no mist left. "Sarah will go with me," Rory said, and Sarah confounded Kate by saying, yes, she would.

They left before dawn, and by sunrise, they had come to the top of Vernal Falls. As they shared water and sandwiches, Rory said, "Sal, let's climb Half Dome. Shall we?"

This was the mountain that towered like a giant granite eagle over the Yosemite Valley. Only expert mountaineers could climb its sheer face, but cables installed on its curving stone back permitted hikers to crawl up to the summit, eight thousand feet in the air.

They set off, and she kept pace with his long-legged stride on the trail through the tangle of chaparral, sweet-smelling pines, and shattered boulders that led to the base. The mountain loomed over them. The steel cables went straight up, but at intervals, narrow wooden resting perches were hammered into the rock.

"It just looks like a ninety-degree angle," Rory said. "It probably isn't. Tell you what, you go first. That way if you fall, I will too."

The harsh metal cables tore at her hands, but Sarah clutched them in a death grip. The ground below them receded, the air grew thin, and her heart hammered as she tried to breathe. She couldn't look down but she couldn't look up and she couldn't close her eyes, because then she would fall, and Rory would fall too. By the time she reached the last wooden rest, she was sure she was brain-dead from terror and not breathing. The broad, flat summit of the mountain beckoned, but she could not pry her fingers loose from the cables until Rory offered her his hand and hauled her forward.

"Wow," he said. "Look how high we are." Sarah tried but failed to look down at the valley far below them. Instead she looked up. Rory, sweaty and triumphant, kissed her. It happened so fast she almost missed it. She sank down onto the rock, Half Dome.

He stretched out beside her; comfortable, he had not recently been hit by lightning. "We're all alone," he said. "It feels like we could touch the sky. I wish we could stay all night."

"It might be cold."

"Might." He grinned at her. "Might not."

She searched through the remains of her brain for something to say. "Not as cold as the moon. I mean, it's like being on the moon, but not exactly. I mean, it's strange to think that we can see the moon and there are people on it right now."

He looked puzzled, although he had been quite excited that

morning when they had talked about the landing of Apollo 11, the first men on the moon. But then he smiled. "I'd rather be here. Why didn't you come with us last year?"

"Oh," she floundered, possessed by a notion that would not revisit her too much in her life, that the boy next to her could read her mind. "I — I — "

"I — I — " he repeated teasingly. "I guess we'd better get back. But, do you realize we'll always be able to look up at this mountain and say, I was up there, on top of everything?"

They returned after dark, exhausted, dirty, and sunburned. Jean was in a state. "Rory, what on earth were you thinking to make Sarah climb that mountain with you? Sarah, go lie down. I will bring you dinner. Rory, go wash. You look like a wild man."

Sarah crawled into the tent. Rory followed her. Kate shrieked, "Rory, I'm not dressed."

"I didn't come to see you," he retorted. "Sarah, did you get blisters?" He sat down on her sleeping bag and took her hands in his. "Yours are worse than mine. Can you get your shoes off?" He began to unlace her boot. Sarah felt more faint than she had on top of the mountain.

"Mom!" Kate yelled. "Make Rory go away and leave us alone."

Jean ordered him out. Sarah lay down on her sleeping bag. Every bone and muscle in her body ached, and when she closed her eyes, her legs were still walking. She examined her hands, streaked with dirt and sweat. She touched her lips. She had been kissed. She had been kissed by Rory McIntyre. It might have been an accident, but she had never felt such happiness in her life.

THEN IT WAS August, and the air was filled with the particular light that belongs to late summer. A Jaguar was towed into the shop. The owner wanted it back and running in an hour. Joe wasn't in. Rory consulted a manual. "It says we need a special part you have to order from England," he told Sarah. "Well, let's try a crowbar."

This worked, and when the owner reclaimed his car, he gave Rory a fifty-dollar tip. Rory and Sarah collapsed in laughter on the office sofa. Overhead, she saw the calendar with its August photo of a bright red Corvette. It was Friday. Rory was leaving on Sunday. "Hey," he said, "Matt's having a party tomorrow night. I said I'd see if you and Kate want to come."

"Wow," Kate said. "It's almost a date. Except it's only Rory."

Sarah spent her half of their tip on a new dress that was white and almost backless. Kate talked her into it, pointing out that Sarah could wear white, and also her long hair covered her naked skin. Sarah was still worrying about it, however, when Rory arrived, and so she missed the appreciative look he cast at her. She did notice that they almost matched: he was wearing a green and white checked shirt and white jeans, and he smelled like pine trees. He was alone.

"Kate went with the others," he said, "but I thought I'd drive the MG one last time. D'you mind?" No, she didn't, but all of her shyness returned as he drove to Matt's house. Rory was quiet too, and she envied buzzing insects who had something to say.

In Matt's backyard, a stereo was blasting "Light My Fire," and couples were dancing on the deck around the swimming pool. Rory was surrounded immediately. When was he leaving? Not tomorrow? Really? God, Boston was so far away. Sarah slid to one side and looked for Kate, who was coping with attention admirably. Someone had asked her to dance and she had said yes.

A hand grazed Sarah's naked back, and she jumped to move out of Rory's way, but he stopped beside her, holding out a can of beer. She had never tasted beer, but she took a sip. He laughed at her wry face and got her a root beer.

"Rory!" A former pom-pom girl named Linda hugged him. "When do you leave?"

"Tomorrow."

"Oh God, aren't you nervous?"

"Would you like to dance?" Rory asked Sarah. The song ended as they reached an open spot on the deck. The next song was a slow one, "The Long and Winding Road." Rory didn't hesitate; he put his arm around her. His hand felt like a flame on her skin. The sun, lingering in the west, filled the sky with wild rose and violet, and in the east, a full moon was rising. This is me, Sarah Glass, she thought, slow-dancing with Rory McIntyre while Paul McCartney sings a long song. She doubted there had ever been a more romantic moment in the history of the world.

"Hey, Rory," someone called. "Do you know it snows in Boston? That's so weird."

"Wow, you're going so far away, farther than anyone else. Has anyone ever been to Boston?"

Rory's hand tightened on Sarah's waist. "Let's get out of here," he said. He held her hand as they went out the back gate. When they were back in his car, he pulled a six-pack of beer from behind the seat. He drank one bottle in several gulps.

"Do you mind if I just drive?" he asked.

His roadster left a trail of dust as they drove up the gravel road into the hills. The wind whipped her hair around, and she had to hold it with both hands. He stopped in a clearing that looked down on the valley, turning smoky blue and serene in the summer twilight.

"Have you ever smoked dope?" he asked.

"I've never done anything," she said, and she didn't know why this made him smile. He took a white, worm-like twist of paper from his shirt pocket. He lit it, inhaled, and handed it to her. She tried to imitate him and choked. She put her hands on her burning ears.

"I didn't know you did this," she said.

"I don't really. It's a going-away present." He stubbed it out. "Sarah, I don't want to go."

"You don't? Why not?"

"I don't know. I never thought they'd accept me. I still don't know why they did. And then everyone said I couldn't turn it down. But they were so serious when I was there. So — superior. 'You're from where?' 'Napa? Where on earth is that?' I don't know if I could be one of them."

She considered this. "I can see where it might be intimidating to go where everyone else is as smart as you are," she ventured. "But it does seem like Cinderella saying, 'Thanks, but I don't want to go to the ball after all.'"

He laughed, after a moment, and bent his head near hers, so close she caught a whiff of beer and smoke, and she had not thought she liked these things. He said, "Let's go to the city."

"San Francisco?"

"There's a place I think you'd like. When I drove David Ilillouette to a meeting, he wanted to stop there. He said it's his favorite place in the world, except for anywhere in Paris."

He put the top up on his car, so she didn't have to clutch her hair, and when they were on the road again, he astonished her entirely by taking her hand in his. He held it against his leg until he had to release it to shift. She didn't know if she should leave it there or move it, but when he finished shifting, he pressed it, and she decided she should leave it there. She never remembered what they talked about as they sped on into the hills of Marin. They went into a tunnel, and when they came out, the Golden Gate Bridge was in front of them, its red towers catching the waves of fog moving in from the sea. Moonlight glimmered on the bay and San Francisco sparkled between the blue sea and the sky. Sarah finally summoned the courage to look at her hand. It was still on his leg.

Rory slowed down. They entered another tunnel and emerged in a noisy, garish place where mobs of people were crowded onto the sidewalks, and cars screeched and honked. Signs were in Chinese and English, but they were all outshone by the colossal image of a woman clad only in light bulbs: it was the infamous Condor Club where Carol Doda danced topless.

"It's a miracle," Rory exclaimed as he zipped into a parking place. "We're here."

Sarah could not stop staring at the naked Amazon. The Condor was not the only striptease club; they lined the street, and barkers were trying to lure people inside. Was this where the great David Ilillouette had brought Rory? It was Sarah's first hint that there might be limits to infinite love, but at least no creepy man was shouting by the door that Rory opened for her. She went in.

They were in a bookstore, a higgledy-piggledy collection of narrow passageways and rooms filled, floor to ceiling with books. City Lights was famous, Rory told her. Lawrence Ferlinghetti had helped found the book store, and it had published Alan Ginsberg. Jack Kerouac had hung out there. Sarah had never heard of any of these people. "Neither had I," Rory said.

They went down a spiral staircase to a cellar filled with more books. "There's a section on anarchy. Ilillouette said it was his favorite." Rory grinned at the awe-struck Sarah. "You thought I was taking you to the Condor Club, didn't you? I don't think they would have let us in."

"I just thought, since he is a politician, it might be his favorite place."

Rory laughed so hard he had to sit down. When they went back up the stairs, he bought a copy of *On the Road* by Jack Kerouac. "Are you hungry?" he asked, and they wandered like two lost country mice until they found a Chinese restaurant. It was crowded and noisy and people were shouting in Chinese. Stammering — he didn't know if they spoke English — he ordered food to go by pointing, and they scurried for his car.

They got lost twice, but then they came to Land's End, the edge of the Pacific Ocean. They ate spare ribs, steamed buns, and fried rice in the car overlooking the deserted beach as mist moved in around them. He opened a bottle of Cold Duck, another going-away gift. Sarah liked it better than beer, but Rory drank most of it, and when he said, "I'll be right back," she was elated, if amazed, that she, Sarah Glass, understood the inner workings of a human male.

When he returned, however, he was a mystery again. The only sound was crashing waves, and he gazed in her direction so intently, she turned to see what he was looking at in the dark. Fog? His hand touched her cheek, and when she glanced back at him, puzzled, he kissed her. This time, he kissed her so many times she lost count, and she could only think how easily he did it. He did not even have to stop as he turned their clothes into tangles. The touch of his bare skin against hers was like nothing she had ever felt.

Abruptly, he stopped. He released her and collapsed back against his seat. He was breathing strangely, but so was she, dizzy with wonder and lack of oxygen. He said, "I think we'd better take a walk."

He helped her put her clothes in order, and he put his arm around her as they wandered along the beach in mist-filled moonlight. When she let her own hand land, like a fluttering butterfly, on his side, he pressed it, so she knew this was all right, but they didn't talk. The tide was coming in. Waves lapped at their feet. Still, they walked until they came to a rock wall and had to turn back.

At his car, he opened the passenger door but then he sat down. He pulled her with him. "I'm a little drunk," he murmured. "D'you mind, can I just hold you?" He kissed her a few more times, her lips, her nose, and neck. Then he leaned his head against her and fell asleep.

Sarah's conviction this would never again happen in her life kept her awake while he slept. She memorized details: the shape of his ear, the feel of his cheek, the scent of his hair, the sound of his breath, mingling with the wind and the waves. She would never be able to discuss this with Kate, and Kate would never know the tongue thing was not at all bad, if it was Rory's tongue.

When a faint light glimmered in the east, she untangled herself from him and got into the driver's seat. Joe had taught her and Kate to drive; she hoped she could find Napa. Rory didn't stir as she drove. When she pulled into his driveway, his parents flew out the door.

"He's not so drunk this time," Sarah said anxiously; and for her final wonder of that night, Joe only laughed, and Jean smiled. Sarah cast one last look at Rory before Joe drove her home.

On Sunday evening, Kate came over to report that Rory was gone. "He asked me to tell you goodbye," she said. "He got all choked saying it to anyone. But he wanted me to give you this. I don't know why. It's weird." It was Jack Kerouac, *On the Road*. "Where'd you guys go? Sarah, I have to tell you: I kissed Matt. I didn't really like it. It was kind of gross and slobbery."

SARAH DIDN'T EXPECT to hear from Rory, and she did not. He didn't come home that Christmas, and the following summer his family drove across the country to see him and visit Washington, D.C., where he was working for David Ilillouette. Kate kept her posted. Rory had met someone; it was serious. He didn't come home, not even for Kate's wedding because, by then, he was married too.

When Sarah heard about his marriage, she felt one last twist of her heart, one last gasp of her dreams before she let them go. She did not think her heart was broken because she knew that technically, hearts didn't break. She went on to other romantic experiments, but nothing ever quite matched Rory McIntyre, not even that first light touch of his hand at her waist, when she was blocking a doorway.

CHAPTER 9

"THERE'S REALLY NOTHING new," Isabelle said. "It's so hot. Why your father wanted to live in Napa, I'll never know. I know I could leave, but where would I go? There's no reason to go anyway. Aaron sent me a book, but why should I read what a man has to say? They're only obsessed with what they can't control. If you ask me, Freud got it wrong with his you-know-what envy. I suppose I should say penis. My group does, but people say anything now. I don't know why Cecily wants to get married again. At least I don't have to worry that he might come to the wedding. At least he's dead, although I don't know how anyone could tell. She's decided to wear ivory, which is better for her than white, but she's chosen the wrong caterer. I won't say anything. She wants to get married in a vineyard this time, and no one can make her believe how bad grapevines look in February. I suppose you'll bring that boy who answered the phone, although I can't imagine you having a boyfriend. You were always so uninterested in love."

The doorbell buzzed. Sarah opened the door to Kate and made coffee while Isabelle talked. "It's a phase she goes through whenever Cecily gets married," she explained when Isabelle had hung up. "She calls me. Then she stops." She yawned.

"Were you out late last night? Where did you and Gabriel go?"

"A place called Chez Panisse. It's a restaurant. But not exactly French."

"Sarah, it's famous! This is a real romance."

"When is a romance ever real?"

"Then maybe unreal is better. Well, look at Rory."

"He doesn't look so bad."

"You should have seen him when he got off the plane after flying with Lucy and Avery. He looked like a refugee from Vietnam, not Boston."

"Is he still camping?" Sarah asked. Kate had said he'd taken his children to the mountains the day after they came to her house, but that's all she had said.

"Yes, and Mom's a nervous wreck about it, but I think they'll survive. So why isn't this thing with Gabriel real?"

"It's so easy." Sarah said. "Every night he turns up. We go somewhere. And it's fun. And then he goes home. It's like he turns into a pumpkin at midnight. Or he thinks I do. He's never — he hasn't even kissed me. But that's my fault. I told him I'd given up sex."

"Have you?"

"I guess so."

"Sex doesn't make anything real," Kate said. "Just sticky. I think even Rory's given it up. When I asked him if he'd gone out with anyone since his divorce, he just rolled his eyes. John — you know he's a priest now? He called Dibby a sure cure for concupiscence. Maybe she was."

"Dibby? That's her name?" Sarah could not resist asking. "What was she like?"

"I only saw her once, at the wedding. She wouldn't come to California. She thought it was contagious. She was okay. Rich. Kind of like a show dog, always perfect. You know Rory; he's always had bad taste in women. But this sounds like your idea of romance, Sarah."

"What does?"

"Remember our stories? Your hero always took ten years to kiss you. And Gabriel is shy."

"Gabriel? Shy?"

"And you are intimidating."

"I am? Why do you say that?"

"I didn't. Rory did."

"He did? Why did he say that?"

"Sarah, what if you have found the real thing?"

Outwardly, Sarah was doing better. She was not anxiously looking for the door. She had not recoiled when Roach swallowed a fish or when Flake offered to massage her ankles. She had not winced when Mildred threw off her clothes, although she had not minded when Gabriel turned up the air conditioning and Mildred put them back on.

Inwardly, however, she was failing. She had driven to Gabriel's hideout with no invitation. As soon as Gabriel opened the door, she knew she had trespassed. The Scoundrels of Leisure cut off her muddled apology cheerfully, but Gabriel said nothing.

She wanted to leave but didn't; she came inside. Gabriel talked to Mildred, who was spinning in the chair. Sarah hated Mildred. She smirked at Sarah, but even the expressionless statues seemed to taunt Sarah's descent into juvenile jealousy and hysteria. She wanted to leave but instead she went to the window and fabricated an explanation for how a cyclotron worked.

"Oh, God, she's smart," Mildred groaned. "I hate smart people."

Only Harry came to Sarah's defense. "She's not smart."

Something flew through the air and fell at her feet. It was a shriveled, dull gold mushroom.

"Eat me," Gabriel said. He had left Mildred. His eyes were no longer cold, but inviting.

Sarah had read about hallucinogenic mushrooms in textbooks. A classmate had made a personal study of various drugs, but he had also dropped out of med school. Sarah's drug of choice was caffeine. Still, as Gabriel darted away, she would have done anything to be included in his flight. She ate the mushroom.

She waited. By nature as well as training, she was an observer, and she wished she could find a more neurologically precise description for what was happening in her brain other than that it had leapt from an airplane without a parachute. There was no going back. The room turned ice cold, but she was sweating. The walls came to life, pulsing to the beat of the music; were they also eating up the air? She tried to organize herself to stand up, but she had grown boneless. She collided with a massive object.

"Need a body?" Harry the Swinger asked.

"I need to find the door."

He hauled her outside. "Some women get really turned on by mushrooms," he offered.

"I think I am going to throw up."

"Damn." He was gone in a puff of smoke. Sarah fell forward into a bed of vines. A spider skittered under a leaf; it reemerged, luminescent white, growing larger. It turned to look at her. It wore a mask of jewels and feathers. It had violet eyes. With each of its eight legs — or were they arms? — it drew lines in the dark, connecting them in a giant web that shimmered with crystals. It exploded, and a cascade of gold, and purple stars rained down, a phantasmagoria of unidentified shapes that sparkled and then dissolved. When the last of the bright images faded, she was left in a preternatural dark. Ghost-like eucalyptus trees emerged from the fog and she found her green Honda crouched like a frog among them.

"ABCDEFG," she recited as she crawled into the driver's seat. "The speed of light is 2.99795 plus or minus 0.00003 times ten to the tenth power centimeters per minute. The law of parity states — something."

She recited the periodic table of elements as she coasted down the hill. The Bay Bridge reared up before her like the glittering jaws of a monster, but she drove toward it.

CHAPTER 10

S HE WAS GRATEFUL that night for the company of the black cat, for the lines between the waking and dreaming worlds were confused but she knew the warm ball of fur was real. Sirens shrieked; the walls danced, and her pot-bellied statue swarmed with other monstrous shapes around her. It was not until dawn that she fell asleep, only to be awakened by the insistent buzz of the doorbell. She stumbled to the door, found the knob, and peered down the stairwell.

"Hullo," Avery announced. "We're back."

"Where is Rory?" Sarah asked, woozy but awake.

"In the shower," Lucy said.

"Does he know you're here?"

The reply came with the thunder of footsteps on the stairs. Rory's face was grim, his hair wet, his shirt half-buttoned. "All right, let's go," he bellowed. "Next time you do this — "

He stopped; the only one he had alarmed was Sarah, who retreated into her flat before her blood supply evaporated. He wilted. He followed her and leaned against the fireplace, mumbling. "Sometimes he prays," Lucy said.

Sarah offered him coffee. He declined. She was relieved. Although Rory's disarray, both mental and physical, was such that he was unlikely to notice her own tatterdemalion condition, she was not sure she was up to the challenge of measuring beans and boiling water.

He was not going to leave his kids with Sterling for long, he mumbled. He had meant to catch a bus to collect his car, which he had left in a garage for an oil change. Then he was going to Berkeley to find a place to live. He had been too particular; he would take a hovel with broken windows and gang fights in the street as long as it was not Sterling's spare room.

"Would you like a ride?" Sarah asked. Rory recoiled. "No, of course not," she stammered. "But you can leave them with me."

"No," Rory snapped as his children danced around him, clamoring to stay. "Dammit, be quiet. No, not you," he added, for Sarah was backing up again. "A ride would be great. Thanks."

She showered quickly, hoping to wash away the residue of a dreadful night, but still she looked ghastly, a red-eyed, green-faced witch. She deteriorated further as they walked to her car and she discovered that she had parked half on the sidewalk. Rory stifled a chuckle. She handed him her keys.

"Don't you want to drive?" he asked.

"I don't know where we're going."

At the garage, to her surprise, he did not leap from the car, but remained, examining the steering wheel with unwarranted interest. "Would you like to come with us?" he said. "Of course, you might rather go to bed — back to bed." His face reddened. "You probably have things to do."

"No," she said, "not really."

He recovered. "Good. You can leave your car here and let them check out the transmission."

"My transmission?"

"You're slipping, Sal."

"I am not," she retorted. "I change my own oil."

He drove an older gray Volvo station wagon, the backseat of which was filled with car seats, stuffed toys, books, and cracker crumbs. He shoved a stack of notebooks and empty coffee cups from the front seat to make room for her. Of course, Sarah thought, the immaculate burgundy MG roadster would be gone.

Crossing the Bay Bridge, it was left to Lucy and Avery to make conversation. Why couldn't Rory drive a dump truck? Why didn't the bridge fall down? Where was everyone going? Why didn't Rory go faster and beat them?

Why had he asked her to come, Sarah wondered, listening to his brusque replies. Why had she said yes? She studied him surreptitiously, trying to discern in this moody, taciturn man what might have caused her youthful self to adore him with such devotion. Had she ever seen him clearly or had he just lost his glow in his fall to earth?

He broke the silence. "The last time I changed my oil, they helped me, and I think we qualified as an environmental disaster."

"How long have you had them?"

He shot her a quizzical look. "Since they were born."

Sarah gave up talking. Rory occupied himself by scanning radio stations, rejecting the golden oldies ("When I Fall in Love"); light rock, less talk ("Nights in White Satin"); and National Public Radio ("New crisis in the Mideast"). He put in a tape of Miles Davis, which sparked an outcry from the backseat.

"Play my music, Rory," Lucy commanded.

"No."

"But I love it."

"I know you do. And we've heard it seven thousand times since Kate bought it for you."

"What is it?" Sarah asked.

"Walt Disney's greatest hits," Rory said, without expression.

Lucy sang, "'I know you, I walked with you once upon a dream.'

That's what the prince sings to Sleeping Beauty, Sarah."

Rory sighed. "Why do women fall for these idiotic things?"

"Some boys like them, too," Sarah said. Avery was singing "Bibbi-di-Bobbidi-Boo."

"They get over it. But Kate's favorite place is Disneyland. She has the Little Golden Books she had when she was five: *Cinderella, Snow White* — "

"Rory likes 'Country roads take me home to the place where I belong because I left my heart in San Francisco.'" Lucy shared this; Avery sang it.

Rory flinched. "I paid my lawyer by playing piano at bars and weddings. Between the two of them, you play every mindless idiotic song ever written."

It was a relief to reach the University Avenue exit. If he rented the first house he found, Sarah estimated she could be back in bed, asleep, by noon; but he stopped near the Berkeley campus. He needed a form, he said briefly, to replace one that Avery had floated in the bathtub.

Sarah stayed in Sproul Plaza with Lucy and Avery while Rory went into the administration building. Students scurried by, heads bent. She had always been one of them, but now she watched the colorful circus they were missing. A one-man band provided music for a woman dancing with a giant blue stuffed frog on her head, a man painted in pink and blue dots was doing Tai Chi, another in a dragon costume blew bubbles over the tables offering information on the calamities bedeviling the world. A whale-shaped balloon from the Save the Whales contingent sailed off on the wind.

With a start, she realized that Lucy and Avery had vanished. She spun around in a panic, and through a cloud of bubbles, she saw Rory approaching, cheerful and unaware that his children might have just been kidnapped to be sold into slavery.

"Done," he said. "They gave me a new form." His euphoria, caused by the unexpected, smooth functioning of a bureaucracy, was mitigated by the stricken look on Sarah's face. "Is something wrong, Sal?"

Just then Lucy and Avery bounded up from Strawberry Creek; they had been chasing a squirrel. Sarah resisted the impulse to flutter to the ground like a discarded flyer for peace, freedom, or whale power.

"What have you two been up to?" Rory asked, but he didn't require an answer. "Sarah, how about lunch?"

"Oh, no." Her recent alarm had mashed into the terrors of the night before with a debilitating thud. She could not let him spend his money to buy her food and then throw up.

"Not up to eating in public with them?"

"I'm sure they're wonderful."

"No, they're not, but we could go somewhere filled with rowdy frat types and fit right in. Or we could get some things and go eat up in the hills. Do you have to get back?"

"No."

"All right, then, to the hills."

CHAPTER 11

A GAIN, SHE HAD said yes, and still she did not know why. They stopped for provisions at a deli. He went into a hole-in-the-wall shop and came out with two paper cups of coffee. She held hers cautiously, slouching down as he drove up into the hills. She was grateful that he did not go near Gabriel's house but followed signs for Wildcat Canyon, which brought them to a wooded hilltop high above the bay. Here, the sun was warm, the breeze light, and the air scented with pine and summer-dried grass. Rory's children sprinted off through a meadow, mostly gold in August but scattered with white and purple wildflowers. Rory followed, carrying lunch and a blanket that he spread out beneath a giant oak tree. Sarah stayed standing, watching the children. Below them, hidden in fog, was the city through which she had fled the night before.

"Sal, come sit down."Rory stretched out on the blanket and sipped his coffee. Had he ever passed such a night? Somehow, she suspected he had. "The kids will be fine. I told them to stay nearby, and Lucy does what I tell her at least twenty percent of the time."

"I'm so sorry I lost them."

"Did you? Just once? I usually lose them half a dozen times before breakfast, but so far, I've always found them." He smiled; it was almost the old Rory, familiar, warm like sunlight. She sat down. "What are you going to do at Cal?" she asked.

He became absorbed in the contents of the brown paper bag, and Sarah, not for the first time, decided she had been in the wrong line when instincts were handed out. Was she not supposed to be curious about his form? He sipped his coffee. "This Peet's is great stuff," he said. "You should try it. It might even cure your hangover."

"I don't —" Did she look that bad? She took a cautious sip. "It's not bad."

He was laughing at her. "So, what have you been up to, kid?"

"Me? Not much."

"Really? You looked like you'd just gone to bed when my kids woke you up."

"I didn't think you'd notice. You were too busy hollering."

"I noticed."

"I ate a mushroom last night, that's all."

"A mushroom? Was it poisonous?"

"Hallucinogenic."

"Why did you do that?"

"I don't know."

He shook his head in a way that made her feel young and stupid. She leaned against her knees morosely and counted the shades of green she could find on the hillside. She was up to thirteen when her inventory halted. He reached out to rub her shoulder, and this wreaked havoc in her brain. Of course, there was a connection, shoulder nerves to the brain, but neurons, as she had seen them in textbooks, were lovely, spidery creations, with wispy tendrils forming elegant connections; they were not raucous, rioting cells, all crashing into each other in pandemonium.

"I'm going to work on a physics project at Cal," he said.

"Physics?" Accidentally, she laughed. His hand fell away, and she was sorry. Despite the hullaballoo in her brain, she had almost been feeling better.

"Why is that funny?"

"Oh, it isn't. It's just — you were never very good at math."

"I wasn't that bad, just not as good as you."

"You wanted to be a politician, when I knew you."

"I used to want to be a fireman, too."

"You didn't study political science?"

"I studied a lot of things, before I dropped out."

"You?" Her eyes widened in surprise. "You did?"

"It's not that shocking." He did not, however, appear to mind her astonished incredulity.

"Why physics?" In the ensuing silence, she answered herself. "It is interesting. It's clear, when it's not vague. There are answers, sometimes. I had a roommate, an English major, who had to take a science class, so she took Physics for Poets. She was amazed that anyone thought there were universal laws. She loved entropy. She thought it was a metaphor for our time, an expanding system becoming increasingly chaotic. She said it explained everything, even Congress."

She paused; he said nothing. "I can see how being married might make you want to study physics." she added and then he looked as if she had just opened a door and come upon him naked. "Rory, what do you think of quarks?"

"Quarks?"

"The little — "

"Yes, I know what you mean."

"I was just wondering."

He cleared his throat. "I think I favor quark physics without quarks, searching for the smallest particle but not finding it."

"Why?"

"Because when you reduce nature to its basic elements, it's a web of interactions."

"And do you think the pattern is repeated, like a ripple effect in the rest of life?"

"Yes, but quarks are better at it than anything else." He picked up his pocketknife and examined the blade. "I think there's another way of looking at it."

"What is that?"

"It's possible to reduce anything to nothingness."

"Oh." He was rubbing his thumb along the blade in a nervous-making way. She asked, "Was it so awful, being married?"

"Yes."

"Why did you do it?"

"I don't know."

"You were in love." She offered this reluctantly, but necessarily.

"Was I?"

"I don't know," she admitted. "You might have been lonely or cold." Or drunk, she wanted to add, but did not. "It gets cold in Boston in the winter."

He snapped the knife shut. "Why do women always talk about love? I asked my mother, how did you do it, how did you stay married all these years? She said they loved each other. I thought, what the hell is she talking about? What did love ever do for them but get them six kids, one worry after another? Love? It's nothing but a bizarre, biology-driven myth, a trap as useless as religion, a delusion based on nothing real."

"Oh."

"You don't believe in all that, do you?"

"In powerful external forces, yes," Sarah said, "but whether it's God or love or biology, I don't know."

He rolled onto his stomach and began disassembling a sandwich, balancing the pieces, tomato, pickles, turkey, into a tower. "After I was married, I used to walk a lot. I always ended up at MIT. I started sitting in on classes." His voice hit a rough patch, and with a swift motion, he toppled his creation.

"It's an odd place, isn't it?" she asked. "I went to a lecture there once, and it took them twenty minutes to figure out how to dim the lights. They never got the microphone to work, and the slide projector got stuck on automatic advance. A security guard had to turn it off."

Rory bent his head. His shoulders were shaking, and it was a moment before she realized that he was laughing. Sunlight glinted off his hair, and, irresistibly, she touched it. He looked up at her and dropped his head down onto her lap. Her brain fell into another frenzy, worse than before. "I don't know why she married me either," he was saying when she could hear again, past the roaring in her ears.

"Hormones," Sarah suggested faintly. "They can make you do odd things."

"Hormones? Is it possible to have transplants?"

"Not yet."

"I'm going to build a radio receiver for an astrophysicist," he said.

"A radio? In space?"

This was inspired, if inadvertent. He began to talk. "It turns out that where you can't make an optical image of an object in space, you can detect radio emissions from it. Take, for example, a star-forming region millions of light years away. To our eyes, it looks like a patch of dark sky, but really, it's a cloud of dust and gas so dense that no light can escape it. Inside it, stars are forming — or were, millions of years ago. A new star blows off its covering and becomes visible; and millions of years later, the light reaches us. But a radio receiver can detect emissions from within the cloud as the star formed, and these frequencies can be mapped and turned into images with elements in different colors."

"Maps of the dark places of the universe? I'd love to see one."

"I'll get you one."

Unaware that he had just said more to her than he had said to anyone in many months, she was trying to imagine a dark world transformed into colors, when he said, "I couldn't study, Sal. I couldn't think. I couldn't sleep. I dropped out before I flunked out. I had to get a job, so I went to work in an auto shop in Cambridge because it was the only thing I knew how to do. A professor from MIT brought in his old Bentley. He recognized me because I had been sitting in on his class. Frank — he writes formulas to describe the mysteries of the universe, but he can't figure out life on earth. He's been divorced three times, never remembers to pay his bills, and doesn't understand practical mechanics. The next thing I knew, I was building a radio receiver for him. It worked. When I finally got the court's permission to move to California, a guy from Cal wanted a receiver, too. So that's what I'm going to do at Berkeley."

"You're interested in stars?"

"Not really. Stars are too far away. I just like to build things, to see if it can be done."

"Stars are incidental?"

"Why did you decide to go to med school?"

"I had to be something, and I really didn't want to be a lawyer. It's not that funny," she added.

"Yes, it is."

"I thought I might learn something about life."

"Have you figured out the difference between men and women yet?"

"Well, yes, it's — "

His green eyes were twinkling; he was teasing her. She stopped in confusion. He settled himself more snugly against her, munched on bread, and offered a piece to her. "So, Sarah, are you going in for psychiatry or brain surgery?"

"What? Oh, no, no — why — " She shredded the bread and tried to stick it back together. She caught Rory's eyes, dropped the bread, and pressed her hands against her head; usually, this worked to push herself back into a cave, dark and devoid of senses. This time, she tripped at the entrance. He had sat up and put his arm around her. He leaned back against the tree. She found no cave, just a confusion of blind bats colliding in her head. Of all things, kindness was most rare in her life, and she didn't know what to do with it, but she listened to his heartbeat; it was always a comforting thing, hearts working.

"Sal, isn't it a bad thing to stop breathing?" She nodded. "So, what's going on, honey?"

Honey? She remembered that Joe McIntyre called everyone, including the clerks at Buttercream Bakery, honey. "I saw a ghost, Rory."

"Last night?"

"No. In a hospital."

"Did you?"

"And I've taken a month off from school. At least, I think that's what I've done."

"Because you saw a ghost?"

"No. Because I can't do it. I am no good at it."

"It's easier to believe that you saw a ghost."

"Do you believe in ghosts?"

"No."

"Neither do I." She sighed. "But that's why I'm here. You asked me. Yesterday."

"I heard — did you go to Yale for undergrad?"

"No. UCLA."

"But they accepted you?"

"Yes. I just didn't go."

"Cinderella saying thanks very much but I'd rather not go to the ball?"

"Who — "

"You."

"Oh."

"It's a good thing you were so cute."

"I just liked UCLA better."

"It's a great school. But now you're back east? Do you like New York?"

"It's not bad. I've only been mugged once. It was my fault" — his hand had paused in its helpful head-rubbing — "I wasn't paying attention."

Later, she wondered about the medicinal effects of a hand, even it if was just resting still on her head; she began to talk as if it had melted away the ice of many winters, unearthing long-buried, lost, and frozen things in a flood.

"At first, it wasn't so bad, Rory, med school. The first two years are mostly classes and tests; that, I can do. But sometimes you have to go into the hospital. The first time, we were following Dr. Mitchell through the wards, and he said to Cheryl and me — she was the other woman in our group — 'You two, go see if Room 302 is dead yet.' We were scared to death, but we went to 302. An old woman was lying on a bed. She looked dead, but we were afraid to go close enough to touch her. We just stood there, saying: 'Do you think she's dead?' 'I don't know. She might be dead.' It was probably a good thing that she was dead. A resident rushed in and said they were just waiting for someone to take her away. He said Mitchell gave women a hard time, but he wasn't so bad; just don't go into a supply closet with him.

"Then next, I was in the emergency room and they brought in a man who had been speared with a pitchfork. He'd been sitting on a fence, watching a woman in her bathroom, and when she saw him, she went out to push him off. No one knew where she had got a pitchfork in Harlem, but she accidentally speared him instead. She was hysterical, almost worse off than he was, except he was dead."

"So I knew I was not good at emergencies, and my advisor said why didn't I spend time in the psych ward because there were patients who didn't speak English, not that I can speak Spanish, really, but it turned out to be more than more than anyone else could. There was one patient, Roselda; she had schizophrenia. I thought she was old, fifty or sixty, but she was my age. She had her first psychotic break when she was nineteen. She said it was like half of her brain disappeared. She heard voices no one else could hear, saw people no one else could see. Her ghosts, she called them. She asked if I believed they were real. I said I believed that she saw them and heard them. I asked, 'What do they say to you?' She said, 'They say I have to kill you.' But she was nice when she took her meds. I told her about a professor at UCLA who said that we are only aware of twenty percent of what our brain perceives, and I wondered what we were missing. She liked that.

"But she got discharged, and then she hung herself. She died. Dr. Mitchell said only a woman would feel bad because a schizophrenic was crazy, but he asked if I wanted to have a drink and talk. He was almost nice, except he called me sweetie, and also, Dr. Carmen, and when I realized he meant go with him to his apartment, I — I said no. He said, 'Suit yourself,' but it was so creepy, I ran all the way back to my room. My roommate said I was an idiot; he wasn't that ugly, and I had probably just ruined my career. I knew it was true. I went for a walk and that's when I got mugged. He wasn't bad, the poor mugger, just desperate. I liked him better than Dr. Mitchell. I wished I'd had more money to give him but I only had a quarter. Would you like me to stop?" She had perceived with concern Rory's strangled expression.

"No," he said feebly. "You haven't got to the ghost yet. Did someone murder Mitchell in a supply closet?"

"No. It was one night. I was at the hospital. There is a big test you take at the end of second year and I'd been studying a lot. I fell asleep in an empty room, and when I woke up, there was a woman in the room. Luz Moreno, an art prof from UCLA. When I was a senior, I had to take a fine arts class to graduate, and the only one that fit my schedule was drawing, so I signed up and hoped I wouldn't fail it and ruin my GPA. I'd never met anyone like Luz, so joyful and irreverent, always laughing, making crazy jokes, driving the serious academics crazy. She had a sketchbook she called *Things I Might Not See Again*. She said she had twenty-seven volumes at her home in Guanajuato. She decided academia wasn't for her and went back to Mexico. She said send her a postcard from New York, and I did. She wrote back, 'Someday, come to Mexico and take the leap into life.'

"And there she was, in this room, wearing a hospital gown. I saw her. I felt her touch my arm, and then she was gone. I checked the hospital records but no Luz Moreno had been admitted. Then I got a letter and package from her son. She had asked him to send me a pottery statue because she was dying of cancer. And she had died, the night I saw her in New York.

"I had read everything I could about schizophrenia; this is a time when it often manifests." Sarah sighed. "I decided to leave school. Except the dean said, why didn't I just take a month off instead. I didn't know you could do that. I had a check coming, money I hadn't expected. I got in my car and started driving. I didn't know where I was going. I just wanted to go —"

"Home."

"I don't know where that is."

Something brushed her hair; she thought it was his lips. She perceived an audience: Lucy and Avery were standing in front of them, wide-eyed.

"What happened?" Lucy asked. "Did Sarah fall down?"

Sarah detached herself from Lucy's father. Rory said, "What have you two been up to?"

They were digging a hole to China, but first, they were hungry. Rory gave them supplies. They bounded away. He leaned back against the tree, but Sarah stayed sitting upright. He stretched out again, and his head fell back on her thigh. He picked up a cluster of grapes, broke one off, and offered it to her.

"Thank you for listening," she said. Another grape. "He was nice, the dean."

"He's not an idiot. He doesn't want to lose you."

"But it is too bad that no matter what you do, everyone dies."

"Not always right away?" The next grape, he held up to her lips. "So, what about — have you had time for any great, romantic adventures?"

"Me? No."

"No?"

"None."

"Really?"

"No. Nothing. I don't think I've ever been in love." Puzzled by the faint frown that flickered over his face, she reflected, "I did get somewhat involved with a bio major when I was a junior, but only because he got bad headaches and dizzy spells when we studied together."

"The first life you saved?"

"I think I can live without love, too," she added, ruefully, recollecting that experience.

This time, when he gave her a grape, his fingers touched her lips. And he wasn't even drunk, she thought; it's a good thing I'm not fourteen or I'd have been dead half an hour ago.

CHAPTER 12

"RORY!" KATE OPENED her door. "Here you are! Where — oh!" It was not so much the sight of Rory with his sleeping children, but of Sarah beside him that stopped Kate mid-question.

Rory said, "Let me put the kids to bed, honey, and then I'll take you home."

"Honey?" Kate mouthed the word in curious confusion.

"We've been hiking," Sarah said.

"I wouldn't put them to bed now." Sterling advised from the sofa. "They'll be up at dawn."

"Sterling, they're asleep now," Kate said. "Have you two had dinner?"

"Dinner?" Sarah repeated, and Rory looked equally vague. When he'd stopped to buy his children hamburgers, she had declined one, and he said perhaps they could leave the kids with Kate and eat somewhere later. Perhaps, unanswered, dangled, like an unfinished bar of music.

Kate, perceiving that neither knew if they had eaten, asked, "Can you stay for dinner, Sarah? That must have been some hike," she added as Rory carried off his children. "You both look so — glowy." She had considered and discarded several adjectives, including "witless."

"Assuming there will be dinner," Sterling said.

"It would be ready, Sterling, if you had baked the casserole."

"I put it in the oven. It's not my fault the oven didn't turn on. It's not my fault it's broken."

"Could it be a fuse?" Sarah asked.

"Maybe," Kate said. "Where's the fuse box, Sterling?"

"I don't know why you expect me to know things you don't."

"Neither do I. Rory," Kate called, "do you know where the fuse box might be?"

Sarah opened the hall closet. "Here it is. A fuse was tripped. That's all."

"Sterling, did you put your television in the kitchen again?"

"Only while I had to fix my lunch."

Kate sighed as Rory appeared from the bedroom. "Never mind. Sarah fixed it."

"Oh."

"Yes," Sterling sniffed. "Amazing, isn't it, that someone besides you might think of fuses?"

"Sterling has been feeling somewhat inferior lately," Kate said to Sarah as they went into the kitchen. "Rory fixed the stereo and the television. I am a bit sorry about that one. Now Sterling just plays this weird game where you hit balls back and forth. And he gets so upset when Avery beats him."

She stopped talking; Sterling had followed them. "What are you cooking?" he asked.

"Steak."

"Steak? What made you buy steak? And you bought the most expensive mayonnaise, too."

"Rory likes that kind."

"He certainly is free with my money."

"His money. He bought the groceries."

Evidently, feeling inferior again, Sterling changed the subject. "Are you frying the steak?"

"No, grilling."

"I prefer fried. Oh! Why are you salting it? Never, never salt meat!"

"My mother salts her meat."

"Your mother is not exactly the world's best cook. Now you've ruined it. What are you going to serve with it?"

"Potatoes."

"I prefer rice."

"Can I do anything?" Sarah asked.

"Could you cut up the potatoes?"

Do no harm, Sarah reminded herself. Would this apply if she put the knife into Sterling's back instead of a potato? She picked up the knife and Sterling was distracted from the menu.

"There really are better ways to hold a knife," he said. "But not being married, you might not know this. Let me show you." He put his hand on Sarah's and she released the knife.

"Kate," she asked, "would you like me to go get a bottle of wine?"

"What a wonderful idea!" Sterling exclaimed. "I'll go with you."

Sarah would have refused this honor, if Kate had not looked so grateful. "Will you get some ice cream, Sterling?" Kate asked. "It will be like a party. What fun."

Sterling opened the apartment door for Sarah and rushed ahead to hold the building door. "Well," he panted as he kept pace with her. "You certainly are aging well, Sarah. You must run. I'd be happy to run with you anytime. You can't be too careful in this city. You never know who you might run into." He opened the door of the liquor store, too. "I insist on paying," he said as she picked up a bottle. "What have you chosen? Ah, seven dollars? How delightful."

As they returned to the apartment, Sarah realized that Sterling had been diligently opening doors so that he could choose which ones to keep closed. He propped himself in front of the doorknob. "One day we will have to go for a hike, too—" The door opened, and he fell inside.

"I thought you might have forgotten your key," Rory said.

"But you forgot the ice cream," Kate pointed out.

"Well, Sarah, we'll just have to go out again."

"Sorry," Rory said, "but Sarah really does have to learn how to hold a knife."

"Will you come over tomorrow, too, Sarah?" Kate asked her when Sterling was gone. "It's so nice to be with people." She fumbled with the corkscrew and handed the wine bottle to Rory.

"I have to eat dinner with Cecily tomorrow."

"I remember Cecily," Rory said, much as he might have said, "I remember Attila the Hun." "What is she up to?"

"Her fourth marriage."

"She was always so tiny and beautiful." Kate was too kind to suggest any deficiency might exist in Cecily's worldview or character.

"So are black widow spiders," Rory pointed out.

"You always thought she was pretty, although you'd never ask her out."

"That's because I could either afford to take her out or go to college."

"Do you want to come, too?" Sarah asked. "Kate," she added, for Rory looked alarmed.

"I'll ask Sterling."

Rory rolled his eyes and began to set the table. "Are we going to pray tonight, Kate?"

"Do you mind?"

"Not as long as I'm forewarned."

"Rory makes fun of me for believing in something," Kate said. "But when I first got married, it was — hard, and then we went to Kansas. Everyone always says 'You're not in Kansas anymore,' but I really was in Kansas. People were so nice and happy, and one woman told me if I let Jesus take over my life, I could be happy too. And so I tried—" She stopped; Sarah was looking stricken. "I forgot you don't believe in things."

Jiggling the wine bottle unmercifully, Rory filled the wineglasses; Sterling was back.

"Rory, you've set the table all wrong," Sterling complained as they sat down to dinner.

Rory had put two places on each side of the table, and now he took the one next to Sarah.

"Oh, damn," Rory said and he picked up Sarah's hand. "Okay, Kate. Pray."

As if she had fallen through a hole in time, Sarah missed the prayer, owing to the fact that she was holding hands with Rory McIntyre. Both Kate and Sterling's eyes were on her hand too until Rory released it. "Rory," she said, "did you find out how old the universe is?"

He had just taken a sip of wine and while he swallowed, Sterling undertook to answer Sarah's question, providing, as well, a history of physics and its shortcomings. This, too, Sarah missed; she was observing the ink stain on Rory's shirt pocket. His top button was unfastened; the copper-colored hair on his chest was just visible. His beard had brown, gold, and several gray hairs, but mostly it was auburn. The beard obscured the curve of his jaw; his hair hid his ear. She traced the veins and muscles of his forearm. His fingers were long and slender, his nails bitten short, his hand restless. He touched a scratch on her wrist. "What happened here?" he asked.

"The cat —" The only person more startled than Sarah was Sterling, who stopped talking for nearly three seconds.

They moved into the living room for coffee. Rory sat down next to Sarah. His thigh pressed against hers and made her knee tingle. Stop it, she told herself; it's only his leg. It's only because you didn't sleep last night and you drank a glass of wine. The fly-like hum of Sterling's voice was making her drowsy; he was explaining why science was infinitely unreliable.

"Calculus isn't." Rory, enjoying dinner with Sterling more than usual, stretched out his arm along the back of the sofa and, accidentally, Sarah listed toward him.

"What use is calculus?" Sterling asked. "I know I would have done well, if I had studied it, but really what is the point?"

"Sterling, all physics is predicated on differential equations. F equals ma: acceleration is nothing but the second derivative of the position vector with respect to time. That's classical mechanics. Quantum mechanic's fundamental equation is Schrödinger's, which is a partial differential equation. The only way to describe nature is with calculus."

Sarah opened her eyes, saw Rory's shirt beneath her head, and straightened up.

"Well, I am glad to know you can talk, Rory," Sterling said. "He usually doesn't have anything to say, Sarah, but I suppose you are entitled to be gloomy if your marriage has failed. I am glad Kate and I have been able to make things work out, although Kate is not my ideal woman and I am sure there are women who would suit me better, but it was a question of she was available when I wanted to be married. It might be helpful for you to see how we do it, Sarah. I think you could make a good wife, even though your family is not quite normal."

Rory murmured, "D'you want to go home, babe?"

"Yes." Sarah scrambled to her feet. "But you don't have to go. Goodbye."

Even as Rory stood up, she was out the door.

CHAPTER 13

SARAH RAN UNTIL a stabbing pain in her side forced her to sit down at a bus stop. The world came back into focus, illuminated by a blinking pink and green sign on a tavern. Her heart slowed to a mild thundering, eclipsed by the raucous drumbeats erupting from the bar. A bus lumbered up. She didn't know where she was, so she didn't know where she might go, but her legs wouldn't move anyway. She would sleep where she was and learn what it was like to be a person who slept on city benches. She might be murdered, but then she would not have to wonder what she had been doing all day. "It's not possible," she said.

A trampled newspaper fluttered by, a day that would not come again. Footsteps scuttled the gravel behind her, and her heart, recently calmed, lurched like a worn-out car making one last effort to run.

"Ha!" Gabriel crowed. "I knew I'd find you even though it might take years, as I tragically turned one way, while you turned another." He sat down beside her. "Hello."

Sarah felt a rush of something, but whether it was guilt, relief, or happiness, she wasn't sure. Such words had been buried by the exotic new vocabulary she had packed into her head for the past two years: homeostasis, hypernatremia, pneumothorax, myocardial infarction.

"So, are we waiting for the bus?" Gabriel asked, capturing the page from *The San Francisco Chronicle* and fashioning from it an airplane. "I've never ridden a bus. Shall we? Or we could just sit here." He shot his airplane into the street. "It's such a charming place, and I've never been mugged. Maybe we'll get high on bus fumes. If only I hadn't been chosen to tell you there is a distinct possibility the food dish is empty. Your beast pronged me every time I tried to sit down on the steps. Ah, I knew this would get her to her feet. You can lean on me if you like, Sarah. One of my best fantasies is me as a tower of strength. I won't ask what you've been doing all day. You and all of California never stop running, do you?"

He kept talking as they walked, a soliloquy that had the comforting quality of a chirping cuckoo. "When I was looking in windows tonight, I saw an ice blue room with a crystal ship on a glass table. I'd love to see what they put in their garbage can. Then I thought, why don't I see if Sarah's home yet, even though she hasn't been home all day, but that's none of my business. The beast was pronging me for the umpteenth time when Kate turned up. She said Sterling said she could go to dinner tomorrow. Who is Sterling, and does she ever tell him where he can go? Home at last." They had come to her front door. "Can you make it up the stairs or shall I carry you, like Rhett Butler? Of course, then I have to ravish you at the top."

"I can make it."

"Crushed again."

The room was cold. As she fed the cat, Gabriel unpacked her box of books, and made a chair out of textbooks, draped with her sleeping bag. He sat down and opened *On the Road.*

"Thank you," she said. "You might have saved my life."

"Really? Really, Sarah? Do you know, I've always wanted to be a knight. It's what I told my counselor when she said I could be anything. Then she said I had a reality problem. I said I was working on it, and any day I'd be rid of reality. Kate told me your dark secret," he added, tossing Kerouac aside. "Med school. You know, it's not a bad idea. If you're a doctor, we could be Mr. and Dr. Dinesen, and I wouldn't have to worry about finding myself."

"I don't know if I want to go to med school."

"Oh. Then don't. Why not?"

"I don't really like hospitals. Or sick people. Or doctors. Or medicine. Or the way you're supposed to make people well that doesn't really heal them."

"Well, if you feel that way, Sarah, maybe you shouldn't go to med school because then you might feel obliged to be a doctor. Still, it could be a fine thing. 'Doctour of physik, magyk naturel, wearing silks, fortuning ascendants.'"

"What?"

"Chaucer's doc. I liked him almost as well as I liked the knyght."

"You've read Chaucer?"

"Not all of him, of course. But fundamentally, I'm a medievalist. It's my favorite time. You knew what you were. It was best if you were Richard the Lionheart. I saw a great table in the place across the street. You could sit there and throw bones to serfs, if you were the Lionheart."

"Does it ever bother you, Gabriel, to always be looking through windows?"

"No. Why?"

"Don't you ever want to be inside?"

"No. So tell me: have you always wanted to be a doctor?"

"I don't know. I like science. I like life; at least, I think I do. I'm just not sure how much I like people —"

"Do you want to be something else? What? Is it wild? Secret? Illegal? Oh, tell me, especially if it's weird and kinky."

"I don't want to be anything."

"Oh, bravo! We can be nothing together and be happy forever."

"You don't make it sound so bad."

"It isn't."

"But you can't always just be watching, not if you really want to understand things."

"Who said so?"

"Einstein."

"Oh no! Here comes the real world. Shoo! Vanish! Begone!" Sarah gave up and laughed. "It's the least I can do," he explained. "After last night. Sorry: I was pretty drugged. Tonight I'm not. Not much. Did you like the mushroom?"

"It wasn't so bad," she said, "after I threw up. And when I saw the purple eyes, I wasn't sure I wanted to. I wonder, why purple? And I saw shooting stars in rainbows of colors: where did they come from? Were they outside or inside my head? They were beautiful."

"Why shouldn't you see beautiful things? You're beautiful."

"You don't have to say that."

"I have eyes, Sarah. I can see."

"What you see is wrong. What you should see is something twisted and ugly, odd and old."

"You need glasses, lunatic. And, you know, if you ever wore anything besides sweats, you'd be a complete knockout."

Despair swept over her. "How can I make you understand? You're like light. But it's no use for me. I'm not like you. I'm not like anyone I know, and I don't know what has made me this way. Even when I'm with people, having a good time, something is always beating inside my head saying, 'You're not like them; you'll never be like them.' I've never been part of anything. I am always just watching everyone, like they're on the other side of a glass. If only just once, I could smash this glass and be as light as you —"

"Stop that!" He clamped his hand over her mouth. "Don't say things like that!" When he spoke again, his voice had regained its banter.

"Now, Sarah, if you'd said you lusted after your cadavers, I might think that's weird."

"I didn't, but I did think about how long they'll be dead."

"Sarah!" He thumped her on the head. "Do you know what? I think I should eat dinner with you and Cecily and Kate. Only let's make it lunch."

"Did Kate tell you about Cecily?"

"You may rest assured, my lady, that anything useful to know, Kate has told me. Methinks," he added, "that I shall find a dragon, perforce. And I shall slay the dragon for you."

"Gabriel, you are wonderful."

"Am I?" he asked. "Am I really? We're friends, aren't we? And we are alike: batty as the west wind and dancing on the wild gold shore, waiting for the fall. Sarah, did you like that place in the hills?"

"Yes."

"Good. Because it's going to be ours one day." He jumped to his feet. "And thus, with a kiss, I fly."

He dispensed with the kiss, however, and merely flew.

CHAPTER 14

CECILY GLASS OWENS Baker Younger was as lovely as a stalk of deadly delphiniums fluttering in a spring wind, although the men who had fallen victim to her blue velvet eyes, petal-soft cheeks, and spun gold hair had not died of love; they had merely been divorced and forgotten. To be fair, she had not been married as many times as she could have been, and she had not been married at all in the last year. She was now engaged to the heir of a founding family of Castroville, California, which is also known as the artichoke center of the world.

Cecily was something of a snob, and never more so than when she was in the company of her younger sister. "I suppose it's an accident that you chose a place that doesn't have paper napkins," she remarked as they were seated at Chez Cezanne.

"Gabriel made the reservation," Sarah said. "We've looked in the window several times." The table was set for five, which only puzzled her until Mildred arrived, although Sarah did not immediately recognize her fully clothed.

"Gabriel invited me." Mildred sat down, looking over the group without enthusiasm. "He thought he might be bored." Her eyes slithered over the trim body of the server. He twitched, like a bug pinned to a board, but retained a Gallic sangfroid as he offered aperitifs.

"Bring me something tall and sweet," Mildred purred, "With a straw that I can —"

"Bring her a Coke." Cecily rescued the man and turned the conversation to the more engaging topic of wedding gifts. Her mother-in-law had just given her an entire set of Bavarian.

"Bavarian what?" Sarah asked.

"Isn't she embarrassing?" Cecily asked Kate. "I should have known that her idea of a date would be to walk around looking in windows."

Mildred observed that there were other things to collect besides Bavarians and turned her attention to the menu; the waiter had returned to take orders. "Asparagus," she murmured. "I love the way it slides down my throat. I have a wonderful recipe for it, Asparagus Erectus."

"I thought your friend was coming," Cecily said to Sarah.

"I told him he didn't have to."

"Gabriel is so nice," Kate put in.

"Gabriel," Mildred said, "is a doll. And when I heard he was dating Sarah, I thought, oh, fuck Sarah. He is the handsomest man I have ever seen part of."

"I am sure it's wasted on Sarah," Cecily said. "She wouldn't notice a handsome man if he picked her up on the street and ran off with her."

"I think he's brave to come," Kate said. "I couldn't get Sterling to leave his TV game, and Rory, since his divorce, has just turned into a hermit."

"Rory," Cecily mused. "I remember him. He was very good-looking."

"And divorced men are so starved for sex," Mildred added.

"I was surprised when he asked you to go to Berkeley with him, Sarah," Kate said. "He likes you. Not like Gabriel does, of course. I think Rory wouldn't mind just having a friend."

Cecily and Mildred looked doubtfully at Sarah. One admirer was possible, but two strained all credulity. "Sometimes," Mildred said, "the only explanation is a link from a past life."

"I'll bet you've had quite a few past lives," Cecily remarked.

"I have. I feel it all the time, and the last time I felt it was when I met Gabriel. And when I heard he was with Sarah, I thought —"

"Yes," Cecily said, "we know what you thought."

Just then, Gabriel flew, comet-like, through the door. "Late," he cried, "but I couldn't find a parking place. I was going to pay someone to drive my car in circles, but I feel so insecure handing my keys to a stranger. Ah, look! A place! Sarah, my love, if I stand in it, will you go get my car? It's on the sidewalk around the corner." He dragged Sarah from the room. "I have my trusty rusty sword in hand," he said. "I invited Mildred to be my squire."

"Do you know anything about Bavarian?"

"Coming right up."

"That is a nice car," Cecily observed when the car was properly parked. "What do you do?"

"I drive it. Sometimes I park it. Not too often. You know what parking is like in the city."

Cecily was not to be deterred. "Do you work?"

"Alas, I have a profession but no job. I'm a lawyer."

While Sarah choked, Cecily said, "There can't be too many lawyers." She had drawn extensively from the pool, both for husbands and divorces. "So much depends on where you went to school."

"It does," Gabriel agreed. "Absolutely."

"Where did you go to school?"

"Yale."

"Like Sarah, almost!" Kate exclaimed.

"But she was an idiot and threw away the chance," Cecily said.

Gabriel merely lifted his eyebrows. "Excuse me," he said, picking up Cecily's plate and studying its underside. "I thought as much. This is a poor imitation of my grandmother's Bavarian. When she died, the baker stole her entire set. We found out because my mother ordered a cake for the funeral and he accidentally sent it on one of the plates."

"That's shocking," Cecily said. "Where did you live?"

"Chicago."

"Well," she said, as if that explained it.

The waiter returned. Gabriel waved away the suggestion that he order. "Sarah will share her sole with me. I always love whatever she orders. Sarah! I'm an idiot! I keep forgetting to tell you that we have the uncle's tickets to the opera. Opening night. I suppose we'll have to dress, but whatever you wear, you'll be beautiful. Especially if it's a dress. Oh! I almost forgot." From his pocket he drew a box. "Happy birthday."

"But how did you know?"

"I told him," Kate said.

Cecily sighed. "I suppose that I should pay for lunch,"

"What a sweet thought!" Gabriel kissed Cecily's hand. "Waiter, bring the check to this lady, please. And now, I must run." He kissed Kate's hand too, patted Mildred's head, and, with the darting motion of a bird, he kissed Sarah, half on her lips, half on her cheek, before he rushed out the door.

All eyes turned to Sarah. "We both feel the same way about the city," she said, quite calmly studying the remains of her sole. "That it's really exciting and full of exciting things to do."

"Well, open it," Cecily said, when Mildred had followed Gabriel out the door.

Sarah studied the box, wrapped in yellow paper printed with blue bears blowing horns. In her family, birthdays reminded her mother of her marriage and were best forgotten. Once, in fifth grade, on her birthday Sarah had found a white paper bag hidden in her desk by the teacher. It had her name on it so she knew it was for her. She spent the morning imagining what might be inside and was slightly let down when she finally looked inside and found a frosted cupcake. She rattled Gabriel's box. It didn't sound like a cupcake.

"What will you wear?" Cecily asked.

"Wear?"

"To the opera, idiot."

"Oh. A dress, I suppose."

"Do you have one? Do you have any money?"

"Are you really paying for lunch?"

"Do you have an account at Magnin's?"

"I don't have an account anywhere."

"Sarah," Cecily said. "That very attractive man likes you. You might make an effort."

"I don't know how."

"Here is how: you open your gift. It's obviously jewelry. You buy a gown that goes with it. And you wear it with proper shoes. She wore running shoes to my last wedding, Kate. I was mortified."

Inside the wrapping were two boxes. One was perfume. Cecily and Kate oohed, so Sarah surmised that Joy ranked up there with Bavarian. "It smells good," she said.

Cecily opened the other box. A tiny shoe made of diamonds dangled from a gold chain.

"Oh, of course," Kate exclaimed. "It's Cinder —" She caught herself and blushed bright guilty red.

"Why are you laughing?" Cecily asked Sarah. "Those are real diamonds."

"So," Sarah said, "what goes with diamonds and Joy?"

They went shopping, and when they returned to her apartment,

Sarah was in a state of shock, sorry that there were no scholarships for a night at the opera.

"You'll need a wrap," Cecily said.

The cat strolled in. Sarah draped him around her neck. "My fur."

"You are hopeless. I don't know what Gabriel sees in you."

"Neither do I."

With a few last admonitions — "Try to be serious about serious things" and "Don't forget the shoes" — Cecily departed. Kate left, too, after offering to loan Sarah the fur stole Sterling's mother had given her. "It's ugly," she said. "But it is real."

Sarah, alone, tried on her new dress. She had been searching through a sales rack when Cecily brought her this gown, shimmering with the colors of a sunset. (*"There's no top." "It's just strapless." "It will fall off." "It won't." "It costs more than my car did." "Charge it."*)

She scrutinized the mirror. She never expected to see any reflection looking back, but she really did not recognize this woman. Was it possible that the unlikely combination of Cecily and Gabriel had given her entrance to a forbidden, mysterious night world of love and beauty? Did she still believe in love, despite so little evidence that it existed? A feeling descended over her, like a silk veil floating down from the sky: could she be in love?

CHAPTER 15

"YOU HAVE FURNITURE!" Kate exclaimed. "A bed and a table and chairs, too?"

"The woman downstairs was moving out, so I bought a few things. The opera isn't until September seventh, so I asked the landlord if I could rent the flat for one more month."

It wasn't all Sarah had bought in the past three days. Kate inspected earrings, gold slippers, six pairs of stockings (in case she ran five putting them on), and a sack full of makeup.

"I only asked for a lipstick," Sarah said, "but somehow I bought all this. The saleswoman made me a map of how to put it on."

Kate was enthralled. "It's like the prom we never went to. It's like getting married, only you won't wake up married."

"And the music will be better."

"What does Gabriel think of all this?"

This was a disconcerting point. Sarah hadn't seen Gabriel since their lunch. The telephone being forbidden, she had summoned the courage to drive to Berkeley to ask him when the opera was. He'd gone home for his mother's birthday, the Scoundrels informed her, but they'd give him her message when he called to make sure they hadn't burned down the house. Gabriel did call. Did she really wanted to go to the opera, he asked. Yes, she said, a little. If you insist, he said. Did she know when it was?

"He went home for a few days," she said to Kate.

"Rory's gone home too," Kate said. "He found an apartment, but the landlord wants to paint it, so Rory took the kids to Napa. He wouldn't go before. Mom's in heaven. She said he even left the kids with her and went out with someone."

"Oh." Sarah felt herself droop, unaccountably.

"I told him about Gabriel, Sarah."

"Told him what?"

"That you'd met Prince Charming."

ON THE MORNING of the opera, Sarah went to Union Square one last time. She returned carrying a gilt bag. She called Kate to ask if she could borrow Sterling's mother's fur wrap, after all. "I went to buy one this morning when I got my hair done, but I bought something else instead. Underwear. French. I can't spend any more money, Kate."

"I'll bring it over after work," Kate said. "This, I want to see."

From the salon, Sarah had filched a magazine that had a timeline for preparing oneself for a significant event. As she began to follow it, her stomach twisted into knots, as it always did before an exam. She soaked in a tub and examined her waxed legs. She put on lotion and her new underwear, a handful of silk and lace, artful, insubstantial, and decadent. The knots began to untangle. She felt a tremor of excitement, as if someone inside her who had been sleeping a hundred years was awakening. The phone rang. It was her mother. Sarah listened, surveying her toenails. What a bizarre thing to do, to paint your toenails burgundy.

"Why not go out with him, Isabelle?" she asked. "You could just ask him what his first wife died of. It might have been natural causes."

The doorbell buzzed. Sarah opened the door, gasped, dropped

the phone, clutched her head, slammed the door, retrieved the phone, ended the conversation, put on her robe, and opened the door again.

"Your fur," Rory said, grinning.

"Thank you."

"My pleasure."

"Would you like to come in?" she asked, hoping he would not; but he did.

"I thought you were Kate."

"She has to work late."

"She works hard."

"Yes. She does."

"That was my mother on the phone."

"How is she?"

"Not as crazy as she used to be, I think."

"Good. That's — good."

He examined the pottery figure on her mantel. Sarah sensed that something was on his mind, but it was up to her to guess what. "Would you like coffee?" she asked.

"No, no, don't go to any trouble."

"Where are Lucy and Avery?"

"With my folks." He picked up her newspaper, squashed it, and tried to smooth it out. "I took them to a daycare center but they cried when I tried to leave. The teacher said they'd be fine once I left. She said they were. But the next day, they cried again. Today, they're with my folks."

"Are you moved into your apartment?"

"No. Mom's still cleaning. It looked all right to me, but she thought there were germs. I came over to get some things I'd left at Kate's. But I'm interrupting you."

"I was just going to put on makeup."

"Go ahead."

Bewildered, Sarah went into the bathroom. It wasn't rude since she didn't close the door. She applied moisturizer and foundation. Blend, blend, blend, the saleswoman had said. The eyes were next; they were tricky. She had three colors, two liners, mascara, and a fixer to hold it all in place. She looked up to see Rory watching her from the doorway. She put the mascara brush in her eye.

"I didn't know you do all this," he said, as she scrubbed black blotches from her eyelid.

"I don't. It's why I'm so slow."

He came into the bathroom. She looked down because she had only one eye finished and so she was lopsided.

"Do you do the hair stuff, too?" he asked. "Curlers and all that?"

"No, my hair is too long," she said, quoting the hairdresser.

"No, it isn't." He touched the stiff back of her upswept hairdo. Nothing moved.

"I think he put a gallon of glue on it."

"You smell good."

"It's Joy. It's a perfume."

He sniffed the bottle. "It smells better on you."

"That's chemistry," she said, and he smiled. He examined the objects on the sink, reading the labels and twisting the caps. She finished her second eye, except for the mascara, because he was scrutinizing the spiky brush. It was odd enough to be doing it, let alone with an audience. How would she put on her dress?

"Would you like a glass of wine?" she asked. She had bought a bottle of wine, too.

"Would you?"

"Yes."

"I'll get it."

When he went into the kitchen, she jumped into her dress. She came out of the bathroom just as the setting sun was filling the air with golden light. She pirouetted, and the dress sparkled like a thousand stars. Rory, bringing in the wine from the kitchen, halted. To be staggered is not a bad thing to happen to a man who has said that calculus explains it all.

"You're beautiful."

"It's a lot of makeup."

They sat down at her new table and chairs. Sarah swung her feet. They both were looking at her toenails. "Why do women do it?" he asked.

"I suppose it's the ritual transformation," she speculated. "You have to go through it once. Usually you get married or go to the prom. It's the closest thing we have to magic: makeup."

"Transformation to what?"

"Who was ever loved without magical help?" She smiled at him daringly. "Oh, I forgot: you don't care for love."

He raised his eyebrows, and she felt as if a heater had been turned on inside her. She hoped her eye shadow would not melt and run. "I care about some things," he said. He took a scroll of paper from his pocket, a blur of colored spots, red, yellow, and blue, on a black background. "I brought you this."

"How pretty! Did Lucy make it?"

"No," he laughed. "I did. That is, my receiver did."

"It's the dark part of the universe?"

He nodded. "Well, a part of it."

"Rory, do you really think calculus is the only way to describe nature?"

"Did I say that?"

"Yes."

"I wish it were true."

"Galileo said mathematics is the language in which God has written the universe."

He did not appear inclined to pursue this interesting topic, and Sarah formed a resolution because she was beautiful, for this one evening, and taking a chance on love. She asked, "Is there something else you wanted to talk about?"

"Yes."

A triumph; disguised by beauty, she'd done it. He said, "When do you go back?"

"I said I'd be there by September ninth."

"Are you flying?"

"No, driving."

"Did you get your car checked out?"

"I forgot."

"Do you want me to do it? I hate to think of you driving that car across the country alone."

"I've already done it once."

"Yes, but I didn't know you were doing it."

She sprang to her feet and spun about nervously. The sunlight had left the room, but the dress still sparkled. He stood up too, but he didn't spin.

"Rory, did you ever think that you left school because you had to learn something?"

"No."

"I do. I feel like I've spent my whole life inside a cave, a hole with no light or windows, wishing for something, for life or love or anything, but always just waiting in the dark. If only twenty percent of what we see ever reaches our brain, what are we missing?"

He made no answer. The sun's last colors were flaming across the sky. She wasn't ready; she'd be late. She picked up the box with the diamond necklace. She wasn't sure she liked it, but she had to wear it, didn't she? Her fingers fumbled with the clasp. Rory took it from her and fastened it around her neck. His hand stayed on her shoulder, sending sparks shooting through her spine, landing on her knees.

"You don't need to learn what I've learned," he said, and when she looked up at him, he kissed her. He said something — she never knew what — and then he was gone.

"It must have been the underwear," she said to the cat. "French, you know."

CHAPTER 16

"NO WONDER YOU don't like music," Gabriel grumbled, "if this is the kind of music you don't like."

"But I love it."

It was intermission, and they were flocking with the other finely feathered guests into the lobby of the opera house. Sarah paused to marvel: this set was as splendid as the one on stage, a grand, marble birdcage, gilded, lit with crystal chandeliers and filled with rare birds. Then she hurried to catch up with Gabriel near the exit.

"Where are you going?" she asked.

"You don't want to leave?"

"It's not over."

"You really like it?"

"I do."

"Then why do you want to have a serious conversation? Is something wrong? Has your virtue been threatened? Your mother victimized? Has your lover been faithless? Have you been locked up and forced to drink poison? You have to admit that life has been good, but tame."

This had been his mood since he'd arrived to pick her up. She said, "I didn't know you went to Yale."

"I didn't. I just said it to impress Cecily. God, she is beautiful."

"You could get on the waiting list and marry her next year."

"Touchy, touchy. I'm being strangled by my suspenders. Want to see them?" He moved to a corner, opened his jacket, and extracted a vial of cocaine.

"You'll get arrested, Gabriel."

"Not a chance." He turned a knob, held it to his nose, sniffed, and offered it to her; she declined. "No one will notice. We're the best-looking people here. Is that Cecily's dress?"

"No."

"I like it. It reminds me of a picture I saw when I was a kid. Insects were playing instruments and a fairy was dancing on a spider's web. She looked like you. You should have been a dancer. Shall we?" The cocaine was doing its work. He spun her in a circle. "Damn," he said as they veered near a wall, "is that a door or a window?"

"One of Kate's brothers walked through a glass door once."

"Let's!"

"No."

"Then let's go to Hamburger Mary's? We'd get more stares than the waiters."

"You really don't like the opera?"

"No, I hate it. I hate all this passion and suffering. Why doesn't she just admit he's a bastard and throw a knife at him? No, she has to love him. Why? Why doesn't she find herself a nice fisherman or prince and settle down?"

"Maybe she doesn't want one."

"Of course she does. Everyone does."

"That's an unfair generalization."

"She's missed his whole character."

"She has not."

"Then she's missed half of it, which is just as bad."

"Which half?"

"The half he doesn't show her and she doesn't see because she's too good to see it."

"She's not two-dimensional; why should she assume he is? There has to be some trust for what she doesn't see."

"And look what it gets her. A knife in the heart."

"It's her choice."

"No, it isn't. How can it be? He got her entangled with his great magic show: here I am, and here's my yacht, and aren't I grand, and isn't this fun?"

"It doesn't mean that's all she thinks he's capable of."

"She doesn't know what he's capable of."

"Why not?"

"She's innocent."

"Gabriel, look at the times they lived in. There was no innocence."

He shut his eyes. "Well, if you insist, we'd better go back in. I'll just leave before she croaks herself. I used to do the same thing before the battles in the cowboy and Indian movies."

After the final curtain, Sarah found Gabriel slumped against a wall in the lobby. She was humming; her eyes were dancing. She hadn't noticed when he'd left.

"Did she do it?" he asked.

"Stab herself? Yes."

"Are you hungry?"

"I am. Starving."

They went to Hamburger Mary's. Gabriel ordered coffee and a beer, Sarah, a hamburger.

"You're right, people are staring at us," she said. "Some feat for San Francisco." Still he didn't smile. "Thank you, Gabriel. I loved it. And I'd never have found it on my own."

He tried stick his fork in his forehead, shrieked, and fell forward onto the table.

"She's not really dead. You could go backstage and talk to her."

"It's not her I'm worried about." His voice was muffled. "It's you."

"Me?" She looked from the knife to the catsup bottle and put the knife down.

"But it doesn't matter. You're leaving."

"I don't have to. I paid my rent for September."

Sarah had not thought it was possible to see the blood drain out of someone's head, at least not in a restaurant. "Let's get out of here," he said.

She trailed after him as he flew down the street. She couldn't run in her shoes; her dress tangled around her legs. Gabriel turned into an alley. A green sign flashed one word: "Dancing." They entered a smoked-filled, cave-like room lit only by a rotating strobe light. The disco music muffled any other sounds. Gradually Sarah's eyes adjusted to the pulsing light and dark.

"Shall we dance?" Gabriel asked.

"Is it all right?"

"Why not?"

"Because," she whispered, "I am the only woman here."

He dragged her into the center of the room. He danced. She gripped her necklace, acutely conscious of every stab of light on her diamonds and her dress, until she realized that no one was looking at her. She began to move more freely. She let her dress swirl; she was dancing.

Gabriel stopped first. "Okay, let's leave."

No, she thought, let's not.

How many miles did they walk in silence as the fog thickened around them? They passed the pawnshop where they had met. The necklace made of lovers still dangled in the window. They came to the abandoned house with the Gypsy caravan. They sat down on its steps. A bell, tolling midnight, broke the silence. Sarah's feet were throbbing; she took off the gold shoes.

"Do you go there a lot?" she asked.

"I've never gone there before. I've just wanted to."

"Why didn't you?"

"I knew once I went in, I'd never come out."

"But if it's what you want —" He said nothing. "I should have known."

"Why? Why should you have known? How could you know what I don't know myself?" He picked up her hand, something he had never done. His hand was square, his fingers thick and cold. "It's why I came here, Sarah. Everybody knows what they are, but I don't. You don't know what it's like to spend your whole life knowing you don't feel like anyone else, wondering why, and if it's good or evil, and if it means you'll always be alone."

She cleared her throat. "Gabriel, it's me you're talking to."

"That's a point," he admitted. "When I got here, Sarah, I lost my nerve. I panicked, and then I saw you. Didn't you wonder why I didn't try to make love to you?"

"It was kind of a relief."

"Oh."

"And I told you I gave up sex."

"Did you really?"

"I guess so. I just decided I wouldn't—"

"Unless you were in love?"

"Unless I wanted to, that's all."

"God, do I know what you mean. I haven't had sex in six months. Sarah, I'll kill myself if you like."

"We're not at the opera, Gabriel. You might rather just be, you know, gay."

"I don't know. I don't know. Why don't I know?"

"I'd probably be gay if I were a man," she offered. "I like men better than women."

He laughed bleakly. "Oh Jesus, I should be in love with you. I'd be crazy if I weren't. So I must be gay. You're so rare, Sarah. When I saw you tonight, I thought we really are made out of the same stuff as stars. She really is someone to kill dragons for. I'll never forget you."

She felt the curious stab of an unnamed memory. What was it? He kept talking. "I don't know anyone who is gay. I look at men and wonder, is he, is he? I thought about going to a gay rap in Berkeley. I walked past one once, but they all looked a lot more gay than me. There's one tomorrow night. What are you doing tomorrow night?"

"I don't think I could go to a gay men's rap."

"No, but I don't want you to sit home alone if — if we don't see each other anymore."

Now she remembered: it was her first thunderstorm in New York. The afternoon sky turned black. A bolt of lightning whizzed past her window, so close she heard it sizzle. Thunder roared and rocked the building. When it was over, she was sitting in the dark.

Gabriel twisted a rose until it stained his fingers red. "I see you and I get all mixed up. I don't know why you like me."

She laughed, a hollow imitation of his own manic style. "You make me feel normal."

SHE WALKED HOME alone. The cat was waiting. He climbed the steps with her. She opened a can of cat food and sat on the floor by him while he ate. She looked again in the mirror. Her hairdo had unraveled; her stockings were tattered. Her necklace — she clutched her throat — it was gone. She'd lost her shoe.

She threw off her clothes. The cat attacked her dress and wrestled with her French underwear while she took a shower, scrubbing the glue from her hair and the perfume from her skin. She burrowed into her sleeping bag in her new bed by the window.

"I should have left at intermission," she said, "when my head was full of splendid images."

The night was cold. She jerked the window shut, and the spider's web ripped into shreds. The spider scuttled for shelter.

"I'm sorry," Sarah said, heart-stricken. "I forgot that you were there."

Her pain took the shape of a huddled spider, crouched in a hiding place. She opened the window and cold air filled the room, but the spider did not emerge again that night.

CHAPTER 17

"HELLO, SARAH!" AVERY opened the door of Kate's apartment. "Why are you all wet?"

"It's raining." Since dawn she had been walking, looking for her lost necklace. This must be like anesthesia, she speculated, the baffling notion that there is pain, but you can't feel it. In theory she was appalled by the idea of making herself numb, but now she was afraid of what she might feel if she were not so oddly insensible.

"Is that you, Sarah?" Kate called. "You're up early."

"I brought back your wrap. I'm packing."

"How was it?" Kate asked. "It was on the news, all the people arriving at the opening. We didn't see you but Rory said you were gorgeous."

"He did?"

"Well, I said did she look gorgeous, and he said yes. He's at his new place in Berkeley." Kate had caught Sarah's swift glance around the room. "Sterling went to pick up a mattress for him, and he is supposed to collect us on his way to Berkeley, but he just called and said Rory gave him the wrong address in the wrong city, so it's going to take much longer."

"But you can take us to Berkeley," Lucy concluded.

❦

"THERE IT IS." Kate pointed to a brown shingle Craftsman shaded by an oak tree. Sarah killed the engine as she glimpsed a tall, auburn-haired man standing beside a truck. Then she saw three of them. The twins, Pat and Mike, and Tim, the youngest McIntyre, were on their way to pick up pizzas for lunch. Lucy and Avery opted to go with their uncles. Kate went too. Sarah said she would carry up the box of odds and ends. She just wanted to see it; that was all.

The landlady lived on the ground floor. Sarah climbed the stairs and stopped at the door to a room that smelled of fresh paint. It had dark wood beams and built-in bookshelves. The window looked out at the oak tree. She loved it.

"Good heavens! Sarah! What a surprise! Come in! Here, let me take that box. It's much too heavy for you." Sarah found herself relinquishing her box to a woman who was twenty-five years older and one inch shorter than she was: Jean McIntyre.

"I'm just doing a few things in the kitchen," Jean said. She was cleaning, unpacking, and cooking, but in Sarah's experience, this trim, impeccable woman never did fewer than three things at a time, and she talked while she did it all.

"It's not as bad as I expected, and certainly not as bad as some of the places he's lived in. The stove needed a good cleaning, of course, and the shelves weren't lined. I wanted to put a few things in the freezer but I had to defrost it first. Rory insists he can cook, but you never know what that means. I made spaghetti sauce and macaroni and cheese, Avery's favorite, and a meatloaf. Rory makes fun of meatloaf, but he always eats it. At least I know the children won't starve. Well, I know Rory wouldn't let them starve. Joe says don't worry, but it's hard not to. How are you, Sarah? You look pale. Are you working too hard? Let me get you some coffee. Rory should be back any minute."

Sarah knew she should leave, but she took a cup of coffee.

"Do you remember these?" Jean asked, unwrapping salt and pepper shakers shaped like ears of corn. "Avery tried to eat them, just like Rory did when he was three. I've brought Rory thirty years of mismatched dishes, but he's happy with them. He doesn't have anything. That woman took everything, except the children; thank goodness for that."

Jean paused. Sarah knew she suffered from a notion that God might be listening to her at any random moment, but generally with encouragement, she overcame this. "Her name was Dibby?" she asked.

"I think it's really Doris, but no one calls her that." Jean glanced upwards. "I did try to like her, Sarah. Her parents liked Rory, although her mother carried on as if he had only learned to use a knife and fork at Harvard. And her father didn't have to so amazed that Rory had brains. At the wedding he boasted about Rory so much, Dibby got upset and threw a platter of lobsters at a wall. She said she had to express her feelings, but I can't imagine what kind of feelings make you throw lobsters. I was worried because I know Rory can be difficult too, but what could I say at a wedding? We weren't happy, of course, about the divorce."

"You weren't?"

"We knew it wasn't a happy marriage — actually, it was the worst disaster I'd ever seen —but once there are children, you have to try to make the best of things. They were very young, although I don't know if five or ten years would have made any difference. I still can't believe a woman would just give away her children."

Jean, as close as Sarah had ever seen her to being confused, rearranged a shelf of mismatched coffee mugs. "Rory always wanted something more — not things, just something. But Joe and I are simple people. What could we do for him? You can't show your child the way to a place you've never been, but he got there on his own, and then I was never sure where he was. He was so homesick when he first left.

He would call, but Joe and I had to do all the talking. And it was worse after he got married. Then, he didn't call. At least he's finally come home, not that Berkeley is home. I wish he would live in Napa, but I know he must do things his own way. He always has. I worry because he is so alone, but I suppose it will take a long time for him to trust anyone again. It's an awful thing to watch your child be hurt, no matter how old he is. He does have a good heart even if he doesn't always know what to do with it."

From the doorway came a jangle of musical notes. Rory, steadying a piano on a dolly, backed into the doorframe and swore. "And I was just about to tell Sarah how much your temper has improved," Jean said. Rory turned, lost his grip, and left his father to push the piano into the living room.

Joe McIntyre was not as big as Sarah remembered him but he was still as handsome, dark, lean, and vigorous, with eyes full of laughter. He came into the kitchen, crooning, "Hey, good-lookin', whatcha got cookin'?" It was the song he always sang to Jean. To Sarah he sang "Jeepers creepers, where'd you get those peepers?" He kissed his wife as if he had not seen her in weeks. He kissed Sarah, too. They really were a family where everyone kissed everyone all the time.

"If this isn't like old times," he chuckled, "seeing Sarah look at Rory like he's walking on water instead of the floor."

"Joe!" Jean said, as Sarah choked on her coffee. "Don't embarrass Sarah."

"Why would that embarrass her?"

"No one likes to remember when they were young and silly about love."

"Why not? When you were young and silly, you chose me." Joe patted his wife, and she frowned with poorly repressed delight.

"It was a long time ago that Sarah admired Rory so much."

"And I say it never hurts to have a fine woman think you are wonderful," Joe countered, winking at Sarah. "I enjoy it."

"Is that your old piano?" Sarah asked weakly. "And your sofa?" She had only survived the conversation because Rory was nowhere in sight.

"Jeanie's redecorating," Joe said, adding cream to a mug of coffee.

"I am getting a new kitchen, Sarah. We're thinking about selling."

"Jeanie is," Joe said cheerfully. "But when she gets her new kitchen, she'll stay put."

"Joe is just happy because everyone wants to buy his grapes, Sarah. You know Rudy sold his land to Joe before he died, and someone bought the Langley's land because he thought he could build eight houses on it but he couldn't because of the Ag Preserve, so the man had a fit and sold it to Joe too. Now I don't know how many acres of grapes Joe has, and Pat and Mike are at Davis studying how to make wine, which is an odd thing to study at college, but it makes them happy. I have to say, Joe's wine got so much better after he met that man from Russia who had studied wine at college, too, but in Europe; they take it so seriously there. I really don't mind drinking Joe's wine now. And then that odd thing happened in Paris where someone put wines from Napa in a tasting of French wines, and no one knows how it happened but the judges thought the wines were French and gave them the top marks."

"They're calling it the Judgment of Paris," Joe added.

"Now, Sarah, people keep driving down the lane and knocking on the door because they've seen Joe's grapes. And they sit in the barn with him and taste his wines and think it is exciting. I said, 'Joe, let's sell everything while this craze is going on, and then we can take a vacation in Hawaii.' How many years, Sarah, have I wanted to do that?"

"Quite a few." Jean was always saving for a trip to Hawaii, but then she'd spend the money on school clothes or a new pump. Hawaii would wait, she'd say; it wasn't going anywhere.

"Here come the pizzas," Joe announced.

"Did you get salad?" Jean asked the twins. "No? I knew you'd forget anything healthy. Sarah, we'll have to make one."

She rummaged in the fridge and handed Sarah a head of lettuce. She found a salad bowl and commenced cutting tomatoes, cucumbers, and peppers. Sarah examined the lettuce uncertainly. She broke off a few lettuce leaves and ran them under water. She put the lettuce on cutting board and picked up the knife. Jean gave her an odd look, but said nothing. It was either too much lettuce or not enough.

"Sarah, don't you know you're supposed to tear lettuce, not cut it?" Rory was leaning against the doorframe. The knife sliced through her hand, and blood spurted over the lettuce. Jean gasped, and amidst the cries for bandages, Sarah tried to apologize for ruining the lettuce. "It's nothing," she insisted, transfixed by the sight of blood spilling down her arm. Her head began to spin.

"I've got her." Rory's voice came from far away, yet he was holding her upright and dragging her away from the spotlight. Sarah was so relieved, she didn't wonder where they were going until they were outside on the sidewalk. The rain, falling steadily, cooled her hot face.

"I'm all right," she said.

"Good, then let's go get your hand stitched up."

Sarah sank down onto the curb. Rory fell beside her, amidst a clutter of empty cans and dead leaves. "Are you going to faint again?" he asked.

"I didn't faint."

"You didn't? Then you came close enough for me."

"I'll just leave now."

He was fixated on the blood seeping through her makeshift bandage. "I don't want you to bleed to death, honey."

"I won't. I already would have by now."

Rory rubbed his head. The rain was falling harder. A police car passed them and slowed down. "Come on, Sal," he said. "Let's go." She shook her head. "Why not?"

"I hate hospitals."

The police car returned and stopped. "Everything all right?" the officer asked.

"Yes, fine." Rory stood up. He was dripping rain and smeared with blood and dead leaves, and Sarah knew she must look worse. She wondered if the man would believe that Rory was building a machine to help solve the mysteries of the universe and that she could soon be qualified to remove his appendix. "I was making a salad," she said.

The policeman could not talk Sarah into going to an emergency room either, but Rory did persuade her to go back upstairs. Joe made her lie down on the sofa and drink a restorative glass of wine. Jean worried that Sarah was too thin to lose so much blood, and Kate wished she was so thin, although Sarah knew she was not thin at all. Pat and Mike insisted blood added to the taste of a salad. Tim described how he had once sliced his arm open with a saw. Avery and Lucy sat beside Sarah and examined her bandage, and Sarah, who had not worried about bleeding to death, was in acute danger of expiring from too much attention. Only Rory stayed apart, staring out the window. "Just think," Tim said, "somewhere out in that storm is your mattress."

"I can't believe you sent Sterling to the wrong address in the wrong city, Rory," Jean said. "It could take him all day."

"I know," Rory said. "Otherwise I'd have told him it was in Nevada."

"Sarah," Pat said, "is it true you're going in for surgery?"

"Sarah will make a fine doctor," Joe insisted.

"As long as she only faints at the sight of her own blood," Tim added.

Mike said, "Remember the time Sarah brought Dad that dead bird so he could fix it?"

"Dead?" Sarah said. "But Rory told me it flew away."

"Rory was afraid to make you cry," Pat said.

"And it's no crime to have a tender heart," Jean interceded. "Remember, Rory was the one we could never take to the zoo because he'd stand in front of the cages and cry so sadly."

"Oh no," Rory said. "Who gave Ma wine?"

"For that matter," Jean continued, "I was just telling Rory not to worry because the children cry when he leaves them at school because no one could have raised a bigger fuss than he did when I first took him to kindergarten. Every morning for a month, he would hang onto my knees, begging me not to leave him."

Rory was wondering aloud if someone might change his mother's wine to water when Sterling's voice reverberated in the entryway: "Rory, I am sure I got you a better deal than you would have gotten if I had found the place you told me to go to. Oh! Is everything moved in? Did I miss it all? Why did you put the piano there? It is not the best arrangement to put the sofa by the window —"

Lucy asked worriedly, "Is he going to move in too?"

SARAH HALTED IN the doorway to Rory's bedroom. He was lying on the new mattress.

"Come in," he said.

"I didn't know you were here. I have your sheets. They were packed with the pans. Your mother said —"

"You don't have to make the bed."

"Good, because I don't know how to do it the right way."

"Ah, the right way." He sat up and held out his hand. She stepped forward then backward; he was only reaching for the sheets. "Did you hear about the dilemma of divorce, too?"

"It's all right. I'm used to it."

"Offending God?"

"It must be hard if your parents didn't get divorced before you did. You may have offended God, but at least God —" She stopped talking, for he had tossed the sheets aside and taken her bandaged hand in his.

"God?"

"Doesn't call you up to discuss it," she faltered. He was pulling her closer, and she had nowhere to go but directly into him.

"How was the night at the opera?" His voice was nonchalant but his coolness vanished as tears filled her eyes. He tugged, and she landed, startled as a cat, on his knees.

"I just came to say goodbye." She dashed the tears from her eyes. "Sorry."

"It's all right." He patted her shoulder. "I've gotten used to all kinds of things. Except diapers. I never got used to them. Mom said when it's your own baby, it's different. I said, then we'd better have blood tests." He had got her to smile, however wanly. "What's wrong, Sal? Did you have a fight with that guy?"

"Something like that."

"It's not usually fatal, honey."

"This is."

"Are you sure?"

"Yes."

"Damn. I shouldn't be glad."

"I know. And I shouldn't be glad your marriage was such a mess."

"Oh, Sarah." He was laughing. "Neither should I."

He kissed her and so they both missed the approach of Sterling. "Rory, I bought what you wanted, but if you want to return this mattress for a single bed, which is what I would recommend, I could let you have, for only three-fourths of what I paid for it, the frame I had in college. This way you won't have to put your mattress on the floor. And since you have no need for a bigger bed, and I explained this to the salesman, he agreed that you could return" — Sterling halted at the door, flabbergasted but not speechless — "it. Sarah!"

Rory raised his head. "What did you say?"

Sterling repeated his speech, with only marginally diminished conviction. "I hope you aren't drunk," he added to Sarah.

"The mattress isn't on the floor," she said. "It's on the box spring, which is on the floor."

"And Sterling is just the person we need," Rory added. "Sterling, do you know how to make a square corner?"

By mid-afternoon the move was complete. Joe carried off Jean while she was still giving Rory instructions to make sure the children bathed, ate, and slept daily. Sarah, following Kate and Sterling out the door, felt a hand on her arm. "Stay," Rory said. "Will you?"

She stayed. They unpacked his books and filled the shelves with *Major British Writers, Letters to the Earth, Sea Wolf,* and *Galactic and Ex-tra-Galactic Radio Astronomy.* They walked to a grocery store, and he detoured into a pharmacy, leaving the children with Sarah.

"What did you buy?" Lucy asked when he rejoined them.

"Something for Sarah," he replied with a mysterious twinkle in his eyes.

"Bandages," Lucy said.

Rory cooked pasta for dinner, and while the sauce simmered, they built a fire of packing materials. They ate at the painted wooden table in the kitchen. The boiling pasta and bubbling sauce had steamed up the windows and warmed the room. Rory pulled off his sweater; Sarah, watching him, managed not to upend her wineglass. Lucy, aware that no attention was being paid to her, decorated her head with pasta. Avery, not to be outdone, put his whole plate on his head.

"I'll just give them a quick bath and put them to bed," Rory said. "Don't do the dishes." She did them anyway, while she listened to Rory reading a story. You should not think these things are wonderful, she told herself: old flowered dishes in a chipped enamel sink, two Christian Brothers wineglasses, the smell of Ivory soap, and *The Tale of Two Bad Mice*. How could this be the stuff of enchantment? She knew she should leave while she could, but instead she watched the rain falling against the dark glass of the window. She could see her own face, off center, ghostly, blue-gray, and streaked with rain. She bent her head down into the dishcloth. "Oh please," she whispered. "Please love me."

The sound of the piano drew her into the living room. Sarah remembered the piece, "Trois Gymnopédies." She had always loved it when he played it. He hit a wrong note and stopped. "I'm out of practice."

As he stood up, she felt a vivid bolt of fear and nerves. "I should be going," she said.

He walked with her down the stairs. A burst of rain hit them as he opened the front door.

Her voice was barely audible. "You don't have to go out into the storm, Rory."

"Neither do you, Sarah."

SHE LAY MOTIONLESS, her eyes closed. If she opened them, the clock would strike midnight and she would be wandering somewhere with one shoe and a shattered pumpkin. If she opened them, a witch would offer her an apple and she would eat it. If she opened them, the man lying beside her would turn into a frog.

"They're still asleep," Rory said. "Maybe there is a God." Sarah nodded. "I have to hand it to Sterling. His square corners are holding up." He drew her closer to him. "Talk to me, Sarah."

She opened her eyes. The room was dark, except for a blurred bit of light from the street. Rory's face was shadowed, but it did not vanish in a puff of smoke. She said, "Do you know if it really is possible for a mirror image to exist of something that has no counterpart in nature?"

He was only mildly surprised. "It is true that parity isn't conserved, but it's deceptive to extract too much from that experiment. You might as well break a glass and ask if physical laws are reversible in time. The answer is yes."

"But the glass is still broken."

"To your eyes or mine. Nature seems to be able to tell the direction of time, as well as right from left." He hesitated. "Sarah, was that too fast for you?"

"No. Oh no."

"But you —" He looked uncertain, unexpectedly shy.

"Oh! Don't worry. I've never had an orgasm." His expression disintegrated; she had forgotten that physics could be far more theoretical than biology; they probably should return to discussing the direction of time. "I never usually make it past the door."

"Why is that?"

"I don't — usually — like going into the dark, with someone."

"Why not?"

"Because, it always seems like he turns into everyman, and then —"

"Daddy!" Lucy's cry rang out. Rory sprang out of bed. Sarah listened to him comfort her frantic weeping. Lucy always called him Rory, except now, in the middle of the night.

"Is it you?" Lucy asked.

"Who else would it be?"

"Monsters."

"No. No monsters, baby."

Sarah turned to the wall but felt his warmth against her as he returned to the bed. "Go on," he said. "Everyman."

"I forget."

"Do you?"

He was not rushing now, like a wild river, just meandering on a lazy exploration. She tried to distract her nerves by naming the places he was touching. She only got as far as *longissimus*. She clamped her eyes shut, and her head was filled with an image of a panicky cat clinging to a pine tree swaying in a wind created by a thousand butterflies. A goat trotted into the meadow. It looked like Yosemite. Why Yosemite? Why a goat? Clouds swirled in. Thunder clapped. The cat sailed through the air and landed on the goat who began to gallop towards a cliff. They plummeted over it. They became a firefall, tumbling down a mountain. They plunged into deep water. They were sinking. They were drowning. No, they weren't. They bobbed to the surface and the hot sun poured over them. She opened her eyes in astonishment.

"What goat?" he asked, and as she explained, they collapsed in laughter.

He fell asleep, but she did not. What was next? Could she wake up in the morning and drink coffee with him while his children ate their Cheerios? Would they ask where she had slept and why she was still there? And then what?

Her bandage had come loose. She didn't want to get blood on his sheets. She heard a car whistle past on the wet pavement, and moments later she was flying down the road too.

PART TWO

SEPTEMBER, 1976

CHAPTER 18

B Y THE FOLLOWING afternoon, Sarah had reached Winnemucca, Nevada, although she made the last part of the journey in a tow truck driven by burley tattooed man who chewed tobacco and said "Nope," when she asked if he minded the cat riding along with them, and "Yep," when she ventured her theory that a problem with the transmission had caused her car to stop so abruptly.

"Could be," he added. "Where you headed?"

"New York."

"In a hurry?"

"It's serious, isn't it?" she asked, recognizing the same fearful tone in her voice that others used in talking to doctors. Patients' humility and dependence had always depressed her, but not as much as her own did now. A transmission, she knew, was terminal.

Yep, he confirmed after they had reached his shop, it was the transmission. Yep, it was serious. He could rebuild it, if she could spend a few days in Winnemucca.

"Sorry," he said gruffly. "Hell, look, I'll buy the car from you. Even if I fix it, there's no guarantee you'll get past Wyoming."

Sarah sold her car and bought a bus ticket and a carrier for the cat, who yowled plaintively as the Greyhound roared out of town. She sat next to a woman with four children. The woman was pregnant and the children all had colds. One boy kept complaining that his throat hurt, and Sarah tried, inoffensively, to call his mother's attention to the rash on his neck. The woman moved her tribe away, but not before one of them sneezed on Sarah.

A woman wearing a battered fake leopard coat took her place. She had long, glitter-flecked eyelashes, and her eyeshadow was layered, purple, orange, and gold, like a sunset. Her name was Charlotte, and she was on her way to Elko. She told Sarah her life story. She had been a hooker, a high-class one. She'd had a pretty good time; now she had some kind of disease. No one knew what it was. "You afraid to sit next to me now?" she asked.

"No," Sarah said. "I expect it's more dangerous to sit next to someone who smokes." Charlotte chuckled, took a bottle of whiskey from her gold purse, and offered to share it. Sarah declined. She asked where Sarah was going, listened, said, "Good for you, kid," and fell asleep. Someone turned on a radio. A song called "Omar the Vampire" was playing as the bus pulled into Elko, Nevada.

"Fifteen minutes," the driver said.

Sarah got out, carrying the cat, who was clawing at the cage. It was dusk, but the heat hit her like a wall. She sat down on a bench and studied the curious oasis of buildings and signs in the middle of the endless desert. "I hope you wanted to come with me," she said to the cat, and when she opened the cage door to pat his head, it sprang to freedom.

Panic-stricken, Sarah searched for it, down the street, under cars, and between buildings. She was four blocks away when she saw her bus pull away. Stupefied, she watched it shamble out of sight with her belongings. She'd gotten off the bus with the carrier but not her handbag. She sat down beside the empty carrier in a daze. "I don't know a person in the town to call," she "I don't have a dime to call anyone collect. I don't have anyone to call. I am hopeless at living." Horns honked. Brakes screeched. The cat was sprinting toward her, and then it was flying through the air. Sarah dashed into the street, picked up the ragged ball of black fur, and broke into tears.

"I DON'T KNOW what kind of doctor you're going to make, if you can't tell a live cat from a dead one," Charlotte observed. "Well, probably no different from the rest of them. Have another?"

Sarah nodded. Two nights ago at this time, she had been at the gala opening of the San Francisco Opera. Last night, she'd been in bed with Rory McIntyre. Now she was sitting in a bar in Elko, Nevada, and an ex-hooker was buying her drinks.

The cat was sleeping. Charlotte had taken them to a vet after she had hauled them both out of the street. The cat was all right. Charlotte paid the bill and offered to buy dinner for Sarah, who was in worse condition. Sarah, tipsy, had just finished recounting her life story. Charlotte was clucking sympathetically.

"I always wondered if my life would of been different if I'd had any brains," she said. "But now, I think, maybe not. So what are you going to do?"

"I don't know."

"I expect," Charlotte added, "if you called that boy, he'd be here in a minute to get you."

"No," Sarah said. "Which one?"

"Oh, any of 'em. Myself, I'd call Harry the Swinger. It's a funny thing about love," she mused, studying her brandy. "I read some place that if it wasn't for all the people writing about love and singing about love and looking for love, it might not exist. I wonder. I've given it up lately. I don't really miss it, but I still kind of believe in it, if you know what I mean."

Sarah nodded.

"I wish I could give you some advice, honey, but I don't have any. I can loan you some money." Charlotte brought out a roll of wrinkled bills from her purse.

"Oh no, I couldn't."

"Take it."

"I'll pay you back when I get my purse back."

"Take it," Charlotte said, putting the wad into Sarah's hand. "And get going before you miss the next bus."

"Where can I write you?" Sarah asked.

The woman waved her away. "Just pass it on, honey, when you can. Now get out of here, and go home. Don't forget the damned cat. And take care of yourself, too."

CHAPTER 19

FOR TWO WEEKS Sarah lay in bed suffering from a condition she diagnosed as scarlet fever or an allergic reaction to life. The black cat lay beside her, recovering from his own excursion into the greater world. Sarah was not so ill, however, that she could escape wondering what she would do now that her month was up and she was on the wrong side of the continent. The money Charlotte loaned her had been enough to buy a ticket to either Omaha or San Francisco. Sarah returned to San Francisco to wait for Greyhound to ship back her purse and boxes. She called her school with her diagnosis. The secretary said she would talk to the dean; they would be in touch.

The spider was gone from the window, dead, no doubt; and the question of who would feed the cat if Sarah died, too, worried her. When she dragged herself from her room to buy more cat food, she stopped in at the People's Clinic, where she sat amid a collection of grubby, coughing people who all looked as if they had been on her bus. She counted needle marks in the arm of the man rasping next to her and told him he might have pneumonia. He said, what do you know, and she said not very much, she had only finished two years of med school. This caused a crowd to gather around her. One man showed her his shingles. Another described his psychotic tendencies. A third man's symptoms sounded like hepatitis, and she told him not to leave until he had seen a doctor. After three hours she went home and back to bed. She would get well or she would die, and perhaps it really did not matter which. There was no antidote for an allergy to life.

It could be schizophrenia. Her head was crowded with the faces and voices of sick people she had met. She apologized to them if she had been unsympathetic and thought they were not making much of an effort to live. She had not liked medicines that removed the symptoms but not the cause of an illness, but now she thought she might not mind such a thing. Her roommate in New York might be able to get her something. She and Lesley had been roommates but not friends. Lesley marveled that any medical school had accepted Sarah, who was unimpressed by white coats, who didn't take offense if someone thought she was a nurse, and who lagged behind to talk to patients instead of keeping up with the attending doctor on rounds. Lesley had warned Sarah that she had been overheard agreeing with a patient that doctors didn't know everything. She didn't call Lesley.

She also thought of Stephanie, her roommate at UCLA. Steph had majored in psych and relished every emotional crisis she read about in textbooks. She fell in love, overate, starved, took drugs, and exhausted sexual liberation. Steph would have gotten Sarah drugs, although probably illegal ones. She didn't call Steph either. After living together for four years, they had gone their separate ways and Sarah doubted they would ever see each other again.

She and Steph had had other roommates, too, a procession of students, actresses, and surfers, all united by a tortuous pursuit of a rainbow; but if they found a pot of gold at its end, they still wanted a man to be tending it. They sought love and, in consequence, sex, or perhaps it was vice versa. Sarah knew more about physiology than most of them. She had read excellent papers comparing humans to other species, including loons, reindeer, and puffer fish. She thought

other mating rituals were more interesting and certainly more effi-
cient. What she did not get, Steph had told her, was the connection
between body and heart. The heart, Sarah replied, was an organ that
worked or did not, to the advantage or disadvantage of its owner.

Sarah also did not call Kate, although she saw her twice from her
window.

On the first day of autumn, a letter arrived from her school. It was
thin, which was ominous. She put off opening it. The cat food supply
was low. She decided to replenish it before she learned that her life as
a med student was over. She went outside, feeling brittle and lifeless as
a leaf on the wind. She bought cat food and stopped at the Land of Oz
cafe for tea before she walked home. There, she stopped and dropped
her parcel; the tins rolled down the hill. She had been having trouble breathing but now she could not breathe at all. The cat was on the
steps where he had often waited for her, but his head was in a white
cardboard bucket. Next to him, unless she was hallucinating, was Gabriel Dinesen, cracking a crab claw.

"Oh," he said. "Hello. I brought you cioppino, but Widdershins
might have eaten it all." He ran the claw through his hair, making it
stand on end. "I think he missed me. Sarah, I tried to call you, but
there wasn't any answer, and I thought you might not be answering
the phone because you thought it might be me. So I thought I'd drop
by. Your phone's ringing. Shall I go answer it? It's not me."

"No! No."

"But I don't mind talking to your mother. The thing is, Sarah, if I
never see you again, there are all these things you'll never do, like go
to a rock concert. So, why can't I see you?"

"I don't know," she said because the idea had been his, not hers.

"Then, would you like to go to one?"

"One — what?"

"A concert. You might like this guy. He sings about the end of the world and deep stuff like that. They call him the Lord Byron of Rock. The crowd will be mellow. No one will hit you with a beer bottle. It's at the Paramount Theater in Oakland. Want to go?"

"When?"

"In an hour. But you might want to know, there's a man coming too. Unless you mind, and then I'll tell him he can't. Except he bought the tickets. I've never gone anywhere with him, but he led the rap session I went to. He's all right. At least, he didn't mind buying three tickets."

DAMON FRIEDMAN WAS a solid, pleasant-looking man with dark hair, blue eyes, and an expression as uncomfortable as her own. "He's never been out with a woman," Gabriel explained. "He's really gay. But I told him he'd like you."

Damon mumbled hello and turned his attention to driving. Gabriel put Sarah in the passenger seat and hopped into the back. While Damon drove, Gabriel brought Sarah up to date on the Scoundrels of Leisure, the highlight of which was that Flake had passed out in a morgue and woke up, certain that he was dead. "What have you been doing, Sarah?"

"Not much. Just thinking."

"See, Damon? You two will get along great. Damon thinks I'm frivolous and a drug addict. Speaking of which —"

"No," Damon said.

"Sarah will say yes. That's the difference between men and women."

"With her cough, she would be wise to turn down your dope."

"Damon went to med school too, Sarah. He was supposed to be a good Jewish doctor, but he couldn't stand blood so he became a shrink. Take the Broadway exit, Damon."

"Who are we going to see?" Sarah asked.

Gabriel shrugged. "Forgot. I just want to see the Paramount Theater.

I hear it's very Art Deco. Damon didn't know what Art Deco is. He may be an intellectual, but he's very ignorant."

Midway through the concert, Sarah had an attack of coughing. Damon helped her into the lobby and went to get his car. "I don't mind leaving early," Gabriel said, strolling about the lobby, which resembled the inside of a lavish gold clam. "So, what do you think, Sarah?"

"I liked it." Her words were punctuated by wheezing. "I liked the part where he forgot the lyrics and beat his head on the piano."

"I mean, what do you think of Damon?"

"He seems nice."

"He thinks I'm Wamba the Witless."

"He'd like you to go with him to Peter and Paul's Halloween party," she said, thinking what an odd conversation this was.

"I don't know how I feel about going with him. I might rather go with you."

She had another fit of coughing, but resisted going to an emergency room. They returned to her flat. Damon told Gabriel to make her a cup of tea while he went to find a pharmacy.

"I adore him for his drugs," Gabriel said. The phone began ringing and before she could stop him, Gabriel answered it.

"Well," Isabelle Glass said. "I didn't think she'd finish medical school. You have to be smart to do that. Not that it did my husband any good to be so brilliant. You still had to talk to him like he was the village idiot. He'd still ask you where his left foot was before he tried to find it. One time I asked him to put away the laundry and he put his socks in my underwear drawer, and when I said I hoped he would never have to find my gall bladder, he sulked for two weeks. How could he not know where his socks were kept? For so long I thought I had just had the bad luck to marry an idiot, but in my group, every woman had married the same kind of man.

"Why would anyone want to try to be a part of their world? Men don't want women in it because they will have to stop being idiots. Aaron is smart and he could have gone to medical school, if he had gone to college, and he would make a good doctor because he never minds saying awful things. Cecily might be bright, but no one will ever know until she stops getting married. There are other things in life besides marriage, although I don't know what."

"How is your group?" Gabriel asked.

"Oh, that. I've quit it. They were always telling me what to do. They said I should write a book about what it's like to be a Mexican. Mexican! My family came from — other places."

Hanging up, Gabriel asked, "So, my lady, is there any other way in which I can slay reality for you with my trusty, rusty sword?"

"Could you read a letter?"

He opened the med school missive, read it, and collapsed on the floor, pulling his hair. "You scare me to death, Sarah."

"What does it say?"

"Let's see: In light of the fact that you got the highest scores in the history of the universe on some test or another, and so forth, and because of your outstanding promise and potential — they've given you a year to live."

Damon returned with medicine and told Gabriel they had to let her sleep. Sarah watched from the window as they drove away.

"I love him," she said, with wonder and despair. "And I will love him all my life."

CHAPTER 20

I N OCTOBER IT did not rain at all, and Rory McIntyre discovered, to his confusion, that many people assumed he would know why. To his landlady he replied courteously, yes, the volcano in the South Pacific might have affected the weather. To the journalism student who wandered into the Space Sciences Lab, he said he did not know if it was the result of a hole in the ozone. Only to Mother Earth did he reply, curtly and firmly, no, it had nothing whatsoever to do with the influence of the planet Neptune.

This last conversation took place not long before Halloween. By then, his days had assumed an unbreakable pattern: he got up early and took his children to the day care center, where they wept, clung to his legs, and implored him not to leave them. Each day the teachers assured him that as soon as he left, they were fine.

He went next to work in a windowless lab where his human contacts were monosyllabic exchanges at the coffee machine and telephone conversations looking for parts for his receiver. At six, he collected his children and they stopped to eat burritos, noodles, or burgers at cheap student restaurants. Once home, Rory would survey the growing wreckage of his apartment, and sometimes he would wash the dishes.

Laundry was the bane of his life. In his youth, dirty clothes had always disappeared from his floor, only to return, clean and folded. At college, he had sent it out in a bag and a laundry service dealt with it. When he was first married, his wife had insisted they do laundry together, more than once a month, but he had been unable to fathom the mysteries of her methods. She would not put everything in one load. When he accidentally washed half of a two-piece silk outfit, she was unforgiving. She would not try his solution, to wash the other half so both pieces would look the same. After this, she did the laundry alone. When he was on his own with the kids in Boston, an elderly Russian immigrant named Olga cared for the children, and also cleaned, cooked, and did his laundry, because otherwise he filled the bathtub with it.

Perhaps because someone else had always done his laundry, he hadn't thought to rent a place with a washer and dryer. He was now living on a stipend from Berkeley instead of a mechanic's salary augmented by work at MIT and piano playing. He had found no kindly Russian lifesaver. He could not afford to send his laundry out, and at the end of a week, he had more than would fit in any bathtub.

Laundromats with Lucy and Avery were harrowing places. On their first excursion, Avery ate the remains of a candy bar he found on the floor and hid in a dryer while Lucy went off in pursuit of a stray cat. The one time Rory left the clothes washing, someone stole everything, even his underwear. He rarely got the clean clothes put away before they were dirty again, and the mountain of clothes in the living room had become the children's favorite playground. His recurring fantasy was to own a washer, a dryer, and a dishwasher.

He tried to read after his children were in bed, but he always fell asleep. His children alternated the nights on which they awoke with nightmares, and always, in the dark, he stepped on invisible, sharp objects.

He did not know why anything in his life would give him insights into the workings of the universe. He was beset by mysteries he couldn't explain. Why, when he cut the crusts off toast, did his children change their minds, and want them put back on? Why didn't it bother them to wear their shoes on the wrong feet? Why, if he read nothing else, did he always check the weather in New York? And why did Lucy only want to be a pink fairy princess for Halloween?

It was the latter question that brought him, in late October, to San Francisco, to Kate, whom he held responsible for Lucy's mania for princesses. Kate happily led an expedition to Haight Street. He was steadfastly steering Lucy away from the people sleeping in doorways and Avery from interesting objects on the sidewalk, as Kate discussed the merits of being a pink or blue princess. He was thinking that women were born defying comprehension, when Kate halted. "Hello!" she exclaimed.

"Fair Kate!" A man danced around her in circles. "What brings you out this morning — ah, it's afternoon, isn't it?"

"A princess costume."

"You're going to Grimm's?"

"Of course."

"I've already been there! Oh!" Gabriel had noticed Rory, standing woodenly to one side. "Well. Hello."

Kate made an introduction that confounded Rory. This was Sarah's Gabriel. Rory surveyed him with instinctive dislike; he was about to take his kids and depart, when Kate asked, "Have you heard from Sarah?"

"Heard from her?" Gabriel pulled a puzzled face.

"Let me guess. You send her sourdough bread each week."

"Why would I do that?"

"Because she's in New York —"

"She is?"

"I haven't heard from her either."

"Well, she's been sick."

"Sick? Sarah never gets sick. She's not pregnant, is she?"

Rory felt ice forming around his spine even as Gabriel answered, "No, someone sneezed on her in Winnemucca, and then she was run over by a bus, or was that the cat? Kate! I have an idea! Let's go dancing!"

Kate glanced at her brother. "Have you got a headache, Rory? Would you like to go get some coffee? We can take the kids to Grimm's, can't we, Gabriel?"

"And then we can all go dancing. Come along, young fellow," Gabriel added, retrieving from Avery half a doughnut, newly discovered on the sidewalk, only stepped on once. "What if we buy a whole new one? A fairy princess, Kate? Oh, I have always wanted wings."

Rory went to the Land of Oz cafe, and after two cups of coffee, the sensation that a meteor had crashed on his head subsided. When he had awakened to find Sarah gone, he had tried to call her, again and again, throughout one long day. He finally concluded she was already on the road to New York. She knew how to reach him if she wanted to, but apparently she did not. As his life took shape, he felt a slightly guilty gratitude. How could she fit into the never-ending chaos that was his life? And why would she want to?

But, if the half-wit could be believed, she was still in the city, and the impulse to see her was strong enough to get him back on his feet and carry him toward her flat. At her door, he wavered. A light was on in her window, but he was not sure that he really wanted to ask her any questions, let alone hear her answers. He continued on down the street and into Mother Earth's, and this is when he was drawn into the conversation about whether Neptune was responsible for the drought in California. It was preposterous, he said, to imagine that distant clumps of gas and dust could direct the lives of inhabitants on Earth. It was appalling that people could not abandon the Dark Ages.

Only when his most compelling evidence — science — was dismissed with a wave of Mother Earth's hand, did he finally leave.

By then, the lights were out in Sarah's flat. Rory went on to Kate's. Her living room was filled with glittery pink stuff. Kate was sewing, and Lucy and Avery were bedecking Gabriel in net and ribbons. No, Rory said irritably, Avery could not be a blue fairy princess, and he was nettled to hear his sister tell him not to be a narrow-minded ass. He joined Sterling in the living room and watched him play his game, endlessly hitting an imaginary ball back and forth, and most often losing to an invisible opponent.

CHAPTER 21

GABRIEL WAS WEARING a Nehru jacket, a cowboy hat, and boots. "I'm cowboys and Indians," he said. "What are you?"

"I couldn't think of anything," Sarah said. "I'll stay home."

"But I can't go unless you go."

"Then I'll go as myself. Consider it a disguise."

Gabriel, browsing through her closet, brought out her opera dress, and draped the glittering thing on a hanger. "Wings," he mused. "But then I'll be dull. Sarah, you don't mind cutting this in half, do you? Do you have paints? No, wait, I do! I keep them in my car for emergencies."

Sarah painted their faces blue and gold while Gabriel fashioned the wings. "Two male birds of paradise," she said. "How appropriate."

"You sound as sour as that ass McIntyre."

"Who?" She skidded blue paint into Gabriel's eye.

"The guy with the great kids. I'd like to steal them and let them have fun. I can't imagine they have any, living with him."

"You met Rory? When? Where?"

Gabriel described the occasion.

"You didn't like him?" she asked incredulously.

"No, I did not. He wouldn't even go dancing."

"You asked Rory to go dancing?"

"He did remind me of the Coeur de Lion," Gabriel admitted. "Oooh, baby, would I like to go on a crusade with you. Wow, what do you think, Sarah? I must be gay. But he was a zero. He pretended not to hear. He makes Damon seem like a barrel of monkeys. Kate would have gone with me, but she had to keep the kids while Zero went off to explain the universe to a reporter. I'll bet that woman had a great time. 'Would you like to see my calculations?' Kate is great, isn't she, but why did she marry that ass Sterling? Was she looking for someone like her brother?"

Outside Peter and Paul's house, Gabriel tried out his wings and fell into a hedge. As he was removing thorns from his thigh, a man wearing green tights and a feathered cap opened the door.

"Gabriel!" he exclaimed. "And this must be Damon — no, it's the divine Sarah! Welcome! I am Peter — either Peter Pan or Pan. I wanted Paul to dress as a two-headed candy bar and write 'Joy' across us, but he wouldn't. Well, enter and live out your fantasy!"

"Thank you," Sarah said, inadequately.

The room had been divided into two sides: the silly and the solemn. On the silly side were the Big Bad Wolf, Don Juan in drag, George III of England, and several U.S. presidents. The solemn side included Mary Wollstonecraft and Shakespeare's sister. Gabriel and Sarah lingered in the center. "We seem to be in that place where people who aren't baptized Catholics go," Sarah said. "I thought it would be larger."

"Limbo," Gabriel crowed. "Sarah, I love you."

He flapped off down a hallway; Sarah stood motionless. Had the doors of the universe just swung open? Had Gabriel just said he loved her? No one had ever said that to her before, except the bio major, and she'd known that was more for what she could do for his headaches than for who she was. Gabriel loved her? But he had been talking to a wildly painted bird of paradise, a mirror image of himself. This might not be love for her true self either. Still, she followed him down a hallway filled with artwork, the most distracting of which was a sculpture titled "A Six Pack of Cocks." She tripped but was saved from tumbling out the back door by Damon Friedman.

"Thanks," she said. "I nearly had to use my wings."

"I'd hate to have to rely on them if Gabriel made them," he replied. Alone on the landing, he was carving a pumpkin. Sarah had not seen him lately, and it was hard to tell from Gabriel's conversation if he was seeing Damon or only considering it.

"I didn't know you were coming," she said.

"I promised Gabriel I would, although it doesn't seem to matter to him now. He only got mad as soon as he saw me because I wasn't wearing a costume. I hate costumes."

"So do I."

"I can see that. He wouldn't have made me a costume. I wonder why I bother with him."

"I think he's rather fine."

"Yes, and he thinks you're perfect. It's because you're not in love that you can think each other is so wonderful."

"You just can't judge Gabriel by normal standards."

"Why not?"

"He's trying to open the door to infinite possibilities."

"Is that what you think? I think I'm chasing a chimera."

"But Gabriel is real. He's elemental, like light."

"I'm glad it's not his gravity that attracts you," Damon replied, handing her his pumpkin. He had made two stars for the eyes. "If you see him, tell him I went home, will you?"

She found Gabriel carrying a bottle of wine. "I've been looking for you," she said.

"Oh? Why?"

A beaded curtain parted to reveal a man wrapped in a smoke-colored robe. "Ah, the wine," he said. "And Sarah? Are you joining us?"

She felt her blue and gold face turning red. "No. No, thank you."

"Did you want to leave?" Gabriel asked. "Take my car." He tossed his keys to her and she dropped the pumpkin. He disappeared behind the curtain.

Sarah leaned against the wall. "I will be wild," she mumbled. "I will. I will."

"Will you?" A silvery laugh came from a woman dressed in a patchwork velvet gown and a turban trimmed with peacock feathers.

"No," Sarah admitted. "What I really want is dull relief."

"Could I offer you a cup of coffee?"

"You could. You really could."

They went into the kitchen. Sarah sat brooding on a stool, while the woman brewed coffee. She said, "When I saw you with that boy, I thought of a prince and princess of moonlight."

"We don't usually dress like this."

"I should like to paint both of you against a silver background, fading in and out."

"Are you an artist?"

"I aspire. I'd paint you as a woman wrapped in webs. Of course, I'd prefer to paint you in nothing at all." She leaned forward and kissed Sarah's lips.

"Oh," Sarah sputtered. "It's late. I'm late. I have to go." As she fled out the door, she heard the woman's laughter, like an echo of the doors of the universe slamming shut.

"It's Harry," a furtive voice said. "Is Gabriel there?"

Such was Sarah's confusion that she had answered her telephone on the first ring.

"I have to tell him I blew it," Harry said. "I answered the phone, and damn, if it wasn't his mother, saying who is this. I tried to say

I didn't know who I was, and it was a wrong number, but now the phone keeps ringing. I thought I'd better warn Gabe."

"He's still at the party."

"Really?" Harry's voice perked up. "You know, I only answered the phone because I was so damned lonely. Did Gabe tell you Mildred and I split up? You know what my problem is? I'm a romantic. I'm probably the last fucking romantic in the universe. All I want is a little romance."

"I know what you mean," Sarah said, astonished that she and Harry the Swinger were speaking the same language.

Fifteen minutes later he was at her door. "Trick or treat," he said.

Sarah hesitated. The thought that she would not mind some kind of company this night had slipped through her mind as swiftly as a shooting star, but Harry's keen radar had detected its flight. Now he stood at her door, the last romantic, so uncomplicated an offering of pheromones she could not find it in herself to turn him away.

"First we'll build a fire," he said.

"I don't have any firewood."

"Well, I have kindling." He pulled a white packet of cocaine from his pocket.

Sarah found newspapers, and lit a fire, which would be brief but splendid. Harry stretched out on the bed and unfortunately lay down on the cat. "There's nothing wrong with the floor," he said, moving quickly. He tossed more paper into the fire and took her in his arms.

"I don't have any diseases," he said. "Do you?"

"No. Do you have condoms?"

"I knew you'd think of things like that." He drew a box of condoms from inside his jacket.

"A whole box?"

"You never know. What first?"

"I don't care. Anything."

"Anything? I may never go home. But first —" He looked around for his white packet. "Where'd it go? It was right here."

"Did you throw it in the fire?"

Harry searched through the fire and for this paid more grievously than for sitting on the cat. "Oh well," he said, finally abandoning his hunt. "On to anything."

After this night, Sarah still believed in love, but she did not take it so seriously.

ON THE MORNING after Halloween, also known as the Day of the Dead, the doorbell buzzed early. "I hope I didn't wake you," Kate said. "I'd been meaning to come by but I've had to work overtime. Gabriel said you were still here and — oh!" Her eyes grew large.

Sarah glanced around. Whatever other magic the night before had wrought, it had done this: Harry the Swinger was gone, and sleeping on the floor instead, lay Gabriel Dinesen, naked, his wings broken and discarded, the shimmering remnants of her gown his only covering. He stirred drowsily. "What fairy wakes me from my flowery bed? Ah, it's me."

Casually, Sarah snatched up Harry's box of condoms and retreated to the bathroom. When she emerged, Kate and Gabriel were drinking coffee. Gabriel was wearing Sarah's bathrobe.

"Sarah, you are not going to believe this," he said, "but for the first time in thirty years, Jean McIntyre is not going to be able to cook Thanksgiving dinner because her kitchen remodel isn't finished. But Kate and I have solved the crisis. We are going to cook."

Kate had to go to work. Sarah joined Gabriel for coffee; she had the oddest notion that the expression on the pottery statue had changed. She was sniggering, if not guffawing.

"How did you get in?" she asked Gabriel.

"I flew. No, that's not true. I came up the fire escape and through the kitchen window, which you, you careless woman, left open. But why did you leave so early, Sarah? You missed the Sisters of Perpetual Indulgence."

"Is your mother upset?" she asked, still confused on many accounts, not the least of which was that Gabriel would need a place to sleep.

"About Jean's kitchen? I'm sure she would be, if she knew."

Sarah gave him a modified version of Harry's Halloween visit.

"Damn," he said, "we may end up cooking the Last Supper instead."

"I thought you were going to tell her those guys are living with you."

"The time hasn't been right yet. Sarah, I thought we'd established that it's sometimes desirable to wear something besides sweatpants."

"It's morning. I was in bed."

"All the more reason to follow the desirable rules. What were you doing in bed? Reading, no doubt. Imagine this: there are other things to do in bed besides read. Tomorrow, we will go shopping. We'll buy a rug — that floor is damned hard — and a new bathrobe. This one has died from old age. But first, I'd better go deal with Harry's calamity."

The next day, however, Gabriel and Kate began planning their Thanksgiving feast, and Sarah went shopping alone. In a second-hand store, she found an Indian wool rug woven in green, gold, crimson, and blue. She bought a green velvet quilt and two down pillows. She wondered if she should look for a job. Her funds were going to run out, especially if she kept shopping. Instead, she bought paints, and in the tower, a fantastic garden grew up the walls. She painted the ceiling blue, with stars that glowed in the dark. She painted the kitchen bright yellow, and the bathroom ruby red. She painted the table and chairs and the telephone too.

Gabriel applauded the results, but he did not spend the night again. Kate worried that she was taking up too much of his time, but Sarah only said no. Just as she had not asked Kate about her marriage, Kate didn't ask why Sarah was still in San Francisco. They seemed to have an unspoken agreement not to discuss what they were doing with their lives.

Sarah neither saw nor heard of Rory, except when Kate said she did not think he was coming to the Thanksgiving feast. Kate didn't know why, or what his plans were. She hadn't talked to him. She thought he might be busy.

CHAPTER 22

"WHY ARE YOU putting brandy in the cranberries?" Sterling asked.

"To make them wicked and decadent," replied Gabriel, who viewed conversations with Sterling as an exercise equivalent to jousting.

"Really, I prefer nuts," Sterling said.

"Mirror's in the bathroom," Gabriel said. "Kate, are you sure my stitches are right? It seems so brutal, sewing the poor bird shut, but it is dead, isn't it? And it is better than having the divine oysters fall out. So, are we ready? Let's knit."

Kate was teaching him to knit, and under her patient tutelage Gabriel had created a lumpy rectangle. "Who would ever think that two sticks and string could turn into anything?" he asked.

"I doubt it will," Sterling said, "since Kate is teaching you the way her mother knits."

"Sterling," Gabriel asked, "how was your job interview?"

"Sarah," Sterling said, "it might be useful for you to learn to knit now that you are not going to medical school. But you should have someone who knows how to do it teach you."

"You had an interview?" Sarah asked. "How did it go?"

"I don't know," Sterling said. "The man turned on the air conditioner — in November — just after I began to talk, and I don't think he could hear a thing I said. But since Kate just can't earn enough money, Sarah, you might like to rent Rory's old room. You are not entirely unemployable, although it may take time."

The phone began ringing and Sarah escaped to answer it.

"Kate," a hoarse voice said, "are you — could you come over?"

IT WASN'T UNTIL Rory opened his door that Sarah acknowledged it might make a difference if he had thought he was talking to his sister. She had borrowed Gabriel's car, and he, decorating turkey cookie place cards, had not asked why.

Rory was wearing only boxer shorts; his face was flushed, his hair uncombed, his eyes bloodshot, but when he saw Sarah, his demeanor worsened, like a man who has been hit by a truck and has staggered to his feet, only to be run over by the arriving ambulance.

"You called" — Sarah's voice faded — "Kate."

"Rory has a headache," Lucy whispered. She and Avery were sitting with unnatural stillness on the laundry that filled the living room, like an erupted volcano. Rory retreated to his bedroom, where he fell onto his bed with the appearance of a man about to die from one pain if not another. Sarah followed, unsure how far she could go without hastening the process.

"Is it bad?"

"Yes."

"Have you taken anything for it?"

"No. Never mind. Just go away."

She went into the bathroom, wondering why it was so marvelous that he had such things as toothpaste and toilet paper. She found an empty aspirin bottle. She searched through her handbag, took out a vial of pills, and brought him two, which he swallowed without water.

When he didn't tell her to go away again, she sat down beside him. She put her hand on his head and felt a hurricane beneath her fingers, a storm filled with crazy winds and burning embers.

A crash broke the uneasy quiet. Lucy and Avery stood in the door. Lucy was holding a dripping glass of chocolate milk, and Avery was looking fearfully at a pile of tattered bread and butter on the floor by a shattered plate. Tears welled in Rory's eyes. Lucy dropped her glass and jumped on the bed to fling her arms around him. Avery followed. Rory was buried under a mound of children. Sarah, blinking back tears herself, gathered the soggy bread and broken glass and carried it into the kitchen. She was mopping up the milk when Rory's ragged voice called, "Sal?"

She peered into his room; he beckoned her closer. He asked Lucy and Avery to go play in their room, and they complied with an abnormal docility. He took Sarah's hand in his hot, dry one and put it back on his head. She sat down, listening to his raspy, labored breathing.

"I almost hit him, Sarah."

"Why?"

"He cut up the screen in his room. It's the third time he's done this. He cuts holes and climbs onto the roof. Maybe he's trying to leave home. They've been out of school for three weeks. First it was head lice, then chicken pox. Lucy, then Avery. It's like the plagues of Egypt."

"Have you been able to work?" She revised her question. "I mean, go to work?"

"I tried hiring babysitters, but no one came back. I took them with me to the lab to get some things to work here. The phone rang, and in half a second, they were gone. I found them in the lunchroom. They'd raided the refrigerator. They ate three lunches."

"The chief of pediatrics told new parents the main thing was to remember to keep breathing."

"I wanted to clobber him, Sarah. My parents never did that."

"You don't know that they didn't want to."

"That's true." The thought cheered him a bit. "What did you give me? I think it's working."

"It's for menstrual cramps. Sorry, it's all I had."

"Thanks, doc. I am turning into a mad housewife. Sarah, I didn't call you."

"You didn't know I was still here."

"Yes, I did."

"It doesn't matter now. Will you rest? I'll look after Lucy and Avery."

"Sarah —"

"Rory, I once watched a faith healer, who said he could draw out pain and give it to Jesus. He demonstrated on a woman who had four children. She had to lie down for twenty minutes while he waved his hands over her. She said it was a miracle, but I wondered if it might not have been just because she got to lie still for twenty minutes."

"Sarah, I have nothing to give you. Nothing."

"Don't worry about that now. Just go to sleep."

His voice sank, weighted, to the bottom of a well. "My ex-wife is coming over."

"When?"

"Now."

"Why?"

"I asked her."

"Oh."

"She called. I hadn't talked to her in a year. She said she was in town, and could we talk."

"Would you like me to take the kids to Kate's?"

"God dammit, why are you so kind? Oh hell," he added as the doorbell rang. "I have to find my pants."

Sarah was not predisposed to like Rory's ex-wife, but she was curious. No amount of speculation, however, had prepared her for the woman at the door: a towering golden goddess, so beautiful she might have glided to Berkeley, Venus-style, on a gilded clamshell.

"Hello," Sarah said, feeling quite hollow. "Please come in. Rory is looking for his pants."

The woman emitted a rippling, full-bodied laugh. "Why not? Rory without his pants is pretty enticing."

Sarah nodded in extreme confusion. "He's got a headache."

"I know. He sounded terrible when I called him this morning. He said he was fine, but he always does. You have to jump up and down on him to get him to tell you if anything is wrong."

She could do it, Sarah thought. She could pick him up and wring the truth out of him. She could hold him upside down and shake it out of him.

"Poor guy," the woman went on. "Those headaches really knock him out. I've told him he needs more exercise."

Woefully, Sarah imagined her idea of exercise. The woman stepped inside, looking around, no doubt, for the enticing sight of Rory with no pants. "Where are the kids?"

"Playing in their room."

"Lively, aren't they? Especially the little guy — what is his name?"

"Avery?"

"Right, the elf. Isn't it his birthday soon?"

Sarah gave up to total astonishment. "I don't know. Don't you?"

"Me?" The woman scrutinized Sarah. "No. Aren't you —?"

"No, aren't you —?"

"The ex? Good lord, no. I'm Jane Rowley, humble journalism student, pretending to be madly interested in whatever it is Rory's building up on the hill. Who are you?"

"Sarah Glass."

"Oh! Rory's told me about you, sort of. Our conversations always go in fits and starts because someone falls out a window or floods the bathroom. Actually, his kids told me about you. Rory just said you're his very old friend, and perfect, like everyone's first-grade teacher."

Sarah had not thought it was possible to feel lower, but now she did, as Jane Rowley burbled on: "He told me the ex was coming over, and he sounded so sick I thought I'd better come and give him moral support. I have to admit you didn't look like a nut, not that Rory has ever come out and called her nuts. I just figured she'd have to be to — oh, hello," she said as a third woman came to the door.

This new arrival was dressed with care in tawny silk; her dark blond hair was expertly streaked and her makeup flawless. She would have been quite attractive had she not been so eclipsed by the Venus in a sweat suit.

"I am Dibby McIntyre," she said. Her voice had qualities of an irritated Siamese cat, but she did not look crazy, at least not until she had fully seen Jane Rowley. "Who are you?"

"His fan club." Jane grinned. "Waiting for a sighting. Rory's lost his pants."

"His pants?" Dibby echoed. "Why has he lost his pants?"

"What a guy, eh? I wonder who else he invited to his Thanksgiving party."

Dibby's eyes narrowed. Feebly, Sarah made introductions and offered to make tea.

"We may as well," Dibby said. "If Rory is looking for something, it will him take all day."

They went into the kitchen. Sarah put the teakettle on, mopped up the spilled milk and chocolate powder, and tried not to stare at the woman Rory McIntyre had married.

"I'll have a beer," Jane said. "I brought him a six-pack last week, but I bet it's still in the fridge. He doesn't really like beer."

Dibby said, "I may as well have one, too. I know he won't have juice. He never buys anything healthy."

Jane brought out the beer and dusted the cocoa powder off a chair to sit down. "Looks like he's been cooking."

"Not him," Dibby said. "He is the fussiest person I ever met about cooking."

Jane chortled. "Wait, are you the one who stuffed the chicken with marshmallows?"

Dibby bristled. "I can't believe he told you about that."

"Well, he didn't say who'd done it," Jane admitted. "It was just one night when I tried to cook dinner for him and overcooked the damned rice and burned the beef, and he said it wasn't the worst meal he'd ever had, and he told me about the chicken. I just figured he was being his usual sweetheart self."

Dibby sniffed. "Rory would be much better off if everyone would stop saying he is a sweetheart. You have no idea how it made me feel to always hear, 'You're married to Rory? But he's such a sweetheart.' He is not a sweetheart."

"Fortunately, he has other talents to make up for it." Jane wiggled her eyebrows. "He's a great baseball player."

Dibby finished her beer and opened a second.

"So, Dibby, is it true you want him back?" Jane asked.

"Did he tell you that?"

"No, I'm just checking, since I'm shamelessly pursuing him."

"I am used to that. That's why I'm here. I've forgiven him."

"Really?" Jane asked. "Is there that much to forgive?"

"You cannot imagine what it was like to be married to him."

"No, I can't," Jane agreed. "I have a poor imagination, but I think the guy's all right."

"You don't know him very well, do you?"

"Nope. That's always disillusioning. Learn the basics, I say, and don't probe. He's an amazing two-strike hitter and he's nice. I don't care how he feels about his mother."

"If you don't know how he feels about his mother, then you don't know him at all," Dibby said. "His mother is perfect. His mother has never done anything wrong since she was born."

"She bought him a purple acrylic sweater once," Sarah recalled. "He complained about it so much she finally cut it up into pieces and threw it away."

Dibby, noticing Sarah for the first time, said, "He did like a sweater I bought him. It was gold cashmere, just his color. We never fought when he was wearing it. Who are you?"

"She's Rory's old friend," Jane said. "Hey, Sarah, did you ever see him play baseball? He's good now, but he says he's past his prime. He's so modest."

Dibby sighed; Jane the journalist continued her probe. "Why do you want him back? Because he is so good in bed? Now, don't worry; I don't get him into the sack that often. He's always so tired, and he's got those two kids stuck like Velcro to him. They never sleep at the same time. And I think he takes things more seriously than I do."

"He's working-class Catholic," Dibby said. "It explains everything."

"Does it? Jeez, and I thought he was just too much of a gentleman to say no. Did you always have to drag him into bed, too?"

"I did not."

"Now, don't get huffy. It's nothing serious. Just fun."

"Fun? How can you say it's fun?"

"I don't know," Jane said. "It seems like fun to me."

"But there was nothing else to go with sex. He used to leave and be gone for hours, and I thought he had a lover, and then I found out he was sitting in physics classes. And while I was trying to tell him how I felt about it, he wrote an entire page of formulas. He said he was seeing if he could solve quantum harmonic oscillators, even though it had already been done."

"Yeah, and he could have played baseball. Major League," Jane said.

"What do you think, is it love or marriage that makes people crazy?"

"Crazy, why do you say crazy?" Dibby demanded. "This was real. You've never been married, have you? You don't know what it's like to get married and have to wonder who am I now? And be afraid to find out because it might not be what you are supposed to be. He never understood that, never. And even when he tried to be nice, I knew he wasn't doing it because he loved me." Dibby had finished her fourth beer, and her words were becoming blurry

"The tea is ready," Sarah said anxiously. "It's herbal."

"But he only has white sugar, I'm sure," Dibby said. "That's what his mother uses. I read a book that said it's a serious mistake to want to marry your mother, even though he insisted that he didn't. Maybe the problem was I really didn't want to marry my father. I did like Rory when I met him. He was so different. He knew how to do things. Once, my father was in a fit because his car wouldn't start, and Rory just did something and it started. We were so amazed. The one time my father tried to do something — hang a picture — he put the nail through his thumb and fell off the chair and hit his head on a table and had to get stitches, and then he was mad at my mother for putting the table in the wrong place.

"The book also said if you don't want your husband to be like your father, then you don't know what you want him to be like, and your husband gets confused messages, although I couldn't even give Rory confused messages because he is so emotionally closed. Even when we had sex — but I shouldn't be talking like this," she said to Sarah. "You've just put a pound of sugar in your tea."

"It might not be enough," Sarah mumbled.

At last, Rory appeared, carrying Lucy, who clutched him with one hand and a doll with the other. He had found his pants, but he still did not look like a well man.

"Sorry," he said. "Avery fell asleep." Seeing Sarah's face, he reached out to rub her shoulder. Jane and Dibby stared. His hand stopped in midair and he batted at an invisible fly. He sat down, took a sip of Sarah's tea, and choked.

"Well, I should be going," Jane said. Her mission to ensure that Rory did not reunite with a woman who had put him off relationships was complete. "Rory, there's a game tomorrow. If you want to play, you can be an honorary journalism student again."

Sarah rose too, but her exit lacked Jane's efficiency because Lucy had attached herself to her, like an oversized set of skis. "Lucy," she pleaded, "let me walk."

"Rory," Dibby said, "why are you dressing her like that?"

"Like what?" Rory asked. Lucy was wearing an orange shirt, a pink overall, and socks with monkeys on them.

"You know how I feel about pink." Dibby reached for the last unopened beer, caught Rory's eye, and pulled back. "I am not drinking."

"I didn't say you were."

"You know I don't like beer, although that Amazon who's been warming your bed apparently does. But why are you buying pink?"

"I didn't. My mother did."

"I suppose she bought the doll, too."

"No, that was Kate."

"Do you realize what you are doing? She only likes these things to please you."

"I don't like dolls."

"They just train women to like babies."

"Some women do."

"Are you saying I don't?"

"Oh, for Christ's sake." Rory shoved his chair backwards with a violence that knocked Sarah out of her fascinated trance. Her legs were free. Lucy was gone. Sarah found her huddled in Rory's closet.

"Tell you what," Sarah said. "Let's get Avery and go for a ride in Gabriel's car.

CHAPTER 23

O N THE DRIVE back to San Francisco, Sarah was no longer astonished that Rory had mortal items in his bathroom, but her meditations on this subject were interrupted when she arrived at Kate's,
and Avery, who had been unnaturally quiet, was sick on the sidewalk.
She put him in Kate's bed and watched him with the anxiety of one
who could extrapolate, from a single incident, a range of possibilities.
Common sense warred with what she could imagine and lost. A sleeping child will be still; nonetheless, she asked Kate to call Rory one
more time.

"No answer," Kate reported.

"Maybe the ex is taking care of his headache," Gabriel offered. "I
vote to keep his kids."

"We could call Mom," Kate said. "But they're probably on their way
here."

"Couldn't Avery be sleeping because he is tired?" Gabriel asked. "I
understand this happens, even with kids."

"Chicken pox can develop complications," Sarah said. "Pneumonia. Encephalitis. Meningitis." Now that she had said it, the possibility grew like an inflating balloon. "I saw a baby die of meningitis. Oh,
forget Rory. Gabriel, will you take us to the hospital?"

The emergency room was filled with the early victims of

Thanksgiving: burns, gashes, food poisonings. One person had been popped in the eye with a cork and another had suffered a concussion when he tripped, carrying the turkey, and hit his head on a doorframe. Howls were coming from a room guarded by two policemen; this patient was due to be charged with felony assault as soon as he was stitched up.

"Lions and tigers and bears, oh my," Gabriel chanted. "No wonder you don't like these places, Sarah. This lights are never out. And it must be worse for you; you understand what they're saying. Sorry, Sarah, but you know I am not good at reality."

"Then, will you go find Rory?"

"Find him? Where?"

She told him the address. "Don't upset him. Just get him."

"You'll survive? Right. Find Rory." Relieved, he galloped off but her fearful face went with him. Inspiration struck; he found a telephone and called Damon Friedman.

"Are you the child's mother?" the receptionist asked Sarah.

She swallowed with difficulty. "No."

"A relative or caregiver?"

"Not exactly." Sarah felt her voice rising. "But you can check him. I know you can."

The receptionist called a resident, who looked concerned but calm, precisely as Sarah would have aspired to look if she were confronted with a hysterical person holding someone else's child. "Meningitis?" he repeated. "What are the symptoms?"

Sarah flinched, feeling the extent of her descent into irrationality. "He threw up."

Just then, Damon arrived, looking confused, and the shrieking felon hurtled out of the exam room, abandoning his hospital gown as he ran.

✲

For several hours Gabriel worked diligently at his task. He found Rory's flat and ate crab dip with Rory's landlady. He learned that she adored Rory and wanted him to come to her single daughter's Thanksgiving dinner. But he had go to work, how terrible! He was not looking well, poor boy. Did she know where he worked? Oh yes! Somewhere on the Berkeley campus.

Next, Gabriel struggled through a conversation with security guard who finally located R. McIntyre in a directory. Space Sciences was on the hilltop. The building was locked. Only one light was on, in an office on the second floor. He tore his pants climbing a tree. He banged on a window until the man, sleeping with his head on a table littered with tools, looked up. "What are you doing here?" Rory asked with poorly concealed distaste, after he opened the window.

Gabriel did not like Rory any more than Rory liked him, but Gabriel's irritation had the edge because he knew the button on his turkey had popped by now, and he had missed it.

"Sarah sent me to find you."

"Why?"

Gabriel made a note to tell Sarah that McIntyre was an ass, in case she had not noticed. "Your son has meningitis."

Rory instantly looked so deranged, Gabriel felt obliged to drive him to San Francisco. As they crossed the Bay Bridge, Rory said three words: "Where's Lucy?" and "Oh."

The receptionist at the emergency room sized them up as victims of an accident: in addition to his ruined pants, Gabriel had twigs and leaves in his hair; Rory was holding himself upright with difficulty. She offered him a wheelchair. He declined, unevenly, and asked for his son.

"Avery McIntyre?" she asked. "Oh, his grandparents have taken him home."

"Oh, thank God your mother is here," Gabriel exclaimed. "I was so worried that Sterling would make the gravy."

"But Avery's father is still here," the receptionist added.

"Who?"

"The poor man was knocked down by an escaping felon," she explained. "He's got a concussion, a dislocated shoulder, and a badly sprained ankle. Have you come for him?"

"Avery's father, indeed," Gabriel muttered, as an aide wheeled out Damon.

"I never said I was," Damon said. "When I walked in the door, Sarah burst into tears and for some reason, they assumed I was the father. Then I was unconscious after the felon knocked me down. You must be Rory McIntyre," he added. Painkillers did not squelch his curiosity about a man whose mere name, he had perceived, had a remarkably powerful effect on Sarah. He hoped, for her sake, that the man did not always look so poor-spirited.

"Where is Sarah?" Rory asked.

"She was here," Damon said. "She said she'd wait for me when your parents took Avery home. Your mother very kindly invited me to dinner. But Sarah — where is she? She does seem to have taken this all very much to heart."

Sarah, slumped in a plastic chair, was mumbling, "Do no more harm." Charging herself with responsibility for Rory's ghastly, suffering face, she rose to her feet before she had time to think that she might rather hide under the chair. Rory saw her; he sprang toward her and this was his undoing. He crashed to the ground.

"I may be wrong," she said with painful humility to the doctor who rushed, almost as fast as she had, to Rory's side. "But he might have chicken pox. He never had them. I asked his mother. She thought he was immune. Sometimes the lesions aren't visible. I read that."

Rory's subsequent sufferings were not insignificant, but they paled in comparison to Sarah's, for he had the advantage of being, for the most part, unconscious. The fact that her blunders alone had not leveled him was no comfort; she was acutely aware of all that was transpiring, a condition compounded by just enough knowledge to be a torment and her conviction that whether one lived or died in a hospital was largely a matter of luck.

Rory was carried off. Gabriel departed with Damon to tell the McIntyres. Sarah faced a stack of paperwork with a blank mind, emptied by the sight of Rory lying motionless on a gurney. His slight wince as the IV pierced his arm had rendered her witless. She, who had spent a significant percentage of her high school career writing Mrs. Rory Daniel McIntyre on the margins of her notebooks, could not remember his middle name. She had nearly written Rory David McIntyre when the resident descended on her.

"Great diagnosis," he said. Yes, it was chicken pox and the blisters were internal, on his throat and lungs. The disease was far worse for adults than kids, and this particular condition was rare, dangerous, and damned painful. Interesting, wasn't it? Did she want to see?

No.

They wanted to give Rory a new drug and see how he dealt with it. Inspired, he added, how she'd gotten him to the ER. He doubted Rory would have come on his own. "Med student, eh?" Sarah felt she must somehow justify her school's misplaced faith in her abilities and complete Rory's forms. Rory D. McIntyre, she wrote. Born: July 12, 1951; birthplace: Napa, Calif.; height: 6 feet, 1/2 inch; weight: 180; allergies: myths, love, and purple sweaters.

The resident took her to Rory's room. She sank into a chair, stricken by the sight of him in a hospital bed. Time passed; the room darkened. She tried to visualize his invisible wounds. She touched his throat, and his hand closed over hers.

"Where am I?" His voice was husky, but she knew this was from the pain.

"Hospital."

"Why?"

"You have chicken pox."

"How did I get here?"

"You fainted in the lobby."

"Jesus, Mary, and Joseph. Where are the kids?"

"With your parents."

"I feel higher than a kite."

"You probably are."

"No, I think the drugs are wearing off."

"Are you in pain?"

"Excruciating. Mortified pride." He smiled drowsily. "I thought you hate these places."

"I do."

"Isn't that a professional handicap?"

"Yes."

"Do I have to distract you to keep you here?" She nodded. He drew her head down near his. "Will you marry me, Sarah?"

In two years of medical school, Sarah had received forty-seven proposals, six for marriage, from men in hospitals, so she knew she did not have to respond. The resident returned to check on Rory. "Looks good," he said. "You can take him home. He's all yours."

"Oh, but he's not," she protested, although no one seemed to believe her.

Joe McIntyre burst out laughing when Sarah rang up Kate's to explain that she had taken Rory home with her. She had not wanted to risk his life by taking him to Sterling's, nor could she pay for a taxi to Berkeley. In the background, she heard Jean protesting, "We can't just leave him for Sarah to take care of."

"Why not?" Joe asked. "She said she doesn't mind."

"Where will he sleep? Does she have an extra bed?"

"If she doesn't, he'll recover real fast."

"Joe!"

"Tell him not to worry about the kids," Joe told Sarah. "We'll take care of them. But don't be too nice to him, Sarah, or he might never get well."

CHAPTER 24

RORY SLEPT FOR three days, but Sarah, watching for signs of chicken pox pneumonia and other fatal complications, hardly rested at all. She had no solace for her wild and morbid thoughts. She expected him to die momentarily of fever, discomfort, and restlessness. She knew it was not a bad thing for him to sleep, yet she was sure her textbooks overlooked a fatal manifestation of chicken pox: death by sleeping. She could only banish her collective terrors by drawing in her notebook of things she might not see again. She drew thirty-nine images of Rory.

On the third day, he woke up. Puzzled by the soft, warm bed covered with green velvet, the painted garden around him, and the black cat sleeping on his feet, he doubted this was a hospital; then he saw Sarah, drawing in a notebook.

Any embarrassment he might have felt at having collapsed ingloriously on her was so eclipsed by Sarah's abashed and addled explanation of how he had come to be in her bed, he found himself reassuring her that it was all right. He showered, the first time in years he was not interrupted by visitors announcing that they were cooking breakfast or other news that caused him to leap, naked and soapy, from the shower. He drank a cup of coffee. He asked if she had changed something about her apartment. He said he should be going, and he fell back asleep.

Sarah was drawing again when Damon Friedman came to call. He was limping but otherwise recovered. He was interested, for Gabriel had been highly provoked by Damon's speculations on the subject of Rory McIntyre. While qualifying that his specialty was lunacy and not infectious diseases, Damon offered an opinion that Rory looked fair but Sarah looked terrible. Had anyone ever died of someone else's having chicken pox? Missing his point entirely, Sarah was only worried that Rory had not eaten anything.

"Have you?" Damon asked.

"Have I what?"

"Eaten. Would you like to go get dinner?"

"No. Oh no."

Damon left and returned with Chinese take-out and a bottle of wine. "I hope we can eat at the table," he said, "or is that too far away from him?"

She lit candles so they wouldn't disturb Rory with electric lights, and after checking once more that he was still breathing, she sat down with Damon.

"How did you ever make it through two years of med school?" he asked, pouring the wine.

"I don't know."

"It isn't easy, but, if I may say this without being offensive, I think it's harder for women. There weren't many in my class, and I was glad I wasn't one. But your dad is a doctor, isn't he?"

"He was. He's dead. He — died."

"Of what?"

"Gunshot."

"Good god. Where?"

"In the head. That is, in Baltimore. He was at a conference. He went for a walk in the wrong neighborhood."

"Did he run into a gang?"

"No, a policeman. They apologized and paid my mother a set-tlement. It's how she lived." Sarah stared at the candle; the wine was making the world blurry, soft, and golden. "When he left, he said to me, 'I'm just going on a trip.' But I knew he had told my mother he wanted a divorce. I don't know if they were ever happy. I think he was supposed to stop being Mexican when he became a doctor and married her but instead he started going to Mexico. His parents had moved back there when he finished school. He was teaching at UCSF but he wanted to build clinics in Mexican villages like theirs. I went with him to visit them once.

"I had this crazy ritual: whenever he was leaving, I had to get up to say goodbye to him because if I didn't, he might not come back. It had always worked, until it didn't." Sarah finished her wine. "I always wished I could see him one more time."

Damon refilled the glass. "Your mother is not Mexican?"

"I don't know what she is, except unhappy. She didn't — she doesn't — like me very much. It didn't matter; I pretended that the McIntyres were my family. And they were, when it mattered. My se-nior year, when I began to get accepted by colleges, it made my mother angry. When I got the letter from Yale, she told me to get out of her house. 'Leave and don't come back.' It was night. I didn't know what to do, so I walked to Joe McIntyre's repair shop. I knew where the key was and I knew he wouldn't mind if I slept there. I meant to leave be-fore he came to work but when I woke up, there he was. I wanted to die, but instead we went to Buttercream Bakery for breakfast. It's his favorite place. I think he saved my life.

"He and Jean said I could live with them and I did until I gradu-ated. But that summer they were going back east and, well, I couldn't go. I decided to find my grandparents. I had a card my grandmother had sent me a long time ago. A teacher at Napa High helped me find the village it had come from. I wrote and my grandmother wrote back.

She said it would too hot in the summer so maybe we could meet in Los Angeles. I caught a bus to LA and I met them there. We stayed at the house of some relatives. It was wonderful to think that this was really my family, not pretend. My grandmother spoke English well, and so we talked a lot. But then I had to leave for school. She said maybe I could come to see them at Christmas."

"Did you?"

"No." For a long moment, neither said anything until she went on. "I had applied to Yale because I wanted to be like Rory McIntyre — I had liked him, even though he was a star beyond my reach, the baseball hero with brains, too — but when I got to New Haven, I thought: I don't know who I am but this is not me. I called UCLA, where I'd been accepted too and I asked if I could come there, after all. They said yes. But I didn't have much money and I had to work. We wrote letters, my grandmother and I; and then I got a letter from a Mexican lawyer to tell me they had died, one week apart. They had left their little house for me, and a woman from the village would look after it until I decided that to do with it. I want to go see it, one day."

"After you graduate?"

"If I ever do." Sarah described her med school catastrophes, concluding with the ghost of Luz Moreno. "I don't know what else to call it," she said.

"Generally, I like to go for the simplest explanation," Damon said. "Schizophrenia?"

"No, that you saw a ghost."

This made her laugh. Shyly, she added, "I think you must be quite wonderful at what you do. Did you really choose psychiatry because you don't like blood?"

"I like blood, but in its proper place, pumping through the heart." He emptied the wine bottle into their glasses. "Here, you had better eat something. I am eating it all."

"You bought a lot."

"Food is my downfall. Possibly because I grew up with a mother who didn't cook."

"Maybe it's because you like food."

He grinned at her. "Did you get your fertility statue in Mexico?"

"My what?"

He gestured to the pottery female on her mantel. "Isn't that what she is?"

"Fertility? I thought her markings might show the chakras."

"Chakras? Those Eastern whatnots?"

"Some people say they are psychic openings in the body and blocks in them cause illness."

"As compared to, say, germs?"

"You don't believe in them?"

"I wish I did. I know a woman who makes a whopping amount of money clearing them." He leaned back in his chair. "So, tell me about Rory McIntyre. A nice guy? You know, I had a crush on a baseball player in high school, too."

Sarah firmly returned the conversation to magic and healing, East and West.

WHEN DAMON DEPARTED, she unrolled her sleeping bag on the floor and fell asleep. She dreamt: she was wandering through a tunnel full of doors. She opened one to find an artist sculpting a man with wings. "It's too beautiful to be real," she said, and the statue jumped up and ran away. Chasing it, she came upon a group of men in white coats floating above the ground. "There you are," one said. "Go see if he is dead yet." The lifeless man lying on a gurney was Rory McIntyre. "It's too bad that he's shaved off his beard," she said. The floor evaporated, and she tumbled through empty space.

She awoke with a gasp, but her relief in realizing that she had been dreaming and Rory was not dead was undone when she perceived that he was holding her and talking softly, and she was strangling him. She released his neck and the world gyrated around her. She pressed her hands against her eyes. No, it was his hand and she could not make herself let go of it.

"Sal?"

"I thought I was going to throw up. But I won't. I hate to throw up."

"I didn't know we had a choice." He smiled at her, and she concentrated on counting his pulse. "Do I have one?" he asked. She nodded. "Good." He leaned his head against her hair. "Why are you sleeping on the floor, babe?"

"Because you're in the bed."

"Ouch." He pulled her up and dropped her onto her bed. "I'll sleep on the floor."

"Oh, no."

"Good." He lay down but she remained upright. He prodded her back. "Sarah, my darling, you're letting in all the cold air." She didn't move and abruptly, he gasped. "Oh! I'm so dizzy. I may faint. I may throw up, and I don't know how to force myself not to. I will probably tragically expire, unless you lie down."

She lay down, but not too close to him; but the warmth of his body drew her closer, like a magnet. She touched his face. His beard was still there. "What were you dreaming about?" he asked. "Sarah! Stay put. I can't wrestle with you. I'll lose."

"I thought you were dead."

"Wait now, you said I had a pulse."

"No, it's what I dreamt. You were dead, and all I could say was it was too bad you had shaved off your beard. It's not funny," she protested. "I hate it when people die."

"I know; it's almost as bad as throwing up." His voice softened again. "Sarah, I didn't know — any of that."

"You were listening?"

"Who was that guy anyway?"

"Damon. A psychiatrist. Making a house call. Rory! Would you like some Chinese food?"

Watching him eat lemon chicken and spareribs, she began to feel revived herself until he said, "My folks never told me you were staying at the house."

"It doesn't matter now."

"Doesn't it?"

"I wish we could talk about something else."

"Okay." He cleared his throat. "Are you taking the pill?"

"Me? No. Why? Oh! Rory, are you thinking about sex?"

"Of course I am."

She sighed deeply and contentedly and fell back against the pillows. "I am so happy." She smiled at him with delight. "You are getting better."

"And maybe we had better talk about psychic whatnots."

"You won't believe in them."

"I might. Try me."

"Well, apparently, there are seven of them, in a row. The first is the crown chakra." She put her hand on his head. "And here is the third eye." She touched his forehead. "It's my favorite. The next is your throat." She left her hand resting on his neck and rapidly recited, "And then it's heart, solar plexus, abdomen and, well, the root."

He was laughing heartily for an invalid. "Now I am going to die, crushed; your favorite is the forehead? Oh, Sal."

CHAPTER 25

ON THE FOLLOWING morning, Rory awoke feeling restored to life. He lay listening to the pleasant rattle of pots and pans in the kitchen. Smiling, he got up; but with an appalling drop of spirits, he realized he had been on the verge of calling to his mother to come and show him his chakras again. She was the one washing dishes. He retreated to the bed where he lay, appalled, horrified, and devastated.

"Rory?" Jean emerged from the kitchen. "Are you awake?"

"No."

"Can I get you anything?"

"No."

"Then I'll leave you to Sarah. She seems to know what to do with you."

There was no reply.

"She will make a good doctor, won't she?" Jean mused. "You are looking so much better. Thank goodness you didn't get hit as hard as some people do, but you still look a bit peaky. Joe and I were thinking we could take the children to Napa, so you can get some rest in your own" — she glanced at Sarah's bed — "place. But they wanted to see you first. You were asleep when we got here, so Joe went to Kate's to fix her dishwasher and that nice boyfriend of Sarah's took the children out. I think he's uncomfortable with your being here, Rory. I'm sure you wouldn't want to make trouble. He is a charmer, but — I hope Sarah doesn't leave medical school for him. You should talk to her, Rory, and tell her how hard it is to catch up. You could. She's been such a good friend to you. A sister couldn't have been kinder." Rory scowled; she continued, "I bought you a pair of pajamas. I know she's a medical student, but all the same —"

"Where is she?"

"She went to lunch with that other man, Damon. He seems to like her too. She certainly is blossoming. Of course, she was always so pretty."

Rory went into the bathroom. He opened the cabinet to look for aspirin. He saw, instead, Harry's box of condoms. He slammed the door and limped back to bed, where he lay fanning a moody fit as his children bounced in with Gabriel, who was wearing a bow tie that blinked red and green. Lucy and Avery climbed onto the bed to inspect Rory. They told him there was no laundry in the living room, and they had not had to go to school, and the big kid had taken them to Mr. Mopps' toy store. They had presents for Rory: a book of fairy tales and a tie like Gabriel's.

"It almost was pantyhose with Santa Clauses on it," Gabriel explained. "Where's Sarah?"

"She went to lunch with that nice man, Damon," Jean said.

"Behind my back?" he asked. He wrote Sarah a note and left.

DAMON'S OBJECTIVE IN inviting Sarah to lunch, aside from the altruistic notion that someone had to care about her, was to talk about Gabriel. He and Gabriel had quarreled again, and the regularity of these events was discouraging for Damon, who counseled others on how to manage relationships. Sarah had accepted Damon's invitation for an equally self-serving reason: she thought she might rather be elsewhere when Rory woke up.

"You look like you had a good night," he said, as Sarah alternated between yawning and smiling. "I'm sorry I woke you up."

"Oh, you didn't. Rory's mother had already called, and before that" — Sarah looked squeamish — "his wife."

"I thought she was the ex-wife. What did she want?"

"Not too much — I think she might have been drunk." But who was she to talk? She, who had drunk half a bottle of wine and fallen into bed with her patient? She, who had never spent an entire night with anyone, had slept so well and warmly, curled against him.

"I am glad to see that you have better taste in men than I do," Damon remarked, and Sarah refrained from pointing out that their taste was remarkably similar. "He's a good choice for you."

"Who?"

"Sarah, Rory's family is a case study in stability, a museum piece. At least one of you will believe that things can work out. There are challenges, of course, two children, the ex-wife, and so forth, but if you balance these with how much you are in love with him —"

"Me?" She choked on her water. "But I'm not."

He chuckled. "Even Gabriel has noticed it. It's one of the things we fought about. He has this absurd notion you're an asexual creature who belongs to him."

"AND THEN SHE woke up."

"He kissed her, and she woke up," Lucy corrected Rory.

"Why do they have to kiss?" Avery asked.

"They have to or she won't wake up," Lucy said.

"If you know this story, why are we reading it?" Rory asked.

"He kissed her," Lucy prompted, "and she woke up and they lived happily ever after."

"Can we read the story about goats?" Avery asked.

Sarah watched them from the door. In love? Maybe her fourteen-year-old self had been better at recognizing it. She felt no giddy leap of her pulse, no misguided confusion of Rory with mythical heroes. She admitted her aborted medical training had gone awry, but she doubted this was the manifestation of passionate love. In love? What did it mean except the activation of a lively interior life that had no relation to reality? Didn't she have a superior version with Gabriel, a lively exterior life that had no relation to reality?

It was Jean who noticed Sarah standing diffidently in her own doorway. "What a lovely dress, Sarah. I love patterns of roses."

"Gabriel —" Sarah stopped short of saying that Gabriel had made her buy it. Rory, with a scowl, had slumped down behind the book of fairy tales.

Jean, perceiving a slight tension in the room, said they would go meet Joe now. "Gabriel left you a note, Sarah. Good luck," she added, glancing at Rory. "I have never known a man to get sick without becoming impossible. Even Joe."

She and the children departed. Rory, prey to the same impulse, swung up out of the bed, reeled, and sank back down. Sarah, in what would be her one wise action of the afternoon, refrained from jumping to his assistance. "Have you had lunch?" she asked.

"No."

"Would you like —"

"No."

"I'm sorry — "

"Why?"

"I don't know." Sarah reminded herself that incivility was a sign of imminent recovery. "I am glad you're better." His dark look indicated she had committed yet another error by implying he had been ill. "Sorry —"

"Why?" he demanded. "What are you sorry about?"

She focused on Gabriel's note. "Your wife called."

"She is my ex-wife. What did she want?"

"I'm not sure."

"Alcoholism is a disease." Sarah was far better at defending anyone else than herself.

"I don't need anyone to tell me about it."

She turned to leave, but, unfortunately, walking blindly, she went into the kitchen, not out the door. He followed her and she was trapped. She began to scrub the sink, although Jean had left it spotless. Stiffly, Rory said, "I seem to have gotten into a bad habit of wanting to be the first one to strike."

"It's none of my business."

"It is if it upset you." He took a shaky breath. "I do want to hear what you think."

"I think — if I were you, I'd prefer Jane. Either way, I'd keep plenty of aspirin on hand."

A dumbfounded look overtook Rory's face. "Are you jealous?" he asked, oddly elated. "Sarah, when Dibby is drinking, she'll say anything. It didn't — it doesn't mean anything."

"I know. Men can make love to anyone."

"What? Men? I'm not the one with a box of condoms in my bathroom."

"I hate this," Sarah whispered. "I hate this, I hate this, I hate this." She repeated it until her heart stopped hammering with fright and the sink was a new shade of white. She looked up. He was gone from the door. He was sitting at the table studying the pages of her notebook of things she might not see again.

"Oh, don't!" She darted to snatch the book away. "Don't look at that!"

"Why not?" She didn't answer. Rory sprang to his feet and caught hold of the mantel. He was trembling but his voice was like thunder. "Sarah! You are driving me insane! Why do you do this? Go so far and then slam the door and run off with that babbling idiot? Does anything matter to you? Are you ever going to do anything besides hide out in this damned attic?" He spun around to face her; she flung up her hand as if to avert a blow. He was wounded beyond measure. "What do you think I am? Never mind — go on, run away. It seems to be all that you can do."

GABRIEL'S NOTE SAID he would be at High Waves for a haircut. He was there, draped in a cape and discussing how short to go when Sarah plummeted through the doorway looking ghastly, pale, and anguished. He waved.

"Come in! Sarah, do you know Tony? He just got a job as a female impersonator. Can you advise him on female things? What have you done with Damon? I thought it over; I forgive you. I'm glad to see you've dragged yourself away from the Bedside."

Sarah burst into tears.

"He hollered at you?" Gabriel asked when he had dragged her into the nearest bar and ordered gimlets. "That's it? I thought he had at least dropped dead on you. So he's not dead? There's a lowering thought." He rubbed his unfinished haircut. "Why did he holler at you?"

"I don't know."

"That's what you get for fooling around with straight men. Did you? Ah, she says nothing. How was it? Oh don't — don't cry again. Tell you what: let's go shopping. I wouldn't trust Tony to finish my hair now anyway. Female sensibility throws him off."

Several hours later Sarah and Gabriel, laden with packages, paused for another drink. "I love the castle set," he chortled. "I might keep it. Kids could eat the pieces, right? I'll give Avery the Lincoln Logs and

Lucy the puppets. But they're such great puppets. Maybe I should buy two sets. I love toys. My dad never allowed them. He said they cramped creativity."

"Maybe it worked."

"But, Sarah, you haven't bought anything — for anyone, not even yourself."

"I'm not very good at Christmas."

"You're not really Hindu, are you?"

"No. I like Christmas. The McIntyres" — her voice wobbled sadly — "I don't know what's wrong with me, Gabriel."

"It's nothing I can't cure." He ordered more drinks. "You have to buy your heart's desire."

"Buy it?"

"Absolutely. If you wait for someone to give it to you, you'll wait forever. What is it?"

"I don't know. Maybe I don't have a heart."

"You will never graduate from med school if you don't improve your anatomy, dummy. Sarah! Look at that man going into the bath shop. Maybe your heart's desire is bubble bath."

"Just because he's handsome doesn't mean he is gay." She drooped and drank her gin.

"Want to bet? God, Sarah, if all you are going to do is mope, let's go talk to that ass McIntyre. We'll ask why he was behaving like an ass, and if he turns out to be a bigger ass than I already think he is, and he hollers at you again, we'll go get Damon and Damon can hit him. Better yet, let's go get Damon first. He's doing his married couples thing tonight."

"WHAT ARE YOU doing here?" Damon met them, with more surprise than enthusiasm, in the reception area of his clinic.

"I came to apologize," Gabriel said; and Sarah felt her brain begin to shrink.

"This is hardly the time or place to talk. I have people waiting."

"But I want to talk to you now."

"Go home, Gabriel. I'll call you."

"No, you won't. You didn't before."

Damon turned and walked away. "I think we'd better leave," Sarah said.

"No!" Gabriel grabbed a dish of hard candy from the counter and flung it after Damon. The glass splintered. Sarah pulled him towards the door.

"I hate this!" he burst out wildly. "God, I hate this. It's never happened to me before, and it matters. I go see him, and he's not home. I call, and he doesn't call back. I make an ass of myself, and I can't stop. It matters; God, it matters, and I hate it."

FOR SEVERAL MINUTES after Sarah's departure, Rory sat limply on the bed, rubbing his head. The times he had lost his temper and scared his children had caused him a degree of guilt and anxiety he had never before known, and he had learned to confine his explosions to solitary exercises in which he went into the bathroom and pounded on the wall, but not too hard. Now, he had gone up in flames, after an alarming display of emotion, and he could not say who was more alarmed. Nothing was left in his head except smoke, ashes, and a recognition of the paradox of reversibility in time: things said could not be unsaid.

He dressed and left the flat, noting testily that there was no way to lock the doors behind him. He intended to catch a BART train to Berkeley. He got as far as Mother Earth's, where he sagged, feeling bloodless. Passively, he accepted her advice to begin eating organic. He dragged himself back up the hill and fell into Sarah's bed. It was dark when he awoke again; the doorbell was buzzing. It was the psychiatrist who made house calls.

"We've met at the hospital, but you may not remember," Damon said. "I am sorry to disturb you. I'm looking for Gabriel."

"Gabriel?" Rory echoed him, bewildered.

"He's not here? I'm under strict orders not to go to his place in Berkeley, but tonight my inclination is to say to hell with that."

"Berkeley?" Dimly Rory recognized that the Fate he didn't believe in had tossed him a gift: a ride home.

MUCH LATER, SARAH and Gabriel tottered, zigzagging, into the dark, quiet flat. "I can't believe your heart's desire is a book about God and physics," Gabriel said. "But that was a great bookstore. Even Damon might be impressed with an autographed copy of *Howl*."

Rory was gone. Sarah saw this before she noticed, on the mantel by her statue, an orchid with three lilac-colored blossoms. A folded piece of paper lay beside it. *Sorry. Thank you. R.*

"Have we got anything else to drink?" she asked Gabriel. It was cold, and she put her bathrobe on over her clothes.

"Yes. I knew we'd need it. Sarah, how about this: your heart's desire is a new bathrobe."

"What is wrong with this one?"

"If it's what you wore when the Heartbeat was here, no wonder he left. Joking, Sarah, I'm just joking. I thought we agreed that he isn't worth it, and we're going to introduce him to Damon and let them be asses together."

"Would it make a difference, Gabriel?"

"Having something in common?"

"No, bathrobes."

"Stuff of dreams, kiddo. Sarah! I've got it! We'll go away. It's just not the same, wandering in the fog, three weeks before Christmas. You're supposed to rush around in the snow on Christmas Eve. Let's go to Paris. Let's go tomorrow. I'll get tickets. You pack."

"Paris?"

"Paris."

"Oh, Gabriel! Maybe that's my heart's desire."

CHAPTER 26

"WE WILL BE cruising at an altitude —" the flight attendant recited.

"Cruising at an altitude," Gabriel hummed. "I love it."

"I don't see how we can cruise," Sarah said. "We hardly have time to take off and land."

"In the unlikely event of an emergency water landing —"

"A crash in the Great Salt Lake," Gabriel said. "Sarah, do you believe in the Devil?"

"No. Why?"

"Last night a man came into the bar dressed as the Devil. What if he was the real thing? It worries me."

"Why? He might be your type."

"Thanks, friend. Because I'd sell my soul."

"For what?"

"Anything. I've probably already lost it."

"I'd worry more about losing my mind."

"Speaking of which, Damon said I should tell you: I'm going to tell my parents I'm gay. He's so damned full of shoulds."

"What am I supposed to do?"

"Vouch for me." Gabriel rolled his eyes. "And be ready to run."

Gabriel's father met them at the Dallas airport. He was a fair, substantial man, who wore a hunting cap pulled down over his ears. In the same way some people come to look like their pets, he greatly resembled his beige Cadillac.

Neither father nor son said anything as they drove. Sarah commented that the weather was clear in Texas, whereas it had been cloudy in San Francisco. They turned onto a street lined with mansions, English Tudor, French Country, and Southern Colonial. An automatic gate swung open at the driveway of a sprawling, modern, beige house, another relative of the Cadillac. Sarah observed that the lawns, like everything else, were quite large, and Christian Dinesen said, "You're in Texas now." Later, Sarah realized that this might have been the highlight of the trip.

They stepped into the entryway, where a portrait of a man in a helmet glowered over a wrought-iron cage filled with stuffed birds. "This style is Early Inquisition," Gabriel said. "But the living room is pure Louis XVI, don't you think?"

Sarah, glancing at the red brocade furniture, red satin curtains pouring onto the floor, and a collection of marble heads, agreed that it lacked only a guillotine to evoke revolutionary Paris. The house also had a Gothic dining room, a Chinese den, and an Early American kitchen. It was Henrietta Dinesen's method of decorating to buy any showroom that struck her fancy, Gabriel explained as he escorted Sarah to a bedroom done entirely in white. "High Arctic," he said.

"Lunch!" A woman strode past them, a mustard-colored caftan billowing about her like a sulfuric cloud. Cigarette smoke trailed behind her. "Lunch!"

"It's not going to work," Henrietta Dinesen said as Gabriel and Sarah entered the dining room. "She won't listen to me. I told her three times how to cook the roast, but she would not listen. What did she do? She browned it. I did not tell her to brown it. I said to put it in the oven. I will not have it. If she won't cook the way I tell her to cook, she can leave."

"Hello," Gabriel said. "This is Sarah."

Christian Dinesen joined them. He had replaced his hunting hat with a leather aviator's cap, fastened under his chin.

"She put red frosting on the cake," Henrietta continued. "Red! She said it looked Christmassy. I said Christmas is a serious time, and not a time for red frosting."

"We had a good flight," Gabriel said. "It was cloudy in San Francisco, but it's clear here."

"And what do you suppose she said to me? 'I work best if I am left alone in my kitchen.' Her kitchen! It is not her kitchen. This is not going to work. If I do not want the roast browned, it is my kitchen, and she can leave if she does not like it."

It was evident the cook had done something odd to the roast, for what was on Sarah's plate looked like a chicken leg. It was also possible that the cook had already left before preparing anything else; the leg was the only thing on the plate.

"It looks good," Sarah said.

"What?" Henrietta asked, distracted.

"This — er — this. I don't think browning hurt it."

Gabriel dropped his fork and pulled Sarah under the table with him. "The roast was last week," he whispered.

"She said the French brown things," Henrietta was saying when Sarah resurfaced. "If she wants to cook French, she can go to France. This is America. We are Christians here. And it is my kitchen. I will have to let her go. Hurt what?" she asked Sarah.

"This — chicken."

"Chicken? It is certainly not chicken. It is a fricassee."

"Uncle George's house is holding up well," Gabriel said.

"Why wouldn't it?" Henrietta retorted. "If you are appreciating it properly."

"Oh, everyone does," Sarah said; then she took a hasty bite of chicken.

"Who?"

"Everyone in Berkeley," Sarah stammered. "It's such an interesting city. Everyone appreciates — everything."

"Sarah and I are going to be married," Gabriel announced.

"Berkeley is the realm of the devil," Henrietta said. "That's why I said to Gabriel, if you stay in your uncle's house, I do not want one person from Berkeley entering it."

"Sarah is Jewish. It's like Ivanhoe and Rebecca. I'm going to convert."

Henrietta turned a look on Sarah that should have transformed her into a pillar of ice — or was it salt? — and Sarah, who had never known herself to exhibit any kind of courage under duress, said, "He doesn't have to. No matter what, our children will be Jews." Then she reverted to form and thought she might faint.

"Chicken," Henrietta said. "It is not going to work out, Christian. I will have to let her go. I will cook. I can cook. I most certainly can cook. Red frosting indeed."

Christian stood up. "That was a good dinner, Mother."

AFTER LUNCH, SARAH had several questions she wanted to ask Gabriel, including why he had chosen such an obtuse way of coming out of the closet and if his father always wore a hat. Gabriel, however, went into the Chinese den with his mother, where they settled down to watch a television game show in which contestants were asked questions like what foods made Americans say yuck, and who said, 'Wherefore art thou, Romeo?' in *Romeo and Juliet*. It was Henrietta's sport to answer these questions, as in: a very silly person had said that, and yes, she certainly did know what made Americans say yuck. Regrettably, this reminded her of the cook. Sarah retreated to her bedroom. She opened the white curtains. She sat for some time looking at the view of endless, flat land, before she dialed a number on the white telephone.

"Sarah!" Kate said. "Are you in Paris?"

"No, Texas."

"But I thought you were going to Paris this morning."

"We had to stop here first, so I could meet his parents."

"Is this getting serious?"

"No. They just wouldn't give him any money to go to Europe unless he brought me home."

"Er, Sarah —"

"I was wondering, how is —"

"I fed him. He's fine."

"Who —"

"Your cat. And I will water your orchid. It's so romantic. Did Gabriel give it to you?"

"I'll probably kill it."

"Oh, you non-believer, you remind me of Rory. 'Sigh, groan, what shall I do about all these women pursuing me?'" Kate broke off with a squeal of protest. "Stop that!"

"How is he?" Sarah asked, with only a faint, forlorn quiver in her voice.

"You'll have to ask him. He's right here, throwing sponges at me, being a bad example for his kids. Do you want to talk to him? Oh, oops, sorry, he's gone. He's going to the airport."

"He's going away?"

"No, no. Do you remember that congressman, David Ilillouette? The good-looking one? He and Rory have stayed friends, and Rory writes things for him from time to time. He's flying back to California today and Rory is going to meet him at the airport so they can write something about that crisis."

"Which crisis?"

"I think it's the one in Iran. Or maybe it's the one in Korea, where there might be a coup. Or maybe it's that bad guy in Africa, Gaddafi or someone. I can't keep them straight. But don't worry. I'll feed your cat and water your flower, and then if you don't mind, I might just sit there a little bit."

Sarah hung up and sat on the white bed, looking out at gray sky, and after a while, she ventured out of her room. In the kitchen, she found Henrietta, watching *As The World Turns* while another woman, a smaller version of Christian Dinesen, shaped a mix of ham and cream cheese in holiday molds of wreaths and trees. The younger woman glanced over Sarah.

"I am Gabriel's sister, Vicki."

"I didn't know Gabriel had two sisters."

"That's not my fault, I am sure."

"I was wondering," Sarah said, "if you heard any news —"

"Of course, we know," Henrietta said. "The cook has quit. Without a warning. She threw a cake against the door and walked out. Well, good riddance. We are Christian people, and we do not throw cakes."

"Mother," Vicki said, filling the last mold, "this recipe is perfect."

"Everything you do is perfect."

"No, you didn't see the dreadful salad I made last week. My lettuces just didn't blend."

They both looked at Sarah who felt called upon to compliment the cream cheese shapes, and her stomach did growl as she observed them.

"Would you like one?" Vicki asked.

"Sarah is Jewish," Henrietta said. "You shouldn't ask her to eat things she refuses to eat."

"It really is extraordinary that Gabriel brought someone home," Vicki said. "I don't know how anyone could put up with him."

"Now, I will not have that," Henrietta said. "Gabriel is my son and my only son. And if Jane believes Paul, after what he did to Myrtle, she deserves what she gets."

Sarah backed out of the room. "Rebecca!" a voice called. "Come help decorate the tree!"

Lydia was standing amidst boxes of ornaments wearing a sweater with a giant head of Rudolph the Red-Nosed Reindeer on it; his eyes and nose were wooly pompoms.

"Have a drink, Becky," she said. "Make yourself at home."

"Thank you," Sarah said. "I feel right at home."

Lydia lowered her voice. "It's not true is it, that Gabriel is going to marry someone named Sarah? Mother always gets us confused with her shows."

"No."

"I didn't think so, because you are just perfect for him."

"No, I am Sarah."

"Then you are going to marry him! How wonderful! Oh, it's getting late. People will be here any minute! Can you help me with the lights? No, I forgot, you're — what are you?"

"I can help anyway," Sarah said. "What people?"

"Didn't Gabriel tell you? It's why we're all here. It's the reunion for everyone who went to Father's experiment. Ten years ago tonight, they started the commune. It was too bad they had to start in the winter because it was so cold, but it was symbolic. There was nothing to eat, but Father believed we should always be a little hungry, so we'd know what it's like to be deprived. We were so glad when Rosie arrived."

"Rosie?"

"Father's girlfriend. She looked a little bit like you, Sarah, so beautiful, just like Natalie Wood in *West Side Story*. We loved Rosie. She cooked and Father didn't mind."

"What happened to her?"

"She ran away with my brother. When my mother showed up."

"She ran away with Gabriel?"

"Oh no! Gabriel was just a boy. With my older brother, Jacob. We never heard from him again." Lydia refilled her glass. "You don't know my parents. You can just cease to exist for them. Power of life and death. Boom, you're gone."

"To those of us who have survived our dreams." Abe Barkham, co-leader of the collapsed commune, raised his glass.

The room was filled with people. Vicki was playing the piano, and Lydia was sleeping beneath the Christmas tree. Sarah started towards the buffet table, but she was stopped by Abe, who kissed her. "Liberation dies hard," he sighed, "but I can still kiss a pretty girl."

Sarah disengaged herself and was accosted by a sinewy woman dressed in red. "You must be the girl Gabriel brought home," she said. "Where is that bad boy? I am Sylvia Barkham. You just met my husband. I hope we don't seem cliquish to you, but we shared such a meaningful experience. I often think that we might have made a go of it if only we had had a better heater. But I was always warm."

She was carrying a silver flask, and she took a swig before she went on: "How my art blossomed there! I danced; I sang. My only regret is the wine. It was my dream to feel the grapes between my toes and then to drink the wine, knowing it had felt my feet, that it was born of my dance to life. But the grapes never grew. We had to buy some from a man in Calistoga. How he laughed when I explained my need. He was a simple man, a man of the earth, but we reached across our differences, the simple peasant and I. He gave me a box of grapes, and I invited him to taste the fruit of my feet. It is too bad we never made the wine. Someday, I shall write a book and call it *I Was Always Warm*. Ah, you are smiling. What has that bad Gabriel told you about me?"

"Nothing," Sarah said truthfully. Sylvia, disappointed, turned away. Moving toward the food, Sarah was stopped again, this time by a chubby, sad-faced man.

"Gabriel said your brother is a writer," he said. "I envy him. I am sure that if I could write about it, I wouldn't feel so guilty about killing the chickens. I didn't know that they would eat everything you gave them, and we had such a lot to throw out that night because Abe had cooked. I found them lying on the ground, dead, their stomachs bloated; it was a smudge on Paradise. And I really didn't seduce Sylvia. I just found her in my bed. It was only that for a time, we felt free, like anything could happen."

Sarah had reached the buffet table decorated with a plastic Santa Claus; a light bulb inside him gave an exaggerated glow to his belly. The platter of cream cheese shapes was empty.

"I'm not surprised," a voice said behind her. "Henrietta is cheap, and Christian is mad."

"Hush, Milton," a woman hissed. "That is Gabriel's fiancée."

They were Milton and Ann Major, who were now selling real estate in the Central Valley. "We've had a difficult decade," admitted Ann, who had once set off so confidently in search of the other half of her brain. "It is hard to think that those hopeful times really happened. Do you remember, Milton, when Christian put too many prunes in the pressure cooker? What a time we had cleaning them up. Dear silent Christian. What a man he is, if you ask me."

"I did not," said Milton.

"Are you still jealous?" she asked. "But I wasn't the only person who slipped a little. Shall I remind you how you ogled whenever Sylvia did her dance? And Margaret —"

"We do not need to go into Margaret."

"We never did," Ann sniffed. "But why did it all happen that way? In Paradise, too."

Sarah collided with a plump, melancholy girl who sighed, "You must be Rowena. I bet you don't know my name."

"No," Sarah said, "but then I hardly know my own."

"I bet Gabriel never mentioned me to you. It's because there's nothing to tell. But when I heard that he was going to marry the heroine of *Ivanhoe,* I knew my youth was over." Sarah had backed into the only person who had suffered from unrequited love on the commune.

The clock began to chime, and Abe Barkham once more raised his glass. "To those of us who survived our dreams."

A crescent moon was visible from Sarah's window. Gabriel, sitting on the bed, was drinking wine from a bottle. "Come in," he said. "Sit down. Dinner will be late, which means never. Would you like a Life Saver?"

"Maybe your father is doing another psychological thing. Does he always wear a hat?"

"Yes. And my mother never stops talking."

"My family is crazy too," she offered, although she thought, in a contest, his might win first prize.

Gabriel held the bottle up to the moonlight. "Empty," he said. "What'll we do now?" The room grew colder, as if the window glass had dissolved. He darted at her, awkwardly. "Damn," he said. "Missed. Well, try again."

CHAPTER 27

A WILD STORM WAS sweeping down from the Arctic. Before it was over, it would close the Golden Gate Bridge, ice the hills of San Francisco, blow houses off hills in Marin, and flood roads in Napa and Sonoma. First the wind arrived, fierce and frigid.

Sarah turned on the heater for the first time in her tenancy. If she didn't, her orchid would surely die. She had never owned a plant and felt obliged, for the sake of life in general, not to kill it. Why could Rory not have left a bouquet of flowers, doomed to wither?

But the heater did not turn on, and while she contemplated this, a parcel, postmarked Paris, arrived. It was silver cardboard box, elegantly embossed with the words *Nuits de Paris* and an image of the Eiffel Tower. Inside it was a mound of crimson velvet, black fur and jet beads. "Bathrobe," read a note pinned to the fur. "Don't worry. It's not real." As she lifted it, a sheer black wisp of silk fluttered to the floor. It was labeled: "Nightgown." The box also contained shampoo, bath oil, soap, and lotion with flowery labels in French. For a night in Paris.

The doorbell buzzed. A deliveryman handed her a wicker hamper from a San Francisco shop that called itself a deli, much as the Queen of England might call herself a working woman.

"Oh no," she exclaimed. A "Perishable" label was stuck on two limp, live Dungeness crabs. She put them in the kitchen sink. She was cautiously inspecting the rest of the hamper, filled with wine and black waxed boxes tied with gold ribbons, when the telephone rang.

"Hello," a voice chirped, "this is Robert W. Moses and I'm calling from New York —"

"Gabriel," Sarah said, "you've got to stop this."

"But —"

"No, Gabriel, listen," she said. "Don't send any more things. I don't care if your mother is crazy and your father never uncovers his ears, or if dinner was never ready, or if you told them we were engaged instead of telling them you were gay, or even if, for a few minutes, you weren't so gay. Starving people have this urge to procreate. I don't care that you left the next day and Vicki had to take me to the airport. I don't care that you went to Paris by yourself, but if I keep saying I don't care, I may end up not caring about anything. When I'm with you, I forget it's not real, but someone has already gotten the Nobel Prize for proving that parity is not conserved."

There was a delicate cough at the other end of the line. "But I really am Robert Moses," the man said, "calling from *Newsweek* to see if you would like to subscribe —"

Sarah's brain devolved from resolute to feeble-minded. "I thought you were someone else."

"I know. It happens. But to subscribe —"

"No, thank you."

"It's a good deal —"

"I don't want to know the news."

"I understand." He paused. "What is not conserved?"

"Parity. It's physics."

"Ah." He hung up.

The wind rattled the windows, and the heater remained still ice cold, but she could freeze in style. She bathed in Nuit de Paris, anointed herself with lotions, and put on the nightgown and the robe.

She sampled the Saffron Curry Prawns, while the cat tasted Foie Gras with Truffles on Brioche. "The problem with Gabriel is he is always preferable to reality," she explaining to Widdershins when the buzzer sounded again. "That must be dessert."

It was, however, Rory McIntyre.

He looked — he was — cold, wet, windblown, and so wretched, Sarah thought if Gabriel had not kidnapped and sent him too, then the winds had blown him, unwilling, to her door. This wasn't true. He had come of his own free will. After enduring many wretched days, he had finally decided, in a rite of self-torture, to finish himself off by telling Sarah — not that she had asked or in any way indicated that she cared — that there could be nothing between them. He had, however, expected an obstacle to prevent him; yet, there had been no traffic back-ups on the Bay Bridge. He found a parking place within ten blocks of her flat. Her light was on. The street door, unlocked, was flapping in the wind. "Oh," he said. "You're here."

"Yes," she, equally stupid, replied. "I am."

"I didn't think you would be." Sarah had no answer to this. He took in her elaborate outfit. "Are you going out?"

"I was just going to try to fix my heater."

He descended with her to a dusty basement, lit by a single light bulb and cluttered with debris from construction projects. Sarah held her bathrobe closed with one hand — magnificent though it was, it did not have a clasp — while she inspected a large metal contraption.

"That's the hot water heater," Rory said. "Here's your furnace. This probably is the problem." He jiggled a disconnected pipe, loosening a shower of dust and dirt on her. He dusted her off. His hand stayed on her shoulder. "We can probably reconnect it."

He unearthed a ladder and climbed up a few steps. "Oh, look," Sarah exclaimed. "It's a black widow."

"Where?"

"Right above your head."

"Are you sure?"

"Oh yes. They have a distinctive body shape and color. Can you see her hourglass? Oh, don't kill her!"

"They're poisonous, my darling."

"But they're shy. They usually only bite if they're startled or their eggs are threatened."

The light above him flickered. "And what if I startle this one?"

"It wouldn't be so bad for you. Their poison is more potent than snake venom, but they can only administer a small dose. It's really only potentially fatal if you weigh less than fifteen kilos or have a heart condition."

"I have a heart condition."

"There is an antivenin."

"I hate spiders."

"Poor thing; I wonder if she knows she's poisonous. She may just be hanging there, thinking about life."

"No, she's waiting for her mate."

"She does a lovely mating dance. She lies on her back and weaves her legs around and rather hypnotizes the male."

"And then he dies."

"She doesn't always kill him. Shall I go up the ladder?"

"No, I'll fix the damned pipe."

He ascended the ladder. The wind howled, the light went out, and Sarah accidentally gripped Rory's leg. He descended. They blundered into each other. Few things can better ease a meeting after a disastrous parting than a broken heater, darkness, and a black widow spider.

Rory said, "Maybe we should just build a fire and let the landlord deal with your friend."

While she called her landlord, he built a fire from scraps of wood from the furnace room. "Where are Lucy and Avery?" she asked. "At day care?"

"No."

Wrong subject. Even vintage Parisian lingerie could not improve her instincts; the robe had probably belonged to Marie Antoinette. But she tried again: "Rory, are you hungry?"

By degrees, his grim expression softened as he reclined in front of the fire, sampling Filet Mignon aux Champignons en Croûte and Homard á l'armoricaine. Yes, he said, it was fine if all she had to drink was Dom Perignon. No, it didn't matter if it had not been chilled; room temperature would be cold enough. If it was not the conversation he had envisioned, he had to admit that any other might have lost its gravity, if not its pathos, served up with caviar, oysters, and Provençal peaches in Grand Marnier. Still, despite the wine and five kinds of cheese, a residual wariness flickered on and off. Reality still droned around them like a mosquito.

"We need to talk," he said.

"About what?" She trying to hold her robe closed while opening the chocolate mousse with raspberries with one hand.

"Sal, what are you wearing?"

"Oh. Nothing."

"Really?" He tugged on her fingers; the robe fell open. "You do have a secret life. No wonder I can never look at you without wondering what kind of underwear you're wearing."

She studied her hand in his. She knew she had all the props of enchantment. They could be done with talking in an instant, yet she was going to pat the mosquito and offer herself up as its next meal. She said, "Gabriel sent all of this. It's an apology for taking me home with him. He was going to come out of the closet and I was supposed to vouch for him."

She half expected everything, including Rory, to vanish. He only said, "I know."

"You do?"

"Damon told me. He gave me a ride to Berkeley, the day you and I quarreled."

"It's one way around the black widow dilemma —"

"Sarah," he interrupted gently. "Let's stick to the mating habits of humans, shall we?" She made no reply, and he, with a strained nonchalance, added, "So, if that guy is gay, why do you have that box of condoms in your bathroom?"

"Oh, they aren't mine. They're Harry the Swinger's. He had this fantasy about a night of anything." She paused; Rory was looking distressed. "It didn't mean anything."

She was rescued by the ringing phone. A small, sad voice wavered, "Sarah?"

"Lucy? Where are you?"

"Disneyland." The word had never been uttered with less enthusiasm by a child. "Rory said I could call you if he wasn't home. He wrote down the number."

"Are you looking for him?" Sarah asked. "He's right here."

Rory's face was ashen as he took the phone. Sarah fed the fire, but there was no way to escape the conversation as he, in increasingly uneven tones, told Lucy she couldn't come home yet. Wasn't it fun staying in a hotel? They were hungry? Where was their mother? Well, as soon as she was awake, she would get them dinner. Yes, he loved her. Yes, he loved Avery too. Yes, he was lonely for them. Yes, that was why he had come to see Sarah. His voice shifted to a monotone. "I didn't call them, Dibby. She called me. Let it go. Just have a good time."

The telephone clattered as he hung up. The fire was crackling, the room growing dark, and Widdershins was eating the Lobster Diavolo. Sarah touched Rory's back. His muscles felt rock hard but knotted, like the cat had been tangling them for sport. As she rubbed them, his breath steadied, but he didn't look at her. He said, "That feels good."

"A nurse showed me how. I could do it better if you lie down. But it's probably too cold for you to take off your shirt."

He smiled, although wanly, pulled off his shirt, and stretched out on the carpet.

"Do you mind if I use olive oil?" she asked. "It's either that or *Nuits de Paris.*"

"I'll take the olive oil." He sighed deeply as she went to work, and he began to talk.

He began by describing how, as he sat brainstorming with a forlorn congressman ("He's still kind of an idealist, Sarah. Sometimes this gets him down.") on whether or not there was hope for the world, Avery flushed a mango pit down the toilet and flooded the flat. Next, his ex-wife turned up with four tickets to *The Nutcracker.* He was saved by Kate who had taken refuge in his flat after she and Sterling had their annual fight about where to spend the holidays. She went to *The Nutcracker* in his place. Dibby had continued to haunt Berkeley, but he didn't know why. Then his mother arrived and set about cleaning without mercy for any speck of dust. She offered no explanation, but every time his dad called, she was too busy polishing doorknobs to talk to him.

This supply of babysitters had allowed him to do something he needed to do when Jane, the journalism student, arrived with a Christmas basket. He liked her, and he knew he had to end whatever it was they were doing. He asked her to go for a walk. Dibby arrived as they were leaving and greatly expedited his purpose, giving Jane, he was sure, nothing to regret.

He finally asked Dibby what she wanted. She said she had changed her mind. She would take him back. She had money and he was living like a pauper. The blithe assumption that he would never turn her down made it much easier to do so. He only didn't know why, after all these years, it was such a painful conversation. When he saw Dibby next, she announced that she was exercising her visitation rights, something she had never done. She had two weeks; she was taking the kids. If he objected, they could go back to court.

"I had to let them go, Sarah. She's threatening to reopen custody. It's never going to end." He rolled onto his back, gazing at her.

"Shall I do your chest, too?" she asked. As she picked up the olive oil, he caught her wrist. She dropped the bottle and oil oozed over him. He kissed her with a fierceness that matched the storm; then he released her.

"Dammit, Sarah — I didn't intend — it wasn't my intention —"

She ran her fingers over his chest to disperse the olive oil. "In medicine, 'intention' means healing, the process of healing. You have a wound: the two sides intend to come together again."

"We can't keep having one-night stands every time I see you."

"Why not?"

In one swift motion, they tangled in red velvet and fur. Useful thoughts fell away along with her robe. Sarah thought the wild storm had moved inside the room, perhaps into herself, but the room was no longer cold, until a freezing wind gusted over them. The door had blown opened. Sarah sprang to her feet, her gossamer gown shredded and streaked with oil. Kate, dripping rain and clutching a red and green present, was frozen in the doorway.

"Oh! Oh, I am so sorry."

Rory stood up, as flushed and sweaty as Sarah, but wearing even fewer clothes. "What's up, Kate?"

"I wanted to give Sarah — this — I didn't know — Rory, I sent your presents home with Mom. But I'd better go —"

Sarah found her vocal cords and her robe. "Come in. You're all wet."

"It's raining." Kate's voice wavered and broke. "Rory, I don't want to go with Sterling. Once, just once, I want to go home."

Sarah concentrated on closing food boxes so as not to watch Rory comfort his weeping sister. He held her, patted her back, and offered to kill Sterling.

"No." Kate sniffed. "I'll be okay. You smell like salad dressing."

"It was either this or *Nuits de Paris*. Do you want me to take you to Napa?"

"No." She shook her head. "I'll go. Well, Merry Christmas." She ran down the stairs.

The fire sputtered and expired, just like the brief, wild moment of passion on the floor; perhaps, Sarah reflected, it had panicked and fled to warmer, safer climates. They carried the boxes of food to the refrigerator. The two crabs were still languishing in the kitchen sink.

"Rory," Sarah said, "do you think we could put them back in the ocean?"

CHAPTER 28

SARAH AND RORY succeeded in freeing the two crabs without killing them, and this had a salutary effect on their spirits. Rory mentioned that he was planning to head north to see his friend Matt Biagi, who now managed a restaurant in St. Helena. Matt had called him earlier that day with an ambiguous but urgent summons. Did she want to come with him? He did have a working heater in his car.

They drove across the Golden Gate Bridge shortly before the storm closed it. The solid Volvo trembled in the wind and rain pelted it as they discussed Kate's disastrous marriage. They wondered why she had married Sterling and why people went to Disneyland. By the time they came into the realm of hills and vineyards, they were deep in a discussion of a galaxy named M82, which had captivated astronomers with its fantastic starbursts and superwinds. It had what Rory called "resolvable phenomena," as compared, Sarah supposed, to most of the universe.

St. Helena, as they had known it, was a Victorian village up valley from Napa; it had a fairytale quality, bestowed by its cottages, ghostly castles, and the overall air that a disgruntled witch had waved her wand over it, casting it into sleep for a hundred years. In this case, the witch was the federal government and the castles those few wineries that had survived Prohibition. But St. Helena was awakening, or at least it was yawning and looking for a comb. It now had restaurants besides Vern's Copper Chimney. Sports cars or even an occasional limousine mingled with the tractors and pick-up trucks. This was all quite strange for Sarah and Rory, who had thought their valley was the beginning of nowhere.

An abandoned stone building that had been a bordello and then a warehouse was now transformed into a candlelit Italian restaurant. Matt Biagi was waiting at the door. "McIntyre!" he hailed them. "I knew a storm wouldn't keep a New England guy like you away!"

Matt had grown so stout and red in the face, Sarah hardly recognized him, but he gripped her like a football by way of greeting. "Sarah Glass, cute as ever! Rory, I've got a gig for us."

"A what?"

Matt brought them to a table and sat down. "You don't know the Matlocks," he said, "but they came here from LA with a truckload of money, bought an old winery, and, wow, you should see what they've done with it. Mrs. Matlock wants to bring art to the farmers, so she set up the Budapest String Quartet to play a concert in their new wine cave. This place — it'll blow your mind. Of course, it's not a concert for the farmers, but for a bunch of ritzy people. Thing is, this storm has shut down airports, and her quartet is stranded in Hawaii. I said not to worry. The Napa High Jazz Band will save the day."

"The what?"

"I told you Jack and Steve and I have been playing gigs. We need a piano player, however."

"When?"

"Tomorrow night."

"You're out of your mind."

"Come on, you said you'd been playing in clubs back east."

"In bars. At weddings. The lowest common denominator."

"Perfect. These are tourists. Do you know any Christmas songs?

The Hallelujah Chorus?"

"No."

"Hell, we can do the Spring Show. They'll love it."

"Not if they're coming to hear the Budapest String Quartet."

"But they aren't. They're coming because this is a cool new thing, to pay big bucks to hear music in a cave. We'll give them lots of wine. They'll never know the difference."

"You'd have to give me lots of wine."

"That I can do." Matt summoned a waiter.

Rory, perceiving Sarah's amusement, asked, "You don't really want me to do this, do you?"

"I'd like to hear the Spring Show."

"Done!" Matt chortled. "The guys are heading over to rehearse. Sarah, can you sing?"

The restaurant had only a few patrons that night and they didn't mind impromptu entertainment. The former Napa High Jazz Band played old songs — "The Way You Look Tonight," "Unforgettable," "Only You" — and no one was in a hurry to go back out into the storm. Sarah, not drunk enough to believe that she could sing, made drawings on paper cocktail napkins, and she wondered: was this how they had figured out what love was?

"How about a song from *Oklahoma*?" Matt suggested.

"No," Rory said, emphatically. When they were only sophomores, Rory and Matt won the starring roles of Curley (Rory) and Will (Matt) in the high school musical. This was before Sarah had fallen in love with Rory, and later she suffered greatly to think that she had only gone to one show and had missed five other chances to hear Rory sing "People Will Say We're in Love."

"'Some Enchanted Evening'? 'Till There Was You.' I've got it! 'Stranger in Paradise.'"

"No. No musicals, Matt."

"Have some more wine, Rory. Look, these folks think they've bought a ticket to Paradise. What's wrong with feeding the fantasy? Sarah, what do you want us to play?"

"I would like to hear 'Till There Was You.'"

"You got it."

"You'll pay for this, Sarah," Rory warned, but he played the song. Matt was warbling out the last notes when the restaurant door slammed. A tall blonde woman in a black satin trouser suit with a lavishly beaded red bodice strode into the room.

Tanya Matlock was the daughter of a real estate developer, who, along with his brother, a plastic surgeon, owned Matlock Family Vineyards. The Matlocks were part of a new wave of vintners who did not live in the valley but had purchased part of it, having discovered that owning a winery was an excellent tax write-off. The Matlock team had built a stylish new replacement for an old ghost, and hired vineyard crews to plant and tend grapes, winemakers to make wine, and an artist to design a label with their name on it. People did joke that in order to make a small fortune in wine, you needed to start with a large one.

Tanya was a walking testament to how far money could go in purchasing the good things in life. When she had decided to be a rock star, her plastic surgeon uncle redid her original face with flawless results, although it had not been possible to create a new voice. She performed wherever engagements might be purchased; but she was now thinking of being a lawyer and considering more revisions to her appearance.

She found the Napa Valley dull past endurance. She approved of efforts to bring the civilization to the farmers — a kind of Republican Peace Corps — but when she learned that her mother was substituting the Napa High School Jazz Band for the Budapest String Quartet, she forewent a holiday party to come north and thwart this disaster. A high school jazz band? The Robert Mondavi Winery had presented

Ella Fitzgerald. If necessary, Tanya, herself, would take the stage. "Matt, what is this?" she demanded.

"Let them sing," someone called out. The audience applauded. Matt bowed. As Tanya looked over the band, her eyes lingered on Rory McIntyre.

"I suppose you might do," she said. "We will need some amusement. I sing, you know."

Rory drained his wineglass and stood up. "I've got to get back to Berkeley, Matt."

"All the way to Berkeley?" Tanya drawled. "In this storm?"

"Rory went to Harvard," Matt said. "He can drive in the rain."

"No wonder he takes offense so fast." She smiled at Rory. "We've redone a worker's cottages as a retreat for artists. You're welcome to use it. You might enjoy it."

On a napkin, Sarah was drawing a creature with unnaturally long legs and arms and an hourglass on her chest when Rory bent down beside her. He chuckled appreciatively. "Shall we take the black widow's invitation?" he murmured. "Can you drive, babe?"

"Who's she?" Tanya asked. "The groupie?"

SARAH PUNCHED THE secret code that caused the ponderous winery gate to slide open. As she drove past the buildings and up a hillside, lights blinked on to show the path. At the last turn, the automatic lights illuminated a cottage nestled among the oaks like a plump, irradiated mushroom. They sprinted through the wind and rain to the door. Rory deciphered the lock. The door swung open. Lights flashed on. They stood in the doorway, stupefied.

The artists' retreat was made of mirrors, red satin, and black leather, accented with dead animal skins. Swathes of ruby fabric shrouded the walls between gilded mirrors; a chandelier dripped red globes, like drops of blood. A black leather sofa was flanked by two ruby-colored elephant-shaped end tables. Scattered about the room were sculptures of human forms contorted into poses that were not anatomically feasible, reflected infinitely in the mirrors. The centerpiece was an enormous bed, raised on a platform, festooned with ruby silk and fat, zebra-striped pillows, and waiting, like a gaudy carnival queen, to enfold occupants in a rapacious embrace.

The wind slammed the door, shutting out the sounds of the storm. Sarah was seized by the notion that they had become prisoners in someone else's fantasy. What would a mere artist do here, other than conclude that any other creation was extraneous?

Rory, doffing his wet jacket, strolled about the room. He peered behind a curtain made of long, fat, puffy strings of black plastic. He hooted. "Sal, you have to see this."

It was a bathroom, also done in red and mirrors, except for the fixtures, which were all white ceramic hands, cupped and groping hands. The mirror reflected their faces, Sarah's appalled, Rory's amused. "Do you think the water is blood?" he asked. "Want to take a shower?"

She retreated to the weird living room, and opened a curtain. Outside, the sensible world still existed. Rory's image, like a shadow, materialized behind her in the glass. He drew off her coat and wove his arms around her. "I don't think you like this place, Sarah."

"I think it looks like an operating room on a bad day."

"Shall we turn out the lights and go to bed?"

"That sounds so strange."

"Does it? It sounds kind of natural to me, but I don't run in your bizarre social circles."

"It's, none of it, real."

"No? You feel real enough to me." He drew her to the sofa. The back of one elephant was inset with a panel of buttons, and he began pushing them experimentally. Music went on and off. The fireplace flamed up. The lights dimmed. Sarah, knowing he could go on investigating the buttons for quite a while, picked up a statuette from the panther table. A man had wrapped his left leg in a spiral around his right like a coiled snake. No, not a leg, it was a penis. She set it back down and realized he was watching her, grinning.

"How about some wine?" he asked. "I bet there's a button that finds a bottle and opens it."

"No. No thank you."

"Okay." He leaned toward her and kissed her but she, who always responded to him like flower to sunlight, didn't move. "What?" he asked.

"You said you wanted to talk."

"Did I? When did I say that?"

"When you said you didn't want any more one-night stands."

"I don't."

"What else is there?"

"Damn. You really do want to talk." He sighed and went back to the buttons. The flames leaped and subsided in the fireplace. "Go ahead. Talk."

"What do you think of this place?"

"I think it's too bad you can't go home again because LA has bought it and redone it."

"Would you?"

"Go home? I don't know. Would you?"

"I never wanted to come back here."

"Okay." He nuzzled her neck, pulled at her sweater. "Did we talk enough?"

"Rory, I know you came over to tell me what you said to Jane and to Dibby, that you couldn't — you didn't want — but then it was my fault —"

"And the olive oil. And that black thing."

"But now you've been playing love songs, and drinking, and I think you are a bit drunk —and, well, there you are."

"Where?" His eyes were suddenly serious. "Where are we? Sarah, when you look at me like that, it scares me to death. I feel like you're looking at the inside of my brain."

"Would you tell me about your marriage?"

"No."

"Why not?"

"It's history. I was an idiot. You don't want to hear about it."

"I do if you will tell me."

He had never disclosed to anyone the saga of mortifying confusion, missteps, and calamities that had constituted his life of the past few years, but just then he felt remarkably detached from his past.

"Being cold doesn't explain it all," he said.

CHAPTER 29

H E HAD BEEN somewhat unhappy his first months away at school, Rory told Sarah; by this he meant a depth of misery and loneliness so overwhelming he didn't go home that first Christmas because he knew he wouldn't return. The people he encountered, an elite of those either brilliant or entitled, overawed and humbled him; he would never find a place among them.

He met Dibby that spring, when his roommate invited him to Myopia, a hunt club on the North Shore of Boston named for the distinguishing characteristic of its three founders. The breezy, brittle girl surprised him with her interest; and unlike most girls he had met so far, she did not overwhelm him with her intellect or ambition. They took a walk on the Polo Fields, and he decided that drinking Sherry after a hunt was not really such an odd thing to do.

She invited him to her family's palatial estate in the village of Wishing. He was so dazzled, it was only later that he realized that the giant portrait of Elizabeth II in the entry should have been mad George III. The peculiarities, however, were inescapable. The grand house was exceedingly cold. Dibby's father talked so knowingly about Harvard, Rory was surprised to learn that George Mudell had never been a student there. Dibby's mother, Millicent, quizzed Rory relentlessly on his ignorance of art, until, midway through dinner, she fell asleep and only Rory seemed to notice. Dibby's brother sulkily inferred that affirmative action was responsible for giving a Californian his rightful place at Harvard, and her sister was subject to a condition Rory described as "where you eat and throw up." Dibby was, by far, the most normal of the lot.

In turn, the Mudells, members of a rare tribe of Massachusetts Republicans, were startled to learn that Rory intended to spend the summer in Washington D.C. as an intern for a Democrat, Congressman David Ilillouette, who had written a recommendation for Rory. "He'd called to ask how I was doing. I didn't want to tell him I was so fucking miserable I wanted to die. I said great. He said, 'Wow, when I first went to school, I was so fucking miserable I wanted to die.'"

Still, the Mudells invited Rory to a weekend on Nantucket. He sailed, and played tennis and croquet. He expected someone to check his ticket at intermission and tell him he was in the wrong section, but no one did.

He went to Washington and returned with a dark secret: He didn't like politics; everyone lied. Not Ilillouette, of course; he was magnificent. But he had teased Rory, telling him, "I think you belong on the dark side." What was that, Rory asked. Journalism, David Ilillouette said.

His new penchant for the truth brought him to grief that fall with Dibby. At a polo match, she, tipsy on Champagne, introduced Rory as the scion of a wealthy winemaking family and he felt obliged to clarify that his mother's family had lost their winery fifty years earlier and his father made wine in his garage, a hobby he supported by his auto repair shop. Dibby hysterically dismissed him forever; Rory was surprised that his chief reaction was relief.

But then, after the Thanksgiving hunt at Myopia, George overindulged in Scotch and landed in the custody of the Wishing police. He called Rory to see if he might slip up to Wishing and drive him home. He liked Rory, a soused and melancholy George admitted. He

was sorry it hadn't worked out with Dibby; sometimes she got reality confused. Sometimes life was damned hard. He didn't really drink.
Sometimes he just got so damned tired of waiting. Thus, Rory learned
that the grand Wishing estate belonged, not to George, but to his elderly aunt who lived in Florida and refused to come to Massachusetts
as long as it kept voting for Democrats. When she died, George would
inherit and sell it, but as long as she insisted on existing, the family
lived precariously on the edge, paying Myopia dues instead of buying
heating oil. George managed other people's money, and Millicent decorated their houses. They knew precisely how they should live if only
they could afford it. Their knowledge was their torment, their fantasy
was their doom, their debts were prodigious, and yet they had so per-
fected the art of living as they thought they should, no one questioned
how they did it.

Back at the mansion, Dibby was drinking wine from a bottle. He
would hate her, she said, now that he knew. No, he insisted, no. Six
weeks later, she told him she was pregnant.

"I asked her to marry me," he said. "I had to but I thought it couldn't
be that bad. My parents liked being married. I was an idiot."

The wedding was set for June. A marriage, he learned, could not
be accomplished in less time. But what about the baby, he asked.
Oh, that, she said. Gone. A mistake. "I don't know why I didn't run."
Cursed with perception, he began to understand that he was entering
a world more rigidly programmed than the one he had left behind.
The comparative poverty of his own life had allowed for improvisa-
tion; here, money was the inexorable ink with which the description
of life was written. He tried to broach the subject with Dibby, but she
didn't understand. She had never questioned the patterns of life she
had learned. Why would she want to live any other way? Many people
did, he said. The business of life, she replied, was to be sure they had
enough money to be spared that possibility.

On the eve of his wedding, Rory escaped from the rehearsal dinner and went for a walk alone. He ended up at the Massachusetts Institute of Technology, where a flyer caught his eye: a lecture, "The Uses of Infinity," was scheduled for the next day. At the wedding, the noise, the heat, the throng of strangers, and "all the dead flowers" made him feel queasy. He left the reception and went to the lecture. When he returned, no one had noticed his absence, least of all his wife, who was drunk. He kept thinking about the lecture; it was like a gift from an enchantress who had not been invited to the wedding: a fascination.

The honeymoon was a disaster. Dibby had wanted to go to Tahiti but the rich aunt only gave them a Caribbean cruise. She got sunburned; the sun would not have been as hot in Tahiti. He learned just how much his wife drank.

He worked that summer in a law office. He hated it, but it was preferable to their flat. On humid sweltering days, they fought about things he didn't care about: can openers, vacuum cleaners, and laundry. Dibby's discontent sprang from what she viewed as his working-class aversion to spending the money he would earn after he graduated from Harvard Law School. He began sitting in on physics classes at MIT, wondering if he could transfer. The night he told Dibby he didn't want to be a lawyer, she returned to Wishing.

"I never thought it was so hard to be happy," he said.

On a cold winter night, he got a call from the Wishing police. Dibby had been arrested, driving drunk. The chief said the first time she had been picked up drunk she was thirteen. "Do something," he said. Rory went to Wishing. George explained Dibby had only had a drink because she was upset. She was pregnant; this time it was real. Rory mentioned this circumstance vaguely, as if it were a contagious condition Dibby had picked up on the Metro; but the working-class ethics she deplored became the hook that hauled him back into the marriage.

George proposed that Rory move to Wishing, commute to school and keep Dibby happy; Rory complied, and that spring Lucy was born. Rory took a summer job writing for *The Wishing Chronicle;* it almost paid a nanny's wages. He was not unhappy, living in a house filled with unread books and whispers of history, reporting on the antics of Selectmen and the School Committee. Had Ilillouette been right? George, all enthusiasm, read Rory's articles aloud at Myopia and thought about running for selectman so Rory could write about him, too.

He rarely saw Dibby until the August night in the newsroom when he heard over the police scanner that Dibby had been stopped for drunk driving. At the police station, he found her in a panic because this time she could go to jail and her name would be in the paper. Her genuine terror eclipsed their estrangement, but only for one night, because Rory did not keep her name out of the Wishing newspaper. After this, even a mansion was not big enough for both of them.

Rory moved back to Cambridge. He had an idea for a thesis; he started writing it: a novel about an idiot. He didn't know about Avery until Dibby brought both children to him. Avery was three weeks old. She didn't want them, and if he didn't either, she would put them in foster care.

He left school. He told his mother she didn't need to move Joe to Massachusetts. His Russian neighbor, Olga, cared for the children while he worked. They ate a lot of fish soup, but they'd survive. These conversations with Jean had the peculiar effect of persuading him that it might be true, although nothing reassured her as much as the time she called and Congressman Ilillouette answered the phone. Visiting Boston, he had dropped by to see how Rory was doing; Rory had run out to buy milk. Babysitting was part of his constituent service, Ilillouette explained.

George Mudell also visited; he was the only member of his family who did. He promised that when he got his money he would help, and finally, the aunt in Florida died. George and Millicent, celebrating the event they had waited for their entire adult lives, drove into a tree on Topsfield Road.

George's will was read, and, to everyone's shock, they learned that he had divided his estate in half, one part to be split equally among his three children; the other half went to Rory, for George's grandchildren.

Dibby descended on Rory, livid. She wanted a divorce. She wanted everything her father had given to her children, including the Wedgewood Peter Rabbit dishes. She wanted that money; and so she wanted the children. The fight began, and it trudged on until the night Rory got another call from the Wishing police chief. Dibby had been driving on the wrong side of the road. She refused to stop for police officers and led them on a drunken chase that only ended when she spun off the road. She tried to hit the officer who arrested her. The old man was gone; what did Rory want them to do? Keep her, Rory said; let her wake up in jail. That was his choice, the chief replied, but what about the kids, who had been in the backseat? The next day Rory told his lawyer to tell Dibby she could have every dish and every dollar; just give him the kids and permission to leave Massachusetts. She agreed. It was finished. He was free.

"I've put you to sleep," he said to Sarah as he reached the end of his story.

"No," she said. "What happened to the story you were writing?"

"I don't know. I probably threw it away. I hope I did."

"Did it have a name?"

"*The Hero of Paradise Lost.* It's from a quote by Byron. 'Who is the hero of *Paradise Lost?*' Byron answered his own question: 'Satan, of course.'"

CHAPTER 30

THE STORM WAS still raging when Sarah awoke in the giant bed. By daylight, the cottage looked weirder than ever. She was alone. She didn't know where Rory had slept, but if the night before, he had talked himself into a vow of celibacy, she understood. She had asked, and now she understood why love for him ranked lower than astrology and ghosts.

He came out from behind the creepy black plastic curtain, drying his hair with a zebra-striped towel. "Good morning," he said. "Matt called, wondering if you'd like to go have a mud bath in Calistoga while we rehearse. It couldn't be any stranger than this place. There's no kitchen in all this sybaritic splendor. Shall we go get breakfast?"

Only at the door did his easy banter falter. "Thanks for listening to me," he said, studying the doorknob. She nodded. Love, she thought, shoo, vanish, begone.

They went to Vern's Copper Kitchen. He was starving. He ordered the Farmers Breakfast, and his eyes twinkling, he added snails and bear claws. "D'you remember when Dad scared you when he offered you snails or bear claws?"

"He was always doing that. His Buttercream favorites."

"I loved that place. I remember, when I was fifteen we had to write about our dream jobs, and I said mine was to work at Buttercream and eat all the doughnuts I could."

"My fantasy, when I was fifteen, probably would have been to make out with you in the parking lot," she recalled, and then she dropped her coffee while he choked on his. When they had mopped the table free of spilled coffee, she asked, "Did you know I had a crush on you?"

"Yes."

"Did your mother tell you?"

"No! I figured it out for myself."

"How?"

"I knew the night you went on the Zipper with me."

"The what?"

"That ride at the fair. I was there with — who was I with?"

The Zipper. Metal cages on a rotating spear. "Diane Crupack," she said.

"Yeah. Good old Diane. She wouldn't ride on the Zipper, and there had to be two in a basket. Then I saw you and Kate." Kate refused but Sarah went on the Zipper with him, twice. Every time she opened her eyes, she was upside-down. The thrill of crashing into him paled against her fear that they would die together, like Romeo and Juliet. She had forgotten; the brain really did block out traumas.

"It really pissed Diane off. I had to win her a stuffed elephant to make up for it. And I asked Kate if you liked me."

"There is no other reason a person would ride on the Zipper. What did Kate say?"

"She told me I had a terminal case of fat head. And I thought, wow, if Sarah hasn't said anything to Kate, she must really be in love with me."

Sarah looked away from his teasing grin to the window and the rain.

"I loved it, Sarah. Don't you think I'd bring it back if I could?"

❧

RORY ENTERED WITH Sarah, beneath the marquee for "The World-Famous Therapeutic Mud Baths," and when the attendant asked if they were a couple, to Sarah's surprise, he said yes.

"I thought you had to rehearse," she said.

"Oh well. I'd rather get in the mud with you."

They were escorted to a room with two tubs of thick, dark, sulfur-scented mud. Sarah undressed quickly and slipped into her mud before Rory came out of his dressing room. She put cucumber slices on her eyes. She heard the mud squish in the tub next to her.

"Jesus," Rory muttered. "Is this really therapeutic? Do we smell like this all day?"

"Rory," she said. "I wish I could read the novel you were writing."

"No."

"Why not?"

"Because it was terrible. Besides, you won't let me look at your drawings."

"That's different. They're not finished. It's like being half-dressed."

"But I like you half-dressed. Of course, there is something to be said for nothing. I can't believe you forgot about the Zipper, Sarah. It's one of my best memories of you, with your eyes about to fall out of your head. Why didn't you hold on to me?"

"I was afraid I was going to throw up on you."

"But you don't do such mortal things. Have you forgotten about the time we climbed Half Dome, too?"

"No."

"God, I was scared on those cables."

"You were?" She took the cucumbers off her eyes to look at him.

"Yeah, I knew if you fell off, my mother would kill me. I was so relieved when we got to the top, I would have kissed you again except you didn't look like you felt like fooling around." He glanced at her. "I just wanted you to know, it wasn't always a one-way street. But I guess you figured that out soon enough."

Sarah's expression changed, from faintly puzzled to bewildered.

"Oh no," he groaned. "Have you forgotten about the night we drove to the city?"

"No."

"Did you think I had?"

"You were somewhat drunk."

"I wasn't that drunk, baby. Why do you think I stopped?"

"Well, I didn't know what I was doing. I'd never kissed anyone so I didn't know if I was doing right but probably not —"

Mud oozed down his chest as he sat up, looking distraught. "Sarah, it almost killed me, but all I could think was, oh, God, she trusts me. I almost lost my mind. But you thought — oh Jesus, if this stuff weren't so disgusting, I'd drown myself. Sal, I didn't put you off sex, did I?"

"No."

"This is a relief. But —"

"We can't talk about it here."

"Why not? We can't do anything else, up to our necks in mud."

The attendant opened the door. "Time's up," she said. "Now for the mineral bath, and then your massage."

By the end of the treatment, Sarah and Rory were so relaxed they could have believed they were the center of the universe; they could have conversed with Mother Earth without hiccoughs. They might even have returned to the artist's cottage, but Matt was pacing in the lobby.

"Dammit, Rory, what are you doing? You were supposed to leave Sarah here and meet us."

"I was? Oh damn."

"Tanya's having a fit. She has a tux for you to try on."

"A tux?" Sarah echoed.

"Hey, this is no shabby deal. It's black tie all the way. Sarah, can you take Rory's car? Meet us at the winery at six. There's a reception before the concert. Rory, you come with me, and try not to offend Tanya any more than you already have. You can have him back tonight, Sarah."

Rory winked at her. "Tonight," he said.

CHAPTER 31

B Y SIX O'CLOCK that evening, all the beneficial effects of the mud bath had evaporated.Sarah sat in the parking lot of the Matlock Family Winery, enervated if not paralyzed by an afternoon of frantic activity, driven by a question she knew was entirely unimportant in the scheme of the universe: what was she going to wear? Why had she cared? It had nothing to do with Tanya Matlock's rapacious gaze, crawling over Rory. No, he would not even notice what she wore. Yet, she had obsessed, even as she reminded herself that if there was something in St. Helena besides a feed store and Goodman's, specializing in Pendleton shirts, she couldn't spend her dwindling funds on another dress and stockings; she was not going to the opera again. She was wishing Gabriel would appear like a fairy godmother to turn the blood-red satin sheets from the artist's cottage into something with or without wings — she didn't know how to sew; she had not yet done sutures — when a mad idea dropped into her head. And now she was sitting in Rory's car, devitalized, sapped, and knackered. Also, too nervous to get out.

The Matlocks had kept the old ghost winery for storage, but it was dwarfed by a gigantic new building, a design inspired by a French chateau with touches of a Chinese pagoda.

A giant clock on it read six-fifteen. She turned on the radio. Paul

Simon was singing, "Still Crazy After All These Years." She turned it off. She had listened to enough radio news during a wild drive to San Francisco: energy shortages, power outages; a dictator had a terrible new weapon, and a controversy raged over the question: could women climb telephone poles as well as men? Six-twenty: Rain was still falling steadily. It was growing cold. She forced herself to get out of the car for only one reason: she did not want to miss the music.

The Matlocks had blown up most of a mountain to create an underground space to store their wines; the entrance was a towering slab of metal, carved in vines and grapes. At the door, a waiter handed Sarah a flute of sparkling wine and she finished it as she passed the marble statues that lined an entry way: Rodin's *The Kiss* and Michelangelo's *David*, busts of Christopher Columbus, Vince Lombardi, and Richard Nixon. "Not the originals, but just as good," a man near her was saying. "The Matlocks don't do anything by halves."

She came into a huge, vaulted room, a giant's world lit by hundreds of electric candles and painted in Italian-style frescos: two processions of knights, ladies, dogs, horses, and peasants led to a central throne where royalty sat beneath a gilded canopy. Below this was a stage set with a grand piano and drums. Black chairs were set up in rows; beyond them, people mingled, drinking and eating tidbits served by roving waiters. They all looked like they had flown in from the San Francisco Opera, not the least bit disheveled by the flight.

"Here you are, Sarah!" Matt, in his tux, bustled up. Tanya Matlock was with him, draped in black satin, with ropes of red stones dripping down her chest. Another woman with them was older, heftier, and dressed in gold brocade — Sarah recognized her: she was the model for the painted queen on the wall.

"So this is the girl Rory's been waiting for all day!" she exclaimed. "Sarah, is it? What a lovely gown! Where did you get it?"

"Paris," a voice said behind her. Sarah looked up at Rory, resplendent in a tux, and she accidentally chugged her second glass of wine. Tanya eyed her but said nothing. Of course, Sarah realized, she had stolen Tanya's colors.

"Well, isn't this fun?" Mrs. Matlock asked. "And how exciting to meet some natives! Matt just told us, that his father came here to work at the insane asylum and that Rory's great-great — how many greats? — grandfather actually built a winery! What did your ancestors do, Sarah?"

"They picked the grapes."

"And did you learn to be so democratic at Harvard, Rory?" Tanya smiled to see she had riled him.

It cost him an effort but Rory managed to yawn and look bored. "Sometimes I do wish Sarah weren't so much smarter than I am. Excuse us." He gripped Sarah's arm and walked away. His fit of temper abated as he rubbed the black fur of Sarah's bathrobe. "You went to the city?"

"The Bay Bridge was open. You don't mind —"

"Mind? Mind? Why isn't it falling off?"

"Velcro. It just sticks, so you don't have to" — she was interrupted as he kissed her — "sew it."

"Are you wearing that black thing too?"

"No, it was shredded."

"What, then? Nothing?"

"No! But my French underwear —"

He was moving again, taking her with him, behind the stage, through a green velvet curtain and into a tapering space, carved out of rock, covered with mold and dust-filled webs. The ceiling barely cleared Rory's head. Dim lights flickered in sconces.

"What is it?" she asked as they went deeper into a tunnel.

"The old original wine caves," he said. "Chinese workers dug them by hand. One time my dad took us to the ruins of my mom's old winery. We found caves like this, filled with bats and spiders. Snakes."

The tunnel ended at a stone chamber, a forgotten place, filled with old barrels, rusty relics, dusty bottles. The air was still as if time itself had been put in a bottle and left there to age.

"How strange," Sarah said. "The world outside could end and we would never know it. We could be the only ones left in the world."

But he was not inclined to discuss the nature of space and time. He swung her off her feet and set her on a wine barrel so they were eye to eye; his had a wicked gleam.

"I was thinking, Rory," she said, "that it might not be a bad idea if you gave up sex."

"No yet," he said. "Not yet."

SARAH FLOATED ALONG past the audience, whose collective curiosity as to what music they were going to hear had been considerably mellowed by the wine. She wafted into a chair next to two bejeweled women. "That piano player is gorgeous," one woman was saying. "But he doesn't look like a Russian. But the fat one with wild hair, he definitely is Russian."

"We're here for the music, Marion," her companion replied. "And I heard they're natives,"

"Natives? Of where?"

"Here."

"No. Where are the Russians?"

"Lost in the storm."

"Natives. Really. Well. I might slip that piano player my room key."

"Good heavens, is that underwear hanging out of his pocket?"

"Oh dear God, he must be Russian."

Sarah noticed Tanya Matlock watching her. She smiled glowingly, and the music began.

“GODDAMN, RORY, WE were great.”

“It wasn’t too bad.”

“Bad? Hell, half the audience is sure we’re the Budapest String Quartet. Hey, thanks for doing ‘Have Yourself a Merry Little Christmas.’”

“I’ll get even some day.”

“Hey, I’m not the one who decided to do ‘I Left My Heart in San Francisco.’”

“I knew the music.”

“But everybody loved it. You know what it is? It’s romance. That’s all people really want. You hear this music, and you’re back in high school, you’re back in love, the world is simple. That’s Paradise. You believe in love, you believe in everything. You know, we could do something with this. You could give up this science shit and I could get out of the restaurant. You want the mysteries of the universe: here they are. We could be the new Rat Pack. Oh, hey, there’s Tanya, heading this way. Do me a favor, Rory: don’t stand next to me. Better yet, go find Sarah.”

CHAPTER 32

I T IS ONE thing to indulge in a fit of amorous daring in a cave and another altogether to risk being stranded with the object of that passion. Faced with the imminent flooding of the Napa River and an extended stay in the artists' cottage, Sarah and Rory scrambled back to San Francisco. They parted at her flat where she found her heater had been repaired. The rooms were warm. She dared not wonder what might happen next; it was too akin to dreaming. A working heater surpassed her expectations.

Half an hour later, her phone rang. "Are you awake?" Rory asked. She told him her heater was repaired. He'd had a message from his kids. The conversation drifted into sleepy inanity.

"Am I keeping you up?" he asked.

"No, I'm in bed."

"Sal," he said, "can I come over?"

In the morning, she mentioned shyly that she had to go to work and was flustered by his amazement. "It's just temporary. I'm helping out at the Free Clinic; they were short-staffed."

"How long have you been doing this?"

"Since you said I wasn't doing anything," she replied, thereby ending that conversation.

He drove her to the clinic, and when she finished her shift that evening, she found him standing, with a squeamish expression, amid the dazed, drugged, ragged people seeking help.

"I usually walk home," she told him.

"Yes, that's what I was afraid of."

He asked if she wanted to have dinner but looked without enthusiasm at the places offering cheap vegetarian or Chinese food. The jarring music, the dog feces, the drunks in the gutter, and the people in black leather and spiked hot pink hairdos were all unusually abundant. How many cases of food poisoning did they treat each day, he asked. Sarah remembered a Spanish place in Cow Hollow that Damon liked. "Let's go," he said.

The tavern was bustling but Rory was quiet. It was too romantic, Sarah speculated, too hot or too cold, too spicy. How different this was from dinner with Gabriel: she never worried about what he was thinking; it was irrelevant. She never wondered what would happen next, because nothing did. "I didn't realize there would be so many gay men admiring you," she said anxiously.

"Are there?" Rory was knocked out of his meditations. They shared a dish of paella and a bottle of Spanish wine. They drank a sherry; its heat rose to Sarah's brain. She fell onto a gold cloud that drifted toward the stars. Rory paid the bill and they left.

THERE FOLLOWED AN interlude during which Sarah felt that they had fallen inside a shimmering glass Christmas ornament, the kind hanging everywhere just then. She could see the outside world, although it was tinged with gossamer hues. Inside it was their own private nest.

He stayed with her. He slept with her at night and in the morning, he made coffee, got the *Chronicle*, and came back to bed, and she awoke to find him beside her. When they finally did leave her bed, he drove her to the clinic and went on to his lab in Berkeley. When she finished work, he was waiting for her. They tried new restaurants. They went to a movie and to *Beach Blanket Babylon*. He offered to take her to the Condor Club, but she declined, so instead they went to City Lights books. They went to a jazz club; they danced. Some nights they stayed in and he cooked. It was fun, he insisted, to cook for someone whose favorite food was not macaroni and cheese. On those nights, they went to bed early, but they talked, too. They talked about everything except what they were doing, except once, when he asked her to dance and he said, "It's been a long time." And one other time, when Harry's box of condoms was empty. "I hate those things," he said cheerfully. "Hell, I don't care if you get pregnant."

His children called him every night. They couldn't sleep unless he told them a story about two kids and their mysterious friend, the Moonbubble. Sarah listened, too. She knew this time was only temporary, a random quirk, an accidental wrinkle. He was a sociable man craving companionship, a passionate man in need of distraction. Sometimes she thought he liked talking as much as he liked sex, but then she would think, maybe not. She had walked too many times through the shambles of Haight Street to make too much of anything. The dawning of the Age of Aquarius had not survived the fragility of its dreamers. The world they had grown up in had shattered into so many fragments it was impossible to determine what would be included as it was reassembled. What was true one day was false the next; what was touted as healthy turned out to be toxic. The allies of today were the enemies of tomorrow. Styles changed, fantasies and truths were interchangeable, and nothing was meant to last but only to be consumed. When one thing was depleted, society rolled out something new, and the least of this was love; yet in their rose-gold glass bubble, they were happy.

This lasted almost two weeks until a new winter storm moved in. That morning, as they lay in bed, Sarah formed a resolution: Gabriel, with his seemingly limitless income, was always short on cash, but Rory wouldn't let her pay for anything. When he said, "See you tonight?" she replied, "Tonight, I'll cook."

"You will?" he asked. "Really?"

By noon, her impulse had brought her to the edge of a mental breakdown. She left the clinic to buy a cookbook but was overwhelmed by choices: Indian, Thai, Julia Child. Her head became a jumble of menus, none of which could be cooked in fewer than three days. When Rory walked into the waiting room that afternoon, she hid in the back.

"Are you all right?" the clinic director asked.

"No." She explained her dilemma.

"You're worried about cooking for that guy?" Dr. Castro asked. "Sarah, you could give him Wonder Bread and Velveeta cheese, and he'll think it's wonderful." He gave her a friendly pat on the shoulder, along with a shove in Rory's direction. "Don't let it get you down," he said.

Stumbling toward Rory, Sarah detoured to greet Jimmy, a sweet, slow-witted man who had no pressing medical problems, but came by the clinic daily to talk. He wanted Sarah to see his new shoes. She admired them until Jimmy nodded in Rory's direction. "Your boyfriend is here," he told her. "I don't want to make him jealous." He laughed boisterously and shook Rory's hand. Rory looked pained. As they descended the stairs, he asked how long she planned to minister to the dregs of humanity.

"Sometimes I do believe you went to Harvard," she retorted.

He was startled into a moment of silence, after which he chose to chuckle, moderately. He said he would have to get used to the fact that he was sleeping with Mother Theresa and this made Sarah feel unaccountably low, worse even than Julia Child's recipes.

"Don't let what get you down?" he asked. "What was that guy talking about?"

"Dinner," she said sorrowfully. "Are you hungry, Rory?"

"Are you really cooking?"

"I can't cook anything." She stopped in the middle of Haight Street. Breaks screeched; horns honked. Rory caught her arm and sprinted to the curb.

"Tell you what," he panted, "Let's go to that grocery store."

Sarah's relief was immense but incomplete. He had rescued her from her offer, but she knew it was because he was nervous about death by food poisoning. By the time they returned to her flat with pasta, sauce, wine, and a box of Presto logs, her pleasure in his company was demolished. Morosely, she tried to light the fire while he talked to Lucy and Avery. With inexplicable pain, she listened to him telling his children he loved them; then, he was talking to her. "Sal, I think you leave the log in the paper bag, honey. You light the bag to start the fire." Sarah let the match drop and bent her head into her hands.

Rory was flummoxed. He was not unfamiliar with the labyrinth of female emotions, as he viewed them, and he, far more than Sarah, allowed her admission to the club of bewildering women; but as much as he theoretically acknowledged that she possessed emotions that could confuse him, the prospect that she might break down over lighting a Presto log confounded him.

The telephone rang. He answered it, scowled, and handed it to Sarah.

"Sarah!" Flake cried. "Are you coming to New Year's?"

"You don't come to New Year's," she said. "It comes to you. After Christmas."

"But we're starting to party now. It'll be the party to end all parties. Hey, we thought maybe you'd come over tonight. Gabe's under the bed."

She had hardly thought of Gabriel, except to be glad that he had made her dance. "Why?"

"We don't know, but we thought you could find out. I'll put the phone under the bed."

"Gabriel?" she asked the silence. "What are you doing?"

"Everything." His voice was slurred.

"Why?"

"I lost, Sarah. My mother called here and Flake answered the phone. She got the whole story out of him. She told my uncle I'd filled the house with degenerates. We have to leave."

In the background, Sarah could hear the party to end all parties. "Do they know?"

"No. They'll hate me."

"No, they won't. No one expected it to last."

"I did."

"You can find another house."

"Not like this one."

"If you had a job —"

"Why? Why do you want a job? To get a house. Why do you want a house? Because you have a family. I don't. I never will. I went to see Damon, Sarah. He told me he couldn't see me anymore. And you probably hate me, too."

"No."

"I went to Paris without you."

"I know. Thank you for the bathrobe."

"I got a gargoyle for Sterling. I get passionate when I get drunk, Sarah. Passionate and sad. It's why I should stick to drugs. You're probably pregnant."

"That's — unlikely."

"Really? You mean, we didn't do it?" He sighed in relief. "I couldn't remember. I mean, not that it wouldn't have been great, but —"

"I have to go now, Gabriel."

"Well, come over for the party if you want. It will be wild."

She hung up. The fire was crackling; Rory had lit the log properly, and the room was stifling. She wanted to get away from the heat, the absurdity of what she'd been doing, dream-making again. She said, "I think I'll go for a walk."

"Okay." He got to his feet.

"I'd rather go by myself."

"No."

No? What did he mean, no?

"It's late, Sarah. It's dark. It's not safe."

"I don't care."

"I do."

The telephone rang again and she answered it. "Is Rory there?" a shrill voice demanded. "Why is he there?"

Rory seized the phone, and Sarah fled out the door. She did not get far; she tripped on her shoestring and tumbled down the stairs. She clutched her ankle in a daze of pain as she listened to Rory's cold voice. "I didn't call them; they called me, and if you were wise — no, I am not saying you're stupid. Look, I can't talk now. No, I'm not dropping anything on you. Yes, we'll talk, but not now. Don't call me here. Yes, I'll call you tomorrow. Goodbye, Dibby."

Sarah had dragged herself up when Rory flung the door open. He was anticipating a run, and so he nearly knocked her down the stairs again.

CHAPTER 33

"I NEED A GIFT," Sarah said in reply to the sales clerk's merry greeting.

"How unusual! December twenty-third, and you need a gift! Man or woman?"

"Man."

"Well, if he rates a smile like that, I'd recommend our Italian silk boxers. We have them in gold, red, and hot pink."

"No. That's too — too — I thought, maybe a book, but —" From her shopping bag, Sarah pulled *The Tao of Physics* and *The Art of Fiction*.

"How thrilling."

"I am terrible at Christmas."

"We have some lovely sweaters."

"His mother and his ex-wife gave him sweaters."

"Oh dear. We don't want to call to mind the ex. Or the mama. So we are thinking somewhere between a sweater and boxers. Aha! A belt! It suggests interesting possibilities."

"No."

"Oh well. Cologne?"

"I like the way he smells now."

"My, this is serious. How about an inflatable kayak?"

"He has two children."

"A coffeemaker."

"He has one. I was thinking, maybe, a pen."

"A pen? To write with?"

SHE RETURNED TO the clinic with her shopping bag, which now contained five gifts, including gold Italian silk boxers. She would give him the pen and save the other things for another time. Another time? The thought made her dizzy.

"Sarah," Dr. Castro greeted her, "how was your dinner?"

"Dinner?"

"What did you end up cooking?"

"Dinner — oh, I forgot — that is, we forgot to eat."

"Don't tell me," he laughed. "I'm too old."

He handed Sarah a chart, and she went into an exam room. The young man waiting there was dressed in camouflage and his hair was bright pink spikes. He said, "Oh hell."

"I beg your pardon?"

"No offense, but I'd rather have a man doc, if you don't mind."

"But I am not a doctor. I am only going to get a history." She focused on the questions — name, address, birthdate, sex; she was, for a pleasurable second, distracted.

"You okay?" he asked.

"What? Oh, yes. I am."

"You keep smiling."

"I'm so sorry." The most brilliant med student in her class had been told his only flaw was that he smiled too much. It was not always appropriate, for example, if one was delivering news of a terminal disease.

"Got some last night, did you?"

"What?"

"Hell, you're lit up like a Christmas tree. Okay, doc, I'll tell you my problem."

When she had finished his chart, she went into the hallway and slumped against a wall. She, Sarah Glass, had understood everything he'd told her. Somewhere, a radio was playing. The Eagles, "One of These Nights." Sometimes it happens. She admitted this with wonderment. But she had to stop smiling.

Only when she had finished her shift and did not find Rory frowning at patients in the waiting room, did her euphoria begin to dissipate. She waited for fifteen minutes, but only Jimmy showed up. "I am sad today," he told her.

"Where are your new shoes?"

"Lost them."

Finally, she limped home alone. It was raining, and her ankle ached as she climbed the stairs. Rory's socks were on the floor. He had left early, in the dark, and forgotten his socks. Why? She hadn't thought about it till now. Should she call him? No, first, she should do laundry. She added his socks to her basket. What if he felt sick and that was why he left? He might be sick. She dialed Rory's number. The telephone rang five times before he answered. She slammed the receiver down. Seconds passed and it began to ring. Sarah fled with the laundry basket.

Of all settings in which to descend into despair, anxiety, and confusion over a relationship, a laundromat is the most fitting. When Sarah finally found, in the row of dented, rusting machines, a washer that worked. When she had checked to be sure the man sleeping on the floor was not dead, she sat down on a plastic chair and contemplated the sorrowful sight of discarded single socks and empty soap boxes. The rain was falling harder now, and even if her remaining quarters were enough to dry her clothes, they would get wet again when she carried them home.

Amid the lonely thuds and moans of the washing machine, she could either read a six-month-old magazine or ponder the universal question: what had happened? What had she done wrong? Had she got it all wrong? What had she missed? How could she survive, having only the instincts of a badly wired robot that stumbled, visionless, off cliffs? That was five universal questions. She had given Gabriel up, but now she yearned for his inane babble. When she ran out of quarters, she would go find him, and if he was still hiding under his bed, she would join him. Where was Rory? That made six questions, all unanswered.

RORY WAS, AT the moment, swearing vividly as he looked for a parking place. His day had been bad, even by his standards. Of the night, he had no complaints but he had awakened at three in the morning, beset with the chilling thoughts that can plague the mind in that lonely hour — chiefly, what was he doing? He drove to Berkeley, but his flat was too silent, clean, and cold; he couldn't sleep there either. He went to work. He was blearily contemplating his notes when the director of his project walked into the lab.

"So, McIntyre, this is when you work." Dr. Cageman cut short Rory's vague and guilty response. "I was wondering if you might be free to have lunch with me today."

Rory worked poorly that morning, distracted by the notion that he would be fired that afternoon. Why not? His work all fall had been uninspired, when it was not interrupted by the timetables of child care and the calamities of chicken pox. He would probably fire himself.He left the lab and walked to Telegraph Avenue where vendors in the rain were hawking jewelry, pipes, and Guatemalan sweaters. He unnerved himself by examining a tray of rings. He considered buying Sarah a cookbook, but his marriage, however brief, had taught him the inadvisability of having a sense of humor in choosing gifts. He studied a set of colored pencils in a cedar box. His ex-wife would have told him it was not romantic to give someone pencils. Why was her voice clattering so insistently in his head? He chose earrings, fire opals that reminded him of Sarah's eyes, and went to meet Bob Cageman at a Thai restaurant called Lucky House.

He was reconciled to being fired. He did not like Cageman, a short, fat, bald, self-important man whose early attempts to establish a personal rapport with Rory had been limited to complaints about the child support he was obliged to pay. Conversations, even about the receiver, had dwindled in the last few weeks. Rory surmised his chicken pox had been off-putting as well as inconvenient. Cageman seemed to have no interests beyond the vast empty reaches of space. He spent much of each year at the South Pole in frozen isolation; the man who contemplated mysteries of the universe was devoid of wonder.

They ordered. The server brought them Thai tea. Cageman asked if Rory had found an apartment. Housing was difficult in Berkeley. Rory had children, didn't he? Rory decided to cut lunch short and fire himself. "Math is inadequate to describe the universe," he said. "We add nothing but blurred images to our knowledge of the world. The more sophisticated our equipment becomes, the less able we are to communicate."

"How interesting," Cageman said, in the same bland voice with which he had ordered beef satay. "I was actually only curious as to how soon you might be able finish the receiver."

"I could do it in few months, I suppose."

"Good. Beyond that, it may be of little use to me. I have received some disturbing news."

"About your grant?" Rory knew funding was becoming tight, but Cageman, with twenty-five years of research, had seemed as secure as anyone might be.

"No, my grant is fine. But it seems I'm going to die. An absurd statement. We're all going to die. Only I am dying sooner than I expected to. Ah, here comes our food."

When lunch was concluded, Rory returned to his flat feeling as if he had been hollowed out by insects. He fell into a sleep filled with bizarre dreams only to be awakened by the telephone. He knew it was Sarah the moment he heard the panicky click of a hang-up.

He was now battling traffic, grousing. Why did a rainstorm in California cause drivers to abandon their wits? Still, he knew the only way to tell Sarah he wasn't coming to the city that night was to drive over and do it. He had ample time to expand his message as he sat in the pile-up of traffic on the Bay Bridge.

He would tell her he had been out of his mind. This idyll would end; it had to. If he could not bear the thought, it made no difference. She was the best and brightest of women; he had peaked in usefulness at seventeen, when, on a two-three count with two outs in the bottom of the ninth inning, he had hit a grand slam. This would remain his sole achievement, his only justification for using the dwindling resources of the earth. Beyond this, there was nothing to distinguish him from the other lowlifes who hung around her seeking solace. He would tell her all this, if he ever found a place to park. He did, and he strode to Sarah's flat, only to be stymied at her steps. The lights were out. She wasn't home.

THE STRING OF Christmas bells on the door jingled, and Sarah made the mistake of looking up. The new arrival squeezed his sack of clothes into one machine, sat down next to her, and said too bad that it was raining. She did not reply. He asked if she spoke English. He was an English major; maybe they could arrange lessons. She opened a magazine and was reading about a woman who had met an angel disguised as Big Foot when the bells rang again. A shadow fell over her. Rory McIntyre bent down in front of her.

"How did you know I was here?" she asked.

He drew a silk lace wisp of a bra from his pocket. "You left a clue on your steps."

He stashed her laundry basket in his car and drove badly until they ran out of road. He parked in the deserted lot at Land's End. The sea was hidden by dense clouds. She tried not to think about another night, a drunk and frightened boy, a shy, awkward, awe-struck girl. Instead she wondered if anyone had ever driven unknowingly straight into the ocean. In the dark, a hand touched her hair and she was engulfed in embrace not so different from that long ago night. Lights flashed over them. They sprang apart. A police officer peered in the window. Rory jabbered a muddled explanation that they were going to the Cliff House for dinner.

"Jesus," he groaned as the smirking officer strolled back to his car. "Talk about Rebobs."

"Rebobs?" She remembered: they were a Napa legend, winged apes that preyed on teen-agers who parked at the end of the lonely Partricks Road to make out. Rory was far more likely to have encountered one than she.

"I had a weird dream about them," he said. "Never mind. Let's go eat." The wind and rain buffeted them as they walked to the restaurant. Sarah tried to keep up with Rory's rapid pace, but her ankle began to throb. He halted. "What is it?"

"Nothing. I twisted my ankle when I tripped on the stairs."

"Today?"

"No, last night."

He rolled his eyes to heaven; his day, as a series of disasters, was complete.

"I wonder," Sarah said, "could we talk about it inside?"

They were seated in a corner of the Cliff House, so named because it clings the edge of the world above the sea. Rory ordered a whiskey, Sarah, a gin gimlet. His face was so grim, she thought she might go to the ladies' room for a while. She stood up, winced, and sat back down. He fell on his knees and took her ankle in his hands. "Why didn't you say anything?"

"I didn't feel any pain last night."

Rory smiled, but briefly and slumped back into his chair. He ordered another drink. He ordered distractedly, anything the waiter suggested: oysters, soup, steak, salad, wine.

"That's a lot of food," Sarah said.

"I'm starving," he replied. "I went out to lunch with my boss today and just when our food arrived, he told me he was dying." Rory paused; he had not intended to mention this.

"Dying?"

"Well, we're all dying. He's just dying sooner than he planned. The idea offends him."

"Dying of what?"

"Pancreatic cancer."

"Oh."

"Is that bad?"

"What prognosis have they given him?"

"Six months."

"What if he dies sooner?"

"Someone else will map the Milky Way."

"And you?"

He shrugged. "I'll be out of a job, a thesis, a future. I'll go live on Haight Street with Jimmy. I saw him tonight. He gave me directions to the laundromat."

"He has a good memory for faces. He draws them in chalk on the sidewalk. I gave him paper, but he lost it."

"Does he live on the street? He doesn't have anyone?"

"No."

"It's hard to imagine. But you've always been alone, too, haven't you? Do you think you could get used to not being alone? I mean, I've never been alone, except sometimes when I'm driving. And you probably had roommates at school, and then you wished you were alone." Sarah looked at him with courteous incomprehension. "Well," he said, "here come the oysters."

The waiter, however, was carrying a bottle of sparkling wine. "Compliments of the house," he announced. "And our best wishes to both of you."

"It must be for the holidays," Sarah said.

For the rest of dinner they talked about physics, dark matter, and the uses of infinity. When they returned to Sarah's flat, they went to bed, but they just lay there as rain fell outside. "If I ask you something," Rory said, "will you promise not to leap out of bed and fall down the stairs and run naked outside and I'll have to run after you and this time, we'll be arrested —"

"Rory, do you ever still think about being a writer?"

"No. Sarah, why did you hang up on me? Don't you think, under the circumstances, you can call me?"

She bit her lip to keep from saying, what circumstances? "I hate telephones."

As if objecting to this unjust condemnation, the phone began to ring. Rory answered it.

"Well," Isabelle Glass said. "I did it. I went out with that man. I thought, what is the worst that could happen? I could die. So what? So I went. I used to be popular, you know. Men used to like me. Then I realized what had changed: I knew what was going to happen next. In every movie, it was always the boy chasing the girl until they caught each other, and then the movie ended. They never told you what happened next. And so I ruined my life. Well, tomorrow night Cecily is bringing that man over. I can't remember his name, but she will probably divorce him before I learn it. I suppose you are coming too."

"No," Rory said. "Sarah's going home with me."

THIS IS HOW they came to be shopping in a storm on the morning of Christmas Eve. He insisted she did not have to bring gifts. He just wanted to bring her home with him, if she would go. She would, but not empty-handed. It was symptomatic of his state of mind that he not only shopped with her but he enjoyed it. He found her indecision endearing, and she thought he was the model of patience and good humor. For once he did not mind the aberrant collection of humans on Haight Street. They could have sex in the black leather goods store, like those other two, he observed, and no one would notice.

"What other two?" Sarah asked.

"See? You didn't notice."

He disappeared while she was trying to decide on wrapping paper, but returned promptly, carrying a shopping bag of his own. "It's for you," he said solemnly. "New technology. Quite a concept. It answers your phone and it deals with the monster for you."

They passed a lone flutist playing "Have Yourself a Merry Little Christmas." Sarah put her change in his basket. Rory caught her in his arms and kissed her.

"I think it's snowing!" Sarah caught a snowflake. "It is." She tried to remember who had made up the story about rushing around in a snowstorm on Christmas Eve. Kate, no doubt.

"We're doomed," he said. "No one in California can drive in rain, let alone snow. So, are we finished? Can we go back to bed now?"

She had never had sex in the afternoon; she considered this as she lay beside him watching snowflakes flutter past the window. Of course, she had never had sex in the morning or in the kitchen either. "What?" he asked, watching her. "What are you thinking about?"

"The symptoms of a nymphomaniac."

"Well, it's better than being a schizophrenic, isn't it? Dammit," he added as the doorbell buzzed. "I wonder if I could make an answering machine for it too."

It rang again. Sarah detached herself to open the door. At the bottom of the stairs, alone and grubby, stood Lucy and Avery McIntyre.

"Hullo," Avery said. "We're home."

Behind Sarah, Rory was scrambling into his pants.

CHAPTER 34

A S A CHILD, Sarah had watched the McIntyres' Christmas cele-
brations with fascination and yearning. Their house became a
wonderland, bedecked with greenery and twinkling lights, and smell-
ing of pine trees, beeswax, and the cookies that Jean baked all month
long. Jean brought out special things at Christmas: a snow globe
with a reindeer in it, a nutcracker king, and, most magical to Sarah,
a wooden manger and a family who lived in it. Jean created a scene
with shepherds, wise men, angels and all kinds of animals standing on
a bed of glitter-flecked cotton snow, although Rory insisted it probably hadn't been snowing in Bethlehem. Sarah loved to move the figures about; Jean didn't mind. The father was named Joseph, and for a
long time Sarah believed he was Joe McIntyre.

At Christmas, everyone got an Advent calendar filled with choc-
olates, and everyone had a stocking that Jean had made, each name
spelled in sequins. They all went together to find a tree and decorated it
with every odd thing the children had made at school; strings of gilded
macaroni chains, painted pine cones, and popsicle stick snowflakes
hung alongside Jean's glass birds and jewel-colored balls. Everyone
made gifts, hid gifts, and guessed at them as they appeared beneath the
tree. On Christmas Eve, Jean made cioppino, and neighbors gathered at
the McIntyre's house to eat, sing carols, and drink Joe's hot mulled wine.

Secretly, Sarah tried secretly to imitate their traditions. Once she took branches Joe trimmed from the tree, and she made a little tree that she decorated with scraps she pilfered from Jean's craft-making supplies. She took an almost empty tube of silver glitter, but she returned it the next day, and Jean surprised her by giving it back to her, along with a string of fairy lights. Sarah lit her creation at night, but she never expected to find a gift under the tree that was mostly stolen.

All these years later, as they came to the door, everything looked the same, the colored lights strung across the porch, the wreath with silver bells. Sarah's reflection in the glass was of a grown-up carrying gifts, but she would have been less surprised to see a child with pockets filled with ribbons nicked from Jean's craft box.

Jean flung open the door. "Rory! You made it! I was so worried about the roads. Rain and snow! Sarah, how wonderful! And the children — here, Rory, let me take them."

Rory and his mother went off together, he arguing that she could not carry both sleeping children at once. Sarah gazed around the living room lit by candles and the fire on the hearth. Nothing had changed, really, although no one had eaten most of the candy off Jean's gingerbread house yet. But where was Joe?

Rory returned, cheerfully vanquished. "She's putting the kids to bed, since I don't know how to do it. She's put you in Kate's old room. I'll go get our stuff."

The hallway was what Joe called Jean's Rogues' Gallery, school photos of everyone from kindergarten to high school graduation. Kate's room was unchanged, too: the cream wallpaper with pink rosebuds, the canopy bed, the twin pink glass lamps, the poster of *Romeo and Juliet*.

Jean bustled in, bringing fresh towels. "Those poor babies didn't even wake up. They're exhausted. That woman! She just left them at your door? It was too much for her, but at least she thought to bring them to you. Rory said she didn't even wait."

"No. By the time we got out of bed, she was gone."

"Oh."

"Now you've done it." Rory strolled in, laughing. "Sal, I can't find your suitcase."

"Suitcase?" She had given Rory her bag of gifts to take to the car; then Avery had wanted Cheerios and Lucy peanut butter on toast. "I forgot."

"I can loan you a nightgown." Jean left the room.

"Is she all right?" Sarah asked.

"Are you afraid she'll make you go to church?"

"I would go."

"I know you would. Confession. That's what you need."

"I have enough sins."

"No, not nearly enough." He pressed her hard against him. This is really me, Sarah Glass, she thought, and this is Rory McIntyre, and we are here, in this moment, alive.

Jean returned with a flowered flannel gown. "This should be good. It's so cold —" She stopped talking even after Sarah removed her hand from Rory's groin.

"She'll be warm," he told his mother.

Jean recovered. "We'll put the roll-away in with the children for you, Rory. Pat and Mike and Tim are in your old room. John said he doesn't mind sleeping on the sofa."

"John's here?" Rory asked. "If he marries Sarah and me, can I sleep with her instead?"

"Rory, behave."

Jean left. Rory said, "You wouldn't do this to me, would you? Wear my mother's nightgown in my sister's bed? Let's go find John."

❧

JOHN MCINTYRE WAS in the kitchen, eating a sandwich and chopping onions for the cioppino. He was two years older than Rory, and although he had never been as talented, tall, handsome, or popular, he had excelled in one area where Rory presented no competition: goodness. He was a priest, presently at St. Rose's in Paso Robles, but he had left his flock on Christmas Eve, drawn home not only for Rory's homecoming but also because of a troubling conversation he'd had with Sterling. Typically, John avoided these conversations as much as anyone in the family, but the last time he called Kate, she was out, and Sterling, with undisguised glee, had recounted the story of Jean's solo visit to Rory.

John adored his mother. He loved his father, too, of course, but he considered the picture-like perfection of their life to be a reflection of his mother's excellence. The suggestion that she might be unhappy was as unthinkable as the Virgin herself announcing she needed more in life than motherhood. He came home as soon as he could. He found his mother as brisk and busy as ever. Nothing seemed amiss until he realized that his father was sleeping in his workshop. He didn't know how to ask his parents if something was wrong, and so, with what he recognized was a child's simplicity, he was trying to make his mother happy by eating as much as possible.

"Sarah!" he exclaimed. "What a pleasure! What brings you here?"

Rory said, "I'm coming out of the closet, and Sarah is going to vouch for me,"

John blinked; Jean remonstrated: "Rory, you had better watch yourself. You remember how Kate was about Show and Tell. Here, you can peel the garlic. "

"Where's everyone else?" Rory asked.

"They went to Vallerga's for me." On cue, Pat and Mike came in carrying bags full of mussels, crabs, and clams. Tim followed with loaves of bread.

"Sarah!" Mike called. "Just in time to make a salad!"

"You can bleed all over cioppino," Pat added, "and no one will ever know. Ma, we got mistletoe, too. You forgot it."

"It's poisonous." Flames shot up as Jean set a pan of onions down hard on the stove.

Sarah scrambled to say something: "Your new kitchen is beautiful."

"Dad finished it," Tim explained. "Where is he anyway?"

Jean jiggled the pan fiercely. John said, "He went to get Grandma and Aunt Margaret."

"Oh lucky him," Rory said. "I'd rather clean crabs."

"Here comes a car," Mike said. "It must be them."

Jean sighed. "Why does he do this? He was supposed to take them to their hotel and keep them there, but they always want to come here early, just to see that I am not ready."

An extraordinary thing happened: the onions began to burn. Smoke surged from the pan, and Jean grabbed the handle. She dropped the pan, clutching her hand.

"Here, put cold water on it." Sarah turned on the faucet for Jean. The others stared at the scattered onions, stunned.

"I'll go get Dad," Pat said. "I think we could use some wine."

Jean burst into tears and ran from the kitchen.

John picked the frying pan up off the floor. "I think something is wrong."

"Hell." Rory shrugged. "I'd cry too, if Aunt Margaret was coming to visit me."

"Sarah," John asked, "could you go say hello to everyone? We'll — pick up the onions."

Sarah remembered Aunt Margaret, the person who had discovered she knew no prayers. When she and Joe's mother visited — inspections, Jean called them — Aunt Margaret had the ability to paint Jean as a sloppy, disorganized rebel, and Grandma was the one who had trained her. Now their practiced stares were fixed on Sarah. Where was Joe?

"Did you have a good flight?" Sarah asked.

"Mother, look at what Jean has done to the house now."

"I'm glad your plane could land in the storm."

"A new sofa and a new rug, Margaret."

"But I suppose you're used to storms in Omaha."

"It was sunny when we left home," Margaret said; clearly California was at fault. "Joe said she was redoing the kitchen, too, Mother. She must have spent thousands of dollars."

"Joe did some of the work," Sarah pointed out.

Grandma sighed. "The poor boy never gets any rest,"

Sarah was relieved to see Jean come into the room. She said hello and offered coffee. "Sarah," she asked, "will you help get it?"

Sarah, who had never known Jean to require assistance with anything, least of all the filling of a coffee pot, followed her to the kitchen. "I'm sorry," she said, "if I — if Rory —"

"Rory," Jean echoed; she hardly seemed to know the name. "Just be careful. Look out for yourself. Men, even the best of them, can trample your heart. I'm so sorry" — she had begun to weep again — "I've had such a shock, Sarah, and I don't know how to get over it."

John served coffee and asked after the health of the parish priest in Nebraska.

"Who is that girl, John?" Grandma interrupted.

"That's Sarah, Grandma. She came home with Rory."

"So he finally brought his wife home? I was beginning to think he kept her in an attic like a loony. Joe said she's odd, but she doesn't seem odd. Little, talks too much, but not odd."

"She is not Rory's wife. She is his friend." Margaret's tone emphasized all the lurid possibilities of the word.

"Friend? He can't have a friend. He's a married man."

"No, Mother, you forget. Rory is divorced."

"Divorced? Rory? No one told me. John, is this true?"

"It is, Grandma. It's been quite a while now."

"You must remember," Margaret added.

"How can I remember what no one has told me? Divorced!"

"You know his wife left him."

"Now I don't believe that! Why would she leave such a good-looking boy? He does look more and more like Joe, doesn't he? I've always said, of my two children, Joe got the looks."

Margaret made no reply. Her mother continued, "It comes of all that tomato sauce Jean fed them. Joe was always nice and quiet until he went to California and married her, but when I met her, I saw why he had done such a wild thing: she puts tomato sauce on everything. A man who eats too much tomato sauce is apt to do anything. Still, I accepted Jean, and if Joe came down in the world when he married her, I've never said it. But didn't Rory have children?"

"They live with him."

"Rory? Well, he must get another wife and keep this one. Can he be married again, John?"

"He wasn't married in the church."

"Then he isn't divorced! Margaret, I wonder you can make up such stories. Well, next time he has to marry her the right way. John, you'll see to that. Who is this friend?"

Margaret said, "If I am not mistaken, it's that Mexican girl who used to moon after him."

"Did she? Well, then she won't mind if he blows up her kitchen. I remember that summer he made that experiment and there went Jean's kitchen. And if she cooks Mexican, he will be able to eat it since he has eaten tomato sauce all his life. She's little, but I learned my lesson when Joe married Jean and I said anyone that small could not be a breeder. Where is Rory? I want to talk to him."

Sarah slipped out the back door. A light was on in Joe's workshop. Nat "King" Cole was singing "The Christmas Song." Through the window, she saw Joe, surrounded by winemaking paraphernalia: bottles, barrels, flasks, and siphons. There was gray in his hair and lines in his face. All her life Sarah would associate this man with kindness, humor, and love, and the sight of him alone and aging was like a cold hand on her heart.

She slid open the door; the grating sound reminded her weirdly of the time she went to confession with Kate, beset by an urge to experience forgiveness, probably for not knowing any prayers. She had sat in the dark closet wondering if she were in the awful presence of God. When the tiny window opened, Sarah, knowing she was a trespasser, had run away.

"Sally!" Joe stood up and kissed her cheek. "Come in! Sit down."

"Everyone is looking for you."

"Then we'd better have a glass of wine." He filled two glasses and handed her one. It was the color of rubies, but the scent was odd, the taste sour. Joe's wines were usually fragrant, soft as velvet. "So you came home with Rory," he said. "You like that guy?"

"I always have. But you know that."

"He'd better treat you right or he'll have to answer to me. Of course" — his voice sank, painfully sad — "a man would have to be an idiot to destroy his happiness, wouldn't he?"

Sarah gulped her wine, reminding herself that she had never seen any doctor burst into hysterical, empathetic tears when listening to a patient. "Joe," she asked, "what's wrong?"

THE HOUSE WAS filled with people when she and Joe came inside. Mrs. Olsen was leading carols, and Jean was arranging Mrs. Orsi's tongue salad and Mrs. Venutti's antipasti on the buffet. Joe took his place serving wine. Sarah slipped back outside and leaned against a tree. She had not realized she was so spineless that she would feel faint just because she had asked Joe what was wrong and he had told her. The air had ice in it, and she began to revive.

"Sarah?" She straightened up, but it was only John. "Are you all right?"

"Yes, fine. I was just feeling — warm."

"Can I get you something? Wine?"

"No. No, thank you. No."

"Rory was coming out but he got caught by my grandmother."

"Oh, God. Oh — oops."

"Don't worry." He smiled at her. "I talk to God all the time."

"I expect he answers you."

"I've been told that if you hear him, you can be sure it isn't God." John's voice had a musical lilt like Rory's. He was not, like Rory, filled with lightning, but he was attractive in a quiet way. "We were wondering if you want to go to Mass."

"Rory was?"

"Well, no. But he'll go if you do, I'm sure."

"I am not the person to make Rory believe in anything."

"I would take issue with that. So would my mother."

"Jean would?"

"Right now, she is somewhat upset with love, that is, with my father; but she will get over it. For her, love is life. Well, I suppose it is what we all wish for."

"Is it why you became a priest?"

"It is more likely why I am thinking about leaving the priesthood."

"I suppose the love of God can be a lonely thing if you can't hear him."

"Yes. Especially if you crave the love of — if you would rather see the face of God in a man — in man. I find I am becoming somewhat

jealous when I have to perform a marriage. Not long ago I did a funeral for a man who had been married sixty years. His widow's face
was something beyond grief, and I thought, I will never in my life be
loved like that. But this is not why I came out — I mean, I only wanted
to thank you for talking to my father. Now he's inside and everything
is right again. I won't ask you to betray any confidences, but you have
more courage than any of us. Now, I had better go rescue Rory. Will
you come in?"

"In a moment."

When he had gone back inside, she walked down the lane. Her
footsteps crunched on the frozen ground. The clouds were parting and
stars glimmered here and there, but the moon was still obscured. The
night had that stillness that comes after a snowfall.

Her old house came into view, dark and dreamlike. For years, she
had imagined returning to it, painting it, putting furniture in it. She
resisted an urge to open the front door and climb the stairs to her old
room. Instead she went to a gate, which opened to a path to the creek.
In summer, it dwindled to shallow pools, but now it was running, and
in its lively burbling, she could hear echoes of Kate and Sarah, sitting on the bank telling each other stories of mad, wild love. Do you
dream when there isn't enough reality, she wondered, or when there
is too much?

"So, I was on my way to Italy."

"Italy?"

"We don't always have to go to Paris, Sarah. So, there I was on the
plane and the handsomest man was sitting next to me. He had black hair
and beautiful blue eyes. We hit a storm, and the plane began to shake. I
fainted, and when I came to, I was in a desert."

"What desert? On the way to Italy? Don't you take the polar route?"

"The plane had gone off course. I don't think you can be passionate if
you're cold. I was going to be kidnapped by a Bedouin so the blue-eyed man

could rescue me. It could be a Mountie, but I might prefer him to the man with the blue eyes. I don't know, Sarah. You do one."

"I haven't dreamed anything lately."

"Why not? Christmas is great for dreams."

"Okay, well, I was in Paris, alone —"

"How could you be alone in Paris at Christmas?"

"But maybe you are. And maybe you're walking, and you pass a house full of lights and music and people —"

"And just then, a car runs over you and breaks your leg. The driver leaps out and you swoon in his arms. He's so overcome, he kisses you. And you don't even feel pain."

"Probably because you're in shock from having a broken leg."

"Sarah! You really aren't romantic, you know?"

Footsteps crunched over the icy ground, and Rory came up beside her. The thin moon slid from behind the clouds and cast glitter on the snow-dusted trees and rocks.

"Make love to me," she said.

CHAPTER 35

THE FOG WAS a white cocoon, so dense they couldn't see the hood of Rory's car as they crawled through it back to the city on Christmas night. Lucy and Avery listened to fifteen minutes of Dave Brubeck before requesting something different, and Rory made no objections to the music of Raffi who sang "Willoughby Wallaby Woo" and "Five Little Frogs." They had said nothing about their vacation, but twice Lucy unfastened herself from her car seat to lean forward and pat Rory's head. Presently, they slept, and Raffi sang "The more we get together, the happier we'll be" to Sarah and Rory alone, until he turned off the music.

"Sarah, do you think it was so bad, what my father did?"

"Not on the scale of the world, no."

"Then why is my mother so upset?"

"She's hurt. That's different from upset."

"But do you understand why? It happened so long ago."

"She's only found out. It's an odd thing to write in a Christmas card. Rather cowardly."

"Yes! Why didn't this woman relieve her conscience when she was living next door to them? Why did she wait until she moved to Idaho?"

"Twenty-two years ago, John was five, you were three, Kate one, the twins, just born —"

"I wonder how he had enough energy to fool around."

"I'm sure she seduced him. Wasn't she the one who always gardened in her bathing suit?"

"It takes two, you loyal heart." He reached over to ruffle her hair. "But why is Mom upset because he said it didn't mean anything? Wouldn't she prefer that? Nothing changed then, so why should it now?"

"If someone drops a rock on your head, it hurts whether a person intended to do it or not."

"But here's a man who has followed the rules all his life. Why can't he have one minute of wildness, even with a neighbor with a dead battery?"

"What rules?"

"There are rules."

"Only no one knows what they are."

"He knew." Rory glanced at her, knotting and unknotting her hands. "If you understand all this so well, why were you crying?"

Why? Why was he singling her out? The morning had unfolded like a movie: excited children, presents, stockings, even one for Sarah. Everyone was laughing over the twins' gift to her, an ornament shaped like a head of lettuce drizzled with red paint, when Joe handed a package to Jean. The film broke. Jean fled the house in tears and drove away in her car. Joe cried, John cried, the other brothers looked sick and stunned, and Avery announced that he had changed his mind and did not want the crusts cut off his toast. Sarah was gluing the crusts back on with jelly when Aunt Margaret and Grandma arrived from their hotel. Sarah, who could not cook, had cooked their ham, wondering how could it be that one minute you were ablaze with fire, mindless of time or place or frozen rocks on the ground, and the next you were arranging maraschino cherries and pineapple rings on a ham according to Margaret's directions. Jean still had not returned when they departed for San Francisco.

She said, "It's just hard to think of them as divorced."

"Divorced?" Rory swerved. "They won't get divorced. They'll work it out."

"How?"

"He'll do something. I don't know what, but, come on, Sarah, why do you think she is so hurt? Why do you think he's ready to kill himself? They love each other. He'll do what he needs to do. It's just taking longer, probably because she hasn't told him what to do. I don't know why. She must know he'd do anything, if she would only tell him."

"Maybe she doesn't know."

"I doubt that. She's always known before."

"Have they ever fought before?"

"They've been married thirty years, my darling."

"What did they fight about?" The scenes she had witnessed resembled nothing in her experience of his parents, and, she suspected, little in his.

"I don't know — dumb things. Isn't that what you usually fight about?"

"But she never left before, did she?" A thought struck Sarah. "Maybe she wants to leave."

"No. She doesn't."

"But everything is always transforming, right?"

"No, it isn't."

"See, you really don't like physics."

"All right, if it's physics we're talking about, then she needs to give him a shred of data."

"Data?"

"Why not?"

"It sounds so cold."

"But data are the only arbiters of the universe. What else is there?"

"Inspiration."

"Meaning what?"

"Why doesn't he take her to Hawaii?"

"Hawaii?"

"She's always wanted to go there."

"She has? I didn't know that."

"Men's minds are really different. You'd hardly think one chromosome explains it."

"Do you want to go to Hawaii?" he asked.

"No."

"You always wanted to go to Paris."

"That was just dreams, crazy stories."

"What do you want? Because I'll tell you, Sarah Glass, what I want is starting to make me awfully damned nervous." The yellow headlights of a car sprang like a tiger out of the fog. "Do you want to get married?"

If Sarah was surprised — in fact, she was shocked speechless — this was of little consequence. Like one who had only just discovered what his brain was planning to say, Rory hastened to deliver, in a flood of words, his oft-delayed speech explaining why it was impossible for her to be involved with him. He described so graphically his lack of time, money, energy, a job, a direction, and a future, that any response from her was superfluous. He had proposed, if indeed he had, and turned himself down in one long, confused paragraph.

In the following days, when he recalled with acute suffering all he had said in this self-induced panic, he need not have worried so much. Indeed, it might have served as a study in perception that of all he said, far less than twenty percent reached Sarah's brain. She only heard that he did not, could not, would not love her.

In the silence, Rory began pushing buttons on the dashboard. Raffi began singing again. Rory punched the music off. From out of nowhere, nausea seized Sarah like the terrifying grip of a stranger. It would not let go. "Rory," she said lowly, "could you stop?"

A glimpse of her face caused him to swing his car across two lanes. She dashed from the car and vomited into dead bushes. She slumped against a chain link fence, hoping that whatever had just hit her was fatal. Rory was holding her upright, one hand tangled in her hair.

"Better now?" he asked.

She shook her head no. "You can just leave me here."

"Sarah." His voice was gentle; he was talking to an idiot.

"Please, Rory, I'll take the train. I just want to go home."

"I know. I'll take you home. But I'm not going to leave you here. Or put you on a train."

He hauled her back to the car. His children, awake, were staring at her wide-eyed. As wretched as she would ever be in her life, Sarah got in. Traffic moved like an endless slug over the Bay Bridge. Raffi ran out of songs. The children were quiet. Rory rubbed Sarah's shoulder but this only increased her misery. When, at last, they reached Stanyan Street, she said, "You don't need to park. I'll just get out."

He double-parked in front of her house. "I can't do this," he said.

"I know. Neither can I."

"Don't misunderstand me, Sarah. You never have before."

In the backseat, the audience was on high alert. "Rory kissed Sarah,'" Lucy told Avery.

"Is she going to throw up again?" Avery asked.

Sarah stumbled up the stairs and fell onto her bed. It came to this: at the stroke of — it wasn't even midnight — everything was as it had been before. She had not just lost the glass slipper; she'd taken off the shoe and pounded it to smithereens. She closed her eyes and tried to fall into unconsciousness, but she went nowhere, and her efforts fizzled entirely when the telephone rang, five times, and then Rory's voice came out of the answering machine. "Sarah, do you need anything, babe?" Drugs, she thought, stupor, oblivion. "I — Avery, why are you up?"

"I want to talk to Sarah, too."

Sarah picked up the phone. "Hello, Avery."

"We played Candyland, Sarah. Rory got stuck in the Molasses Swamp one hundred times."

"Now, scram." Rory said and cleared his throat. "How are you feeling, honey?"

"Fine."

"Will you call me if you — now what, Avery?"

"I forgot to say good night to Sarah."

Rory sighed. Avery said, "Sarah, you threw up."

"Yes, I did."

"One time I threw up."

"Avery!"

"Good night, Sarah. I love you. Now Rory is going to chase me." Delighted giggles faded.

"You can laugh," Rory said. "You didn't play Candyland for an hour."

"And get stuck in the Molasses Swamp." Life crept back into her voice.

"Did I tell you thanks for the pen? I love it."

"Thank you for the earrings."

"Sal, tomorrow —"

"I have to work."

"Oh. Well, David Ilillouette always goes to Paris for New Year's Eve; no one knows why, but first, he's invited some people to his house up on the north coast to brainstorm about the future of the world, is there one or not? I said I'd go. I think I'll take the kids."

"They'll love that."

Silence. Maybe he had hung up. No, he hadn't. "I've been thinking," he said. "We just have to connect all the pieces. Do you think we can, Sarah?"

She whispered, "Yes."

"You do? My darling, if you think that — why do you think that?"

Because I love you, she thought. She dropped the phone; it clattered on the floor. The cat, hopped through the window, yowling. She said, "I'd better go feed the cat."

"I'll call you tomorrow, okay?"

And I will ask, she thought, if there is a future for the world, yes or no.

CHAPTER 36

THE DAY AFTER Christmas, the clinic was quiet. Cheryl the receptionist had brought in a platter of cookies and fudge. "Otherwise I'll eat them all," she said. Dr. Castro had given her the results of a pregnancy test: positive. What a wonderful gift; she was so happy.

He had given a gift to Sarah too: a leather-bound calendar. "Thanks for everything," he said. "I am sorry we'll be losing you." A group of pre-med students was coming in to volunteer after New Year's. He didn't need her anymore.

"I was thinking, if Cheryl is leaving, maybe I could stay —"

"You want to work as my receptionist?"

"I wouldn't mind."

"No," he said. "No. You want a job here? Go finish school. Then I'll give you a job."

They saw three people suffering from problems of the heart. They sent the one with chest pains to St. Mary's emergency room; the other two were depressed and lonely and had nowhere else to go. They had just closed for the day when a man pounded on the front door. "There's a woman lying on the sidewalk," he called. "Someone just left her there."

Sarah ran down the steps to a motionless woman wrapped in a tattered blanket that reeked of vomit and urine. She knelt and felt the woman's pulse as she brushed filthy, matted hair away from her face. For a dizzying moment she thought she was looking into a mirror, so familiar was the blue-tinged face of Dibby McIntyre.

SHE DID NOT entirely understand the compulsion that made her go to the hospital and stay with Dibby, who had been drinking so hard that her body was poisoned, her heart and liver failing. Sarah experienced another attack of nausea, threw up, and felt better, but Dibby was going to die. Sarah sat beside her, watching the lines and numbers on the monitor. People lived and then they died, she thought; they breathed and then they didn't. Hearts beat and then they stopped. Dibby's eyes flickered and her hand clutched Sarah's.

"Rory is coming," Sarah repeated. "We're finding him. He'll be here."

But Rory didn't come, and the resident called the time of death, two fifty-seven. Sarah stood up unsteadily and made her way into the hall. She followed the row of lights, thinking how bizarre light bulbs were, thin, brittle, hollow except for a delicate interior contraption that was rendered useless by the slightest bump and left you in the dark.

"Is she dead?" a nurse asked. "The poor thing. Well, you did all you could. Oh, there's Dr. Friedman. He was looking for you."

Sarah had called Damon when she didn't know what else to do. "We found Rory," he said. "Through the congressman's office. I'll wait here for him. You look exhausted, Sarah. Go home."

She went out into the clear, cold dark. The streets were empty and the wind felt like broken glass. She walked until the sun rose; then she went home, fed her hungry cat, and fell asleep.

When she awoke, it was afternoon. She made coffee, but it didn't smell right, so she poured it out and made a cup of tea. She collected her mail and sat down to read it. Her bank statement reported details of her dwindling balance. The other letter was from her landlord. He had sold the building; this was her thirty-day notice.

She began to feel queasy. She was looking up food poisoning — how long could it last?— when she noticed a red light blinking on that new, strange robot, the answering machine. Warily, she pushed a button. "You have three new messages," it said.

"Sarah," Kate's disembodied voice appeared. "It's so great that you got a machine. I'm coming back early because — well, you know — Dibby died. Mom had gone to Paso Robles with John, so Rory had to leave the kids with Dad so he could to take her body back east. He thought he should. He was pretty shaken up. He'd never seen a dead person before; well, neither have I. I'll help Dad till John brings Mom back. Well, Sarah, I've spent a lot of time thinking. I wish I wouldn't eat when I'm upset. I've gained five pounds, but I've decided: I am leaving Sterling. I'm not sure where I'll go but —"

Here, the machine cut her off, as if it could hear no more. "Message two," it said.

"Sarah, it's Damon. I wanted to make sure you're all right and tell you not to worry about Rory. His friend, the congressman, made arrangements to fly Dibby's body back east. Her family wanted this done, but couldn't be bothered themselves because they have New Year's parties. David is flying with Rory but he's going on to Paris, even though his wife has threatened to leave him if he does. Goodness, he's handsome and so fond of Rory, I wondered if maybe he's not as straight as he seems to be but Rory said no, he is. Straight. Well, I decided to go too. Forget love; I'm going to spend New Year's in New York. Always fly with a congressman. We got upgraded to first class. The Lonely Hearts Club, David calls us —"

"Message three," the machine said, and Gabriel's voice sang out: "Go home, said the man in the moon, go home." And he left a telephone number.

She called Kate. Her machine answered. "You can stay at my place" Sarah said. "I'm going away, but I have the flat until January thirty-first. I'll leave the key in the mailbox."

Then she called Gabriel Dinesen. "Get me out of here," she said.

PART THREE

DECEMBER 1976

CHAPTER 37

A FROST IN THE night had turned every blade of grass a cold, glittering white. Leaves, branches, and spider webs all sparkled. This was a mystery the black cat was exploring as he prowled, touching a minimum of toe to the frozen earth, pausing to examine his feet. He halted, raised a paw, leapt, and landed on nothing in particular. He was, after all, a city cat who had never been in the country before.

A bird darted past him. He sprang to a rock. His ears whirled like radar as he surveyed this strange new jungle. A giant goddess of a bird waddled past him. He slithered off the rock to stalk her. He sprang to attack; the goose, five times his size, stretched out one wing. The cat changed direction mid-leap and landed in a pine tree. The branch bounced up and down. One could almost hear his question: What country, friends, is this?

Nearby, in the overgrown courtyard of the Castle Paradise, Gabriel Dinesen called, "Turn it on!" and the fountain came to life, water spewing from Cupid's head. "You're my favorite genius," he said to Sarah. "You just reconnected a pipe? Someday I'll study physics too."

Gabriel had been living at the old ghost in the Napa hills since the disbanding of the Scoundrels of Leisure. He didn't know why he hadn't thought of it before, but only since Sarah's arrival, three days earlier, had he gotten around to taking the sheets off the furniture and sweeping away piles of rat droppings, dust, and cobwebs. Where were the others, she had asked. He didn't know. Somewhere, he supposed.

"What shall we do now?" he asked. " Look for ghosts? Or shall we have dinner? I bought three steaks, one for the cat."

"But it's still morning."

"Sarah, we can eat dinner whenever we want."

"I forgot. Shall I cook?"

"No, not unless you want to."

"I can make a salad." While Gabriel badgered the stove into working, Sarah browsed through the cupboard and found a jar of artichoke hearts. "Shall I use these?" she asked.

"If you like them."

"Don't you?"

"No. I bought them by mistake. I thought they were olives. But if you like them —"

"No, not much." Sarah set the jar aside and began tearing lettuce.

"There is a knife, Sarah."

"You're supposed to tear it."

"Why?"

"I don't know. Probably I could cut it."

"No, tear it if you prefer." He chuckled. "Sarah, you'd think we're in love, we're being so unnatural."

At length, they sat down to eat. The sun had melted the frost and the day was warming up. "Can you believe there are blizzards on the East Coast?" Sarah asked.

"Poor peasants. Snow in winter." He poured wine and raised his glass. "Happy almost New Year's Eve. Sarah! You're not drinking!"

"No, I — for some reason, it tastes funny — in the morning."

"Oh well." He drank her wine. "So, Ma, what do you think of the homestead?"

"You've done a lot."

"We have. Next project is the fireplace. Just think, Sarah, I have a goal in life: a working fireplace. I know you can do it."

"Gabriel, you promised to take me back."

"What if I lied?"

"How long do you plan to stay here?"

"Forever. Sarah! Come live here with me."

"I can't. I have to go back. I have to pack. Move out. Buy a ticket to New York."

"While I freeze and die. Alone. No fireplace."

"Maybe I could stay for one more week."

"A week to live!"

"WHY ARE WE planting ten-year-old seeds, my lady?" Gabriel asked, dragging a burlap bag through the meadow. "We could buy new ones."

"I feel sorry for them. At least they have a chance to grow, however late."

"You're crazy," he said happily. "I always knew you were. Shall we go see the chickens?"

He had bought three chickens from a neighbor, and when they laid eggs, he was so delighted, he named them Allison, Absolon, and Nicolas, and he had remembered to feed them for three days. After Sarah and Gabriel visited to the chicken coop, they walked on through the grizzled remnants of a vineyard to the pond, a stopover for migrating wild ducks. Gabriel was putting out grain for them and they were lingering.

"You are taming them," Sarah warned.

"I know. There's a new one, out by the edge." He arranged a mound of grain apart from the other ducks. The wild duck darted at it but fluttered away as the others moved in. "She'll be back," Gabriel predicted. "I'll get her."

Near the pond was an ancient apple orchard; Sarah found an apple and offered it to Gabriel who feigned terror but ate it. They went on, following a trail up the hillside to a cave, which Gabriel believed hid the old count's lost treasure, if not his moldering body.

"Today we'll go in," he said.

"Do you think it's safe?"

"Nothing is safe."

"Some things are safer than others," she argued but she followed him to the entrance. "Do you think there are rats?"

"Rat, bats, vampires, Injun Joe —" From overhead came a tremendous fluttering as hundreds of bats swooped out. They ran and fell to the ground. "Nature," Gabriel gasped. "I feel like a Republican. Look for oil and pave it."

Twilight suited them, Sarah decided as they sat in the deep grass: the mysterious gloaming, the pale time between worlds. The pearl-like luminescence of the winter sky wouldn't last for more than a few minutes. Across the valley, the western mountains were turning into shadows, receding layers of blue. A hawk circled above them and flew off with a screech. She wished she knew what it was saying; she wished she knew how nature mixed its colors. She wished she knew why she was thinking such languid, bootless thoughts. She plucked a strand of grass. "Some of these grasses are wild herbs," she said. "You can do things with them."

"Spells. There's a book in the library."

"I saw it. There's one to invoke spirits. We could try it."

"No."

"Why not?"

"It might work."

"That would be interesting."

"And it would be at the expense of your oldest and dearest friend.

I tried the spell to turn myself into a werewolf. Sometimes I think it worked."

"You could ask for Richard the Lionheart."

"And my influence would blow it. We'd get the Old Man, and then I'd sell my soul."

"Do you believe there are spirits, Gabriel?" she asked. "If there is so much more around us than we perceive, we could be sitting here with the first people who lived here —"

"Don't, Sarah. I really believe in those things." Wind rustled the trees, and through the air came a distinctly inhuman call. "Oh hell," he groaned. "Now I know why you have a black cat."

"Let's go see what it is."

"No, let's not." Sarah had already gone into the grove of oaks. "Whatever happens, don't let me sell my soul."

Sarah lifted a tangle of branches. An emaciated horse was trying to reach them over a fence from his own field, which had been eaten bare. A goat was eating the fence.

ONE DAY LATER, Gabriel bounded up the hill to Sarah, who was sitting on the fence feeding oats to the horse. "Success!" he called. "I found the bastard who left her here to starve. She's the victim of a divorce. He bought her for his wife, but they split up. She says the horse is his because he bought it; he says it's hers because he bought it for her. But don't worry, old thing." He patted the horse's neck. "I took care of everything. I bought you. And the goat too."

"How did you manage it?"

"I was at the feed store, getting more oats, when I saw a poster. 'Have a problem? Call Congressman Ilillouette.' So I went to his office and an aide started calling everyone, saying the congressman was extremely concerned about a horse. In two hours, we had the owner. We wrapped up the case by writing letters to everyone, thanking them for their concern, sincerely, Congressman Ilillouette. I wrote one to you, too."

The horse followed Sarah down the hill, while Gabriel tried to tug the goat through the lush green meadow. "No need to eat the whole hill now, old thing," he said. " I think I'll name you Milton. What will you name the horse, Sarah? She's yours, you know."

"Mine? But, Gabriel, I'm leaving."

"Pshaw." Gabriel grinned at her. "Poor orphaned, nameless horse —"

"All right. How about Ophelia?"

"Sarah!"

"Rebecca?"

He chortled with delight. "We'll have to name the five thousand ducks, too. And look at Widdershins, stalking the goat. What a cat we're raising! Sarah, are you happy?"

"I only wish there was something I could do for you."

"Stay. Fix the fireplace. Marry me."

Of these, she decided the most sensible choice was to stay a few more days.

Later, in her notebook of things she might not see again, she drew Gabriel, standing on the hillside, laughing with his goat.

She was filling her notebook. She had the time because she rose much earlier than Gabriel. She was glad about this because of a peculiar circumstance, which was difficult, these two weeks later, to still dismiss as food poisoning from her cooking of Aunt Margaret's ham. Every morning, she felt quite ill, threw up, and then was fine. She worked weeding the commune garden and drawing bugs, weeds, and trees until Gabriel emerged from his bedroom in the north tower. They spent several hours together and cooked supper before they parted ways again. She went to her room in the south castle where she drew and read books from the commune library: *Zen and the Art of Motorcycle Maintenance, The Teachings of Don Juan, The Kama Sutra, Horton Hears a Who.* She didn't know what Gabriel did at night.

The day they brought home the horse and goat, Gabriel wanted to put them in the living room to heat the castle peasant-style but Sarah felt that the animals would be more comfortable in the adobe chapel, so they cleared out the commune's wreckage, the broken loom and potter's wheel, and rearranged the pews into stalls.

That night, instead of retreating to her room, Sarah returned to the chapel-barn to visit the animals. She was dusting off the statues of Jesus and Mary and posters of Ho Chi Minh and the Grateful Dead when she heard an engine start. Startled, she watched Gabriel's red tail lights disappear over the hill, but the uneasy notion that she had been left alone diminished when the goat chased the cat, who fled up to the loft. Sarah found Widdershins behind boxes and abandoned furniture on a balcony that looked out to the western mountains and a sweep of starry sky. She and the cat slept there that night, wrapped in her sleeping bag. She wondered where Gabriel had gone, and why he hadn't said anything; she wondered if she should mind and why she didn't. It was a relief, she concluded, not to be in love.

In the morning, after she put the horse and goat in the meadow near the barn, she went to the house. She was putting out birdseed in the courtyard when a naked man came out of the north tower. When he saw Sarah, he bounced backwards, disappeared, and returned fully dressed.

"I apologize," he said. "I didn't know anyone else was here."

"Neither did I."

"I'll just head back to the city."

"Would you like breakfast?" she asked, for he was looking hungrily at her birdseed.

"Do you have coffee?"

Of all the signs and wonders afflicting her in mornings, this was the most powerful: she, who formerly had lived on coffee, could not bear even the faintest scent of it. She made him coffee; then she went into the garden and threw up.

She spent the morning clearing out the loft. She found a chair, a bookshelf, a desk, and a mattress; the latter, she put on the balcony. When she had finished, Gabriel's car was gone again. She did the evening chores alone, and that night she slept beneath the stars, with Widdershins on her feet.

She had not seen Gabriel for two days when she found him in the kitchen, covered with flour. He was baking bread. "Do you know that you are supposed to love bread in order for it to rise?" he asked.

"I didn't know an emotion could affect a chemical reaction," she said. "Although, come to think of it, love is a chemical reaction."

He sighed. "Aren't you going to ask me where I've been?"

"Where have you been?" she asked doubtfully.

"You don't care. Never mind."

"I do. I care."

"That's better. I've been working. Snigger if you must. I still have my bread to love."

"Sorry." She composed her face. "What kind of work?"

"For Congressman Ilillouette. Volunteer, of course. One of his aides had a baby and I'm filling in for her. I answer the phone and discuss whether we should bomb Iran and if preservatives can cause people to become Republicans. Then I write letters from him thanking people for their concern. One woman came to the office to show me her letter. She'd framed it. And Walter, the guy with the horse, came to see me. He wants me to go to divorce court with him and help him keep his favorite chair. I said I'd go. I'm such a pushover for big men."

"It sounds rather good, Gabriel."

"It's like working for the Coeur de Lion. Oh, and sometimes, at night, I go dancing. If you don't mind."

"Me? Mind? No."

Increasingly she was alone, she and the animals. She didn't mind. One week became two, then three. She knew she had fallen backwards into this world; she knew it wasn't hers. She knew she had to leave, but she began to forget. She was happy.

CHAPTER 38

MILTON HAD EATEN part of the chicken coop, and Gabriel wanted to barbecue him; that was why Sarah took the goat with her when she led Rebecca the horse up the hill where she could draw while the horse grazed. Milton was not so docile as the gentle horse, however; he walked with her briefly, kicked himself free of his lead, and sprang away.

She made no intricate studies of bugs that day, only a half-finished sketch of a narrow-eyed, belligerent goat defiantly mowing grass while dragging a rope behind him. Recalling the communal chickens who had eaten themselves to death, Sarah worried that this might also be possible with goats. She couldn't let it happen. She liked Milton. She admired his individualism, his single-minded pursuit of goals, his disdain for the opinion of others. She set out to recapture him, and he, realizing this, scampered away. They had carried on like this until she employed a ruse whereby she approached the goat by walking backwards while talking to Rebecca. Her victory was brief. Milton rebelled by spinning around and kicking out his hind legs. They hit her, and whether this knocked her out of herself or up into orbit, she never knew. Thoughts of goats and horses, cats and bugs were left below on Earth. Sarah was flying, shooting like a comet through darkness. Sparks began to flash around her. Stars? Ahead of her, a glittering castle took shape. She didn't reach it. Her wings melted. She tumbled out of the sky and landed with a thud. A heavy thing fell on her. She opened her eyes, and presently she recognized the creatures looking down at her: a horse, a cat, a goat, and someone new: a red-gold, brown-eyed dog whose not so distant ancestors might have been full-blooded wolves. The dog licked her face, and she remembered her name was Sarah and she was somewhere on a hill in California. The thing that had fallen on her was a body, hers. She took inventory of her parts and was surpassingly glad to find them all.

"He shot his lawyer," Gabriel repeated in a dazed voice. "I could understand it if he shot his wife's lawyer, but, no, he shot his own lawyer."

Sarah had found him collapsed on the sofa in the great room. She had recounted her own adventure, but it paled in comparison to Gabriel's with Walter at the courthouse. She made him tea and then sagged down beside him, judiciously dividing her attention between patting the red-gold wolf dog who had followed her home, and Widdershins, perched on her shoulder, eyeing this interloper without enthusiasm.

"Of course, I should shoot Milton," Gabriel added. "You saved his life and look what he did: he kicked you."

"You can't shoot a goat for acting like a goat, Gabriel."

"Walter shot his lawyer for acting like a lawyer; a lawyer wouldn't barbecue half so well."

"It wasn't so bad, Gabriel. Maybe it was worth it. I learned something."

"What?"

"Reverence for life." He snorted. She said, "But I'm serious."

"You always are. And I shall have some relief." He roused himself to find his cocaine.

"Why do you do it?" she asked, watching his ritual of chopping and sniffing.

"I want to see purple eyes and gold shooting stars. You do, but I never do."

Sarah looked at the dog, the cat, and the deer outside, grazing beneath oaks against a violet sky and a rising moon. "And yet I prefer this."

She started as he fell back against her shoulder. She hadn't felt a human touch in weeks. "I'm trying to see what you see," he said. "Ah, I'm fading, fading."

"Are you going dancing tonight?"

"Trying to get rid of me?"

"No. Just don't stay home on my account. I'm fine as long as you don't shoot Milton."

"No." He returned to his cocaine. "I'm not going tonight. I'm tired. I wish I could fly away like you did. Why does it happen to everyone but me? How can you live without sex, Sarah?"

"I guess I just can."

"You should be sleeping with someone. Someone should be screwing you blue in the face."

"Why blue? Why not green or purple?"

"You're not being serious."

"I always am," she replied. "Is that what you think love is? A life-affirming ritual that makes you part of the stars and the night, worth getting the breath knocked out of you?"

"I can't explain it to someone who doesn't believe in it." He inhaled more cocaine.

"Gabriel, there is something to be said for reality."

"What?"

She thought about her wild flight and her delight at finding the earth beneath her feet again. "Sometimes, it's like magic: a miracle. I've always wanted to believe that."

Abruptly he stood up. "Well, if you're okay, I guess I will go dancing."

SHE COULD PUT it off no longer. In the morning, Sarah left the mountain driving Gabriel's rainbow-painted Jeep. She stopped first at a health clinic in Napa. She walked past the entrance a dozen times before she went inside. The waiting room was jammed with people, women with children, men with sun-ravaged faces. The clerk gave her a form, say-ing, "Let me know if you need help filling it out."

She sat down next to a white-haired man with a mustache. Blood was seeping through the handkerchief wrapped around his hand. She thought of her grandfather who had told her, "We worked in the fields so that our son would not have to."

"May I see it?" she asked softly. "*Puedo* — ?"

"Sarah Glass?" the clerk called.

"I think you had better take this man first." Sarah said. "Do you need help here?"

It was late in the afternoon when she left the clinic and drove on to San Francisco. She listened to the news. A computer had set off a nuclear alert, and for three seconds the world had hovered on the brink of war, but now everything was all right. She had been uncon-scious on a hillside at the time. She knew she should worry about the incident, but the possibility that the world would annihilate itself had been such a constant theme in her life, she was more worried about running out of gas. She wondered what would become of a world col-lectively running on empty, looking for parking places. A miracle was needed; but, supposing such things really existed, and each person re-ceived an allotment at birth, Sarah feared she had used up hers asking for parking places.

Damon Friedman was waiting for her at Tosca's Cafe. He was

drinking a martini and when he saw her, he drained it. "D'you know, Sarah, I think I like you best with wings."

She ordered two coffees. He took a pill from a case, swallowed it, drank the coffee, and asked for another martini. "You shouldn't do that," Sarah said.

"What? Drink coffee? That's right. You went to med school, or would have except you ran off to the hills with Gabriel Dinesen. So, tell me, Sarah, tell me — I'm sorry — I am tired today, but tell me —" He put his head down on the table and did not move again.

THE RED-GOLD DOG, now named Wolf, sniffed the sleeping man in the Jeep. Widdershins tested his claws on Damon's jacket before he settled down to sit on him.

"Just what we need, another animal," Gabriel said.

"I was only going to talk to him," Sarah said. "But when he passed out, the waiter had to put him somewhere."

"So you think he missed me, do you?"

Sarah did not see them again until the next day, when they came into the courtyard where she was feeding birds. "What I would like to know," Damon was saying, "is how you live here."

"Quite well, thank you."

"Can you ever answer a question straight?"

"Yes. No. I don't know. Why? Why not? Maybe. What? Straight? Egads!"

"I don't see how Sarah can stand to live with you."

"You seem to have stood it for a day. He only loves me for my perfect body, Sarah."

"Believe me, your perfect body is not worth it. I am only asking how you live on the nonexistent salary you get for going into a congressman's office and writing letters to people you don't know from someone you've never met."

"Picky. Picky. Picky."

"Politics might be your perfect world. Everything is as real as you are. How do you live?"

"At least it's not on pills and coffee. I don't pass out on innocent young women in public."

"Who pays the bills?"

"My father. I send them to him. You see, Damon, it's a poor reflection on him if I don't turn out well. He was so relieved to hear I'm living with a woman, he pays any kind of a bill."

"That's blackmail."

"Reality."

"Gabriel, this is not the real world."

"Do you hear someone calling?" Sarah asked.

They went outside to find a man standing by the empty swimming pool. He was young and slight; his mushrooming hair and beard made up the bulk of his person.

"Do you know there is a cow in your pool?" he asked.

"What luck!" Gabriel cried. "We needed a cow. Thank goodness we didn't fill the pool!"

"Who are you?" Damon asked. "What do you want?"

The man's name was Cloud, and he recommended they get the cow out of the pool by contacting it on a psychic wavelength. Gabriel opted to descend into the pool with a halter.

"Here cow," he crooned. "Nice cow."

"You can't just stand there and expect the cow to walk into a halter," Damon objected.

"I love people who stand on the edge of swimming pools and tell you how to catch cows," Gabriel muttered. The cow, however, allowed him to lead it up the steps, but when he crowed, it bolted. Everyone scattered and, unfortunately, Cloud ran into the fence and fell down.

"Oh no," said Sarah, for he appeared to be unconscious.

"Don't worry." Cloud raised his head. "I heal myself."

Gabriel led the cow to the chapel, despite Damon's objections that he could not keep a cow just because he had found it. It must belong to someone, he insisted. When they returned to Cloud, he was sitting up cross-legged and chanting.

"Be nice," Gabriel cautioned Damon.

Damon said, "I see you're feeling better. What do you want?"

"I need a field," Cloud hummed. "I am going to have an event."

"A what?" asked Damon.

"An event of some importance. A gathering of about five thousand people."

"Five thousand?"

"It's a sacred event. A landing." Cloud looked up reverently to the sky. "They are up there. They have finally come. We, the survivors, will come together, and they will land. They will reveal the truths and solve our problems. They only need an invitation and a field."

"Napa Valley is becoming a destination," Gabriel agreed.

"We will have to discuss this," Damon said firmly. "May we contact you somewhere? By telephone, preferably." Cloud gave Damon a card, bowed, and walked to his Ford.

"Another visitor," Gabriel hissed. A woman, dressed in black, was emerging from a silver sports car. "We have arrived!"

She looked familiar to Sarah, but then there was no shortage of thin, blonde women in California. "I've been trying to reach you with no luck," this one said. "I decided to just drop in."

"Call Cloud back!" Gabriel exclaimed. "They're here!"

The woman looked them over and chose to address Damon. "I am a neighbor —"

Gabriel interrupted. "Have you, perchance, lost your cow?"

"Cow," she echoed. "What cow?"

"Cow, big animal, four feet, moos."

"I am thinking of purchasing a parcel above yours," she said to Damon.

"Unfortunately, I am only a guest," Damon gestured to Gabriel. "He is the landowner."

Gabriel, assuming the pose of an idiot, waved. She said, "We need to discuss the road."

"We do? Why?"

"My lawyer says it's necessary."

"Ah, well, they'll say anything. Might as well ask a carrot."

"I intend to plant —"

"Something illegal, I hope?"

"Grapes. But we need to clear the trees and rocks."

"Ah," Gabriel said, "that's fine with me. Because then if it rains, your property will become my property."

"Let's be neighborly," she said. "Let's have lunch." She gave him a card and drove away. Tanya Matlock, it read. Sarah had not recognized her without her red hourglass.

"So, Damon, about the real world," Gabriel said.

"I would only like to know if we are going to eat anything before we go back to the city."

"Don't look at Sarah when you say that."

"I don't think it's boring to eat every day."

"Then cook."

"I don't know how."

"Learn."

CHAPTER 39

SARAH WATCHED THE taming of Damon Friedman, who returned like the ducks at feeding time. Irresistibly, the wild duck had eaten the grain, ventured closer, and stayed longer. She did not understand how she got along so easily with two men who clashed so constantly, but she supposed it was because she was not in love, and she was glad, again, not to be in love.

One night, when Damon did not drive from the city, Gabriel ate too many hallucinogenic mushrooms and passed out. "This is the way love should be," he said as Sarah made him tea. "Why don't you call Damon? He was mad because I went dancing, but he'll be back. And I'm going to make him buy a hot tub."

Damon did return, carrying a stack of mail into the kitchen where Gabriel was kneading bread. Sarah was painting pinecones with peanut butter. "What a long drive," he complained. "Gabriel, the mailbox was overflowing. Don't you ever read your mail?"

"No. Fold, turn, fold, turn. I love you, bread. And don't pester Sarah about it."

"I can see that she is doing something terribly important. I hope that it's not dinner."

"It's for the birds," she said. "You roll them in birdseed and hang them on a tree."

"Luring them in for your cat?" He asked as the phone began to ring. "Gabriel, if you won't read your mail, you might at least answer the telephone. Shall I?"

"No!" Gabriel lunged for the receiver. "Hello? Mother. How are you? I'm so glad. Yes, I'm fine, too. I really am. No, her name is Sarah, and she is fine. Of course, she can cook. No, we don't have a date yet. I don't know if she would raise the children as good Christians. Yes, I love you, too. No, I mean it." He hung up, rolling his eyes at Damon. "Roll me a joint, will you?"

"Do you send your drug bills to your father too?"

"Yes. Damon!" Gabriel exclaimed, as Damon doffed his suit jacket, tie, and trousers. "You can't take off your pants in front of Sarah!"

"Why not?" he asked. "Sarah has seen men's legs. I'd bet she has even seen a penis."

"I've dissected one," she admitted.

"Some help you are, Sarah," Gabriel groused, "when I am trying to defend your virtue."

"I don't know why you carry on as if Sarah is a vestal virgin."

"Because she is." Gabriel opened a letter. "It's from Kate. She was going to rent your flat from the new owner, Sarah, but she got laid off. I know! Let's invite her to come here."

"You can't do that," Damon protested. "I don't think I could live with a woman."

"What is Sarah, pray tell?"

"Sarah is different."

"This letter is from Cloud," Sarah said. "He's confirming that you'll rent him your field."

Damon groaned. "I can't believe you did that."

"I didn't know Harry could write," Gabriel said, reading a new letter. "Mildred is pregnant; they're getting married. You still have to, after all these years. What a gene pool."

"I can imagine," Damon said.

"No," Sarah murmured. "You can't."

"I am getting an idea." Gabriel flourished his bread dough. "First, we get Kate. Damon can bring her. Then, we have a bachelor party for Harry, which can also be a welcome for the aliens, and we can break in the hot tub Damon is buying."

"I am?"

"Will Mildred have to come?" Sarah asked.

"She can jump out of the cake."

"I don't think Sarah likes the idea any better than I do," Damon said hopefully.

"It's your fault," Gabriel pointed out. "You brought the mail."

"Chore time." Sarah gathered up her pinecones.

"When do we get dinner?" Damon asked.

"Sarah, please give him a pinecone," Gabriel said. "I am cooking dinner, Damon. The question is, what are you doing?"

"I feel like I'm doing chores with St. Francis," Damon said as birds swooped down to the pinecones; at this, the horse neighed, the calf mooed, the goat bleated, and the ducks began their march in from the lake. "These animals are terribly spoiled," he added as they walked to the chapel. "Although I have to admit, I do like your wolf."

"Someone must have abandoned her. And Widdershins has accepted her, more or less."

"But why does she make snarly faces at Gabriel?"

"We're working on that. She likes you."

"I always wanted a dog," he said wistfully. "You never found the owner of the cow?"

"Not even the congressman could."

"Why do you feed the cow and goat oats, too?"

"Otherwise, they eat Rebecca's, and she's too shy to stand up for herself."

"Ah. So, what's next?"

"Chickens and ducks."

When they had finished scattering grain, she said, "We're done. Unless you want to climb the hill and look at the cave but not go in."

"I suppose we must do this properly or Gabriel will have another reason to be mad at me." They climbed the hill and sat down in the grass. The sun was setting, rose, gold, and crimson. He said, "You have the only cat I've ever seen who goes for walks with people."

"Watch," she said. "There's a hawk that flies out every evening, like he's saying hello."

"It is beautiful," he admitted, "but I can't trust it. One reason we fight — one of them — is that Gabriel wants me to give up everything and move here. But I can't. How can you do it, Sarah? Don't you want anything of your own? A home, a husband, a family?"

"Me?"

"Why not? Frankly, Sarah, you seem to have something of a nesting instinct."

"No." She shook her head. "In freshman biology, we saw a film about a gorilla who had lived her whole life in captivity in a cement cage. She never mated; she wouldn't, so they traded her to a zoo with a gorilla habitat. They filmed her as she saw trees and grass and running water for the first time. She was so fearful but she touched the grass with such wonder, and then she fell down and rolled around. It was joy. I know hearts don't break but mine almost did anyway, watching her. Still, she never mated. Maybe she was too busy looking at things."

"That's very nice, but what about Rory McIntyre? Good grief, Sarah, you do stop breathing. Rory said it worries him." Ignoring her stricken look, he added, "We had some time to talk, while we were dealing with the dead ex-wife."

She focused on the hawk circling overhead. "Was he all right?"

"No. But sometimes people aren't."

"He wouldn't have wanted me."

"Not just then, perhaps. Not that he wasn't worried sick about you."

"Me? It was Dibby who was dead."

"I told him your greatest challenge will be getting used to being loved."

"But he doesn't."

"Is that what you think?"

"It's what I know. Rory doesn't believe in love. He likes sex and conversation and companionship, but not love. Why are you laughing?"

"My dear girl, that sounds like love to me."

"Is that how you feel about Gabriel?"

"No, unfortunately. Once, I thought it was possible, but it's not what Gabriel wants, and so it died. It happens" She nodded. "Haven't you seen Rory?" he asked. "Why on earth not?"

"I decided — " She breathed, in and out, counting, three, four, five times. "I don't want to wreck his life."

"He doesn't need your help for that," Damon chuckled. "He does it all by himself." He was interrupted by a popping sound, like an explosion of firecrackers. They ran down the hill to find Gabriel in the meadow holding a shotgun.

"What on earth are you doing, Gabriel?" Damon asked. "You scared us to death."

"Getting ready for divorce court," Gabriel said.

CHAPTER 40

"MYTH HAS IT that the man who built this place called it Paradise," Damon said, pouring Kate a glass of wine as they sat in the castle courtyard. He had not been looking forward to a long drive with Sarah's friend who was leaving her husband, but he had been pleasantly surprised by the quiet woman carrying a bag of knitting. He gallantly regretted that he had been too filled with painkillers to remember her Thanksgiving dinner, which he knew he had attended. The journey was shortened by a conversation, which he later realized had been mostly about himself.

Kate gazed at the Cupid fountain with the doubtful air of one entering an enchanted realm long after the confusion of life had stolen away any belief in magic. "It's lovely."

"Sarah has done wonders with it and the gardens. And Gabriel ran mad buying her plants and seeds. I can't imagine what will happen if everything blooms. Unless it all freezes."

"Where are they?"

"Gabriel? One never knows. Sarah is at the farmworkers' clinic. It did cause a bit of a rift when she said she was going to work there. Gabriel roared off in his car and almost hit her dog. It's the only time I've ever seen her angry with him."

"I can't imagine them quarreling."

"Oh, he made it up to her, the usual way, I suppose." As Kate smiled, he explained, "He offers to kill himself." He looked at his watch. "Well, I had better go start dinner."

"May I help you?"

"Yes," he said promptly. "You really might. Because I don't know how to cook, but Gabriel says I have to. First, I'll show you to your room. We've put you in the south wing near Sarah's room. Gabriel and I have the north tower."

Kate blinked, and Damon wondered how much they had omitted in her invitation.

"Sarah, of course, prefers to sleep in the barn with her creatures. It was a chapel and then the commune workshop. The commune rather recklessly bought all kinds of things, but not all of the tools are rusted. I am going to use them to make a bird feeder for Sarah, but first I plan to watch the crew install the hot tub that Gabriel made me buy."

A leaf fluttered into his wine. He fished it out and contemplated it. "You know, Kate. Gabriel is creating a world here that has no connection with anything else. It can't last, and yet, I should warn you, it becomes harder and harder to leave."

"I BROUGHT THE things you wanted, Sarah," Kate said. "The weird vase and the orchid; it's still not dead. And I brought your mail too." She felt it was a lame addition to the dinner conversation, which until then had consisted of Damon's ardent admiration of her cooking and Gabriel's creepy haunted tales, yet Sarah, to whom she had handed a stack of battered manila envelopes, addressed in erratic handwriting, looked as if she'd seen one of the castle's ghosts.

"Fan mail from your retarded admirer?" Gabriel asked. Sarah put the mail aside, unopened.

"Your apartment is all cleared out," Kate went on. "Rory said —"

"How are your parents?" Sarah interrupted

"Well, January was bad. Mom went to visit Tim at UCLA, and Pat and Mike at Davis, and then she decided to stay with Rory in Berkeley. Dad was so depressed, Rory and I took him to Buttercream to cheer him up. And guess who we saw? Your mother and Cecily. Cecily's wedding is coming up, and she is sure you'll forget to go, so I said I would. Your mom is going to China. She said you always get all the chances and she never got any, but now she's going to do something for herself. Dad was so interested. He said how beautiful Isabelle is, and then he went by himself to a travel agent. I thought, oh no, he's given up on Mom, and he's going to run away to China with Isabelle. But he'd bought Mom a plane ticket to Hawaii. He said even she might run out of kids to visit."

"Only one ticket?" Sarah asked, dismayed.

"I know. That's what Rory said, too. 'I didn't mean send her there alone.'"

"Did she go?"

Kate nodded. "With Rory."

"Rory?"

"He worked like crazy to finish the thing he was building at Cal so his boss could test it at the observatory on the Big Island. But his boss was too sick to travel so he asked Rory to go test it. He said use his condo, take the kids, and stay for a vacation. Mom was sure Rory wouldn't worry enough about sharks and jellyfish, and who would babysit, so even though she'd insisted she'd never take the ticket from Dad, she decided she had better go too."

"Wasn't that clever of Rory," Damon said. "How is he doing, Kate?"

"Well, his boss died just before they left and he told me he might stay in Hawaii and be a fisherman. And he doesn't like to fish."

"Would you tell him, from me, that if he ever wants to talk to someone, just as a friend —"

"Aren't we just so interested in Rory," Gabriel grumbled.

"Shall we have dessert?" Damon asked. "Kate made brownies, my favorite."

"I will inhale dessert in my room." Gabriel slouched away from the table.

"Don't worry," Damon told Kate. "He just doesn't like any conversation that isn't about him. Gabriel, why don't you sit down and stop behaving like an ass?"

"Because," Gabriel said with a tremble in his voice. "I miss you."

Damon looked amazed, murmured good night, and left the room with him. Sarah, reading Kate's bewildered look, said, "I have a tea kettle in the barn. Do you want to meet the animals?"

"You sleep in a manger," Kate laughed as they sat down in the pews with their tea. "Are they lovers, then, Damon and Gabriel?"

"I meant to tell you, but I didn't."

"When I met Gabriel, he was so handsome and fun, I thought it was odd he wasn't gay."

"I thought Rory might have mentioned it."

"Rory? My brother?"

"He reminded Gabriel of Richard the Lionheart, that's all. It wasn't mutual."

"You seem to love him, Sarah."

"Who?"

"Gabriel."

"I guess I do. But there are other ways of loving."

"Are there?"

"I don't know," Sarah said. "I hope so. I was in it before I knew what I was in. I couldn't just back out, could I?"

"That doesn't sound so different to me."

"Is that why you married Sterling?"

"No. I was in love."

"With Sterling?" Sarah tried not to sound incredulous.

"No. Another guy. My dark secret. My first date at St. Mary's. My first date ever. I thought I'd gone to heaven, not the movies. I slept with him before Christmas and went home dreaming every crazy dream we'd ever made up. But when I went back to school, everything had changed. It was over, he said. No reason. Still, I had to see him every day, and I wanted to die. When Sterling asked me out, I knew there was no chance I'd ever fall in love with him, and I never wanted to be in love again. But whatever love is, Sarah, it matters. We didn't have it, and it mattered every day.

"I tried; I really did. But when Rory stayed with us, he bought me a sack of light bulbs, because he said we had so many burned out ones, and I had to explain that they weren't really burnt out; it's just that Sterling unscrews all the bulbs but one in fixtures to save money. He didn't say anything, but the look on his face — I had to ask myself, what am I doing?

"And even John — when he and Rory helped me move out, we sat in your apartment that night and drank a bottle of wine, and when I said I knew that Jesus would say try harder, John said, did I really think Jesus was as big an ass as Sterling? He said I was afraid; and he said he is too, although I don't know what he has to be scared of except too many women baking him cakes. And Rory — Sarah, are you all right? You are looking kind of sick."

"I'm just tired," Sarah said. "There was a prenatal clinic today. So many women don't have doctors." She now knew the Spanish word for pregnant: *embarazada*. "What about Rory?"

"Everyone, even my grandmother, thinks he cares for you, a lot. I was sorry because I thought, if you had Gabriel, how could you prefer Rory?"

"I've preferred Rory since I was fourteen."

"You have?" Kate, open-mouthed and dumbfounded, set down her tea cup. "Wait, is that why we had to paint all those posters for him? Why didn't you tell me? I would have told him."

"That's why I didn't tell you. Anyway, he knows."

"He does? But if you — if he — Sarah, Rory looks like someone has cut out his liver and fried it, and you don't look so great, yourself. Are you guys nuts?"

Sarah studied the moonlight glimmering through the stained-glass window; it danced like fireflies over the altar, the candlesticks, the sacks of oats, the statues of the Virgin and her son. "It was just a fantasy with Rory, that's all."

"Er, Sarah — most people would be glad to have a fantasy like that."

"Maybe our species has outgrown love. Rory thinks it's a myth for the masses, like God."

"Yeah, and it's too bad that someone who is so smart is such a dumbhead."

"She lived without love, didn't she?" Sarah asked, glancing at the Virgin, who, despite her serene expression, appeared to be following the conversation with interest.

"She might have lived without sex, but she didn't live without love," Kate said and they both laughed.

When Kate had gone to her room in the castle, Sarah opened her mail: five letters from Jimmy filled with drawings. She had sent him a card via Dr. Castro. The sixth envelope contained only a sheaf of long, yellow, lined papers covered with writing in pencil and pen, crossed out, written over. She read it twice before she understood what it was: a fragment from a novel about an idiot, the hero of Paradise Lost. She put her head down on the desk and wept.

❦

AT DINNER ON Sunday night, Kate asked Sarah if she could have a ride to Napa on Monday when Sarah went to the clinic.

"You're not leaving, Kate?" Gabriel protested.

"I only came for a weekend."

"But, Kate you've worked miracles with Damon. Not once has he bothered me about the real world. He cooked. He washed dishes. Would you like a pet? Sarah will find you one."

Damon said, "Why can't I have a pet?"

"Not until you live here," Gabriel said. "And not until you think of something more original than a dog. But, Kate, you said you want to try weaving. Would you like a sheep?"

"And Thursday is my birthday," Damon added. "We could celebrate it. And my Diplomacy game is coming up. Maybe you could go with me. I wanted Gabriel to go, but he won't."

Gabriel fell on his knees and clutched Kate's legs. "Please, Kate, save me. Otherwise, he will make me go and watch shrinks and lawyers reenact World War I."

"They fight?"

"No, they each declare themselves dukes and kings and never go near the trenches."

"We have a giant map," Damon explained. "We plan strategies and see how history would have turned out if we had been in power."

"Damon plays Queen Victoria."

"She was not queen then, you idiot," Damon retorted. "This year, I am Russia. Tsar Nicholas. You would be a wonderful Alexandra, Kate. I wanted Gabriel to be Rasputin, but I'd much rather have Alexandra. We wear costumes and have an Edwardian banquet."

"And for after-dinner entertainment, they shoot peasants," Gabriel added.

"I do need help deciding about my costume, Kate," Damon said.

"Maybe I could make them."

"That would be wonderful!"

"Done!" Gabriel crowed. "Tomorrow, we'll go get you sewing machine and a sheep."

Thus Gabriel spun a web around Kate, and she stayed.

CHAPTER 41

"Y OU'RE LATE," DAMON said. "Kate and I have already had a cocktail."

"It's Sarah's fault," Gabriel replied airily.

"It's certainly an expensive place you've chosen."

"Nothing is too good for your birthday. It's a good thing you can afford it."

"You could too if you ever did real work."

"Which reminds me, you didn't take out the garbage."

"Sorry, I forgot."

"It's all right. I put it in your room."

"Where is Sarah?" Kate asked.

"Out in the parking lot, looking at a bird or something."

Sarah, however, had managed to drag herself to the door of the candle-lit restaurant in St. Helena where Matt Biagi was standing. "Sarah Glass!" he boomed. "Hey, I've been trying to get hold of your guy. Where the hell is he?"

"Hawaii."

"We had quite a nice day," Damon was saying as she slid into her seat.

"We went to a lecture on new forms of insanity," Kate added. "And we found the medals for Damon's costume; then we went to a barbershop quartet competition."

Gabriel gagged. "How thrilling, doing everything Damon wants to do."

"My mother always let us choose a special thing to do on our birthday," Kate explained.

"And Damon is making up for lost birthdays by choosing thirty-seven special things."

"Shall we order?" Damon asked. "Kate, what would you like?"

"Oh, anything."

"No, Kate," Gabriel prompted. "A little caviar. A big lobster. Steak."

"Why not?" Damon asked. "Let's start with sparkling wine, domestic, Schramsberg, please. I have an announcement: I've been offered a job in Napa. Now, may I have a pet?"

Sarah watched Kate's face as enchantment struggled against the protests of practical intelligence. Here they were, dining in style with two charming, handsome men. Had their teenage fantasies materialized, exactly as they'd dreamt them?

A trio began to play, "Isn't it Romantic?" Sadness fell over her like blanket, one that had been spread in a meadow and was full of prickly weeds.

Gabriel, perusing the menu, said, "I want a child."

"A what?" Kate and Damon asked together.

"Think about it. To grow up, your whole life, on our farm."

"That's ridiculous," Damon said. "You can't get a child and change your mind, like you did with the sheep." Gabriel had bought three sheep on Monday, and returned two on Wednesday, after one had stood in the rain with its mouth open and drowned on Tuesday.

"Pardon me," Gabriel said huffily. "It's only my dream."

Sarah had felt sorry for the sheep, and now there it was on the menu, in a roasted rack. She excused herself, fled to the bathroom, locked herself in a stall, and burst into tears. She tried to restore herself to order by repeating all the parts of the gastrointestinal tract, but she, who had once marveled at the miracle of the human body, could only wonder how life managed to endure. Her own body had become a mystery, and a wreck. Just when she had got used to throwing up every morning, especially if there was coffee within five miles, this had happened: at least once a day at the clinic she had to hide in the bathroom to weep profusely over anything; a diagnosis of cancer, a broken pencil, it didn't matter. She had to do something soon.

As she returned to the table, Matt descended on them, carrying a bottle of wine and glasses. A lady had sent her own wine over, he explained. He opened and poured it, and led the ritual of swirling and sniffing it. "Amazing, isn't it?"

Sarah sniffed it; she knew her present situation might be the reason it smelled quite odd, but Damon, too, was wincing. Kate took a sip and choked. "I don't know anything about wine," she said apologetically.

Gabriel said, "Cat pee."

"And a little *pipi du chat* is not a bad thing," Matt explained as Tanya Matlock strolled up to the table. She was wearing a black silk sheath and a ruby on a gold chain.

"You devil, I knew you'd turn up when I told you I'd be here," she said to Gabriel. "So is my wine *sauvage* enough for you? Is anything *sauvage* enough for you?" She kissed him solidly on the lips, and the others returned confusedly to swirling and sniffing their wine.

"Come with me, you bad boy," Tanya murmured. "I have something for you"

Gabriel rose; Tanya shot Sarah a look of venom and triumph, but Sarah, watching Damon worriedly, missed it. Damon only shrugged. "There's nothing we can do. He will keep pushing his luck until he reaches a law at variance with his own. And he has more lives than a cat."

❋

"You're quiet," Gabriel said, as they drove back after dinner.

"I was thinking."

"Yes, I've gotten used to that."

"It was a long time ago that we made that wild ride in the storm."

"Want to do it again?"

"No. But maybe I should leave now."

"Leave?"

"If Damon is moving in, you might want to be alone."

"Yeah," he smiled. "How about that? But, Sarah, you can't leave. It's even better if Kate stays. Then no one will know what's going on."

"Including us." She summoned her resolution. "Do you really want a child?"

"Why not?"

"Children make everything real."

"Yikes! Shoo! Begone! Sarah, now you've put it in my head: let's fly down the hill."

"I think I'll walk from here."

The night was clear, cold, and still. As she neared the house she could hear Kate playing the piano. Damon was singing "Believe Me If All Those Endearing Young Charms."

"Hi, Gabriel!" Damon giggled. "Where've you been? Do you know what we did? We stopped for Brandy Alexanders. Kate had never had one. And do you know what the bartender said? 'I guess they're not all fairies in San Francisco!" He went off into peals of laughter.

"Degenerates," Gabriel growled. "I'd better stay to chaperone."

Sarah slipped to the telephone, dialed, and listened to the voice, warm and melodic, even on an answering machine: "Leave a message; I'll call you back." It was safe, if he were being a fisherman in Hawaii, and it was not, she hoped, as crazy as driving past his house, just to look at it. She hadn't done that. She dialed twice more and then retreated to her balcony. By flashlight, she read the yellow lined pages, the fragment of a novel about an idiot. She wept, the fifth time that day. The dog and cat came to sit with her. Wolf raised her head and howled at the moon. "Yes, that's how I feel too," Sarah said.

CHAPTER 42

"A LEXANDRA, YOU ARE a goddess!" Gabriel, on his knees, was taking pins out of the ruffles of her green taffeta ball gown.

Kate looked uncertainly in the mirror and adjusted the neckline. "It's not too low cut?"

"It's beautiful," Sarah assured her, putting more roses in Kate's elaborate hairdo. "It's too bad it's only a game."

"If it weren't, someone would have to shoot them at the end of it," Gabriel pointed out. "Ah, here's Damon. Can you walk yet, dear, without cutting your leg off with your sword?"

"It does require practice." Damon, resplendent in a uniform that glittered with gold buttons, medals and fringed epaulets, adjusted his sash. "Kate! You look — very nice."

"Moron," Gabriel scowled. "She looks gorgeous, ravishing, stunning."

"Well, she always looks beautiful. But the dress really did come out well."

"Do you think you have enough medals, Damon?" Gabriel asked. "I can still see some of the white of your tunic. I'm afraid you might outshine your consort."

"I doubt that," Damon replied, with a mysterious smile. "Shall we dance once more, Kate? We probably should try it with your skirt and my sword." He bowed, Kate curtsied, and as they waltzed, with only a few awkward clashes, a burst of squawking erupted from the chicken coop.

"Egads!" Gabriel peered out a window. Sterling was marching up the castle steps. "Fly, fair Kate! I shall do battle! Come, Sarah! No quarter!" He flung open the door grandly.

"I have come for Kate," Sterling announced.

"Kate's busy," Gabriel said. "There's a royal ball tonight."

"Sarah, will you get Kate?"

"Get Kate." Gabriel hummed. "Do you mean summon? Sorry, you have the wrong Kate. If you would like an audience, you have to go through me. But first you have to capture the broomstick of the Wicked Witch of the West. And get a letter from your congressman."

"It's all right." Kate's sparkle was fading as she came outside. "Sterling, what do you want?"

"I've come to take you back."

"I'm not coming back."

"That's ridiculous."

"It's the way I feel —"

"Then it's a ridiculous way to feel."

Kate made no reply. Sterling continued talking, although it was not a speech calculated or destined to win her back. Reduced by many words, this was its essence: if any leaving were to be done, he would leave her.

"I wish you would go away," Kate said wearily. "It doesn't matter who left first."

"Damn," Damon said, listening inside with Sarah and Gabriel. "Even if she does get rid of him, she is going to feel terrible."

"There is only one thing to do," Gabriel said. "And you are the only one who can do it."

"I am not going to run him through with my sword, Gabriel."

"Chicken heart."

"I have a better idea." Damon flung his gilt-trimmed royal cape over his shoulder and strode out of the castle. "Oh, Kate. Here you are. Darling." His delivery was only a trifle wooden; Kate's stunned expression by far surpassed Sterling's. Damon squinted at Sterling. "Who is this — dearest?"

"Sterling, my husband," Kate whispered.

"Ah." Damon dowsed the word with regal indifference and hauteur, and heard his high school drama teacher applaud. "We have to be going — but first, I have these for you." From his cloak he brought out a velvet box. "A mere trifle, my grandmother's. How happy she'd be, knowing I've met the perfect woman to give them to. May I?" He fastened a diamond necklace around Kate's neck. "They're almost as beautiful as you. Does he want something, dear?"

Sterling sputtered, "I've come to take Kate home."

"Indeed? But she is home." Another excellent delivery.

"This is none of your business."

"Ah, but it is. But not yours, I'm afraid, because you've lost her."

Sterling departed in a whirl of dust. Damon mopped his brow with his monogramed handkerchief. "It might not have been the best way to handle it, professionally speaking."

"I should feel something, shouldn't I?" Kate asked. "But I don't feel anything at all."

"It might not have been the best way to handle it, professionally speaking," Gabriel sneered as the royal couple departed in Damon's Honda. "He told me he always had to be the tree in school plays."

"Gabriel, why did you say Kate was a goddess, not a queen?"

"Did I? It just fell into my head." He thumped his forehead. "It's empty now."

"Do you think there is a goddess?"

"Oh yes, and a god and a devil and little elves and werewolves everywhere."

"But what if there is a goddess, and God locked her up —"

"Henry and Eleanor!"

"And what if you — gay men — are setting her free?"

"A bunch of fairies?"

"Wasn't Lionheart gay? He freed his mother."

"Ye gads. Useful. What a thought. But, Sarah, you don't think that Damon will lose his head and make a pass at Kate?"

"No. I don't. It's only a game, Gabriel."

"Then, I guess I'll go out too. Tanya the Dreadlock is taking me in her limo to the city."

"Gabriel, I'd be careful. I don't think she's into fantasies. I think she's a realist."

"Sarah, she's from LA. What's real is what she can buy. The top of a mountain. A winemaker. A nose. Me. She wouldn't know real if she ran over it. She might be my soulmate. Sarah, come with me! She hates you. I'll bet she'd poison your soup."

Gabriel left too, and Sarah went to the telephone. She dialed, hung up, stared at the phone, and dialed again. She held on until there was an answer. "Hello," she said. "It's Sarah."

"Who?"

"I heard you might go to China."

"I don't know," Isabelle Glass said. "It's so full of foreigners."

"I wanted to wish you well."

"It's too bad people never mean what they say."

"Well," Sarah said, "then I just wanted to say goodbye."

CHAPTER 43

THEY WERE ALMOST late for Cecily's fourth special day because they waited for Gabriel, who had gone out the night before and not returned. They finally left in the Jeep; Damon's fuel gage was on empty and it was too late to stop for gas.

Cecily's fourth husband was a Catholic, and they were being married at St. John's in Napa. Sarah had been there once before, during Rory's penance. At that time, it was the relatively new, controversial replacement for the old church, built in 1860 but a victim of dry rot. Some parishioners had complained that this modern creation looked more like the inside of a washing machine than a holy temple, but Sarah had thought it was wonderful; this was because she was sitting next to Rory. Now, she was free to observe the grass-green altar in the center of church, the windows made of bands of colors set with stars, the tall white candles, and flame-red tapestry of St. John, a giant in an animal skin, hand raised, saluting the startled faithful. Even without Rory, it possessed an aura of enchantment but, for her, it was the power of the unknown. How did people believe?

The music began, and Cecily, in a cloud of white silk, floated down the aisle. She looked happy. Perhaps this time she would stay happy. What was different? Love? A whiff of incense from a thurible wafted over Sarah. She abandoned thoughts of love and scrambled for the door. She knelt down, retching into a bed of early daffodils. She had not been sick in several days, but it was a welcome change from weeping.

The wind felt cool and fresh, and she decided to walk instead of going back inside the church, where she would think about love again. A few turns brought her to the street that had, for her, possessed even more magic than a cathedral. There, amidst warehouses and shops that fixed broken windows and mufflers, was the corrugated iron barn with the black and white sign: "McIntyre's Repair."

SHE STOPPED AT the edge of the asphalt parking area. The garage door was open, unusual for a Saturday. Joe always stopped working at noon on Friday and did not return until Monday. As she watched through the chain-link fence, the office door opened, and two people came out, the first a buxom, fluffy-haired blonde, dressed for winter in white shorts and a strapless pink top. It was the Cupcake. She tripped along on high-heeled sandals gazing up at her companion as if he were a Greek oracle in a Giant's baseball cap. They walked to a blue Chevy and he turned to hand her a keyring with a purple plastic cat on it. Sarah's heart fell onto a carnival ride, flipping, turning, and falling. The man, tanned and clean-shaven, was Rory McIntyre.

"I can't imagine how it happened," the woman fluttered.

"Well," Rory replied, "a gas tank holds a finite amount of gas, and when it's gone, the car stops." The Cupcake rippled with amusement, although Sarah would have sworn that this was news to her; then she saw Sarah, standing spellbound in the bushes.

"This neighborhood is getting real strange," she said.

Sarah flew down the sidewalk until she found the Jeep. She jumped in, pulled out, and drove erratically, without an idea of where she was going, and mumbling, "Idiot, idiot, idiot." Thus absorbed in a profitless conversation, she failed to notice the red light ahead until it was too late to brake. She hit the bumper of a truck, groaned, and slumped against the steering wheel.

A man leaped out of the truck. "Dr. Sarah!" he exclaimed.

Sarah raised her head. She knew Frankie. He had come into the clinic for a rash he had developed after spraying grapevines. He persisted in calling her "doctor," although she had explained to him that she was not. Her voice trembled. "I am so sorry."

"But it's no problem," Frankie insisted as cars whipped around them. The light had turned green. "All is fine. No damage. But you are hurt?"

A woman climbed out of the truck. Frankie introduced his wife, Josefina. Together, they decided he would drive the Jeep, and Josefina the truck, and they took Sarah home with them.

"I AM REALLY all right," Sarah insisted. She was lying on a sofa covered with a brightly striped serape. Above her hung a painting of the Virgin of Guadalupe. Not far away, people were cooking in a narrow kitchen, and the scent of and onions filled the air. Several children were watching her from the doorway.

"Es la doctora?" one asked.

"No," Sarah said. "Es la idiota." They giggled and ran away. Josefina came in, carrying two mugs of cocoa, scented with cinnamon.

"Thank you," Sarah said. "Gracias." She was not sure how much English Josefina spoke; all the conversation in the house was in Spanish, of which Sarah understood one in ten words.

"You are Mexicana?" Josefina asked shyly.

"I don't know what I am. Yo no se — anything."

"I speak English, only a little. I study — but — is good for me to speak at — to — you."

"This cocoa is wonderful." Sarah had nearly finished her mug.

"Yes, my *tía*, Aurelia, she makes it. But I should not drink it every time." Josefina patted her pregnant stomach. "Today, I am so big. Even my feet, they are big."

"When is your baby due? *Cuando* —"

"Oh, maybe one month."

"What did the doctor say?"

Josefina shrugged.

"Do you have a doctor?"

"Is no problem. Aurelia, her babies came at home. Me too. And you? *Cuando* —"

Sarah watched her stomach grow, like an inflating basketball. "How did you know?"

"Aurelia. She sees you have — *cómo se dice?* — a special look."

"I believe it is called complete and total panic. *Histeria*."

Josefina laughed. "We must call your husband to say you are here."

"Well, no."

Josefina's eyes widened. "You have no husband?"

"No."

"A boyfriend?"

"No."

"*Eres como la Virgen?*"

Sarah laughed and then she gasped. "Oh no! Damon and Kate! I forgot them!" She insisted she was fine to drive home. She was more worried about Josefina's swollen feet. Frankie was leaving on Monday for work in Lodi, so Sarah said she would pick Josefina up, if she would come to the clinic and see a doctor. She wrote down her telephone number.

The church was empty. Sarah could not remember where the reception was, but she found Kate back at the castle, alone. "No worries," Kate said. "We got a ride. I called home and guess who answered the phone? Rory! He came back from Hawaii, after all. But Mom stayed. He brought the kids home, and he's working at the shop. How crazy is that? You just missed him."

"Oh," Sarah said, calmly despite her erratic heartbeat. "Where's Damon?"

"Gone. Something happened. It was bad. I think it's over, him and Gabriel. Damon went back to the city, but he said he'll call, and he'll be back for the alien landing."

SARAH KNOCKED, THEN ventured into the north tower littered with crumpled clothes, empty beer bottles, pizza boxes, bags from McDonald's. "Gabriel? Are you here? What's wrong?"

His voice came out of the dark. "I did it, Sarah. I had sex with that woman."

"Why?"

"I don't know. Why not? I didn't have to do anything — well, not much, anyway."

"You told Damon? Is that why he left?"

"He just doesn't care. He's supposed to, but he doesn't."

"You can reduce anything to nothingness."

"What?"

"He would care, if you would let him."

"I don't know how," he said. "Sarah, would you have sex with me?"

"Me?"

"Here, now."

"Well, no."

"Then go away and leave me alone."

She left. She and Kate did the chores, and when Kate had gone to bed, Sarah went to the telephone. "This is Sarah Glass," she said to a machine. "I have an appointment on Monday. But I have to change it to Wednesday, if that's possible. I know it's the third time I've canceled, but I will come on Wednesday. I really will."

CHAPTER 44

"D̲O YOU THINK choice is the enemy of commitment?" Rory McIntyre, tilted back in an office chair, his feet propped on a cluttered desk, was doodling on a yellow notepad.

John McIntyre was deep in perusal of a ledger. "Rory, I have no idea if anyone has paid any bills since Mom left."

"He's never had to keep accounts. He's never had to turn on the oven, make coffee, or do laundry. What a life."

"Now that I think of it, neither have I," John admitted, "No, wait: I have made coffee."

KVON radio, playing in the auto shop office, announced a breaking news update on a storm heading toward the coast. Only in California, Rory observed, was rain a banner story. He turned his attention back to his writing and browsed through one of several books piled on the desk. He was looking for a synonym for "fortunate," but got distracted by "forlorn," the etymology of which he followed back to the ninth century *Anglo-Saxon Chronicles*, when it had meant "morally lost" or "depraved." Forlorn was the past participle of a forgotten verb, forlese, "to lose completely or utterly." He shut the book. The lost word was hardly useful in a speech for a congressman eyeing the Senate. Nor did it apply to Rory, who was not feeling anything at all these days.

When had this happened? Sometime after he had looked at the face of his dead ex-wife and traveled with her body on a harrowing flight, chased by a winter storm. Free drinks could not obliterate the sensation that they were on a roller coaster to hell.

Archibald Davis, the Mudell family lawyer, met Rory at the airport and together they followed a hearse from the airport through a blizzard to the Wishing cemetery, established in 1658. As snow swirled around them, Davis, formal and reserved, mentioned that he had felt some concern when Dibby told him she and Rory were getting back together. He had even considered warning Rory that Dibby was flat broke, living on credit, trying without success to tap into the funds the judge had ordered to be set aside for the children. What? Rory had not pleaded with her to come to California? Sadly, Davis had suspected as much when she had tried to borrow money from him. Rory, of course, was in no way responsible for her debts.

The ground was too frozen to bury her; they would keep her somewhere until a thaw. Rory tried to think of something to say to the woman who had been, so briefly and disastrously, his wife, and in the end could only manage, "Good-bye, Dibby."

As he slept that night at the inn in Wishing, an ice storm transformed the landscape. In the morning he walked through a frozen meadow to a forest where the trees had been bent into a fantastic grotto of glittering crystals. He liked this hidden and silent place. If he could, he would stay it it. In a way, he did. He just transported it, in his mind, back to Berkeley. He remained in this cold cave during long nights in the lab as he finished his receiver. He carried it to the Hawaiian mountaintop, Mauna Kea, where he took his machine to test it. The receiver worked better than his own brain. When scientists asked him if he would continue Cageman's work, he only said he didn't know.

After he left the mountain, he stayed a week on the Big Island. He took his mother and children to see lava flows, whales, and orchid gardens. At night he swam alone in the pool. Jean urged him to stay a month, but he said he had to get back, although he didn't know why. He and Lucy and Avery departed, leaving his mother alone on an island where she knew no one at all.

The first night back in Berkeley, a pizza delivery man was shot next door, and as Rory lay in bed listening to sirens, it occurred to him that he was free to leave. He gave notice to his landlady and took his children to Napa. Joe was elated to have the company and continually amazed at the things Rory could do — run the washing machine, cook a chicken, fill the dishwasher. To this, Rory only replied, who else would have done it?

He worked in his father's shop and not once during the course of a day did he doubt the usefulness of what he was doing, given the number of people who knew nothing about the vehicles upon which they were entirely dependent. Lucy and Avery stayed happily with a motherly neighbor who offered home daycare; she had rabbits, chickens, and a garden. Each morning he ran for several miles. After work, he swam in a neighbor's heated pool. At night, he and his father watched television, like two old men.

He saw people; everyone in Napa came to McIntyre's Repair. It was the startled look on the face of his first grade teacher, Miss Wilson, that caused him to shave and get a haircut. The editor of Napa's daily newspaper came in with a car held together with duct tape and wire, and when Frank Havoc learned that Rory, between tune-ups, was revising Congressman Ilillouette's notes on the Future of America — was there one or not — he talked Rory into covering a city council meeting; he was down a reporter and they would be discussing an increase in garbage rates.

He did it all from inside his ice cave. If it was cold, he didn't mind. The worries, doubts, terrors, and dread of laundromats that had formerly filled his head were gone. He had no inclination to re-fill it. He was neither happy nor unhappy, just a well-exercised idiot, and soon, he was sure, he would be able to sleep all through a night.

A gust of wind rattled the office door as Joe came in, chatting with the vice-mayor of Napa, who owned a mortuary and brought his hearse to the garage. The telephone rang; Joe answered it. "Aure-lia! *Como estás?* Wait — what? Who's dead? Slow down, darling. Here, you'd better talk to John — you can *hablas español* to him. He knows what he's saying. Yes, he's here, home for a visit."

He handed the receiver to John. "Aurelia Robledo," he said. "A beautiful woman but she forgets English when she's excited, which is most of the time. She's at the Queen," he added, using the Napa short-hand for its hospital, the Queen of the Valley. "I believe her niece had a baby, and the doctor dropped dead."

"It's the doctor's car that won't start," John said, when he had con-cluded this conversation. "I told Aurelia to wait for us in the lobby. Rory and I will go."

"You will?" Rory asked. "You don't know anything about cars."

"You don't know Spanish," John retorted, sending Rory a mean-ingful look. There was no way he would permit his father to go to the aid of a beautiful woman with a dead battery. "Mom has to come back soon," he mumbled.

The rain was just beginning as John and Rory sprinted toward the giant gold statue of the Virgin that hung over the entrance to the Queen. An elegant, dark-haired woman hastened out through the glass doors, flailing an umbrella and speaking rapid Spanish.

"Everything will be fine," John said to Aurelia. "This is my brother, Rory —"

Rory had come to a halt, staring at the lobby as rain pelted him. He felt nothing, heard nothing, except the crashing of his ice cave around him.

CHAPTER 45

KATE WAS TRYING, without success, to pull the cow into the barn. Neptune and all of the creatures had been recalcitrant since a phone call had caused Sarah to rush off in the night, with only a garbled explanation that Josefina needed help. Four days had passed; she was relieved that Damon had returned to deal with the chickens.

She heard an engine and looked up to see the rainbow-colored Jeep thundering down the hill. It screeched to a halt.

"Thank god!" She dashed toward it. "Sarah, you're finally back —" She stopped. The driver was staring blankly at the bouncing windshield wipers. Rory had restarted the Jeep with a jolt, but not his brain; its flickering currents were mired in the melting shards of his ice cave.

"Rory! Why do you have Sarah's car? She's been gone forever and no one will behave. The dog won't stop howling, and Gabriel wants to barbecue them for the alien landing, and I would fry the chickens myself. Where is Sarah?"

He pointed to the seat beside him. Sarah was slumped over, her head on his thigh. A green Ford bounced up behind the Jeep. John sprang out, followed by Aurelia. She scurried to hold the umbrella over Rory, who had assembled his wits enough to get out of the Jeep and walk unevenly to the passenger door. Aurelia could not reach as high as his head and she pronged him in the neck, but he did not react. He opened the door. Sarah slid out. Her hair was tangled, her clothes wrinkled, her eyes bloodshot. She sagged, limp as noodles, into his arms.

"John!" Kate screeched. "What's happened?"

"Josefina had a baby," John replied. "No, she had two of them."

Rory lifted Sarah off her feet. Her head fell against his shoulder. "Where's your bed?" he asked. Sarah pointed skyward. He bent his head to hear what she was saying. He almost smiled and set off toward the barn, oblivious to the audience following him. Aurelia, with a shrug, held the umbrella over John's head instead.

"I am mercifully unclear on the details," John said to Kate. "Something went wrong and she swelled up. Aurelia called Sarah, who got Josefina to the Queen, which saved her life but they had to stabilize her before they could deliver the babies. Sarah promised not to leave them until they could find the husband in Fresno. Everyone survived, but when Sarah could finally leave, she realized she had left her lights on and her battery was dead."

"So she called Rory?" Kate was incredulous, but encouraged.

"Not exactly."

Aurelia stepped in to embellish John's colorless account. "Oh, and when Rory, *si grande, si guapo, como su papá* — he comes to the door of the hospital. He stops — *su corazón*, it is hit! *Como si fuera alcanzado por un rayo!*"

"Rory looked like he'd been walloped by a bat," John translated, loosely.

"Of course! For she is *bella, como una santa*. She wakes! She sees him. Ah, she weeps!"

"And Aurelia was relieved to learn that they had met before and Sarah does not fall wantonly into the arms of every car repairman she meets."

"*Es muy inteligente pero está embarazada —*"

"*De veras?*" John exclaimed.

"*Sí!* But now we know how happy this will end —"

"Is that why everyone applauded?"

"*Sí!* Of course!"

They arrived at the chapel just as sunlight, breaking through clouds, illuminated the stained-glass windows, filling the room with a rose and gold and rainbows scattered over the altar and statues, and also a goat, a cow and a horse. "The hand of God —" John murmured, and Damon rushed in followed by chickens.

"Oh!" Damon stumbled and stammered. "Oh! I thought I saw Rory but — who are you?"

"John."

"Damon."

"And this is Aurelia," Kate filled the silence. "John, I got that Sarah is *bonita, inteligente,* and *una santa,* but why *embarazada*? Why would she be embarrassed? Of course, if everyone applauded, she would have dropped dead. But so would Rory —"

"*Embarazada?*" Damon exclaimed. "*Embarazada!* Now I understand! Oh, I am so relieved!" Bursting into a fit of manic laughter, he sank into a pew.

"Is he all right?" John asked.

"I'm fine!" Damon gasped. "I just remembered the time in Spanish One, when a huge football player said he was *embarazada,* and the teacher laughed for ten minutes. I had such a crush on him!" Damon went off into another attack.

"It means pregnant, Kate," John said, and he too began to laugh.

"*La mano de Dios,*" Aurelia murmured.

UPSTAIRS, RORY WAS studying a space, as neat and plain as a nun's room, except for the unusual collection of books, an orchid, still not dead, and a sheaf of yellow-lined pages, held in place on a desk by the strange, eight-armed statue. He went back out on the balcony, where Sarah had fallen onto a narrow mattress beneath the eaves. He sat down beside her.

She stirred. "Thank you. It was terrible, Rory. Everyone was so frightened."

"But it's over now, isn't it?"

"Yet, but I think maybe I could do it."

"Do what, love?"

"Anything. If —" She sighed. "I was just happy to see you. I had wished I could see you one more time." Then, she was asleep.

He rubbed his forehead. A feathery tail brushed against him. Sarah's black cat leaped onto the bed, inspected her, pummeled her, and burrowed under the covers. A red-gold wolf followed, carrying what looked like a recently unearthed, muddy, moldy bread roll. The dog put it by Sarah's head before turning dark, questioning eyes on Rory.

"You're a beauty," he said, which proved an acceptable password. He could stay. The dog curled up beside Sarah. Three chickens, clucking, came onto the balcony. Something nibbled on his sleeve. "Good God," he said, looking into the eyes of a goat. "Not you too." He hauled the goat, bleating, back down the stairs. The cow mooed; the horse neighed.

"You are their hero," Kate said.

Rory headed for the door and flung it open as Gabriel strolled in. The two men stopped, face to face. Rory growled, "You shouldn't let Sarah drive that Jeep. It has no brakes." He strode on, out into the storm.

"Who let him in?" Gabriel asked.

CHAPTER 46

THE WEIRD BLARE of a horn broke through Sarah's dreams. The full moon was high in the sky; the valley had become a sea of white ringed by mountain peaks that floated above the clouds. The moon was filling the barn with an otherworldly light as she descended the stairs, accompanied by the cat. Rebecca nuzzled her neck, Milton butted her knees, and even Neptune, generally an undemonstrative cow, licked her hand.

"Where's Wolf?" she asked. A low growl answered. Wolf was sitting in front of the altar, where Gabriel sat cross-legged, wearing the silver wizard's costume Kate had made for him, and blowing on a kazoo. He looked less like a creature of magic than an overgrown, fractious child in the aftermath of Halloween. What would happen if he grew up?

"Lo, Sleeping Beauty awakes," he droned. "Just in time to call off the beast before I shoot it. You missed the party, Sarah."

Wolf growled. "What day is it?" Sarah asked.

"Well, the party is still going, but you didn't help frost Mildred's refrigerator box cake. And you missed seeing her jump naked out of it. Six times."

"Did the aliens come?"

"Not yet. Cloud and his followers, all three of them, are still waiting on the hill."

"Why are you in here, if the party isn't over?"

"Claiming sanctuary."

"From Mildred?"

"No, Maleficent. I didn't invite her, but she turned up. Pissed off. She probably put a curse on me. No, probably on you."

"Tanya?"

"And now I call forth all the powers of Hell!" He blew awful notes on his kazoo. "But I have a plan. We'll set her up with Beowulf."

"Who?"

"Roar, snarl. 'Don't let Sarah drive the Jeep or I will bash your brains to a bloody pulp.'"

"Who said that?"

"Berserker, when he dragged you home yesterday."

"He did?" Reluctant cracks broke in Sarah's memory. "I thought I had dreamt — that."

"Well, you didn't. He would have riven me with a sword, if he'd thought of it. They're meant for each other. Tanya can chew on his flesh, and he can beat her with his club. And you and I can leave. We can leave right now, after I shoot the wolf."

Sarah pulled Wolf away from the altar. Gabriel leapt and collided with the Virgin Mary, who went over with a crash. "I'll be damned!" he said. "Look!"

The Virgin had been standing on an iron ring in the floor. Gabriel tugged on it, and a trapdoor creaked open. "And so the gates of Hell unfurl." His eyes gleamed, and he jumped down through the hole. "It's a tunnel! Sarah! Maybe I told the truth! Maybe the old count is mouldering there in a pit of bones and treasure. Come on, Sarah, jump!"

"No."

"Coward."

"Yes." She stopped; he was gone.

"That was strange." Kate, groggy and disheveled, pulled herself upright in the pew when she had been dozing. She grinned lopsidedly. "Hullo, Sarah!"

"What are you doing here?"

"I think I passed out. Yes, I did. I didn't take the cocaine, because Damon said it can make your heart stop and I thought, wouldn't that be too bad at a celebration of love? I did drink a beer with a nice man, but then Damon said he'd shot his lawyer, and I thought, don't I have the worst taste in men? I met the Scoundrels of Leisure, too. Damon said Gabriel's friends make his patients seem quite normal. Then I smoked a joint with Harry the Swinger. He is sweet."

"Are you stoned?"

"Well, I don't know. I've never been stoned before. But I got so hungry, and a strange woman, Sunrise Sunset, gave us brownies. I ate two and Damon ate three before we found out they were special brownies." The nervous gaiety faded from her voice. "I'm leaving, Sarah. I called Dad, but maybe it was John. He's coming to get me."

"You're leaving? Why?"

"Because it would be the stupidest thing in the world to fall in love with him."

"With who?"

"Damon."

"Damon?"

"Damon. Do you remember our crazy stories, Sarah? He stepped right out of mine."

"But, Kate, he really is what he says he is and not what he might be, or not."

"I know. But he's so kind, Sarah. He's fun. With me, he's free, because he doesn't care. We talk; he listens. It's wonderful how much there is to talk about when you don't have to discuss your relationship. And that night, at his crazy game, we were gorgeous and we danced and it was all the romance I'd ever thought there could be in the world. So, I've had my night of being beautiful. Today, every time I looked around, there he was. I don't know why I think we might have been happy."

Footsteps crunched outside the chapel. "Sarah?" Damon called. "Are you awake? Ah, here you are, Kate! May I venture in without calling 'Man on the floor'?"

He was smiling, rosy-cheeked, and tipsy. "Poor Cloud has decided that the aliens aren't landing today — a miscalculation of time, date, or century — and he is depressed because he had prepared a slide show for them, a welcome and introduction to the planet Earth. So, I said, why not show it anyway? I'm sure it could be just as useful for the rest of us. Showtime is in half an hour; meanwhile, we're going to try out the hot tub. Will you join us, Kate? But, Sarah, I believe women who are *embarazada* are not supposed to go into hot tubs."

"What?"

Kate said. "Tía Aurelia told us. But don't worry, Sarah. I didn't tell anyone."

They left. Sarah stood motionless as images flooded into her head, and the most alarming was not of Josefina nearly dying. Sarah had not taken a shower or changed her clothes since she had returned. She would go bathe. Then she would get on the horse and ride away into the night. She would even ride the goat, if it came to that.

CHAPTER 47

SIX TIMES RORY had told John he had no intention of going to the alien landing bachelor party. No, he did not think it would be fun. Finally, John gave up and went to a movie with Joe. Then, the telephone rang. This was why, as Rory sped up the Silverado Trail to retrieve his drug-befuddled, drunken sister from a den of depravity, his two children were in the backseat.

He wanted to see Sarah again. He had considered this all through the previous, long, cold, lonely, rain-filled night, but this was nothing new. Sarah Glass had figured in most of his sleepless nights; it was because, in the iced forest of Wishing, Massachusetts, he had, only for a moment, thought how much she would delight in this sparkling, frozen vision, doomed to vanish in the sunlight. Then the doors of the ice cave had swung closed, and there she was, with him.

He was not haunted by his ex-wife — she was gone — but nothing could rid his mind of the image of Sarah sitting for hours beside a dying woman. He could not believe that the one time she had called him — he didn't count the time she had called him and hung up — he had failed her so abysmally. While he and David Ilillouette contemplated the future, he had left her alone to cope with his past. To crown this, he had done something abysmally stupid, regrettably insane and entirely past redemption. He found, in a box of notes on Ralph Waldo

Emerson and Edith Wharton, the scribbled pages of a novel about an idiot. He shoved one passage into an envelope with a brief note of apology and thanks, which had taken him three hours to compose. On his way to the airport, he left it in Sarah's mailbox, and then, if he could have bailed out over Nevada to retrieve it, he would have. He had not expected a response from her and there had been none, at least not until weeks later, when he was safely locked in his cave, beyond debilitating agony, remorse, or terror. It was a letter, waiting in his mailbox when he got back from Hawaii. It was written on a page torn out of the notebook she had not wanted him to see. "Thank you. Take care. Good-bye." And that was that.

The news that she had run off to live in the hills with a blithering lunatic did not surprise him, but on the subject of Sarah, he maintained a stone-cold silence, except for one night in Hawaii when a woman joined him at the pool. She had heard he'd been star-gazing up at the Mauna Kea observatory. How fascinating! Which stars were overhead now? He didn't know their names? How funny! She knew Orion's Belt. Rory found himself telling her about Sarah and how he had been wondering what she would think of his odd machine scanning the heavens without the least clue what it was seeing. The woman, clearly uninterested in hearing about Sarah, had gone to the bar, and only then did he realize that he had effectively caused her to abandon any plans for a night in Paradise.

In Napa, Sarah was everywhere. He couldn't drive by Napa High without seeing her in the throngs of students, only she was prettier than any of them. When he slid under a car, she was there listening to him tell her about cars with wide-eyed wonder; when he ran down the lane toward her old house, she was waiting in the shadows. He was sure she would eventually fade away, although it might only be when he was dead.

He had wanted to see her once more, if only to be sure that there was peace between them. He would tell her he might fix cars all his life, and she would remember that Einstein, in his later years, had wished he had been a plumber. They would shake hands and part friends.

How to accomplish this meeting had eluded him. He knew it would be easiest for her if he were to cut off his leg or drop a heavy piece of equipment on his head and be hauled, bloodied and brainless, into the clinic where Sarah, according to Kate, was working when she was not with the lunatic. He had even considered the possibility presented by the black widow spider he found in the shop. "Go ahead and bite me," he offered. It did not, and he, for the record, did not kill it.

Then he walked into the Queen. That night he decided he would go back to see her, but not at a party hosted by Dinesen. As he flew along the Trail in the dark, he resolved this: he would slip in, haul off his sister, and if, by chance, he saw Sarah, he would ask, in the calmest possible way, if she would have dinner — no, breakfast — with him at Buttercream Bakery.

He parked in front of the crazy house. Lucy woke up. "Where are we?" she asked.

"Cloud Cuckoo Land."

"Are there fairies?"

"Yes, all over the place. Wait here, Lucy, will you? I'll be right back."

Raucous music was blaring as he climbed the stairs to the strange castle. By the door, a man in the pose of *The Thinker* was contemplating a beer can.

"You lost?" Harry the Swinger asked.

"I'm looking for Kate."

"So am I! Wow, she is really — wow."

"She is my sister."

"Right!" Harry gathered his wits, like the last few lemons before a frost. "She and that dude Damon just went that way to the hot tub."

Rory heard Kate giggling before he saw her in the hot tub surrounded by men. "Damon, if I fall asleep, will you wake me up so I don't cook, like those people in LA?"

Tonelessly, he interrupted the gales of laughter. "Kate."

"Rory?"

"Rory!" Damon said. "I'm so glad you came, after all. Are you alone? Will you join us? Rory, this is George, Don, Win, Joe, Tom, and Glen —"

"Kate, are you ready to go?"

"Are you going somewhere?" Damon asked.

"I can't go anywhere," Kate said. "I forgot where I threw my clothes."

More hilarity ensued. Damon climbed out of the tub to look for Kate's clothes. "Rory, why don't you have a drink? You look like you could use one."

"I'm not ready, Rory," Kate said lowly. "I have to pack. Could you wait?"

"The kids are in the car. They're asleep."

"Well," Damon said, "let's go get them."

They put the sleeping children in the room that Kate said was Sarah's, although she always slept in the barn.

"I am sure Sarah is somewhere," Damon offered, reading Rory's forbidding expression. "She won't want to miss the slide-show welcome for the aliens."

"At least she was not in a tub of happy bathers."

"D'you know, Rory," Kate said, "you are becoming a narrow-minded prude. And Sarah wouldn't have been in the tub anyway because, you know, *embarazada*."

"What?"

"Oh dear," Damon said.

❧

RUBBER-KNEED, RORY FOLLOWED an anfractuous route to the stairs and down. He propped himself against a wall surveying the motley crowd. He wasn't one of them; he was sober. But he was not a narrow-minded prude. He would not object to sitting in a hot tub with seven naked women, and he was sure he extended the same right to his sister. And Sarah? He did not, of course, have the right to extend any rights to her, although his relief that she was not sitting in hot tubs with other men had just been trampled. *Embarazada.* He banished an unenlightened wish to strangle her. He knew Sarah locked many things in her heart and he could not choke them out of her. He would find her; he would be calm, even as he dragged her away. As soon as he could make his knees work to walk.

With the sweeping notes of *Also Sprach Zarathustra,* the Welcome Aliens program commenced. Holographic lights flashed red, yellow, blue, and green. Strauss gave way to Gregorian chants. An image of Mt. Everest filled the wall; the Beatles sang "All You Need Is Love." With a crash, the lights and sound went out.

The chorus went up: "Earthquake!"

"No, someone just tripped over the cord!"

The power returned, but the slide projector was stuck on advance. A rapid-fire succession of seascapes, cities, islands, and cheerful people waving unfolded as chipmunk-like voices chirped the best of the Jefferson Airplane: "One pill makes you larger."

"Well, hello, Harvard," a voice purred. "I didn't expect to find you in this den of sin."

Through the explosion of colors, Rory recognized Tanya of the weird winery, smiling; if a spider could smile, that's what it would look like. She said, "You need a drink."

He drank a glass of wine, then two, but was still unable to extract his arm from her fingernails. He drank a third glass of wine, and then he was rescued.

Remarkably, he had not noticed Mildred, but after her six leaps, she had put on clothes, a sheer gauze gown and a yellow feather boa. Tanya Matlock had merely thought Rory was looking remarkably fit and smoldering; Mildred identified her platonic ideal for tall and sweet. Drawn to him as if by a celestial magnet — what previous lives they had shared? — she arrived as Tanya was saying, archly, "Contemplating the mysteries of physics, Rory?"

"Physics," Mildred said. "Do you accelerate particles?"

"Do I what?" Rory finished his third glass of wine.

"Accelerate!" Looping her feather boa around Rory's neck, Mildred bore him off, crying, "Dance! Dance the dance of accelerated particles!"

Later, he would insist he was only trying to preserve himself from asphyxiation, but he was whirling around the room to the pulsating question "Don't you want somebody to love?" when he saw Sarah on the sidelines staring at him, her dark eyes enormous.

"Rory!" Kate ran into the ballroom. "Rory! Are the kids with you? They're gone."

CHAPTER 48

"WHOA," HARRY THE Swinger said as Sarah tripped over him. "Sarah! Where're you going?"

"I was going to take a shower," she gasped. "But I think I'll go back to bed."

"Okay." He rose to walk with her. "You okay? Did you eat another mushroom?"

"No. But my heart won't stop beating."

"Isn't that good? I remember one time, I thought my heart fell right out of my head, but then I realized, no, it didn't because it would have fallen out of my chest. One time, I was so stoned I talked to a salad bowl for two hours because it talked back. One time, a chair turned into Father Matthew saying I'd go to hell if I didn't stop talking, so I put a can of beer in my mouth and they had to take me to the emergency room to get it out."

Harry's recitations got them to the barn. Sarah said, "I hope you will be happy."

"Yeah, right. A wife and a baby. Now all I need is a job."

"You'll find one."

"Oh yeah? Why do you think that?"

"Because God doesn't play dice with the universe."

"How do you know?"

"Einstein said so."

She opened the barn door, and he, ever attuned to the possibilities of life, followed her inside. "You know, that night at your place, it was the greatest night of, well, of a long time. And anytime you want another night of anything, Sarah —"

A voice, faint and faraway, echoed, "Sarah?"

"Lucy?"

"And me too," Avery called. The voices were coming from beneath the trapdoor.

Sarah bent down, squinting into the dark. "How did you two get in there?"

"We followed the big kid," Lucy said. "We wanted to find the fairies."

"You jumped into this hole?"

"There was a door, but we lost it," Lucy said. "But you can get us out."

She looked at Harry; he said, "I don't think I'd fit in that hole."

"No." Sarah gripped the edge and dropped down. Four arms wrapped around her legs.

"I love you, Sarah," Avery said.

"Me too," Lucy said.

Avery prompted her. "And you say, 'I love you, too. Avery. Not Lucy.'"

"Sarah loves me too."

Dizzily, Sarah said. "I love both of you. But let's get out of here. I'll lift you up to Harry." She hoisted Avery successfully, but when Lucy saw the face of the man who had reached down to lift her out of the black hole, she panicked. He was hairy, but he was not her father; she wanted her father. She burst into tears. Avery joined in.

"Right! We'll get him!" exclaimed Harry. "Who is he? Don't worry. We'll find him!"

Sarah heard scrambling footsteps. The goat bleated; Harry swore. The children stopped crying to laugh. The noises faded. The barn was silent. Sarah reached up, but even if she jumped, she could not catch the edge of the hole. "Gabriel?" she said. "Where did you go?"

RORY EXPERIENCED A new level of anxiety, alarm, and terror as he searched for his children, and although it abated when they appeared, cheering as a goat chased the man carrying them, he did not know if his heart would ever be the same; he doubted it. While Damon called off the goat, Rory followed the parade into the kitchen. Kate made cocoa but he drank whiskey, straight, no ice. It would clash with the cheap wine he had drunk earlier, but he didn't care.

"Does this party have goody bags?" Avery asked him.

"You were wonderful," Kate said to Harry, who was sharing the bottle with Rory.

"It was nothing."

"No," Lucy said. "It wasn't. Because Sarah got us out of the black hole."

Harry clapped his head. "Damn! I forgot her! We'd better call the fire department —"

Kate and Damon rushed out the door, but Rory finished his third shot of whiskey. He was not as drunk as he wished, for then he would be unconscious, but he had not imbibed so badly since a long-ago Halloween party when he had mixed piña coladas, beer, and Jack Daniel's with immense relief; if he were now combining wine and whiskey with mind-numbing shock, fear, and heartache, he was stopped before he was fully senseless. Four large eyes were watching him.

"All right," he said, "let's go get her."

SARAH TOUCHED A damp, cold, crumbling dirt wall. There must be a way out; she only had to go forward into fathomless dark. There was nothing wrong with the dark except you did not know who else might be sharing it, such as bats or rats. Not all rats carried the plague, and few bats were vampires; still, she could not, just then, summon compassion for the feared and misunderstood creatures of the earth, not even black widow spiders, who were most likely all around her. Footsteps thundered overhead. Kate called, "Sarah? Are you down there?"

"Sarah!" That was Harry. "I goddamned forgot you. But I called the fire department."

"Sarah," Damon said, "do you want Rory? We'll get him."

"No," Sarah whispered. "No."

Silence. A shadow fell over the trapdoor. Another voice: "Sal, d'you need a hand, babe?"

She scrambled into the darkness, blindly hitting walls as the tunnel twisted tortuously. She paused to slow the wild beating of her heart. A boney hand clutched her shoulder. She screamed and ran again. She saw a glimmer of light and tumbled out of the tunnel and into a field of wet grass and mud. She lay on her back, and the stars spun overhead in the night sky. She was on the hillside, outside the cave she and Gabriel had never explored, beyond the entrance.

Rory dropped down beside her. "Who did you think I was?"

"A ghost."

He viewed this philosophically, "At least you didn't scream and run because you thought it was me."

Below them, blue lights were flashing. He offered her his hand. "Either the fire department is here, or the aliens have arrived. Either way, we had better go down."

On the way down the hill, she told him about the ghost of the dead count, which obviated the need for a sensible conversation. Back at the castle, she slipped away from the uproar and finally took a shower, the longest of her life. When she emerged, to her relief, only her cat was waiting for her. The party was racketing on, although the fire trucks were gone. She walked to the chapel. The wind had swept the sky clear of clouds, the full moon had risen; the world was glimmering, soft and silver. Wolf howled to her from the balcony, and she sprinted up the stairs. Prancing and waving her tail, the dog led Sarah to her bed. She often brought gifts, bones, carrots, old bread, to Sarah's bed, but this was her best prize to date. Wolf barked; the large lump moved. "Oh," Sarah said. "It's you."

"Now who were you expecting?"

"You never know."

"We are going to have to do something about that."

"Where are Lucy and Avery?"

"I tied them to a tree."

"You did not."

"I threatened to throw them back in the black hole if they didn't stay with Kate. They said Harry the Swinger would call the firemen again." He yawned. "I went for a walk with your dog and we ended up here. I don't know why, when I can't sleep anywhere else, I can always fall asleep in your bed."

"Are you not sleeping?" He said nothing but moved over to make room for her. She remained standing. "Rory, I don't remember what I said to you. Yesterday."

"Let's see: you said if I carried you up the stairs, I had to ravish you at the top."

"I did? Did you?"

"Sarah!" He caught her around the knees and she fell onto her bed. "I took a rain check." She touched his cheek; without his beard he looked younger, almost like the boy she had once known; except she read in his expression a grim determination to talk, and she doubted she could do this without throwing up or falling into a fit. "Do you want to go back to sleep?"

"Not if you don't, babe."

"But I think you are tired."

"Aren't you?"

"No, but I didn't do the accelerated particles dance with Mildred."

"Watch it, my girl."

Feathery wisps of clouds were drifting into the sky, but stars sparkled through them and a rainbow circled the moon. When he ran his hand through her hair, her brain eased its relentless rattling, its rush of thinking, rethinking, and overthinking. It drifted onto a peaceful river. She sighed. "It's so nice. No, that's not the right word, is it?"

"Nice isn't such a bad word. Cole Porter used it; so did Chaucer."

"Why are you laughing?"

"I was sure we'd be talking about Einstein."

"Would you like to?"

"Not tonight."

"Could we not talk, and just be comfortable for one night?"

"You have an odd notion of comfort, my darling."

"Are you not comfortable?"

"I think I could be comfortable with you on the moon. Why do you sleep out here?"

"I like it. It's the same view, but it's always different, the light, the color, there's something new. I know — I do know — you can't spend your life watching, but for a little while, it seems that the more I watch, the more I feel a part of something. I am not sure what, however."

"'Observations not only disturb what is to be measured, they produce it?'"

She smiled, and he felt obliged to add, "I've only been reading Einstein because David Ilillouette loves physics as metaphor, ever since I told him that if all the nuclei of all the atoms in the world were touching, the world would be the size of a basketball. He couldn't get over how much empty space there is, even though he'd already been in Congress two years."

"Are you working for him?"

"No. I like the writing part, but — sometimes I think I'd rather fix cars all my life."

"Did you know that Einstein said if he had to do it over, he'd be a plumber?"

Rory baffled her by breaking into laughter. "Sometimes, Sarah, I think we left Napa no more prepared to be part of the world than sparrows."

"But they are; sparrows are part of the world. And a car mechanic is a wonderful thing."

"How many sweaters are you wearing?"

"Usually it's cold out here. But tonight even my feet are warm. It's such a funny thing about sex," she mused. "I never thought I'd like it. It was always so creepy, so weird and lonely. But I do like it, just only with you. I don't know why it's so different. Physically, it's the same — well, not exactly the same. It's quite mysterious. Well," she added, "you can go to sleep, now."

"Yeah," he said. "Right."

MUCH LATER, WOLF raised her head and growled. Rory, awakened, formed a hazy impression of a man in a wizard's robe scattered with moons and stars hovering above them.

"It's just a dream, sweetheart," he murmured. "Go back to sleep." But now he was awake. A meteor streaked through the sky, and he thought of his homely machine diligently recording data on a faraway mountain. He wished it well, but if from its observations, anyone wrote formulas to describe the universe, it would not be he. If reaching for the stars was the greatest leap from the mundane world, he had broken no chains; he had only made a pass and fallen back to earth. He had landed here, not far from where he had started, but under the open sky.

It was odd to think that this wilderness was part of the valley where he had grown up and from which he had wanted so ardently to escape. The band of life here had felt to him as narrow as the valley itself, a place untouched by the rest of the world. In this valley, comfortable people had food, water, schools, and a white-haired mayor. They filled their lives with basketball games, pancake breakfasts, and the annual Rotary crab feed. He had judged harshly that they lived lives that made no difference, left no mark; they achieved their goals by owning a minuscule patch of land and decorating it with lights at Christmas. He had left; he was back, but for how long or to what end, he couldn't say; even if he wished to stay, there might not be a place for him. He had gained no knowledge of the greater world and found no place that fit him. Still, as Sarah moved in his arms, an extraordinary thought crossed his mind, an unsubstantiated notion that life would work out. This was something akin to happiness.

CHAPTER 49

IN THE CASTLE kitchen, two small people, the only ones awake, were having a breakfast of cake and potato chips when the telephone rang. Lucy answered it.

"Who are you?" a voice demanded.

"I am Lucy. Who are you?"

"What are you doing there?"

"We came to the party for the aliens."

"And the firemen came." Avery had put his ear to the receiver, too.

"Where is Gabriel?"

"The big kid?" Lucy asked. "He is asleep. Everybody is asleep."

"How many people are there?"

Avery said, "Eleventy-thirteen."

"Would you get Sarah?"

"No," Lucy said. "Because we promised Rory. We aren't disturbing him."

"We love Sarah, too," Avery explained.

"We could get Kate," Lucy suggested. "Or Damon. He is sleeping in the living room because he and Gabriel are broken up."

They shrugged and hung up, for the line had gone dead.

❧

THE EARLY MORNING sky was a garden of roses. Sarah watched the colors change as she listened to the heartbeat of her hairy pillow. They disappeared into the luminescent pearl of storm clouds. If she had not been watching at that minute, she would have missed it. She got her notebook to draw Rory, sleeping naked and tangled in the covers. This brought the number of drawings of him to sixty-two, outnumbering by far any other creature.

She could draw human bodies fairly well. In her first year of med school, she had meticulously replicated the parts of her cadaver as she dissected it. She hadn't known the man's name or anything of his life, but he was her own personal dead body. The brain was the last task. A neurosurgeon told the students he never made a cut without knowing that one wrong move could destroy a patient's memories, thoughts, or ability to dance. Slicing into center of her cadaver's head had yielded none of his secrets; still, she had doubted that she would ever know another body so intimately. Now she knew some of Rory's mysteries but of the jelly of his brain, she had few clues. For herself, whatever might quiver in the depths, she knew what she was going to do. It was as simple as the answer to an exam. She closed the book.

Thunder rumbled distantly as she walked to the kitchen. She stopped in the doorway. Kate and Damon were making pancakes. Gabriel was playing cards with Lucy and Avery. It was their secret card game and he was protesting that it was secret because only they knew the rules.

"Sarah!" Lucy said. "We thought you were going to sleep all day. But we had a good time too."

"The firemen let me blow the horn," Avery said. "And we found the big kid. He's silly."

Sarah nodded and tried to meet Gabriel's eyes but he looked away.

"Shall we go wake up Rory?" Lucy asked.

"I'm up, Lucy." Lightning flashed outside the window and thunder shook the castle. Lips brushed the back of Sarah's head. Arms went around her, many of them, like the embrace of an octopus. The kitchen grew hot. A ringing in her ears made her dizzy; it was only the telephone.

"I'll take it in my room," Gabriel muttered.

"Coffee, Rory?" Damon asked.

He held out a mug, steaming and fragrant. Sarah reeled. She made it to the garden; she sank into the mud, retching miserably. Lightning flared, and thunder cracked. "Please hit me," she said, although she knew that this was statistically improbable.

"There are things I'd rather do," Rory said, kneeling down beside her. "Come on, let's get you inside."

She frowned at him; rain was falling on his head too. A bolt of lightning blazed by, so close it sizzled. The skies opened up. Rory swung Sarah up and sprinted for shelter where the animals were huddled in their stalls. Wolf was howling on the stairs. He set her on her feet, laughing. "I've never done that before," he said. "I felt like a caveman."

Sarah picked up a cloth and began to rub the horse. The goat and cow crowded around her, an effective barricade. Where was the cat?

"Sarah." His voice, grown gentle, came closer. "You know, the times when you haven't been afraid of me have been like nothing I've ever known."

"Please, Rory. Please, go away and leave me alone."

"I can't do that, honey." She looked at him in anguish, buried her face in Rebecca's neck, and burst into tears. He tripped over a bucket to reach her; but he would have had more success trying to embrace the goat. Eventually, she could hear him. Words took shape, comforting, if not remotely true; he was saying everything would be all right. She tried to gather her wits; later, she drew them, looking like daisies that had been trampled by an onslaught of buffalo.

"I wish you'd come out from behind the cow," he said. She shook her head. "Come on, Sal. It's not so bad, is it?"

"Yes. No." She took a shaky breath. "Sorry. It's just hormones."

"I know."

"How — never mind. You knew last night?"

"Yes."

"Of course. It's why you didn't worry — but you don't have to worry about anything."

"Don't I?"

"Well, the laws of probability —"

"Sarah, what if I take Kate and the kids home and then come back and we can talk?"

And what if she opened up the trapdoor and jumped back into the dark? The Virgin was standing on the ring again. Mary's nose had broken in her fall but her smile remained, tranquil and mysterious. Why had someone decided she was a virgin, and how had so much of western civilization come to be based upon this myth? She turned away to a small, dusty window. A beetle dangled in its splintered frame, bound up in a silken death wrap. She watched it, and she knew what she was going to say, even if her voice kept breaking like a frayed old thread.

"I was surprised," she said. "I never thought such a thing could happen to me. I was going to have an abortion. I made three appointments, but I cancelled them. I had another one on Monday, but then Josefina called. I'd seen so many dead and dying people, but I'd never seen anyone be born. It was the most terrifying and the most wonderful thing I'd ever seen. And I thought, what if I want to do this?"

"But, Sarah, that's fine. It's — fine. Don't you think that you and I, that we —"

She looked up at him: so a man might look when he was about to shoot over a waterfall, but still hoped someone might turn off the water. "No," she said. "No. I have thought and thought and thought about what to do. I am going to go back to school and start rotations as soon they can schedule me. Then I think I can take a week or two off —"

"Oh, babe, you don't know what you're talking about."

"I know." She turned back to the window. Beyond the rain-spattered glass, rain was still falling but the lightning was only faint flickers over the mountains. The meadow grass was rippling in the wind and there was Widdershins, dancing through it.

"We think we are so different, Rory," she said, "but we're not. The truth is, I'm just like Dibby and Kate and Mildred. Wanting love is a kind of disease, I think. And you're not so different from Gabriel or Sterling or Harry the Swinger. If you even think of love, it is something so different. I did want it, once, but I don't anymore. I think you are just as afraid as I am, and so this is where you and I — where we part."

Tears were rolling down her face again but she forced herself to go on. "I have loved you for as long as I've known you, which is just about all of my life, but you don't — you don't. I read what you wrote. It was wonderful. You are going to do great things. And all that you have been through will make you even better. You just don't need to repeat history."

Rory stood gray and frozen as a stone. He didn't move, even to take the hand that she offered him, and she went out into the storm.

CHAPTER 50

GABRIEL WAS DRAGGING a rowboat against the wind to the pond where the water was rocking in crazy waves. The boat was a decrepit, rotting thing. Gabriel's shotgun was riding in it.

"I have been looking for you," Sarah said.

He kicked at the boat out into the water. "What do you want?"

"You're not going to go out in that, are you?" she asked.

"Why not?" The ducks, having spied the pair, had begun their happy, noisy march in to be fed. Gabriel lunged for his gun, sank in the mud, and swore.

"What are you doing?"

"Going duck hunting."

"The boat won't float. It's full of holes."

"Then the hands of the dead will pull me under." He swung around. His face was flushed, but his eyes were dull and cold. "My mother called. She knows everything. She always does. She's coming here. She wants you out, and she wants Damon out, and so do I."

He plunged into the restless water, and Sarah, who had never had an impulse to violence in her entire life, sprang. She caught him off guard, and so was able to knock him down into a tangle of mud and weeds and murky water. As he struggled to extricate himself, she shoved the boat out into deeper water. The wind caught it, carried it, and capsized it. It sank.

"Get out of here," Gabriel screamed. "Get out."

THAT DAY SARAH hiked into the hills, and she worked without pause, filling her notebook. These last pages contained no careful studies of bugs, webs, or the lines on a leaf. They were hurried sketches, smudged and spattered with rain and mud, but one after another, they were attempts to capture in one sweep the entire view: the shadowy, cloud-bound hills, the twisted trees, the cave, the chapel-barn, the castle. She was trying to see everything and draw it before it was lost in time. She worked until the light was gone; then she went back down the hill.

Damon was in the kitchen, amid pots and pans and trimmings from carrots, onions, and mushrooms. He had smudges of flour on his face and tomato smears on his shirt.

"I have made Julia Child's Beef Bourguignon," he announced.

The table was set with a bouquet of daffodils and tulips and yellow candles. He pulled out a chair for Sarah and poured her a glass of grape juice. "Kate and I bought Julia's cookbook," he said. "I was afraid to try it without her, but I just followed the directions. Julia says serve it with noodles and green peas, and we'll have salad after, French style. Then, cheese and strawberry tart. Something went wrong with my terrine, however. I worried it wouldn't hold together so I added extra gelatin, and now I can't cut it."

He brought two plates to the table, and served two more for Wolf and Widdershins. He raised his glass to her. "I thought we should do it right, the last supper."

"It isn't fair for you, Damon. I'm the one who sank his boat."

"You deviated from the script in a few other ways, dear."

"I couldn't help it."

"Good heavens, who would blame you? Besides, I loved Gabriel, and I'm sure that is worse in his mother's eyes than anything you've done."

Loved: he said it so calmly. "If it wasn't this, it would have been something else," he added. "What was it Kate said? I should feel something, but I don't." He sighed. "She did the right thing, although I am sorry she did. She's a wonderful woman. She's exactly the woman I would have fallen in love with, if I were straight. What do you think of the Bourguignon?"

"It's delicious."

"It is, isn't it? Do you know, Sarah, I might give up love and go to cooking school instead."

"Then maybe there was a purpose to all this, after all. Damon, maybe you've found the other half of your brain."

"I didn't know I was searching for it. But it was fun while it lasted, wasn't it? I've been thinking it's no small accomplishment if you can say at the end of your life that you had fun. What will you do?"

"I am going back to school."

"But not tonight. You're welcome to come with me to the city. Thank goodness I didn't move out. Of course," he added, polishing his glass with studied nonchalance, "I doubt that Rory would mind if you turned up at his door, even with the goat."

"No."

"Why not?"

"He doesn't have a door."

A flush of ducks flew overhead, so close Sarah could hear the rush of their wings. The candles flickered, and a cold hand gripped her neck, or perhaps it was her heart; it was the unseen hand that had started it all. Go away, she said to it; be gone; vanish. Impulsively, she thrust her notebook at Damon. He turned the pages with excruciating slowness.

"They're rough," she said. "Unfinished. Not good."

"They're wonderful, you nut. Oh my, you did study anatomy."

"No, not that one!" Sarah blushed. "Look at the view ones."

"But I like this one. Goodness, no wonder you were glowing this morning."

She sighed. He refilled her plate. "When I turned thirty," he said, "I decided I would do something I had never done before: I'd learn to swim. I made no progress until I met a wonderful woman in Berkeley who said there was no point telling me what to do with my arms and legs when I was worrying about dying. It was true: I was trying to breathe without putting my face in water, trying to kick while making sure I could touch the bottom of the pool, trying to swim and hold on to the edge at the same time. She said we would stop learning to swim and learn to trust. In two weeks, I was swimming like a dolphin."

"That's wonderful," Sarah said. "But I am sure cooking school would not be so hard."

"Sarah! We are talking about love."

"We are? Why?"

"Because love is like swimming. You may never have learned, or you may have had a terrible experience where you nearly drowned in undertow but —"

"I thought you were giving up love."

"For myself, yes — I have such bad taste in men — but I'm not pregnant, dear. Now, what did you say to Rory that upset him so badly this morning?"

"He was upset?"

"He was an absolute thundercloud. And I was the only one here to say goodbye to everyone —"

"I had already told him goodbye."

"I was afraid of that. May I ask why?"

She showed him a drawing of the dead beetle, shrouded and dangling in the window frame.

"Oh dear. Now, Sarah, when Rory returns tonight —"

"He won't."

"Do you really believe he doesn't love you?"

"It isn't his fault; no one could."

"Not true. Gabriel loves you in his own bizarre way, and I am very fond of you myself."

The hand on her neck or heart tightened its grip until she could hardly breathe. "Damon, will you tell Gabriel something for me?"

"You'll see him again."

"I don't think so. I think I will cease to exist for him. But last night I was thinking —"

"Is that what you were doing last night? Really?"

"You can travel from earth at the speed of light, and when you return, theoretically no time will have passed, but you will still have seen wonders; you may not be older, but those veils we wrap around ourselves will not have survived the flight."

Damon cleared his throat. "Is this what you want me to tell Gabriel, or what you were thinking about last night? Because you might lose Gabriel back at the speed of light."

"Gabriel did something for me. He flew into my life, ripped up the veils —"

"Dear heart, he's in love with the veils. And however much you might consider love to be the capacity to indulge another's fantasies, in the end, you have to stand before your beloved without them. Oh — that's good, isn't it? I'm going to use it in my class."

"What I mean is, I'm glad I met him. I'd do it all again."

She was interrupted by a high-pitched laugh. Wolf went on alert as Gabriel strolled into the kitchen. "Well, well," he said. "Started without me?"

"You had better eat, if you have been drinking," Damon said.

"It's amazing I had any time to do anything besides follow your to-do list, and then I had a calamity. My car stopped. There I was, alone, in the wilderness. But I was rescued. Are you coming in?" he called backwards to the door.

Noodles piled up in Sarah's throat before Harry the Swinger ambled into sight. "I've always wanted to be rescued," Gabriel continued, "but the real thing didn't live up to my expectations. Harry's looking for Kate."

Harry nodded. Damon asked, "Where's your car?"

"At the bottom of the hill. But if that ass McIntyre does come for your strawberry tart, or whatever it is you want him to do, maybe he'll look at it."

Sarah flashed Damon a wild look. "Sarah," he said, "if ever there was a woman who needed a fairy godmother, it's you. I have a theory—"

"You have a new theory once a day, Damon, darling," Gabriel pointed out.

"— that love requires a landing place."

Gabriel sniffed "Do you remember the fit you had when I knocked over your favorite plant?"

"I liked that plant. And you promised to buy me a new one but you never did."

Sarah said, "I can go look at your car, Gabriel."

Their eyes met, and the hand lightened its grip, not entirely, but enough.

"We'll take the Jeep." Gabriel speared a piece of meat. "This isn't bad stew, Damon."

"It's *Boeuf à la Bourguignon*, idiot."

"Well, hell," Harry said. "I'll eat it."

GABRIEL STOPPED THE Jeep at the crest of the hill. Below them was a white pool of fog; above them stars glittered. They were in between worlds.

"Are we running away?" he asked. "Where shall we go? It's too bad you can't ever stay where you are happy; you can't grab hold of time and say, 'Stop. Go away. Leave us alone.'"

"I think that's death, Gabriel."

"Then let's die."

"We will," she said. "Sometimes I can think about it. We live and we die. Everyone does, even Einstein. But other times, when I try to think that we will die, we will never be here again, I get so afraid of everything. Gabriel, I wanted to say — thank you."

"For what?"

"Everything. You made things happen."

"I hope we're not talking about Aethelstan the Unready."

"You didn't really go talk to him?"

Gabriel nodded dolefully. "Damon said I had to. So I offered him the Dreadlock instead of you, but he scorned my plan with a withering gaze. And nearly brained me with a fender."

"He hit you? With a fender?"

"No. His fist. I hit him too."

"Oh, God."

"He insists he's read *Ivanhoe,* but clearly he didn't get it. But it doesn't matter. The minute he comes for you, you'll ride off with him."

"No."

"Yes, you will, even if his idea of love is he can't keep his hands off your ass. Because that's how you are. You love things no matter what kind of blot on the landscape they are."

"No. It's not like learning how to swim —"

"Oh no, you heard about Damon's miracle lessons. 'And now, dear children, I swim with the dolphins. I have become shark food.'"

"You don't want love. Why can't I be like you?"

"I don't? Hell, Sarah, what else is there? All I've ever wanted is for someone to love me."

"But I do," she said softly. "I love you. And you're not a blot."

He glanced at her and then looked away. "It's too bad that cave was just a cave. I had this idea I could find the treasure, I could buy this place. My mother said she's going to sell it, but she can't. It belongs to my father. So vines will grow over it for a hundred years. One day the prince will come —"

"What about the animals?"

"We could have a hell of a barbecue."

"No!"

"I knew you wouldn't go for that. We'll just have to take them to New York."

"What?"

"You don't think you're going to leave me with the most spoiled creatures on the planet, not to mention the Dreadlock? I told her the truth, by the way."

"Which truth?"

"That you're pregnant." An uneasy chill passed over her as she watched him grip and release the steering wheel, but his voice retained his zany, humming notes. "And I have go to New York to be the nanny."

"You wouldn't — would you?"

"New York? Oh, hell, yes. She didn't say another word. Of course, she'll turn up here with a poisoned apple. But we'll be gone."

"Yes, I think we'd better get out of California tonight."

"I say we steal the gypsy cart. We have a horse to pull it now. And a cow."

"And a goat."

"Alas, I fear he is only ornamental. But the chickens can ride on the roof. What an entrance we'll make into New York." He cackled happily. "Sarah Glass, I love you."

The hand released her neck; she felt free and light as a feather on the wind. "You said that once," she said, "I didn't think you'd ever say it again."

"Once?" he echoed. "What do you mean, once? The wild ride goes on!"

He started the engine, and the Jeep rolled down into the fog. It picked up speed, and as they hurtled around a bend, lights of an on-coming car flashed. He swerved. Amidst the shriek of brakes and the savage clash of metal, trees spun in cartwheels, scattering trails of golden sparks.

This time, Sarah saw no faraway sparkling cities. She knew who she was and where she was and heard, all too clearly, the voices swirling around her: "Is she dead?" "No, she's breathing." "She might be dead." "She has a pulse." "Are you sure she's not dead?" "Hey, don't worry. God doesn't play darts with the universe."

An image filled her head: somewhere in the universe, Einstein was waltzing with a spider. Then it was gone.

CHAPTER 51

SARAH LOST TIME, and she never knew where it had gone. As she began to flicker in and out of consciousness, this seemed a dubious alternative to oblivion; it was ringed with knives, spears, nails, and spikes. If she could feel pain, then she wasn't dead, and was that not a good thing? She wasn't sure. She might willingly have thrown herself back into an insensible void except an invisible creature had her in a tenacious grip. An octopus? Had she returned to the sea? She had the odd notion it was willing her pain into its strange, warm tentacles, and sometimes it worked.

She was not so concerned with who she was — enough distant repetitions of her name had established that she was Sarah — as with where she was and why. A chorus kept insisting she was fine, although she knew she was not, and that everything was fine, which she doubted, and avoiding altogether any other questions.

She recognized voices. Joe McIntyre: "Don't worry, Sally, my darling, as soon as we get you home, you'll be as good as new."

And Damon: "Everything is fine, Sarah. All of your animals are fine. We took them to the McIntyres. And everyone loves them. Even the goat."

And — was that John McIntyre? "Yes, it's John. No, darling, you're not dying. See, Damon? I told you this is how I affect people. I come to their bedsides and they think it's the Last Rites."

"That's not how you affected me."

"Oh no," John said. "She sees."

No, I don't, Sarah thought. Sees what?

One voice conjured no face, but it spoke quiet sense. It explained: Two cars had collided in the fog. She had crushed her right side against a door. Broken ribs had perforated her lungs. The darkness? It would soon be gone. He could give her the scientific term, but he preferred: temporary. Yes, he was a doctor.

"At least now I understand why it hurts to breathe," she said. "Would you tell the others that, under the circumstances, I don't mind being in a hospital?"

"It will relieve their minds."

Kate came in, too: "Sarah, I brought your orchid. Harry got it for you."

"Harry? Kate, are you smiling?"

"It's just fun, Sarah. Well, it's just sex. But, boy, is it fun."

"What happened to Mildred?"

"She left the party with that man who shot his lawyer. No one's heard from her since."

"Kate, I can't remember what happened."

"Well, you almost died. I'm not supposed to mention this, but I know you'd like to know."

Images quivered in the dark. "There were lights," Sarah said, "and Gabriel turned —"

"Into the path of the oncoming car, yes."

"And the other driver?" Not knowing the truth didn't make it any less true.

"Tanya? Well, she's going to need a new nose."

"Tanya?" Sarah was certain that it was at that moment that the relentless dark began to clear or at least glimmers of light flickered in it like fireflies. "I thought — I was afraid — why did I think he was there?"

"Who?"

"How is Gabriel?"

"No one knows. He was thrown from the Jeep. Damon thinks he broke his neck. But his mother is here and she won't let anyone near him, not even John. She's going to take him away."

Sarah waited for the return of the quiet doctor. She had created a face for him: honey brown with black eyes and a mustache. "Are you from India?" she asked.

"No, Mexico."

"Will you speak Spanish?"

"I already am."

"How do I understand you?"

"I believe more is possible than we can imagine, and much more than we can see."

"Especially, in my case, since all I can see is dark. Can I go see Gabriel?"

"If you wish."

She struggled out of the bed and went down under an attack of arrows of pain. Amidst a ruckus of voices, she was hustled back into her bed.

"Miss Glass," a nurse admonished, "you must not walk alone."

As she lay in a brume of confusion, a complex blurry light resembling a two-headed chandelier entered the room. "The nurses said you aren't eating," Damon said. "So we made you a quiche. Julia's recipe."

"We?"

"Yes." She could see his smile. "Sarah, it's mutual."

"And wonderful." That was John.

"How long have I been here?" she asked. "I don't have insurance."

"And you're not to worry about that," Damon said. "Both drivers were drunk. Believe me, those families are paying the bills. They've got lawyers with disclaimers, but Joe threatened to kill them if they came near you. What a passionate family, these McIntyres!"

As she mulled over life from inside her mostly dark cocoon, Josefine came into the room. "Tia Aurelia made the cocoa you like. You will drink some?"

"Thank you. I'll drink it later."

"You will like to eat when you will go home, Sarah. Soon."

"Your babies are home now?" she asked.

"Yes! And they are so beautiful. So happy to be alive. Oh — Sarah, I am sorry."

"No, tell me about them."

"The girl, she is Sarah Maria; the boy is Frankie. Soon, we will take them to Mexico to meet their family and be warm in the sun. Sarah, you must not be too sad. A little sad, yes, but you will have another baby. Just, next time, get married first."

When Josefina was gone, the gentle Mexican doctor returned. "I knew it wasn't possible for a fetus to survive," she said. "*Abruptio placentae.*"

"There will be others."

"No. Is Gabriel still here?"

This time she made it to the door. Perhaps she fainted. She woke up in bed, where she lay listening to the nurses. It was no comfort that they were not discussing whether she was dead or alive; they thought she had lost her mind. The hit on the head, had it triggered strange visions, unknown voices? Was it possible that, even if she couldn't see, she perceived something they did not? Could one be mostly blind but see more than twenty percent? Was seeing more than twenty percent what constituted insanity?

That night was the worst. A suffocating iron weight pressed down on her while horrible images swirled around her, charred limbs in flames, jabbering severed heads, and gyrating, mangled bodies that tried to suck her into their macabre dance. She flailed about for something to hold her back. Why? "Maybe it is not so bad to die," she said.

"Yes it is." She recognized the grip of the octopus. Why an octopus? Wouldn't it be squishy, cold, and wet? This one had warm, smooth tentacles. She traced their shape with her fingers. Had it lost three tentacles? A wounded octopus? Did tentacles grow back? She didn't know. It felt strong as an anchor. Or maybe it was an anchor not an octopus. But anchors were not warm. Maybe it was just life that wouldn't let go.

BLOBS OF COLOR were floating everywhere around her. She had been watching them since dawn: dusky shadows, violet, pearl, and pale rose. Now a bright pink bubble bounced into view.

"My god, Sarah, you look worse than usual. You might at least comb your hair."

Sarah was happy to be able to see anything, even Cecily. "Where did you come from?"

"Italy. We were at Lake Garda, having a wonderful time, when we got a call from Congressman Ilillouette, and Greg said we had to come home. Everyone thought you were dying, but I knew you wouldn't. I brought you a robe. I knew you wouldn't have a nice one and you have a visitor."

A restive stirring rippled through the air, a fluttering, like birds at a watering hole when a lion appears at the horizon. An energetic swirl of gold exploded into the room. Cecily said, "Sarah, this is Congressman Ilillouette. Try not to be difficult."

"Your sister?" a voice rich with laughter asked. "Not be difficult? Didn't she already interrupt your dinner in Italy?"

"You did that, sir."

"And you shredded my reputation."

"I only said I had no idea a congressman could be useful. But we could have finished our honeymoon."

"When your honeymoon is finished, I hope you will call me."

"Congressman, you are a dreadful flirt."

"Thank goodness you are not. Where's McIntyre? Having a blood transfusion?"

Sarah's vision went blurry again.

"Poor Rory," Cecily sighed.

"You can handle the advance without him, Cecily. Off with you, then. We'll catch up."

Sarah, amazed, watched the pink blob roll obediently out of the room. "Aphrodite with a hat pin," David Ilillouette said. "I think I'm in love, but I know she won't be divorced and available for another month. So, Sarah Glass, you want to see Gabriel Dinesen. Can you walk?"

"See and walk are relative terms."

"I've nicked a chair from the nurses. Shall we storm the citadel?"

Lights flashed by as they streaked down the hall like a high-speed train. "It feels like a miracle," Sarah said, "to be moving. Not to mention, seeing."

"There are two ways to live your life. As if nothing is a miracle or everything is a miracle."

"Einstein."

She saw a grin, bright and impudent. "Tell me," he asked, "who is Gabriel Dinesen? I know he worked, for a time, in my Napa office. My aides adored him. They called him Adonis. And now he is awakening from a dream of life, poor fellow."

"Who —"

"Shelley. The poet. Shelley, my sister, is partial to him, although I've always thought he was an odd duck. 'I fall upon the thorns of life!

I bleed!' Do you know how he died? He sailed with two others into a storm and when they were in danger, he refused rescue from a larger ship. The captain warned them to take in sail and one of the passengers tried to, but Shelley stopped him. They all drowned, and a Tory paper wrote, 'Now he knows whether there is a God or not.'"

"He chose death?"

"For the others as well as himself, unfortunately."

"They got into the boat with him."

"Is choice the enemy of commitment?"

"Who said that?"

"That would be Rory McIntyre."

"I was afraid that something had happened to him and no one would talk about it."

"Oh, something has happened to him, but it doesn't follow that it's bad. I suspect you haven't seen him because he only comes in at night when no one is torturing you, and then he sits in the dark and make notes for a story in which things like this don't happen. You don't want to make a habit of getting hit by lightning. That's my own quote. I try to think of one on my own at least once a month."

"I see why Rory likes you."

"Yes, and I see why he's a besotted lunatic. Speaking of which — ah, I'll leave you here. I spy Cecily with the Dragon Lady of Texas. That's my cue to go in. Don't worry; I've met my share of dragons." His golden voice rang out. "Mrs. Dinesen? David Ililouette. I am hoping you can tell me about Gabriel. Surely you know more than anyone else." Charm poured like a waterfall over the astonished Henrietta Dinesen as she was waltzed away.

Sarah's right arm was in a cast; so was her right ankle. Awkwardly, she tried to roll the chair into the darkened room with one hand, and it began to glide forward. She gripped the bedrail and tried to pull herself up. She wobbled but landed on her unbroken foot. The room was still, although the blinking lights and numbers indicated the presence of life, albeit bound in white and motionless on the bed.

"Gabriel?" she asked. "Are you here? Or are you gone somewhere else? I hope you are free. But I cannot follow you." She touched his hand; it was cold and unresponsive. She wondered if she could transmit an image into it. She tried to think of purple eyes and gold shooting stars; her head filled with sounds of flight, a rhythmic swishing of hundreds of wings, and the lone call of a duck.

CHAPTER 52

S HE LAY IN bed observing her orchid and her statue, the lilacs from
Dr. Castro, and the yellow tulips from the Napa clinic. There was
no note on the wildflowers in a green vase, although the artists who
had made the drawings of firemen, cats, cows, horses, dogs, and goats,
all smiling, had carefully written her name and theirs. Here was the
wonder: all of this had been there when she could not see it.

Cecily entered the room briskly, but was forestalled in her reproach concerning people who swooned and caused an uproar by
John and Damon who arrived just after her.

"Cecily, you are more beautiful than ever," John said. "What a good
sister you are."

Mollified if not distracted, she said, "Well, Greg says we'll just have
to go on another honeymoon. And I was worried about your poor
brother. How is he?"

"I believe my poor brother will survive."

"He looks terrible."

"He just can't tell the difference between fainting and dropping
dead."

"It has been a frightful experience for him," Damon put in. "You
know he was the first one at the scene of the crash. Harry and I heard
it and ran down the hill just as he arrived. He was coming to see

Sarah. I knew he would. And it was a ghastly scene, all that blood and pain. I did what I could but, dear god, time stood still while we waited for the ambulance. Thank goodness Harry drove us to the hospital."

"Harry was so helpful," John said. "Damon called Kate at home, and she said she would watch the children while Dad and I rushed to the hospital, so Harry went to help her."

"Yes." Damon smiled. "That's our Harry."

"Damon won't admit it, but he was a pillar of strength, Cecily."

"No, John, I was not, not until you arrived. They had rushed Sarah into surgery. She was so white, I knew she was bleeding internally. I knew Rory thought she was going to die and I couldn't tell him I thought so too. And then John walked into the room, Cecily, and it was like someone had turned on a light in a nightmare."

"Damon, you were the one who thought to call Ilillouette to see if he could find Cecily."

"And thank goodness we talked to David first," Cecily said. "If it had been Rory calling, we'd have thought the world was ending and not just that Sarah had broken a few bones."

"But Dad is the one who really knew what to do with Rory," John said.

"And us!" Both men laughed merrily.

"He sent us to find coffee —"

"And there we were wandering in the night —"

"I never knew how magical it could be to look for a coffee machine at midnight."

"And Joe told such wonderful stories. I just loved the one about how much Rory loathed Paul McCartney when Sarah planned to marry him. "

"But what really saved Rory was when the doctor came in to say that Sarah was out of surgery —"

"And he asked who was Rory because he thought that Sarah wanted him."

"The look on Rory's face — John and I were both in tears."

"It was quite an icebreaker."

"But, John, I still think the real icebreaker was when Joe called Jean. He wouldn't admit there was a chance Sarah wouldn't make it, but the way he said, 'Your boy's here, breaking his heart.' Jean caught the first flight back, and Joe asked John to meet her plane. I knew about their problems from Kate, and so I understood, but I was surprised — well, thrilled — when John asked me to go with him. First, we had breakfast at Buttercream, and now it will always be the most romantic place in the world. Then we talked all the way to the airport. We didn't once run out of things to say. When John told me his doubts about his vocation, I could only think, thank God. Of course, Joe needn't have worried; when we got to the hospital, Jean just flew into his arms. And we knew everything would be all right."

"Except poor Rory's wits," Cecily said. "Greg insists that love makes all men's IQs drop fifty points, but it would be so much worse to be in love with Sarah. Rory knows — I told him — that if he asks her to marry him, she'll make a complete disaster of the wedding."

Damon chortled. "Cecily, I can see by the look on Sarah's face that if you say a man's in love, it has to be true. Well, Cecily, shall we go and rescue David from the Dragon Lady? It does look like when he runs for president, he will have one vote in Texas."

"I have a few things to say to Sarah first."

They left, and Cecily said, "Stop pretending to be dead, Sarah. And you have to stop acting like a crazy person, speaking Spanish to no one at all. The nurses are polite, but they think you are insane, and also a Mexican. Oh, hello, doctor," she added. "I am sorry my sister is difficult. She always is. It comes of thinking she's so smart."

"We will walk, you and I," the doctor said, "and you can tell me more." Sarah opened her eyes to see her sister leaving the room on the arm of the dark-eyed man from Mexico.

Damon returned alone. "Sarah, I just wanted to be sure that you are here."

"Where would I go?"

"Now that is a very good and reassuring point. John thinks you are the best thing that could ever have happened to Rory, but I did say 'You don't know how fast she can run.'" His smile lit up his face and she remembered the starry-eyed pumpkin he had caved on Halloween. "Oh, Sarah, do you think it is wrong to be so happy?"

"No."

"I am sorry for Gabriel, but I knew, the first time I ever saw John that he was my Rory McIntyre. I just never imagined being loved in return."

"I guess it's worth a few broken bones," Sarah said, "for all these happy love stories."

"Not the least of which is yours, dear." Damon smiled. "It's just too bad you've been unconscious and missed it all."

CHAPTER 53

"THE NURSES SAID you don't want the pain meds?" This was a different doctor, young, sandy-haired, and serious.

"I want to see what I am feeling," Sarah said.

"No, you don't." He grinned at her. "Trust me. I already tried that too. When I had an appendicitis, I thought, I should experience pain so I knew what patients felt. But I changed my mind. Look, you are doing great. You can even take a shower. But take the damned meds."

Sarah took a shower, half wrapped in plastic and sitting in a chair. She inspected the parts of herself that were not in casts. Her right side was shades of purple and green, an ugly red incision snaked across her midriff, and her left leg was hairy as a coconut. How could the human body, beset with trauma, still grow hair?

She put on the silly frilly pink silk robe Cecily had brought her and limped into the hallway. Gripping the handrail, she shuffled step by erratic step down the hallway until she finally found Gabriel's empty room. She leaned against the doorframe. Now what, she wondered.

"Miss Glass — Sarah — may I help you?"

Her heart leapt up into her head. It was the voice, and she was looking at the same pale hair, the same silver eyes of Gabriel Dinesen. But, no, she caught herself; she had only been mistaken because this was Christian Dinesen without a hat.

"I wish to apologize to you," he said stiffly.

"It isn't necessary. I got into the Jeep."

"It does not follow that you don't regret it."

"Perhaps. But not everything."

"I understand that you are recovering well and you will be discharged soon."

This was news. She had not thought so far into the future, but it appeared that she had one.

"And you will return to school but perhaps you will remember —"

"I will," she said. "If nothing else, I will remember what it's like to lie there looking up at people in white coats. No, I will remember more. That place, your place, it was like living in a dream, and even though I knew it was technically someone else's dream, I am glad to know it exists." She had to stop talking to still her stabbing breath. "Thank you."

She perceived that she had disturbed him, and as he turned away, she watched him pull a hat, a gray tweed driver's cap from his back pocket.

She wobbled on, wishing now that she had taken two pain pills. The red exit signs glared at her. If she reached an exit, where would she go?

"Sal?"

She let go of the rail and plummeted toward the floor. Rory dove to catch her. She winced; he flinched and propped her against the wall. "Where are you going?" he asked.

"I don't know. Somewhere. Anywhere. Probably nowhere. Away."

They stared at each other in pathetic confusion, but at least they were not wallowing in a heap on the floor. "I have an idea," he said. "Can you make it to the elevator?"

He was jittery as a spooked horse as they crossed the great abyss of the hallway. His hands hovered and jumped without touching her until she tripped over nothing and caught his arm. They reached the elevator and stood before it dumbly until he remembered to push a call button. They fell into it and crumpled against a wall as it rumbled upwards. Sarah released Rory's arm and massaged it a little. She was sure she had made dents in it. The doors parted. They were facing two gold statues flanking a gilded crucifix. The air smelled of incense. Sarah looked up at Rory, bewildered.

"I know it's a church," he said, abashed. "But I thought you'd like the view."

They were in a tower made of windows. She sank into a chair; her legs would not stop shaking, but she could see: spring green hills and trees filled with pink and white blossoms. A flock of black birds swooped by and a flurry of peach blossoms whirled through the air.

Rory sat down next to her; he, too, was trembling a little. "I found it by accident," he said. "I was walking with that doctor —"

"Which doctor?"

"The nice guy, from Mexico."

"You talked to him? What did you talk about?"

He shook his head. "Not — not now, Sal."

Like everything else, he was still soft around the edges, but he did not look terrible, only a trifle short on blood in the head. She tried to think of a topic that wouldn't upset him. "You're wearing a tie."

"I've been doing some writing for the paper, just a few things: flood control, budbreak, the tomato plant sale, the garbage collection rate debate."

"You like it."

"I wonder if this is the stuff life is made of."

He was carrying a rucksack. He slung it off his shoulder and rubbed his fingers on the zipper, as if its workings baffled him. Finally he opened it, stared into it, and pulled out a thermos. "Would you like some coffee?"

"Peet's?"

"Yes! The stuff in the newsroom is as bad as hospital coffee."

He unscrewed the cap and the scent wrapped around her like a suffocating cloth. She felt the puncture wound where her rib had stabbed her lungs. I will feel it and then the pain will be gone, she thought, and I won't feel anything at all. She said, "Thermoses are interesting."

"Are they?"

"I don't know how they work."

"It's a vacuum. You remove all the air, so there's nothing to conduct heat or cold."

"Nothing? What about virtual particles?"

"They only wink in and out of existence. They come out of nothing and disappear into nothing."

"Then how do you know they exist?"

"Heisenberg's uncertainty principle predicts them. The product of the uncertainty in energy with the uncertainty in time always exceeds the h-bar, Planck's constant, divided by two pi —"

"I don't know why anyone cares if they exist or not."

"I know, except it looks like they mediate the forces. Every electron is surrounded by virtual photons that carry electricity, but when you go to look for them, they're gone."

She nodded; there was nothing else to say about thermoses. Light was draining from the sky. "We should get you back," he said.

"You can go. I'll stay here a bit."

"Sal," he floundered wretchedly. "Sal —"

The elevator doors rattled, and Damon tumbled into view. He was wearing a white coat but his professional aspect was impaired by a stethoscope hanging askew. Also, he was giggling and carrying two picnic baskets, and one was meowing. A red-gold dog rushed passed him, dragging John by a leash. John's hair was disheveled, face flushed, and his black coat covered with dog hair, but his white priest's collar was intact. Howling joyfully, Wolf sprang from Sarah to Rory and back again. With more dignity, Widdershins climbed out of a picnic basket, cast a disdainful look at the dog, sharpened his claws on Sarah's cast, curled up, and began to purr. Damon and John collapsed into chairs, consumed by laughter.

"We did it, Damon!"

"You, the personification of innocence! I knew no one would question you with a dog."

"Not when I was walking with so serious a doctor!"

"We just couldn't figure out how to bring in the horse, cow, and goat, Sarah. Ilillouette will have to pull that one off."

"He could!" They were off again. Presently they recovered. "So there," John said to Rory.

"I never thought you'd be such fucking lunatics."

"Fucking lunatics," Damon said. "I love it."

"We did it because Rory said we couldn't," John said to Sarah. "He was worried that the creatures would die of missing you, and this would upset you. Damon was a little concerned about bringing Wolf into Sarah's room — so much to knock over — but when the nurse said Rory had brought you to the chapel, I thought, how perfect. Rory does believe in God, Sarah."

"We made you a picnic," Damon deftly changed the subject. "It's all French."

Rory unwrapped a parcel dubiously, extracted a slice of beef, and gave it to the dog.

"Rory, that's our Boeuf Bordelaise!" John objected.

"She's the taster."

"Damon and I have decided to go to cooking school in Paris."

"Thank God."

"I suppose we should not stay too long, John."

Sarah pressed her face into the cat's soft fur before she gave him up. Her half-dead heart was perking up, working again.

"Damon," John was saying as they departed, "I wish we could call our restaurant The Fucking Lunatics, but I don't suppose the world is ready for that."

Rory shook his head. "Those two."

"I think it's love."

"Yes. I wondered what the folks would think, but Mom just said, 'Happiness is happiness.' And Dad said, compared to Sterling, Damon is a gift from heaven." He retreated again to his rucksack. This time, he brought out a long, flat, wooden box. "This is for you," he said.

She opened it with her left hand. It was pencils, rows of them in all colors. She ran her fingers over the blues and greens, reds, purples, and yellows. Her throat swelled up and her vision blurred. "Thank you," she whispered. "They're beautiful."

"I bought them last December. I just didn't give them to you."

"I bought you gold silk boxers last December."

"Did you? Where are they?"

"I don't know."

"Will you find them?"

"I'll try." She shrugged. "They might be lost."

"Sarah, don't look so sad." All of his unease flooded back. "No, I don't mean that. I mean — I don't know what I mean."

"It was just the coffee." She could not make her voice stop shaking. "It smelled so good. I couldn't smell it before. It made me sick. Now, that's gone. But it's for the best. You were right. I was so stupid."

"No." She looked up at him; his eyes were red and filled with tears, and she, who couldn't have run away unless he helped her, leaned against him and wept.

The room grew dark and the sky filled with stars. A giant pearl of a moon floated into view, filling the room with a silver-blue light. The leaves of an unseen tree danced a ballet on the wall. Life, she thought, it pulls you back.

"We're a fine pair." Rory broke the silence. "Am I hurting you?"

"No."

"Sarah, when you get out of here, would you like to go somewhere?"

"Yes," she said forlornly.

"Paris?"

"Paris?"

"You were always going there with Paul McCartney. You know, I never liked that guy."

"Paris. Maybe. Someday." She ran her fingers over the colors in the box of pencils, and suddenly all the shades of blue and yellow, green and red exploded in her head, an unexpected firework, an idea. "First, I will go to Mexico."

"Mexico?"

"I didn't know where to go. I thought I didn't have anywhere to go. But these colors, they reminded me of the sky and the sun and — I think I have a house. In Mexico."

"Mexico," he said. "Mexico, it is."

CHAPTER 54

B Y THE TIME Sarah left the Queen, she had grown so used to the hospital, the doctors teased her that she had just completed her first three-week rotation. She stood blinking in the sunlight like a dazed nocturnal creature, unnerved by a world so rough and raw, so noisy and full of stairs. She was tempted to retreat back inside, but instead she went to Mexico with Rory McIntyre.

Cecily exerted herself to show David Ilillouette that she too could be useful and she contacted the Mexican lawyer who provided a map to the village of their grandparents. Frankie, studying the vague directions, concluded that Sarah and Rory would never find the place without help. He and Josefina were driving to Guanajuato; they could all drive together. And then, in a month's time, when Frankie had to return for work, they would stop by for them, and they would all drive back to California. A month? Rory astonished Sarah by saying okay. Tía Aurelia said that then Rory must then bring his children, and this would be no problem. She was going along to help Josefina. She would look after Lucy and Avery on the road until they got to San Antonio where there would be a village to care for them.

So they had set out in a procession, with Frankie and Josefina leading the way in his truck, and the cousins, Diego, Santiago, and Valentina, driving their mother's green Ford. Tía Aurelia rode in the backseat of the Volvo with Lucy and Avery. The dog and cat had also climbed into the car, but Joe McIntyre had been able to persuade them to get out and stay with him.

The journey took three days because they had to stop in Los Angeles to pick up more cousins with whom Frankie played in a mariachi band. Sarah slept for most of the trip; this was preferable to watching Rory's face as he drove deeper into the desert. She knew he was hearing, inside his head, his mother's dire prediction that he would kill Sarah by taking her where she wanted to go. Jean had put a crate of canned peaches, tuna, and green beans in Rory's car. Joe added a case of wine and said not to worry: if Jean fretted he would take her dancing or, better yet, buy her another goat.

Rory insisted he didn't mind the desert if he had a full tank of gas, but it was not his natural habitat, this endless, sun-bleached vista, where mountains were only barren heaps of abandoned rocks. He admitted that the distant hills were nice, painted purple and orange with lupines and poppies, but he thought the Joshua trees looked like giant, twisted tarantulas creeping up out of the ground. And the ones in bloom? Brides of Tarantula.

His unease increased after they crossed into Mexico and left the highway for bumpy, dirt roads that wandered to nowhere. Frankie, after conferring with a lone rider on a donkey, insisted he knew "exactly more or less" where they were, but when night overtook them, a glittering net of stars was their only guide until lights flared ahead of them: lanterns on the wooden porch of the adobe house that had belonged to Rosa and Teodoro Guevara.

A party was underway. Musicians on a patio were playing guitars and mandolins. Lucy and Avery, wide-eyed, held onto Rory's legs until they saw the tables filled with food — three cakes! Rory drank a beer, from sheer relief at being somewhere, and poured his father's wine. Sarah shook the hands of everyone who had known her grandparents and her father, but when the last guest had departed, she fainted, which was too bad, because Rory was still unable to distinguish fainting from dropping dead.

She slept that night in her grandparents' bed, scented with desert sage and cedar; Rory slept beside her and so did Lucy and Avery, but in the morning, she awoke alone. She looked around with wonder and a little worry. She had visited her grandparents' house once, when she was Lucy's age, and she remembered it only as a place where she had been happy; now, she realized it was one room, made of mud, without plumbing or electricity. The only sound was bird calls outside. Frankie and his entourage had planned to leave early; it was possible that Rory, seeing where she had brought him, was halfway back to Bakersfield.

But it was a neat little house, immaculate and lemon-scented. Wooden shutters set in the thick adobe walls were open and sunlight gleamed on a terra cotta floor. Two rocking chairs, woven from willow branches, sat by a round table that held candles and a yellow vase with jacaranda blossoms. Spanish and English books filled a shelf. A wood-burning stove was surrounded by colorful tiles. A painting of the Virgin hung over the bed. The bed frame was carved with vines and birds; the soft quilt was hand-stitched in a pattern of rings. She liked this place; still, her mind did ease — it danced a happy capriole — when she limped outside and saw Rory, sitting beneath an arbor covered with honeysuckle and grapevines, and Lucy and Avery scampering through a garden beyond it.

He was talking in mangled Spanish-English with a woman from the village who had brought him coffee and *chilequiles*, a dish of eggs, tortillas, and chiles. She was Sofia, who had looked after the house and garden after Sarah's grandparents died. Dr. Guevara, she told them, was revered not only for the clinic he had given the village but also for the way he had cared for his parents. He had wished to build them a big new house in Bahía Kino but they were happy with their little adobe. Why would they want more? So he had the dirt floor tiled and installed a fine cooker and dug a deep well. That is how they had grown such a fine garden and an orchard with lemon, orange, olive, and guava trees. The Guevaras also had the finest outhouse in San Antonio; the doctor had insisted on a washbasin with hot water heated by a clever arrangement that piped it through the stove to a holding tank; they had the only hot shower in the village.

Sofia hoped Sarah would not mind that she sold produce from the garden and honey from the beehives. Four years ago, her husband had gone to California to work and she had not heard from him since. She and her three children lived with her parents. Perhaps, she added shyly, she could help, since everyone knew that Sarah had been ill and might not be able to cook. Rory, on his third helping of *chilequiles,* said, "I think that is a great idea." He tried to say it in Spanish, confused the words for "think" and "grow," and made Sofia laugh.

When Sofia left, Lucy and Avery followed her, based on reports that she had children and donkeys. Sarah and Rory were left alone. Bees buzzed in the flowers and a hawk called as it circled overhead. Dear God, she thought, forgetting she did not believe in Him, what have I done? It was a question that would remain unanswered for many days.

He did not come near her bed again but strung a hammock between two trees and slept outside under the stars. Lucy and Avery had two cots that they moved about, sometimes sleeping inside and sometimes outside, and Sarah slept alone. She could not blame Rory. She was wrapped in casts that were heavy, hot, and itchy. Her bruises were fading from storm cloud purple to the strange yellow of the sky after a storm, but the scar across her midriff was a livid red thunderbolt that would never go away. Most nights, she would have preferred not to get in bed with herself either.

He hardly came near her at all unless he thought she was going to swoon and she diligently avoided doing this. Most strangely of all, he had turned so quiet. Their conversations became: "Would you like more coffee?"

"Yes, thanks."

"I think I'll go for a walk, if you don't mind."

"No, of course not."

She was grateful for Lucy and Avery, who filled the silence. They made a hundred new friends, including seven new grandmothers who gave them hot chocolate and honeycomb. They were learning Spanish. With Sofia's children, they collected eggs, milked goats, and rode donkeys; they loved the donkeys. They built a fort with tunnels through sagebrush. They found lizards, snakes, and the footprint of a panther. They saw owls, hawks, and rabbits. "And we are going to find a tarantula for Rory," Avery promised.

"No," Rory said, "we are not."

When Lucy was an old woman and a traveler in the world, she always said it had all begun one springtime in Mexico.

CHAPTER 55

S ARAH SLEPT AND she sat in the sun and let it bake her bones. She read her textbooks. It was all she could do. One cast nearly covered her fingers, and she was lucky she could turn the pages.

She watched Rory and she wondered: without the distractions of sex and conversation, who was he?

He kept busy. He finished a project her grandfather had begun, an outdoor bathtub. He fixed the radio in the village cafe and repaired several pick-up trucks. He borrowed a guitar and in the evenings strummed it. He worked out the chords to play "Wichita Lineman" because Sofia had told him it was her favorite song. Sarah knew he got up at sunrise and walked alone in the desert. Afternoons, he read in his hammock; he had brought a box of books. Late at night, from her window she saw him writing by candlelight on his long yellow notepads. He had brought a stack of them too.

The villagers liked him. He entertained them with his Spanish, but this was nothing compared to his mother's crate of food, which he gave away, explaining he much preferred Sofia's cooking. No one had ever seen food in a tin; no one had a can opener, and if the village had a museum, Jean's supplies would have landed there. Instead, women reverently displayed their cans on shelves with other relics. Even Juanita, who was eighty and disliked men, kept Rory's can of peaches next to her rosary, blessed by the bishop. One morning, Sarah awoke to find the village women gathered to witness Rory making chilequiles; the miracle of a man cooking could only be the work of the Virgin herself. Sofia told Sarah that Rory's hammock had been observed and approved. This was a fine man. Sometimes, Sarah felt like she was back at Napa High.

When she went to the clinic to have her casts removed, Rory walked with her; he offered her his arm, but only, she knew, because he expected her to collapse in the road. When she emerged from the exam room, dancing on her tiptoes, ready to fly, she found him fixated on the photograph of the clinic's founder, Dr. Raphael Guevara. On the way home, he fell into a brooding silence. When she stopped to watch a falcon circle overhead, he didn't even notice but walked on without her.

Freed of her casts, that evening she tried out the tub, and while she soaked, he took his children into the adobe and read to them. She listened to a Moonbubble story; it had gone to Mexico too. When Sarah came into the adobe, Rory went outside. He lit a candle but he didn't start writing. He only leaned back and looked up at the sky. The moon was new, a sliver of light in a thin silver circle. Sarah made herself go outside. "I didn't mean to disturb you," she said when he jumped.

"No, no, not at all." He seemed to have to travel back from the stars to answer her.

"I wondered, would you like a lantern?"

"I'm fine."

"Oh, good," she said. "I am glad — that you're fine."

"Why wouldn't I be?"

"It is so primitive here."

"Is that what you think?"

"Don't you?"

"Sarah, I've never known such time and space."

Then he was gone again, somewhere she could not follow. She didn't know what else to do. She let him be.

WITH HER HAND free from the cast, she began volume two of "Things I Might Not See Again," subtitled, "Things I'd Never Seen Before." This one was in color. She drew the vast, wild, Sonoran landscape with its shifting shades of amber, sand, and gold. She drew the distant purple mountains and clouds. She drew a cactus, a beetle, and the falcon who had taken to landing on the guava tree. When Lucy and Avery inspected her book, she was careful to let Rory see it too, but of what he was writing he gave no clue. She only knew this: whenever she went out to soak in the tub, even if he was already in his hammock, he got up and went inside.

They worked in the garden with Sofia. Sarah doubted she would keel over into the tomatoes unless Rory's watchful gaze made her disintegrate; but on one sultry afternoon, Avery found a bug and when she bent down to see it, he jumped onto her back and down she went. With a shout, Rory jerked the little boy off her. Avery landed unperturbed, but Sarah, catching him protectively to her, flashed a look of reproach at Rory. He strode off into the desert. Lucy explained, "He thinks you are still broken."

Rory did not return until evening. Sarah fixed dinner for his children and they were sitting on her bed reading stories when a thunderstorm broke the day's muggy heat. Lucy and Avery burrowed under her covers. Through the window, Sarah saw Rory on the patio, and she feared he would stay out in the torrential rain and drown like a sheep. Finally, he came inside. "You can get in bed, too," Avery told him. Rory sat down in a chair.

"Will you tell us a story?" Lucy asked. "Do you know the

Moonbubble, Sarah?"

"I have wondered where it came from."

"The golden prince who talks a lot."

When the storm ended, Lucy and Avery were asleep. Rory surprised Sarah by lingering. "She meant Ililllouette," he said. "One time he told them a crazy story about a Moonbubble and I had to continue it. David said his grandfather raised him and his sister on fairy tales."

"Maybe that's why he believes in politics."

He smiled, faintly. "Sarah, I'm sorry if I upset you, but he can't jump on you. You're held together with stitches." She sighed, blew out the candle, lay back against her pillow, and hoped he would go away. "Sarah," he fumbled, "I've been trying to remember something you told me once, about intention —"

"It's the intention of nature to heal wounds?"

"Yes, that's it."

"Some take longer than others."

"Yes," he said. "Are you still mad at me?"

"I wasn't."

"Yes, you were. And damn, Sarah, your eyes are smoke and fire."

He went out to sleep in his rain-soaked hammock.

THE MONTH WAS up. Frankie and Josefina returned with thriving babies, Tía Aurelia and the cousins. There was going to be a festival because someone had gone to Heaven, Lucy reported, and Frankie would go play music. Sofia's mother made Lucy a yellow dress with red and green ribbons and she made a dress for Sarah too. It was long and white and embroidered with vivid flowers. Avery had a sombrero and a shirt with parrots on it. Didn't Rory want new clothes too? No, he said. He wore his jeans and an oxford cloth shirt, but he rolled up the sleeves.

The air was warm and filled with music as they walked to the town square. People were dancing, flashing bright colors. Lucy and Avery joined them, spinning madly and stamping their heels. Sarah watched. One man had fair hair and she thought of Gabriel Dinesen. She yearned to be dancing. She touched Rory's arm. He asked, "Do you want to sit down?"

"No."

She moved away and into the path of a man who had black hair, a mustache, and sparkling ebony eyes. He was Raul, Sofia's cousin from Hermosillo. Smiling, he murmured, "*Eres como la flor blanca que florece tan dulcemente en la noche.*" You look like the white flower that blooms so sweetly at night. He asked, "Do you know what it means, this song, *Quizás?*"

"Perhaps."

"Yes, and perhaps, if I ask you to dance, your gringo will put a knife in my ribs?"

Sarah laughed and danced with him until she felt a hand fall on her shoulder. Rory was looking grim, although not homicidal. "I hope this white boy can dance," Raul said, and he strolled away, chuckling.

"I didn't know you wanted to dance," Rory said, and they might have danced, except Avery fell into a cactus and this sent them to the clinic. As they waited, the grandmothers bustled in. They had a salve for cactus needles. They carried off Avery, and Lucy went with them.

"Shouldn't we go too?" Sarah asked Rory, who, oblivious to the hullabaloo, was staring again at the photograph on the wall. "That is my father," she added.

"I know," he snapped. He spun around and walked off without her.

SARAH DID NOT mind walking alone back to the adobe. She would soak, undisturbed, in the tub. She undressed, and as she stepped out into the sun, she realized that her bones did not ache. She dropped her robe and stretched luxuriously. She twisted up her hair and felt the sun rub her back. She heard a sound. Rory was standing in the doorway. She toppled into the tub. He came outside. He moved a chair near the tub and sat down. Sarah sank as low as she could without submersing herself entirely.

"Avery is fine," he said.

"Oh, good."

"The kids stayed with Sofia. They are going to have a bonfire."

"They'll like that."

"Yes."

The sun was setting. He moved his hand through the water in the tub. "It's getting cold."

"It's fine."

"Are you ever going to get out?"

"Well, no."

"Why not?"

"Because I dropped my robe somewhere."

He retrieved it and held it out for her. "I can't," she whispered. "I have a scar."

He sat back down and examined the seams of her robe, as if they were interesting. He was deep in the contemplation of one who had discovered that, despite what he had been guessing she was thinking, it bore no resemblance to what she had been thinking.

"Can I see it?"

"No."

"I have a scar," he offered. "Thirteen of them, I think. You've probably seen them all."

"This one is ugly."

He cleared his throat, having judged this was not a conversation to pursue. "I was talking to Frankie. He has a job waiting for him back in Napa. In fact, I do too. Frank Havoc offered me one at the paper before we left. He said he could wait a month."

"I think you would like it."

"Maybe. It depends. Frankie was wondering how soon we would be ready to leave. He was thinking we might leave tonight."

"Tonight?"

"He's been driving at night. His truck doesn't have air conditioning so it's more comfortable for Josefina and the babies. Aurelia's car blew a gasket so they left it behind and the band is riding in the back of his truck. I told him I'd see what you think. About leaving tonight."

He waited. Sarah said, "I think it would be better if Josephina rode in your car with Aurelia and the babies. I think you could all fit."

"And what do you plan to do, ride with Frankie and the band in the truck?"

"No." She had said it; she rushed on. "I don't start school again till August. I could go to New York now, but I'd rather stay here. I don't — Rory! I wish you would stop looking at me like you think I'm going to die. I am not going to die. In fact, I think I am going to live. But I will remember to never do this to any patient ever, to look at them like you do. They would just give up and die."

Finished, she sank down until the water covered her head. Soon, she would come back up to continue her plan of living, but for the moment, she preferred to be submerged. She heard his voice, made wobbly by the water. "Sal, it will be a blight on my life if you drown yourself in the middle of a conversation. "

She came back up. He walked away, but her robe flew back through the air to her. It landed in the water. She got out of the tub and wrapped the wet thing around her. Rory was standing at the edge of the patio, looking out at the desert. The sky was flaming red and orange and gold. She felt, in comparison, weak-kneed, inglorious, and also quite cold.

"Sarah," he said, "do you know how I feel about you?"

"No. Oh don't!" The latter was because he had begun hitting his head on the lemon tree.

"That's what Damon said. He said, 'Does she know how you feel about her?' I said, 'Of course.' He said, 'Why do you think that?' I said, 'Because I know how I feel about her. I just don't know how she feels about me.' And he said, 'I think you should tell her, especially now, when she can't run very fast.' Sarah! Do you really think I don't love you?"

"I don't know. But I know that you don't like love or believe in it."

"I believe in love, Sarah. I do." He paused. "But I don't believe in ghosts."

"I know. That's why it's so upsetting if you see one."

"I didn't just see him. I walked around the hospital with him. I sat in that weird church place and talked to him. I liked him. I can't believe I was talking to a god-damned ghost."

"I wish I knew what Einstein would say about it, but I don't."

A wind rustled the tree, and she shivered. He went to his hammock and beckoned her to him. She lay down beside him. The warmth of his body wrapped around her as the hammock rocked softly. He said, "For the record, when I look at you, I am not thinking about you dropping dead."

"You wouldn't touch me. But it's such an ugly scar."

"Sarah! I love your scar. I will always love that scar." The owl flew over them, wings white against the darkening sky. Stars were coming out. "Dammit," he said. "Sarah, you are not like Dibby and I am not like Sterling."

"What?" She sensed she had missed part of this conversation, perhaps the effect of feeling so nicely warm.

"You said that and I'll remember it till I die. So I am trying to do this without reminding you of Sterling again."

"Do what?"

"That day in the barn, Sarah, did you really think I would only ask you to marry me because you were pregnant? I had asked you before."

"You had?"

"Yes, when I was in the hospital, I asked you."

"But men always propose in hospitals."

"They don't."

"Well, not always marriage."

"Oh god," he said, revolted. "But on Christmas Day, I asked you again. You didn't say anything."

"I thought you were talking theoretically. And I threw up."

"It wasn't as bad as telling me I was like Sterling; then I thought I should just give up and go hang myself."

"It was the dead beetle, Rory."

"The what?"

"It was just hanging in the window, all wrapped up in spider webs. It might not have been dead yet, but the spider was watching it like she was deciding when to have dinner. I didn't want you to be a dead beetle. It isn't funny," she added because the hammock had begun to shake. "Rory, what you gave me to read was beautiful. I don't know what you've been writing now, but I do know that you can write like you are pulling words down out of the sky."

"Did you think I'd made it up?" he asked. "Sarah, you've never asked me why I didn't call you when I went away to school. I wanted to, every day, but I didn't because I knew I'd just fall apart and start bawling about how homesick I was, and then you'd get over your crush on me. I tried to write but it was so sappy, I couldn't send it. Then I met Dibby.

"I know I did it all to myself. I didn't think I could ever go back. But then, one night I was out walking. It was winter; it was snowing.

I went into a pub to warm up and across the room, I saw a girl. She was standing by a fire with her back to me, but she had long, dark hair like yours and she was wearing a blue coat like one you used to wear. I was halfway across the room before she turned around and I realized it wasn't you.

"I wondered, why did I think of Sarah, here and now? I called your house and your mother said you were at Yale. The next day I drove to New Haven, but they said, no, you weren't. I called your mother again, and she didn't know where you were. I thought, I'll find her. But then, life closed in again and there I was with two kids and no future. Still, when I started writing that terrible novel, I thought, let it happen, let her turn around, and it's her. Maybe it's why people write fiction, so an idiot can find the girl he wants. I just didn't think it could happen, really, until I walked into that room in San Francisco and there you were. I'd forgotten, Sarah, what it was like to be happy."

Her throat closed up, but she touched his hand and pressed it to her face. She did not think it was so violent a movement, but he rolled out of the hammock as if she had shoved him. He landed on his knees. She sat up, bewildered. And Lucy, Avery, and Sofia's three children scurried into the yard, pulling a donkey.

"Rory!" Lucy called. "The donkey is going to have a baby and another donkey bit her, so we brought her here. Please."

More voices: Sofia and her parents appeared. Lights flashed and music blared from a radio as Frankie drove up in his truck. The donkey broke loose and ran into the orchard. Everyone chased the pregnant donkey, and by the time she was caught, most of the village had arrived. They had come to say goodbye.

"Why?" Lucy asked. "Rory, why do they want to say goodbye?"

Rory bent down in front of his children. "Because we are driving Josefina and her babies and Tía Aurelia back to Napa tonight."

"And Sarah?" Avery asked.

"Sarah is staying here."

Avery burst into tears. So did Lucy, Sofia's children, and all of the grandmothers. Rory sagged into a chair and leaned his head into his hands. It was either that or go beat his head on the lemon tree again.

There was little to pack. Sarah retreated to the shadows watching Rory move about, opening and closing doors, adjusting carseats. She could not change her mind. She had promised Lucy and Avery she would look after the donkey, and there was no room for her anyway. Avery held onto her knees and refused to let go until Frankie offered to let him ride in the truck. Then they were all in the vehicles, except Rory. Hearts could not break, she reminded herself, and hers would not stop beating if Rory left without saying goodbye, but he didn't. He walked over to her, glanced over his shoulder at the crowd watching, and put a flashlight in her hands.

"You'll be all right?"

She nodded. "Rory!" she called as he started for his car; he came back. "You asked me how I feel. At least I think you did." She gripped the flashlight; no, it was his hand. She counted his fingers. "I knew you were there all the time even when I thought you were an octopus."

"Wait — what?"

"Never mind. Goodbye. Drive safely." She would have run into the desert but he still had her hand.

"We were interrupted," he said. "I'll call you. Or you can call me. No, I'll call you. Unless you want to call me."

He kissed her and they were gone. Forlorn, Sarah went into the adobe. "I think he forgot," she said to no one. "We don't have a telephone." She lit a candle and then she saw, sitting on the bed, his yellow notebooks.

CHAPTER 56

THREE DAYS PASSED. Sarah, who had been alone for so much of her life, was lonely.

The desert, she discovered, loomed large, fathomless, and immeasurably dark at night when Rory was not sleeping outside her window. The first night she slept in his hammock with his flashlight on, reading his notebook. Halfway through the second night, the batteries died, and she lay awake, listening to owls and watching bats until there was a glimmer of dawn.

She and Sofia made a pen near the adobe house for the donkey, and they constructed a shelter from the sun. Sarah brought her water and talked to her. She drew the donkey in her notebook; she also drew a crazy-looking woman and an octopus.

She talked to the falcon when it landed near her. She felt closer to the wild heart of life than she had ever been, but she wished it were not so lonesome a place.

THE SUN WAS setting in a fiery show of crimson, scarlet, and gold, and the lone car on the dirt road, a burgundy roadster, picked up speed despite the bumps and holes and rocks. Rory McIntyre drove as fast as he could until he came to a fork in the road. Either way looked the same, and neither was familiar. He had driven this road twice but both times had been in the dark and in Frankie's caravan.

Now, he was alone and the desert night was closing in. He turned right. The road grew rougher, the landscape more desolate. There was no sign of life, not a truck, a house, a shed, or a donkey. There was nothing except rocks, dead-looking bushes, and cactus. The road ended at a deep, dry gulch. Frankie had mentioned treacherous canyons. Rory backed up, returned to the fork, and went left. The road smoothed out. He estimated he had an hour left of light. He sped up and then screeched to a halt when he saw a shadow on the road ahead. A tarantula, as big as his steering wheel, was crossing the road.

"God, you are ugly," he said. It stopped; it was looking at him. How many eyes did it have? He could see its fangs. "I didn't run over you," Rory pointed out.

Another tarantula appeared, and another and another. Did they roam in packs? He didn't know. He watched the weary procession with horrified fascination and thought of Napoleon's army in retreat from Russia, bloodied, limping, missing limbs.

He reached under the seat for his thermos. He sprang back as he touched a furry thing: Lucy's stuffed rabbit. He wasn't that thirsty. He should save his water in case the spiders took a year to cross the road, in case he had to live forever, alone in the desert with tarantulas.

He closed his eyes and one comforting thought appeared: maybe he was hallucinating. He had been driving now for three days, one thousand and sixty-six miles to Napa, and, so far, one thousand and sixty-two miles back. When he opened his eyes, the tarantulas were gone.

He drove on, and his thoughts, which had been scattered over the desert like so many bones of long-dead lizards or antelopes or whatever else lived in the desert, coalesced into one question: What if one tarantula had crawled up under his car and was riding along with him munching its way through the floorboard. In the dark it would crawl up his leg and he would drive off the road into a canyon, where he would be found years later, a bleached skeleton sitting in a rusted roadster, inhabited by hundreds of its spider descendants.

Before the light was entirely gone, he stopped his car, got out, knelt down in the road, and peered up underneath the car. There was no tarantula. What he would have done if he had seen it looking back at him did not bear inspection.

As he got back up, the impulse to leap back into his car and hurry on was suspended. He leaned against the fender and studied the landscape. In the fading light, the land took on an eerie, chiaroscuro aspect. Ghostly. A breeze brushed against him. It prickled his neck. No, not ghosts.

He was doing a crazy thing. But it was a crazy thing of his own choice. The prospect terrified him. But not as much as tarantulas. Or ghosts. He jumped back in his car and drove on.

THE SUN WAS setting as Sarah went into the garden. She thought she might sleep this night with the donkey, but first she would find some dinner. A wind was rising and it rippled her hair and her long white dress as she picked a melon, two peppers, and a tomato. She held them up to the sky to compare their colors and added them to her basket, which also contained two notebooks, hers and Rory's, and her pencils. As she left the garden, the falcon swooped in, calling. It alighted on a fence post.

"The world draws you back," she said to it. "It casts out its net of colors, grander than anyone could imagine, and it draws you back. But you have to catch your own dinner."

The first stars were coming out. Two, she perceived, were twinkling closer, as if they had fallen to earth; and then her heart soared up and away as she recognized the burgundy roadster.

Rory, sunburned, sweaty, dusty, and dazed, came up to her. To the end of her life, Sarah would always be amazed when anyone kissed her.

"Did you forget we don't have a telephone?" she asked.

"No, I came back to hear about the octopus. And to see your scar."

The donkey brayed, came up to them, and nudged Sarah. "Go away," Rory said and he pulled Sarah with him, away from the donkey and toward his car. "I knew there was a reason I drove the MG. I kept wondering why I'd decided to drive it. It's running great, but it doesn't have air conditioning. Now I know: it's because only you and I will fit in it and not a donkey too. Sarah! I am going to finish what I was trying to say, but don't look at me like that because it makes me faint-hearted." He paused. "What?"

"Rory, I think it's a tarantula. Yes. It is. Look —"

"Where?"

"There. By your car."

"Oh, Jesus Christ."

"But it's extraordinary." She released him and bent down to inspect the hairy creature wandering in the twilight. "He's so early. They don't usually come out till the end of summer."

"They don't?"

"Hello," she said to the spider. "Are you confused? Or just over-anxious?"

"Oh god, Sarah, you don't want him, do you?"

"We could name him Harry the Swinger."

"Sarah!"

As she stood up, he sank to his knees. "Are you all right?" she asked. "Did you faint?"

"Sarah Glass, will you let me be the dead bug in your window frame?"

"Rory?"

"Sarah, I'm asking you to marry me, even though I know you'll make a mess of the wedding. Stop that. You're not supposed to laugh."

"But I never thought you were crazy. Well, yes, I did, a little bit —"

"I can't kneel here forever, Sarah. That thing will crawl over me."

"But why —"

"Because I love you, Sarah. And I will tell you this every day of our lives until you are so sick of hearing it —"

"Oh no."

"Sarah, I didn't think I could ask you because I come with two children, but I've figured out that you, my darling, come with every stray creature that crosses your path. It'll work. Sarah: if you want me, I'll go east with you, or wait for you, or live in a barn, or stay here, although I wouldn't mind having indoor plumbing. If you want something else, we'll look for it. We'll find it. I think we might be happy, Sarah."

"You do?"

"I know it. Sarah, when I am alone, I can think of all the reasons why things are impossible, but when I'm with you, I forget them. I don't think calculus can explain it."

The moon was up, half full, bright gold. The tarantula crawled on.

"Sarah," he said, "stop looking at the god-damned tarantula."

EPILOGUE

JUNE 1977

CECILY WAS CHIEFLY responsible for those touches that rendered the wedding of Sarah Glass and Rory McIntyre recognizable as such. Happy, and destined to remain so, her world had begun to expand to include territory beyond herself. Her mother was traveling and their brother sent word that he would come to Sarah's next wedding. She knew that Sarah, on her own, would never manage things properly. Besides, having always been a bride and never a bridesmaid, she was determined to have a good experience.

She approved Sarah's choice of a site, the McIntyre's backyard. Jean had an arbor covered with yellow roses, and Joe's vineyards in the background were nicely green. This provided her color scheme. "But stop saying it's so those animals can attend," she instructed her sister.

She rejected, however, Sarah's choice of a dress, the white one embroidered by Sofia's mother. "Rory likes it," Sarah pointed out.

"Of course he does, you idiot; it's sheer and it looks like a nightgown."

"Sofia's mother made him a shirt to match."

"Which reminds me: I can't believe you gave away that house to that woman. Did you never think I might want it?"

"No," Sarah said. "I never did."

Cecily's chief objection, however, was to Sarah's plans. "You are going to marry him, and leave him in Napa while you go to medical school in New York? You are crazy."

"I'll see him as much as I would if he uprooted his children and moved across the country, again. They're happy here. He likes the job at the newspaper. And it's only two years."

"Only two years? Sarah, you are an idiot, so you probably haven't noticed this, but the McIntyre men have quite the eye for women. Well, except John, of course."

"It will work out."

Rory was even more recalcitrant than Sarah. He insisted on choosing the music, a jazz band called the Budapest String Quartet II and Frankie's mariachi band. He wanted no dead flowers and refused to wear a tuxedo unless Sarah wore a red velvet bathrobe, which did not fit Cecily's color scheme. He further alarmed Cecily by pointing out that Einstein had wondered why should anyone wear both shoes and socks.

Nonetheless, Cecily managed to pull together a wedding. John, although no longer a priest, had got a mail-in certification from the Church of the Sacred Sky and would perform the ceremony. He and Damon organized the food, which included Tía Aurelia's tamales. Joe took care of the wine. Greg and Rory's brothers were Cecily's willing slaves in securing chairs, tables, and potted plants.

On the day of the wedding, Grandma and Aunt Margaret showed up, Margaret rife with delight at the disorder in the McIntyre household — Kate divorced, John defrocked, and Jean and Joe as silly as newlyweds. Joe suggested that Cecily manage his relatives, and although Jean insisted they could not put such a burden on delicate little Cecily, she was astonished to find the terrible duo meekly tying green and yellow ribbons wherever Cecily wanted them.

Thus absorbed, Cecily did not notice that the groom, ignoring all the rules, had carried his bride off in his burgundy roadster three hours before the ceremony. He left Cecily a message that they were going to fulfill Sarah's fantasy. Cecily could only imagine: when Rory asked Sarah where she wanted to go for a honeymoon, she said Buttercream Bakery. Rory's unruffled response was he would think of somewhere, and no, he promised his mother, he would not make Sarah climb Half Dome again.

The guests were arriving: Josefina and her babies, farmworkers, journalists, doctors and nurses, Harry the Swinger and the Scoundrels of Leisure, and Congressman Ilillouette, but the bride and groom were nowhere to be found.

"So," Rory said, as they sat in the parking lot at Buttercream. "Are you sufficiently distracted from the upcoming ordeal?"

"But are you sure you want to do this?"

"Yes."

She looked at him so uncertainly, he was seized by a notion that the bones in his head were melting; although he might have wished to extrapolate some meaning for this according to Heisenberg, he did not try.

"You're not going to tell me about the barren gorilla again, are you?" he asked. "Sarah, I've never met a woman who reminds me less of a barren gorilla than you." He tapped the package she was holding. "Are you going to open it?"

Packages addressed to Mr. and Mrs. Rory McIntyre had not made her nervous; even the ones to Mr. and Dr. McIntyre had not; but this one was addressed to "Rebecca-Sarah Glass."

She broke the seal. Inside were two envelopes. The first one was a card:

Dear Rebecca,

I hope you won't mind me calling you that, for I will always think of you that way, ever since we saw you standing on the street in San Francisco and I thought that you were so beautiful, just like Natalie Wood in West Side Story, that it didn't matter what you were wearing.

My father decided to get rid of the Napa property, and when Vicky and I went to clear it out, we found a box in Gabriel's room. I'm sure he meant to give it to you but forgot, because that is what he was like. The doctors want Mother to turn off the machines, but she won't, so I still go to see him. I told him about finding the box and how I might send it to you. I know it isn't possible, but I think he smiled. You never know about life, do you?

My father asked me to include this letter from him too.

Pete and I wish you all happiness forever.

Lydia

In the box was a necklace fashioned from two gold acrobats wearing enameled tiger skins and dangling by their knees from a golden chain; each held the edge of a gold star.

Rory said, "If you wear it today, Cecily won't notice if I'm wearing a tie or not."

Sarah read a second letter from Dr. Christian Dinesen and handed it to Rory. He scanned it, frowning. "He can't give us that place, can he?" she asked.

"I don't know," Rory said. "Do you want it?"

"No. Well, maybe. Joe might like the old grapevines. Do you?"

"Not if we have to live in that church with goats and cows and horses downstairs."

"No, but not in that castle either."

"I suppose we might build something different."

"Why would he do it?"

"He came to see you when you were, you know —"

"Unconscious. It's different than dead, Rory."

"We talked. He was weird, but at least he wasn't a damned ghost. He brought you some flowers. He said you had grown them."

"The wildflowers," she said. "They grew."

IT'S CURIOUS HOW many questions remain for lives that flicker in and out of existence so quickly they almost disappear before you notice them. The answers can only be determined by that notion that does not really exist: time. But on that day, Sarah Glass did marry Rory McIntyre, and for their honeymoon they went to Paris. A woman David Ilillouette knew loaned them her pied-a-terre on the Ile Saint Louis, but this is another story.

Aunt Margaret was horrified to discover that Jean had invited Russians, Mexicans, and Democrats to the party, but then she accidentally ate Tía Aurelia's hot salsa and was rendered speechless for the rest of the party. Grandma, however, danced with the Democrat, who gained one vote in Nebraska. She had a bang-up time, as did Widdershins the cat, Rebecca the horse, Milton the goat, Wolf the dog, and the chickens, Allison, Absolon, and Nicolas. Neptune the cow, however, vanished that day as inexplicably as she had appeared, but to be mysterious is a fate not often allowed a cow.

ACKNOWLEDGMENTS

THIS BOOK DID not start out to be a historical novel, but time and life have rendered it nearly so. Two small children may have slowed the progress of my writing, but they also made it come alive. As I finally finished this story, it was with no small pride that I could turn to my son Sam, the doctor, for medical fact-checking, and to my daughter Ariel, the linguist, for expert editing.

I want to thank literary agent Laura Langlie for believing in the work for so long. When it still seemed that it might never happen, artist Kelly Doren created a logo for Tempest Books, Ltd., which ignited a project; and an extraordinary team transformed a story into a book.

Dorothy Carico Smith did the exquisite cover and interior design, and Casey Dawes navigated the minefield of publishing, each with infinite patience and good-humor. Betty Teller provided eagle-eyed copy-editing; Dr. James Jackson double-checked the science; Prof. Anne Connor from Southern Oregon University corrected my Spanish; Don Hirsohn kept my computer running, and Tony Lu Priori provided support at every crisis with his special coffee spiked with something Italian and delicious. I also want to thank Bridget Ring, Paul Franson, David Kerns, and Diane De Filipi for their ongoing support.

I started out with a question: is love incompatible with intelligence? It soon became: is love even possible in our crazy world? If my characters were able to come up with an encouraging resolution, it is probably because Patrick Revoyre and Cedric Garnier invited me to work on revisions at their incomparable Chateau de la Barge in Burgundy. There, in an ancient setting, sustained by their memorable meals and their own delight in love, I believe I found an answer: perhaps.

Chuck O'Rear

After studying journalism at UC Berkeley, Sasha Paulsen lived and worked in Europe and New England before returning to her hometown, Napa, California. While raising her two children, with the help of their dog, Pippi, she was features editor for *The Napa Valley Register* where she wrote about food, wine, art, and travel. *Dancing on the Spider's Web* is her first novel.